Nondum Fidelis

by

Gerald Rubin

PublishAmerica
Baltimore

ISBN: 1-4241-4354-3
PUBLISHED BY PUBLISHAMERICA, LLLP
www.publishamerica.com
Baltimore

Printed in the United States of America

This book is dedicated to my mother, Elizabeth. She was always an avid reader and would have really enjoyed this story. She left us before it was completed.

Acknowledgments

There are a few people who need to be thanked for their assistance with the writing of this book.

My wife is first and foremost. Nancy not only encouraged me to write, she gave me several ideas for the story. She also helped out with the computer problems I faced daily.

Karen Wilson was truly an outstanding helper to me. Not only is she a true computer wiz but she took on the job of early editor.

A big thanks to Orlo Strunk for his excellent advice and for leading me in the right direction.

Last but not least is Bob Welker. Bob was constantly on my back to finish the book. His opinions and criticism were just what I needed.

Thanks to all those friends and acquaintances that are mentioned throughout the book.

I'm grateful to you all.

Chapter 1

"Mr. President, the study shows that approximately 23,000 men are resisting the draft in numerous ways including fleeing, false deferments, false statements of illness, etc., etc. Another 3,000 already on active duty have deserted or gone AWOL." Secretary of State Lloyd paused to look at the president, who was gazing out the open French doors. Lloyd knew the president was absorbing all the facts, but he also knew that those damn roses the president loved were getting his attention as well.

Lloyd lit another cigarette and decided to just keep on reading. "The commission found that the 26,000 number has a plus-or-minus error factor of 2,000 either way."

"That's some plus or minus," said President Barringer, "about eight percent or so." As the president turned, he looked right into Lloyd's eyes. Lloyd stared back briefly. As a trickle of sweat rolled down his back, he broke the stare. He knew from the moment he began reading the report, the president would be pissed off at the way the numbers were tossed around. He disliked the way figures could be used to sway an argument. Figures could lie and liars could figure.

"Mr. President, you must understand that the draft boards are trying to come up with the most accurate figures, but these kids are just disappearing. We estimate about 20,000 are in Canada, some in Mexico; but the rest is a guess. We suspect that many are just roaming around the country trying to stay out of harm's way. Our agents, taken from every department available, are chasing all over hell's half-acre to try and locate as many as possible. The figures are changing daily."

"Okay, Henry, lets talk about those figures. Let's say the 23,000 figure is close to accurate; what am I supposed to do about it?"

The president was staring out the French doors again, but not at the roses this time. Instead he was watching a rather large group of protesters along the south fence of the White House. He detested what he saw, men with long dirty-looking hair, beards and rag-like clothing. Many of the females closely resembled the men in their dress and demeanor. The only way he could be sure that some were females was because they were pushing carriages or had babies on their backs, papoose-style. The group walked back and forth chanting something he could not hear. He was glad of that. *It's no doubt about me,* he thought. Even sadder was seeing members of the clergy in the group. From their dress he observed they were from several different faiths. Earlier he had been told the protestors numbered about one hundred or so with ten being clergy. *Shit, why don't they leave war and politics to us and just take care of people's souls? This world is changing so fast, why can't we just be solidified in this war like we were in the past? Damn, why me? Why couldn't we just have peace? Why, why, why?* "Why?" he said aloud.

Lloyd looked up and said, "Why what?"

"Nothing, Henry, nothing. Let's get back to this report. What are your thoughts?"

Lloyd had looked forward to this, but now he almost dreaded it. Barringer was a middle-of-the-roader. He would listen to both sides and usually make a rational decision. He had stated when he took office two years before that he would be a one-term president. He entered office at sixty-four years as a healthy, physically fit man. Some questioned his mental state; but then anyone going into politics should have their mental state questioned. Two years earlier not that many questioned his mental state, but having his wife, Jennie, die suddenly of a massive heart attack and his oldest son killed in the war, all in the first year of office, had taken a terrible toll. Lloyd knew the anguish his friend had and still suffered, but he also knew he was as sharp as ever.

Henry Lloyd had argued with anyone who would listen. President James F. Barringer had full control of his facilities. Yes, he still suffered from his losses, but made the decisions that a president needs to make; and ninety-nine percent were damn good choices. Lloyd knew the president better than any man alive. They went back a long way together. They grew up in the same neighborhood, attended the same high school and college. They double-dated and played ball together. After college they both went to law school, but not the same one. For six years they hardly saw each other, except for a funeral or at Christmas when visiting family, but not much more. Their first reunion came at the end of the war in Europe. They faced each other at a court-martial in France just as the war came to a close. After the trial they got drunk and talked all night about old times and the period they had been separated. The reunion lasted two days. For the next eight years they were again separated by life. They each got their law practices going, along with marriage and family. Barringer got into politics very fast and moved up not as fast; but faster than most. He was as a second-term senator when he welcomed his old friend Henry to the Senate. From that day on they were as close as ever and remained so to this day.

It is not unusual for the president of the United States to ask the advice of his secretary of state. Not unusual indeed; it was his job to advise the president, but Henry Lloyd also knew this wasn't just routine advice. This was a personal view; his own thoughts on this terrible issue that was tearing the nation apart. Thousands of young men had turned their backs on their country in time of war. This war was very unpopular but the previous administration dumped it on him and it was the top concern of all Americans. The whole country wanted to stop Communism, but not if war was the only way to do it. The draft dodgers had torn apart their families by their decision and it was also tearing the country apart. The president had an idea.

Lloyd knew the president was up to something big but he wasn't sure of what. He also knew that he would be the very first to know and he was slightly uneasy with anticipation. He knew he first had to tell his friend his thoughts and was running the text through his mind as he fixed his coffee, just how he would say what he wanted. *I know what I need to say and I've gone over it a hundred times but how will it be received? Hell, I guess I'm about to find out.* He turned to face the president just as the president said, "Henry, sit down. Before you start, Hank, I want to say something." He stood and then sat on the edge of his desk and looked Lloyd right in the eye. "You know how hot an issue this is; it's nearly as big as our involvement in the war. I'd like you to tell me your feelings, your gut feelings. Tell me what you would do if you were sitting in my chair." He stood, walked to the French doors and closed them. He returned to his desk and sat down. "The bug sweep was done just prior to your arrival. Nobody here but you and I, and I want to hear your intimate thoughts."

Henry started, "Mr. President…"

"Stop," said the president. "It's just you and I. We go back a long way, first names please."

"Okay, Jim, if that's what you want. First let me say that I have spent many hours thinking this issue over. As a former military officer, raised by patriotic parents and the father of boys and girls who could possibly be drafted, I have very mixed thoughts. Yesterday flying home from Turkey, I had time to myself and actually reached my final decision. I knew this was coming and I wanted to be prepared."

The smile on the president's face caused Lloyd to stop. "I'm sorry, Hank; I'm just chuckling at you. You know me too well. You are prepared because you knew I'd ask. You're an amazing man. I'm sorry, Hank, please go on."

"Mr. President, I mean Jim, my idea is that the majority of America wants some action taken against these bastards. I think you have to do something concrete in the form of punishment. No matter what you do, you'll be criticized by forty percent of the population and God knows how many of our allies. I hate to think of the political ramifications if you use punishment." Lloyd reached for his coffee and then lit a cigarette. "Jim, what I propose is that we use all possible agents to round up every resistor we can find and get them into an internment camp similar to the type used to house the Japanese during the war. I would intern them for the duration of the war or until…" and his voice trailed off to silence.

The president stood again and walked to the French doors and opened them. "I wonder," he said out loud, "how many times a day I open and close these." He walked out a few steps and stood watching the protestors with disdain. He picked up a set of pruning shears he kept nearby and snipped off a deep-red rose and held it to his nose. What a wonderful aroma. Turning back to Hank, he said, "I wonder if someday all I will have to do is raise my roses and enjoy by garden. Jennie used to say I loved my roses more than her. God, how I miss her, Jennie and Jimmie both." Tears welled in his eyes and one rolled down his cheek and hit the red rose he was holding. Abruptly he turned, cleared his throat and said, "Hank, I like your idea, it's not bad. A lot of logistical problems, but no matter what, there's going to be problems. Where would you get the manpower to make the roundup?"

"From every agency we can, from every level of law enforcement and military," shot back Lloyd.

"How many would it take do you think?"

"Probably a couple thousand."

"Where would you put the internment camp?"

"In a warm climate, it would hold down heating costs."

"Damn, Hank, you really have thought this out, haven't you?"

"Yes, sir, I have. I've also thought about how much hell this is going raise at home and abroad. I felt I had to be prepared when and if the question came up, and it did."

"What kind of reaction do you anticipate and will we bend to it?"

"Jim, the reaction will be bad, of that I have no doubt, but to many it may be just the opposite. I expect a lot of reaction from the religious groups, but I expect a lot of support from others. Remember this idea is to intern American boys like prisoners. The Russians are going to have a field day with it. I will say that in many talks with our allies, we are losing a lot of respect because we have done nothing about this before. Again, I think the biggest objection will come from the religious community and I think we can handle that."

The phone rang and stopped the conversation. The president picked it up and listened for several seconds, said "thank you" and hung up.

"Hank, I have to go now, but I want you to do something right away. First, call Coreblu, I think he may be at the UN for a speech. See if he can see you right away. What I want to know is will he allow our people to enter Canada and arrest our draft dodgers without a lot of paperwork and details; and let us take them immediately out of his country?"

"Jesus, Jim, are you serious? You know the legal system; it's totally contrary to law."

"Hank, I'm not just talking here, I mean business. A lot of things we may have to do in the near future could be contrary to law. I want to move on this and want answers right away. I have other ideas beside yours; this is only the tip of the iceberg. You do what you have to do with Coreblu to get an okay to our plan. Throw him a bone. He wants us to sign that gas agreement raising their prices, promise him I'll sign it. Most importantly, I want our people to have free rein in Canada to arrest those we can find and to bring them home unmolested and fast. I also expect them to lend a hand with manpower, giving us a man or two on each stakeout and arrest. That's what I want and I want it fast. We also want his vow of silence on this matter."

President Barringer's voice had taken a noticeable turn deeper and Hank knew the president was back in command, not asking but commanding. Hank also knew he would do the president's bidding without question. He stood and walked to the door.

"Hank, one more thing. While you're in New York, look up Cardinal

Foote. I'd like for you to get a feel from him on this. Don't be specific about our thoughts. I'd like a viewpoint on the Church's side of the issue. You might mention jailing them and see how he reacts. I'd like this part wrapped up fast, say forty-eight hours. I would like to make a final decision by Wednesday."

Hank breathed deeply, thinking how he had seen his wife and kids for maybe two hours since returning from Turkey yesterday, now this.

"Hank, this is really the last thing. I'm really sorry about you and Betty and the family, and not seeing them much. As soon as I can spare you, I want you to promise Betty that you will be off for a week. I want you to take the whole family if you like and go away from the world and relax, as a family."

"Thanks, Jim. Betty will like that." He turned and immediately walked out the door. As he left he noticed Bob Kilgore seated in the waiting area.

Bob stood, shook hands and asked, "Is there anything I could be told to prepare? It's a little unusual to be called in on a Sunday to see the man."

Lloyd smiled and said, "Bob, I'd rather he tell you what he wants. I'm not even sure we're working on the same matter."

"Mr. Kilgore, the president is ready for you now." Marge, the president's secretary pointed toward the door to the Oval Office.

"Well, thanks, Hank. Can't keep him waiting. See you."

Hank walked to his waiting car, got in and left the White House grounds. His thoughts wandered and flew in various directions. *Jeeze, what I heard and what I said, what part of history am I going to be involved in, good, bad or indifferent? Is this a good idea, is it the right thing to do, what reactions, what ... shit. Let's see just what comes about in the next days. If he had the head of the FBI going in right after me I guess he's dead serious.* Like waking up from a dead sleep, he realized the car was moving and his driver was talking to him. "What, Mike?"

"Where to, Mr. Secretary?"

"I'm sorry, Mike, I was thinking. Well, you'd better head for home and please get me the office on the line." *What if Coreblu wants more than the gas agreement? Damn, he did say at any cost. How much is any cost?*

Mike said, "Phone," and Lloyd quickly picked it up.

"Hello, Linda. What? What's the code for the day? It's, it's... hell, I don't know. I'm not sure I know what day it is."

Softly Mike said, "Shadow."

Henry gave a nod of thanks to Mike. "Shadow, and Linda, we are on scrambler, aren't we? Okay, first call my wife and tell her I'm on my way home. I want to meet with Canadian Prime Minister Coreblu as fast as possible. No, not tonight, but maybe in the morning or for lunch. Also call Cardinal… I can't remember his name. The head guy for New York. Who? Foote, yes, that's him. I want to see him right after the prime minister, figure four hours later. Okay, got it all? Get back to me at home when you have something. Make arrangements for flying up to New York City so that I can be in time to meet with the prime minister. No staff, just Mike and I. Okay? Bye."

As he hung up the phone Lloyd couldn't help shake the same nagging fear he had since the idea came to him. *How will America react to arresting and interning other Americans? Yes, we did it in the '40s to those poor Japs, but we didn't think they were Americans at the time. This time we'd be putting Americans of one hundred percent American parentage in jail. Would I have told him of my idea if my son were on the run? But on the other hand what if I had a son who was killed in the war, what would my thoughts be then? Hell, I don't know just what my thoughts are right now.*

To be summoned to Camp David means different things to different people, but all that were called felt it was different, this time. Each had been contacted individually and in person by the president's closest aide, Ron Jennings. Each man was told where and when he would be picked up and to be prepared to stay at least twelve hours and possibly slightly longer. The strongest point stressed was that each person was not to say a word to anyone about this call to Camp David coupled with a veiled threat that a slip of the tongue could have dire consequences for the slipper. Each was told to dress casually. Military men were told to wear civilian clothing. No further orders were given and no questions were answered.

Three days later they arrived at Camp David, each vehicle slightly more than fifteen minutes apart. The array of vehicles arriving was very unimpressive to say the least; a ten-year-old Chevy, a Ford pickup with a camper in the bed, a red and white Jeep, and so on. The Marine MPs usually manning the gates had been replaced by Secret Service agents, and very senior agents at that. Each guest had to present proper identification and be recognized by picture before allowed entry. Everyone from the guests, the MPs and the agents knew something big was up, but all were guessing just what. The camp staff observed the president arrive by chopper and it was very unusual for him to do so midweek, so they too were wondering. Security was very heavy, so much so that it too raised more questions than answers.

Each guest was ushered into the meeting room by his driver, who promptly disappeared. The first arrivals were Vice President Calley and Secretary of State Lloyd. By design these two were first in the hope it would have a calming effects on the other guests.

"Henry, what in the hell is going on?" asked the vice president.

"I'm sorry, Mr. Vice President, I'm not sure if I know and if I did I'm sure we all got the same instructions on silence."

"Yes, dammit, we did, but this is highly unusual and has me jumpy."

You're jumpy all the time, thought Henry Lloyd, *a good politician, but not a manly bone in your body. Nevertheless, he did in fact draw the party together and assured the president a victory in the election.*

Every ten to fifteen minutes another guest arrived, again by design. Each man seemed relieved to see the others present. Each of the Joint Chiefs of Staff arrived and appeared by sight to be just ordinary citizens, dressed in civilian clothes and carrying no briefcases or having no aides to fawn over them. The vice president and secretary of state talked to each man upon arrival and kept the conversation light. Coffee and rolls were available to ease their minds and keep them occupied. At 11:00 a.m. the last guest arrived and, by an unseen pair of eyes, a tally was taken. Everyone was here.

Those present included the top of the administration and some not quite to the top... the vice president, secretary of state, Joint Chiefs, FBI director, attorney general, secretary of defense, Speaker of the House and majority leader of the Senate; with most not noticing, the doors to the room were closed, waiters and guards disappeared and the president walked in.

The president stood at the head of the table and said, "Gentlemen, let's be seated and get this show started. First let me thank you all for clearing your calendars for me, and secondly I am sorry for all the secrecy, but you will all appreciate it later on. At this time there is not another human being within one hundred yards of this building. From this moment on feel free to speak openly and without reservation. You are all very well aware of the present situation regarding our draft evaders. I have decided to make a move to correct that situation and we are here to discuss it. Please give me the courtesy to hear my presentation before you leap all over me. You will each have your turn to speak with ample time to present your thoughts.

"The plan, hereafter known as 'The Project,' is very simple. To put it into action, carry it out and live with the results will not be as simple. What I plan to do is to move on the dodgers, arrest them, take them to a military base to be determined here and either train them to fight or they go to prison; it will be their choice of the two." The president picked up a glass of water to sip, not wanting it but giving him a pause to observe his audience and their reaction to what they just heard. He had expected shock from some and jubilation from others; he wasn't disappointed. He set his glass down and continued. "We will use every agency we can for arrest teams, including military, federal, state and local. After the lists of known dodgers are received, two-man teams will go after them aided by locals.

"Once the arrest is effected, the prisoner will be taken to the nearest military base and placed behind bars. When the arrests start to add up, they will be taken by military transport to a training site to be determined. Once the final group is assembled, they will be given the opportunity to be trained for military service of some type or be interned in a prisoner-of-war-style camp for the minimum of the duration of the war. In this camp they will work their ass off doing some type of manual labor such as building roads, cleaning roads or similar type of work, chain-gang style." Once again he reached for his glass, sipped some water and tried to read his guests' reactions. They told him what he already knew, shock and disbelief.

Down went the glass and he went on. "Each team will have a packet of info on his target and an executive order signed by me for the arrest and detention of said target. There will be no local paperwork, no proceedings, no extradition, and no lawyers, no nothing. I expect everything and anything to happen. In fact, I fully expect the shit to hit the fan, hopefully after most of the arrests are effected. I hope each arrest team can make their arrest as quietly as possible and disappear before anyone knows what was going on. If it can be quiet and quick, it will make things a lot easier on me, or us as the case may be. If a confrontation occurs, hopefully it can be resolved peaceably, but if need be, our teams will defend themselves. What I am saying is, if they have to shoot they will and kill if they have to." This last sentence forced him to pause and let the group stir for a minute. They were all edgy and wanting to talk. He held his hands up and said, "Let me finish up first.

"I know that what I have proposed here is so radically different it scares even me. I know it is totally alien to our form of government and way of life and that it staggers your imagination, but that is my plan. Just remember what is happening to our country; it too is radically different and it too staggers the imagination." President Barringer reached for and lit his cigar. After a few puffs he said, "Before I open the discussion I would like to take a few minutes. It will give you a chance to think about what I've said and what you may want to say. Please feel free to visit the bar; you'll notice it's well stocked. I know I need one and I'm sure most of you feel the same."

Twelve of the thirteen present moved to the bar. The only sounds heard were of ice hitting glass and liquid hitting ice. As if drugged, each man moved back to his chair and sat. The president sat down and looked at Henry Lloyd and smiled. Lloyd smiled back and nodded.

The president said, "George, as the vice president, you're number one up."

Vice President George Calley, a handsome man in his early fifties, was well tanned and normally very healthy looking, now he looked white as snow. He took a sip of his drink, set it down and looked the president right in the eye. "Mr. President, I think you're out of your mind. I would expect this kind of a plan from the Russians, even some of our supposed allies, but us? It's inconceivable, un-American, it's crazy. It's totally against everything we stand for. You'll be impeached at the least and jailed at the worst and wreck us all politically." George Calley was shaking; it was evident to everyone present. His voice rose higher and his complexion paler. He took a large gulp of his drink and continued. "I am one hundred percent against this and pray to God it goes no further. I'll resign first."

President Barringer looked directly at the vice president as he sat down. Outwardly he was the picture of calm but inside he was in a rage. Waiting to regain his total composure before he spoke, he thought, *If the only good thing that comes out of this plan is the resignation of this coward,* a man he despised but needed initially, *it will be a partial victory.* Finally he said, "Thank you, George," and no more, though he wanted to. "Mr. Secretary of State Lloyd is next at my throat," a direct reference to the last speaker.

As Lloyd reached for his drink, the president said, "I know some of you won't understand this, but Henry and I batted this around three days ago. Hank will be his usual modest self, but I want you all to know that a lot of this talk is Hank's idea. He has been working on this for some time, very hard the last three days. Hank, will you elaborate on the feedback you received from our allies on this matter."

The secretary of state began talking even before he stood and walked to the wall bearing the charts. He turned towards the table and continued his sentence. "Ninety-nine percent of our allies and all of our enemies are laughing their asses off at us for our soft stance on our deserters. Naturally nobody knows of this plan except the Canadian prime minister, and he knows almost nothing. All he does know is that we may want to enter his country and grab our deserters and leave just as quickly."

"And what did he say?" interrupted the vice president in a raised tone of voice.

The president glanced at Lloyd, knowing the bad blood that existed between the two. But Hank was a diplomat and calmly turned toward the vice president. "Mr. Vice President, the prime minister will allow us to retrieve our lost citizens. In fact, it's become a problem for him. Our dodgers are taking jobs away from his people and Canada is not too happy about it. This would solve both our problems and he is, in fact, very happy with the idea. He promised to help us in any way possible to clean this matter up as quietly as possible." Lloyd sat in his chair, leaned back smugly, knowing full well the vice president was pissed beyond belief... He quickly added, "That's all I have for now, but I can honestly say, I think they will all go along with us on this."

"Mr. Secretary of Defense, you have the floor," said the president.

Ralph Springstead stood, a fifty-four-year-old craggy-faced man with a remarkable tongue. An articulate speaker, who gave up a job as chairman of the board of a very large corporation to join his friend as a cabinet member, a definite hawk on defense of his country, but a peace lover of remarkable proportions, a true oxymoron. He rose from his chair and everyone was waiting for a long oratory. Ralph cleared his throat, more of a cough, and looked right at the president. "Mr. President, I think every man here would like time to digest this. At this time my initial thoughts are favorable with major reservations. I think we all agree that something needs to be done to rectify this issue, harshly if necessary. I have grave doubts about the method you have chosen; it's a blatant abuse of our Constitution. Tell me, sir, do you plan to suspend the Constitution during this period?"

The president looked at this longtime friend with admiration and calmly stated, "Ralph, I agree with your assessment about the Constitution; it would be an abuse and I know it. I have thought about asking Congress for temporary executive privilege on the matter, but it would become public knowledge and ruin our surprise tactics. We'd lose more deserters who would go further underground and violence would surely ensue when the arrests began. No, I'm afraid I have to go without approval and face the wrath of Congress and the people after the fact. Is there anything else, Ralph?"

"No, sir. Like I said I think we need time to digest it all before we can say yes or no. You have a very radical idea, Mr. President, one I think the nation could use right now if they don't lynch us all first."

The president half turned his head and eyeballed his next to comment. "Mr. Speaker, it's your turn in the barrel."

Terrell Stonewall Jackson, speaker of the House for the last seventeen years. Friend and foe to several presidents, a man in the twilight of this life, stood and walked to the bar. He poured himself a full glass of bourbon, said, "My doctors would have a shit-fit if they saw this," and drank half of it. He turned facing the assembled group and saw every pair of eyes on him. He raised his glass, said, "Nectar of the gods," and drank the rest. "Well, it seems to me that I have been at this type meeting several times before. The last time was with that arrogant son of a bitch who got us into this war. He didn't live long enough to see what he did, so I guess I have to let bygones be bygones. I'm not about to bullshit any of you with a lot of empty words. Plain and simple facts have always been my motto. This draft thing has become a national disgrace, even an outrage. Not many people over thirty-five can actually believe these long-haired, dirty bastards are too scared to fight for their own country. It seems most I talk with feel these bastards are getting a free ride out of this life. We of the senile group have always remarked that each generation has it easier than the last, but this last generation is the God-awful worst yet. Well, now our president has come up with a very novel idea. Speaking for myself, I like it a lot. Speaking for my colleagues in the House is another matter. The older members, I think, can be convinced on the matter. The young assholes we have are another story. Impeachment is a very nasty business, but so is this shame we bear right now. As outlined so far, I am in favor of it." The glass came up to his lips, but all he could taste was cold water. He turned to the bar for a refill and said, "That's all I have to say right now."

President Barringer stood, walked forward and stopped. Facing everyone he said, "It's now 12:40, we have heard from half of you and it's lunchtime. Suppose I ring for lunch and we'll return afterwards." He didn't wait for a reply, as he expected none. Picking up the phone, he made the call. "This subject is closed until after lunch and we are all here together. No outside calls, none. General Harmon, as the head of the Joint Chiefs, I ask you to take your people to the next room and discuss this matter quietly while lunching. I will ask for a consensus answer from your group rather than five different speakers. Each of the five may speak if he so desires, but I would prefer one main speaker, yourself."

"Yes, sir," Harmon snapped and all five stood and walked towards the door.

Lunch was very typical of the Barringer administration, plain and very unpretentious. The president disliked fancy food, especially the sauces with all the cream and cheese in them. Today's fare was venison stew or baked trout, both obtained right from the campgrounds. Maybe even caught or shot by the president. He had done both on many occasions. Everyone who ate with or around the president had come to expect this type of meal and few complained. At this level of government meals were outrageous with names that most couldn't pronounce. Being forced to eat extravagant meals so often, it was actually a pleasure for most to eat such simple fare.

"What do you think of the stew, Hank?" the president asked.

"Tasty, but your cook never made a bad stew in his life. I prefer his omelets to anything else, but his stew is good."

The same types of conservation continued among the guests for some forty-five minutes. Some ate in silence, one being the vice president. This fact did not go unnoticed by the president, not much did. He suspected he would have problems with Calley on this, but he had decided that he didn't much care what George said anymore. Since Hank had called him and informed him that Canada would assist, he simply moved forward with the plan, regardless of who said what or why. *This well may be my last hurrah in life and it's going to be a big one, the biggest in fact.* For some time he had felt that what was happening to his country was not good. It needed a shot in the arm, an issue, a big issue to rally around. From all he had heard and seen from his constituents and all the extraneous bullshit aside, he thought, *An awful lot of Americans are totally pissed off at these draft dodgers. If most can be taken without a big fuss, I think they will back me. If I'm wrong, I'll be impeached and retire in disgrace or at worst, jailed. That wouldn't bother me as much except for Pauline, she's all that's left for me. With Jen and Jim gone, my life isn't too meaningful anymore except for her. I wonder how all this will affect her, will she agree or not? Worse yet, will she and her family be harassed for my decision? She and John can live with it, but their kids, can they? Kids can be terribly cruel to each other. Damn, I don't want my grandchildren told their grandfather is a... what am I? What will I be if I do this? Will they call me the American Hitler, Stalin, who?*

"Mr. President."

Out of the depths of his thoughts he suddenly realized that Charlie Dombrowski was talking to him. The communications room director was telling him that a communication had come in and he was handing it to him.

"Yes, Chas, I'm sorry."

"Sir, this just came in and I thought you would like to see it immediately."

He quickly read the message and put it in his pocket. He stood and said, "Gentleman, let's get back to work and walked to the meeting room."

The majority leader was next up, but the president reached for and lit his cigar first. Larry Townsend, a small New Englander of nearly seventy years, stood with some difficulty and leaned forward. Pointing a finger in the president's direction as if they were alone he began. "Jim, you and I go back a long way and you know I would never tell you anything but the truth. I doubt you can get away with this in the House without a long and drawn-out fight. From what you're saying, you don't intend to ask for approval; that's good because you would never get it. What you are going to get is a hell of a lot of flack, if not impeachment or both. On the other hand, if I read my fellow lawmakers right, you could have a majority who would back you. We are all disgusted with what this generation has done to the country and we're all in favor of doing something to change that. What you're proposing, and it's been said already; is against the Constitution. It could backfire on you and us; and ruin a lot of careers." Townsend was shaking like a frail tree in a winter wind, but not from fear. Everyone present knew of his physical condition, but admired him for his courageous fight against the cancer that was slowly killing him. Cancer along with Parkinson's is more than one man should have to bear, but Larry Townsend did and with dignity.

"Mr. President, as you have outlined the plan, I would back you with everything and everybody I can muster. Don't wait too long though, I can't promise you my vote too far down the road, time is passing me by. The good doctors are giving me three months before I go and join my beloved Jane. That's the time frame you have for my help." As Townsend sat, several clapped softly.

President Barringer, his eyes brimming with moisture, stood clearing his throat. "Larry, thank you; thank you very much. The American people owe you so very much for your lifetime of devotion to this country. It's very easy to see why your forefathers were so involved in our Revolutionary War and the founding of our country. I personally salute you." Ten men stood and clapped with pride, only two stayed seated, Townsend and the vice president both sat. The president starred at his vice president and thought, *This man will have to be reckoned with soon.*

"Gentleman, let us continue. We have more comments yet." Larry Townsend had made the president's blood tingle with pride and he could feel the adrenalin coursing through his body. Patriots always made him shiver and got him all pumped up. "I observed during lunch that the FBI director and Justice Department director had a long quiet conversation. Would you both care to be heard?"

Both men stood. "Mr. President, as director of the bureau, I will say that Mr. Quentin and I concur on your plan and agree that our full staffs will work to the very end for your plan to be successful. We both see a long list of logistical problems, but feel that they can be worked out without too many problems." FBI Director Bob Kilgore sat, but Jim Quenton remained standing.

The attorney general, a Rhodes scholar and the first black to hold that post, stood full of military bearing and proud. "Mr. President, I would like to add one thing. If you are not impeached, you may become the greatest president this country has ever had. If this plan of yours is successful, you will have changed the destiny of a country who has been slowly deteriorating to the status of a third-rate nation. The figures I've seen indicate that eighty percent of the dodgers are white and middle-class. The black and Hispanic population is going to rally to support you, as you could never imagine. This plan is similar to those who first split the atom, if I may use the analogy. What they proposed could have blown them all to hell or change the course of history and they took the chance. For you and the American people, I hope your plan is the latter."

"Thank you, Jim. For the sake of the people, I hope you're right. For my part, I just hope this works and I'll let history be the judge. I've saved the Joint Chiefs for last, for a very good reason. They will be the bearer of the heaviest burden. Not only will we need the military for the arrest process, but they will have to house, train, protect and decide later if and how we can trust and use these people after training. They will also have the burden of living with and fighting alongside of this group of American dropouts. General Harmon, what are your feelings on this matter?"

General Robert W. Harmon, head of the Joint Chiefs and the highest ranking man in the Army, looked more like a schoolteacher than his title indicated. His civilian clothes were slightly out of style, hair closely cropped and military eyeglasses right out of Army supply. A rather plain-looking man, who could be mistaken for anything but a general officer with twenty-eight years of service and a chestful of medals that would be the envy of any man. It was Harmon's ability of telling it just as it is, not mincing words and beating around the bush, that was most admired by all who knew him. It was also well known that when excited or aroused he could utter some very colorful language. "Sir, per your request, we have discussed the matter and at this time I shall speak for the unit. We are unanimous in our answer and that is we wholeheartedly agree with this plan as outlined, in fact we think it's fantastic.

The boost in morale to our forces to see these pricks... I'm sorry, sir..."

Everyone was laughing, including the president.

"General, you can say what you damn well please here; we're all grown men and have heard worse."

Harmon continued, "Our draftees and the regulars will love to see these pricks arrested and jailed. I hope they're trainable. I can't say how they will be accepted later if they are integrated into regular service units, but for now the morale factor will be worth it. We do foresee problems. For instance, if we use Parris Island as a training site, that will mean the Marines' training of regulars will suffer to a great degree. The staff needed for training and guarding will be a great number. The greatest burden will be on the Corps, but we all will loan personnel to get the job done. Training our regulars, keeping the war supplied and training these assholes is going to stretch us rather thin. The additional finances will have to come from outside our budgets. Mr. President, we will do whatever we have to, to adjust and get the job done. The only thing I can't back is the money part, we just don't have it."

"Thank you, General. I know we can count on you and your staff. We'll get the money needed. We've all been heard from and I would like to add some comments and we'll close. Firstly, I want to thank most of your for your support," looking directly at his VP and not unnoticed by everyone present, least of all George Calley himself. "I honestly didn't know how you would react to such a plan knowing our form of government as it has been and is, but it's going to be very interesting to see if it stands the test. What I want now is for all of you to spend the next week kicking this over, laying out plans that affect your departments of concern. Find the problems and work them out. If you can't, we will be meeting right here one week from today to discuss it all over again. I want to begin arrests in fifteen days and have them all completed within sixty days. I know you all think this is too hasty and you can all see the bureaucratic problems. Cut through them, no red tape, do what has to be done. Finally, you will get everything you need including finances. I don't know from where yet, but I'll get it. Next week I want projected figures and keep it lean, no pork barrel stuff.

"I know as president that I alone make the final decision and I alone face the consequences for failure. I am aware of these facts and I accept them, but let me tell you something else. I can accept defeat for my own failures, but I will not accept it from those I trust. You are here because I trust each and every one of you and each and every one of you is needed to complete this project. Listen and listen carefully, for your life depends on it. From this minute on, no person is to know of these plans, no one. In order to succeed nobody is to know a single detail until we are ready to move and nobody is to know the destination of those arrested. I said your life is on the line and let me not be melodramatic, but in plain language let me say I consider everything said here today to be war plans. Treason will be the charge for disclosure, punishable by death."

The lack of sound in the room was awesome. The only sound was breathing. Those not wrapped up in their own thoughts were looking into the faces of the others and all wondering, *What are we into?*

The voice of the president brought everyone back to the reality of what was happening. He continued, "Believe me, when I said I was ready to go against our Constitution that I am ready to go to any lengths to succeed. If anyone thinks he can leave here and get me impeached for this idea, thus stopping it before it begins, listen to me: Many a death certificate has read 'heart attack,' 'stroke' or whatever when, in fact, that person was eliminated for reasons. I say this to instill in all of you that I'm not just talking and I am not insane. I strongly believe in this project and I will go to any lengths to see it to the end. Speak outside this room and there won't even be time for a treason charge, you'll be dead.

"You will leave the way you arrived. My aide will show you the schedule of departures. He will also show you the details for next meeting, but no copy. Memorize the details, nothing on paper. None of you will contact me or anyone else about this matter outside this room. You are all planners; it's really nothing new except the scenery. Do what you have to and question next week what you need to. Not a word outside this room."

The president rose and walked towards the door, stopped and turned. He reached into his pocket and retrieved the paper he put away during the day. "This is the message the communications officer gave me earlier. It reads, 'Approximately 300 protestors have chained themselves together in St. Patrick's Cathedral, New York City. They are calling for the president's impeachment and the abolishment of the draft.' Goodbye, gentlemen."

Chapter 2

"Mr. President, you wish to speak to me?"

"Yes, George, come in and sit." He continued to read. He wanted his VP to stew for a bit. Finally, he put down his papers, reached for the phone and said, "Marge, hold all calls until I get back to you.

"George, the normal sweep was done this morning. I want you to feel completely free to express yourself." The sweep was the daily sweep for listening devices; an electronic check of the Oval Office by Secret Service agents every morning and sometimes evenings. Paranoia was not the issue, the facts of life were the issue and in the real world bugs are planted every day where someone wanted to ease drop on the conversation. The Oval Office had no immunity. Both sides of the political world and our enemies would love to hear what was being said here.

"George, I want to know if you still feel as strongly about my project as you did yesterday?"

The VP looked at his superior and with a smug expression on his face said, "You know I am under a death threat not to speak on the subject outside the Camp David location."

"Yes, you're right, and I now relieve you of that oath for the purpose of this conversation only."

"Okay, you're absolutely out of your mind and I refuse to consider it any further. The only change of mind I have is my threat to resign. I have decided you're going to hand the presidency to me on a silver platter and I'd be a damn fool to refuse it. If I'm right, and I feel strongly that I am, you're going to be impeached or worse. Having disavowed any dealings with your project or my agreement to it, after you're impeached I will take over and get what I've always wanted. You knew from the beginning I wanted to succeed you. Your venture will speed this process up by two years. Please understand my motives; I don't want it this way. I would prefer you drop your plans for this craziness and finish your term. This thing could have devastating effects for years to come."

"George, I need you on this. I need all the help I can muster. I was relying on you and your wide range of friends on both sides of the aisle. You can settle a lot of people down if you were on my side. Is there anything I can do to change your mind?"

Without a moment's hesitation George Calley said, "No, sir, not a thing."

The president stood, turned and walked to a huge painting of General Douglas MacArthur. It was widely known the president was a devoted admirer of the general. He looked up and into the face of the general and softly said, "You were one bold soldier and cared little of public opinion. I guess I'm about to find out what you went through when you wanted to follow the Chinese army across the Yalu River into Red China. You caused one hell of a stir with that idea." He reached out and touched the painting and smiled.

George Calley was completely mesmerized by what he was watching and at the moment said to himself, *He is crazy. He's touching that painting like it was a female body, as if he were caressing her.* Calley nearly jumped out of his shoes as the president slid the painting to one side and revealed a wall safe. He was numb as he watched the dial being whirled one way then another. Finally the safe was open and the president reached in and removed a large envelope.

He returned to his desk and placed it right in front of Calley and said, in a rather brusque tone, "Open it."

Calley reached for it but withdrew his hand as if he was touching a snake. "Where did the safe come from? I never saw it before. I had no idea one even existed in this office."

"Nothing of extreme value is ever left in it overnight," the president said in a softer voice. "I had it put in some time ago, just to house this envelope."

The things he was seeing and hearing were all racing though his mind to fast. *Why was he bugging me so much to agree to this project and what in hell is in this envelope? Could he really be insane? Could I?*

"For the last time, will you join with me in this project?"

"No, sir, there is nothing you can do or say to change my decision."

"Damn it, George you're forcing me into a contemptible act." With obviously shaking hands he pushed the envelope to Calley and harshly said, "Open it right now." He turned abruptly and walked to the bar. He picked up a glass and filled it with ice and poured scotch some four inches deep.

As he lifted the scotch to his lips he heard the gasp of the VP and immediate sobbing. "Oh my God, oh my God, no."

He gulped another inch of scotch and heard the man run to the bathroom and retch his guts out. He had all he could do to continue drinking while the man in the bathroom vomited like a sick child. The president finished his drink, walked to his desk and sat down. He waited like an expectant father while the VP washed his face and drug himself back to the chair.

He sat heavily, and was still sobbing softly. He took his handkerchief, dabbed his eyes and began to speak, yet no words came forth. He stood, walked around the office once and sat again. "Where did you get these?"

"What difference does it make, I have them."

"I want the details, all the details, I have that right."

"I really see no need to go into details, George, what does it matter."

"God damn it, I said I want the details and I meant it."

President Barringer looked away towards his beloved rose garden and thought, *What the hell, I've gone this far, why not all the way.* "About ten months ago I came into contact with a man who told me he had something of vital importance to my administration. He had these pictures and I obtained them from him for a price."

"Who is he? How much did it cost and who has the negatives?"

"Come on, George, what's the difference?"

The VP turned very red in the face and in a low voice growled, "I said all the details."

"If that's what you want. The man was a Russian agent working in Germany. Apparently on your visit there before the election, you became involved in this affair. He had your room bugged and videotaped. When he approached me he wanted to trade. He wanted out of Russia, but cleanly; no publicity, no questions, no nothing. He asked for asylum here and a new identity. After he passed numerous polygraph tests, I agreed and we traded."

"Why the polygraph?"

"I wanted several answers. Did I have the only set of pictures and negatives? Was he a double agent? Was he to spy on us or was he truly what he claimed? The answers to all my questions were positive. I then had the safe put in here and put them in the safe I never thought I would use. After I left office, I planned to burn them."

George Calley stared straight ahead for a long time. The president neither said nor did anything thinking time was on his side.

Finally Called asked, "What exactly what do you want from me?"

"You know full well what I want. You will back me on this project fully, right to the end. You will do your job of plying your political friends and allies to get them on our side. That's what you do best."

"When do I get the photos and negatives?"

"As soon as the project is complete."

"We have an agreement. Can I go?"

"In a minute; first, I need to know is this practice still part of your life?"

"God, no, please believe me. That was a one-time aberration. I think it was a latent desire that was suppressed for most of my life. That night in Germany I was with an old friend and we had too much to drink. Apparently I said something he picked up on and the next thing I know is that he is in my bed and it all happened. I've been sick about it ever since. I even talked with a specialist about it, naturally in the third person. I relayed the story and told him it was a close friend that I was trying to help. I've dealt with it since then, so help me, that's the truth."

"Alright, George, fine, I'm glad it's over. I am truly sorry I had to do this, but I'm so committed to this project that I felt I had to. I pray someday you will forgive me." The president picked up the envelope and walked to the safe. He placed it back into the safe and closed the door, whirled the dial and moved MacArthur back into place. He turned back to his VP and said, "The vow of silence in back in place, do you understand?"

"Yes, Mr. President." He turned and walked towards the door.

As the president sat down he immediately began wondering, *Will he keep his word? I guess he has to, the very thought of those pictures must scare the shit out of him. I wonder if I could bring myself to reveal them. What choice do I have? To ruin a man's reputation, his marriage and the chance for the presidency? If the thought revolted him, imagine what the world would think of the vice president of the United States engaged in the act of sodomy and fellatio with two young men.*

Seven days had passed and now the project planners were again assembled in Camp David. It had already been agreed upon that the project was a go and now the rough draft had to be laid out. For five solid hours they talked, cajoled and re-wrote the following plan:

1. Arrest teams will consist of two men who will be as familiar as possible with the area they are working in. Each man will be authorized to carry a handgun with an automatic rifle close at hand.

2. The most up-to-date material will be made available to each team. Once an arrest is made the team will confirm by phone the identity of the arrestee and any known subjects connected to him.

3. In the case of several targets living in the same location such as a commune, everyone in that location is to be rounded up and the identity of each person verified.

4. All French-speaking officers will leave immediately to locate targets.

5. Teams will be briefed that the arrest is the most important task, with silence secondary, but equally important. Anything within reason is allowed to achieve that goal. Examples of what is allowable are, but not limited to gags, chloroform, costumes, needles and just about anything within reason.

6. On the day the roundup begins, every base commander in the U.S. is to be notified to expect the arrival of arrestees. Team leaders will use the words "The Project" to gain entry to any military base.

7. Tomorrow the secretary of defense will notify all base commanders that all leaves are cancelled until further notice.

8. All teams will carry a presidential order demanding complete access and compliance to any requests of the team. The Joint Chiefs will have one phone number available to answer any and all questions base commanders might have and to report that they have a number of arrests at their reservation.

9. Parris Island Marine Recruit Depot has been designated as the training site to which all arrestees will be transferred. The commandant of the Marine Corps is designated as the ultimate responsible party for the training of these individuals.

10. Once an arrestee is in custody, he shall be bound with plastic handcuffs and leg irons until such time as he is placed in cell-type security. Each and every time he is taken out of that security, he is to be bound.

11. Each and every team is to act within the boundaries of civility. If they are fired upon by any person or persons, they are to protect and defend themselves by any and all means available including DEADLY FORCE.

"Jim, what about the press? If they observe an arrest and they try to interview or question our teams or those arrested, it could be ugly." Every head in the room was wide-eyed, not at the question, but who was asking it. The VP was asking and they were all asking themselves, *Is the VP actually involved in this?* At the beginning of this meeting the president had said they were unanimous in their agreement to continue, but nobody had believed that George Calley was. For five hours he had sat there like a stone and not said one word, now this. The silence was overwhelming. President Barringer's heart rate was slowing and he hoped it didn't show on his face. He looked face to face at every man in the room knowing, *They must be thinking the same things I am. Well, what the hell, now's as good a time as any to test his sincerity.* "It's a good point, George. What would you suggest?"

"Well, I've been thinking about it for several days. I've been asked by the press on a constant basis just what's up. They sense it. Henderson of the *Washington Post* has been the most insistent. It hasn't gone unnoticed by him that your chopper is nowhere to be seen without the usual explanation. Our own White House press secretary is bugging me for details. He knows something big is up and he also knows better than to ask me for details, but he's getting a lot of heat from the press. I guess I should get back to the question. I think the best thing we can do is to ask the local cops to handle the press. They usually do anyway. We say the following, 'It's nothing more than a criminal arrest,' period. If we do the job right, we can hope the majority of the arrests will be completed in the first day or two."

"Excellent idea, George, I concur. Anyone disagree?" No one spoke or showed any inclination to disagree. The president looked squarely at his VP and smiled and surprisingly the VP smiled back. *He's on my side; he's the asset I needed.*

"Alright, gentleman, make yourselves an after-lunch drink if you want and let's get back to work. I want to go over the last-minute details and set a date. I want each of you to tell me just what problems you have now or perceive you may have." The president was in high gear now. He had been so keyed up over this project that sleep had been fleeting. Physically he was exhausted, but mentally ready to leap forward. He too had been harassed by the press and had purposely avoided any press conferences. He figured if he was under the gun at a press conference anybody could ask him anything. Every person in Washington politics knew something was up and speculation ran rampant, but to the ultimate surprise of those present, their secret was intact. How long it would stay that way none knew, but they counted their blessings.

"Okay, let's go. Henry, as overall coordinator of this project, give us your view."

Henry Lloyd, secretary of state and longtime friend of the president, stood. Walking slowly to a large blackboard, he picked up a pointer and removed a cloth covering the blackboard. "We have assembled 3,500 arrest teams and are working on 500 more. We have used or are using every man we can spare from any and all justice agencies, including a large group of military police. They have been or will be assigned to any area of the country they know best. If you don't already know, we have several thousand targets right here at home. The bulk of the targets are in Canada, so roughly 2,500 teams have left or are ready to leave now to our northern neighbor. Hopefully they will get a few days to scout around with the Canadian locals to spot their target.

"The home team, those staying here to man our information centers and phone lines are in place and ready to man their posts. The order to all military base commanders is worded and ready to be sent. All military transport planes and vehicles are on standby to fly or drive where and when needed. The present training site, Parris Island is a slight problem. Their present training cycle is up in nine days, but we can work around that. All new volunteer recruits will be sent to Camp Pendleton in California. Parris Island will be used exclusively for our dodgers. Every available drill instructor is in or on the way to Parris Island. Former drill instructors on regular duty are being taken back to P.I. to help out. Many instructors from other services may be used in certain situations. All physical features of P.I. have been reinforced by man-made obstacles and security posts. An additional 500 marines will be assigned to P.I. security. We have grabbed a bunch of medical personnel and assigned them to P.I. We expect we could have an unusual amount of medical problems.

"We have drafted a press release if and when it's needed. If the press gets wind of a lot of arrests and they start to add up two and two, we're ready to say that they are criminal arrests and military deserters being rounded up. When the truth comes out we say that we had to protect our arrest teams and civilians around the arrest sites." Henry Lloyd put his pointer down, turned and faced the president. "That's it, sir. Any questions?"

No one said a word.

"Fine, Henry, thank you. You've all done a fine job and my thanks to each and every one of you. I hate to wait too long to start, the secrecy factor bothers me but under the circumstances I should give your people a few more days to work things out. How does next Monday at 0600 sound? That gives you six more days to work with. Anyone? Questions? Comments? Not a one? Okay, then that's it. Let's wrap this up. I've got to get back to D.C. I need not remind you, gentlemen, that the secrecy factor you all agreed to is still in effect. In fact, it's in effect until I tell you you're released from your oath, we all understand?"

Each and every man in the room verbally said "Yes, sir."

The president stopped at the door, turned and added, "Let's all be here this Sunday afternoon around 4:00 p.m. We can go over the last minutes details and make sure one last time."

The president was staring out the window, but not seeing anything. A light snow had coated the Catoctin Mountains making the scene look like a postcard. His staring continued, awash with details and nagging doubts. *Would the arrests go smoothly, how quickly will the press get involved and what's the reaction going to be? Some will be bad, but how bad? Will I survive to carry it through?* Questions and more questions.

A shudder jolted him to reality. The chopper was adding on power to make its landing at Camp David. Once down, he unbuckled, stood up and left the plane.

As President Barringer entered the room the sounds went from soft conversation and tinkling of cups to silence. "Gentleman, please, this isn't a wake, is it?" Everyone smiled and began the usual good afternoon gestures. "Okay, everyone, get your refills and let's get to work."

When everyone was seated the president started. "I expect this meeting will be short and sweet or long and tiring. As far as I know we have but one question: Are we ready to launch 'Operation Roundup'?" It took less than twenty minutes of listening and the president had reached his decision. "Gentleman, the operation is approved by me and me alone. If the shit hits the fan, each and every one of you has my approval to say the president alone made the decision. You have asked for an additional twenty-four hours and that's fine. We launch at 0600 on Tuesday. That gives me another day to get my speech in order."

The president stood and turned to leave when he suddenly stopped and turned back to the group. "I know how hard you have all worked on these plans. I'd like to thank each and every one of you for your time and dedication to the task. I hope we can wrap this up in ten or fifteen days as planned, but more importantly, I want to stress to your people to be careful. I pray this project goes smoothly and without anyone getting hurt." As he turned to the door his final words were "God bless."

Chapter 3

Charlie Rose looked like anyone else window-shopping. In truth he was biding his time debating with himself. The restaurant he was going to was just right next door. He still didn't know if he wanted to go in or not. He had a feeling his former coworkers from the police department were playing with him. They were always known to be major jokesters and he really didn't want to be part of it. Maybe even a post-retirement party--but no, he had been retired for over a year so that's not plausible. As he glanced at the shoes in the window he kept asking himself, *Why would a senator want to see me? What in hell did I do or what did he do? Use your brain. What's this all about? Is it a practical joke or real? Shit, I don't know.* He walked to the door and slowly opened it just a crack, looked in and observed a lot of people eating. He saw nothing to cause him concern. *What the hell, I'm here let's see what's up.*

He walked up to the maitre d' and said, "I'm here to lunch with Senator Concannon."

"Your name, sir?"

"Charles Rose."

"Please follow me, sir," and he walked towards the rear of the dining area. In a far corner sitting at a table Senator Concannon sat reading a paper. He was gray-haired, slender build and close to sixty-five years of age. The maitre d', with a wave of his arm motioned towards the senator, turned and left. As Rose approached the table the senator looked up.

"Charlie Rose, I presume?"

"Yes, sir, I am."

The senator rose and extended his hand. As they shook hands the senator said, "Please, sit. Is it okay to call you Charlie?"

"Yes, sir, that's fine."

"Listen, I don't need the 'sir' title. Out in public 'Senator' is fine. Away from the public, I prefer Carl."

Charlie thought to himself, *Yeah, me calling a senator by his first name.* "Okay," he said, "that s fine."

"How about a drink? I already have one."

Rose replied, "It's a bit early for me."

"Well then, let's order lunch and then we can talk." After ordering the senator looked directly at Charlie and said, "I guess you must be quite curious about all this. First, let me say that I am very aware of your very illustrious career with the D.C. police. I have been following you since some friends told me about you and your uncanny ability of solving crimes... 'Common Sense Charlie' is a unique name and I'm sure you deserve it."

Rose sat perfectly still, letting him talk on. He had never trusted any politician and was on very high alert. *I know something is coming and I'm getting the feeling he is greasing me for what he wants. Well, it's his game and he's got the ball, so let him run.*

Concannon stopped talking, picked up his drink and said, "This isn't the best place to be talking, but it will have to do. Please keep your voice down when you speak and I'll try and explain. For now I can't tell you a whole lot, but if you'll humor me, I'd like to ask you a very pointed question."

Rose smiled and replied, "Senator, you can ask, but please remember, I'm retired and my answer could be very caustic. I don't have to watch my backside, I speak my mind."

"I'm very aware of that, Charlie, that's one of the big reasons you're here. What I want from you right now is a completely honest answer, no bullshit."

"Okay, ask away."

"If you had complete authority to do anything you wanted, use any means, could you stop our drug problem and how?"

Rose tingled with excitement. This was one of his favorite topics; for years he had espoused the fifteen-cent theory; it was always a great conversation piece. *I wonder if he knew about it.*

'Well, Senator, I call it the fifteen-cent theory and it's been in my head for maybe fifteen or sixteen years now. Back then, fifteen cents was the price of a bullet. What I proposed was to set up a table of drug quantities and types.

If a person was caught with a certain type of drug over the limit in quantity, they were shot on the spot, dead in full public view. I conservatively thought it would take a year, maybe two to eliminate our drug problem. Naturally the bodies would pile up, but I don't think they would be missed by most of society." Rose stopped and waited. He was fully prepared for the senator to say he was crazy; many had said just that many times before. He had been told he was a murderer, a Hitler and the devil himself.

Concannon never blinked nor hesitated and replied, "Could you kill a drug dealer that easily?"

"Well, it's my theory, so I guess I would have to say, yes, I could. But you have to know that I have never killed anyone before. Many a druggie I have arrested needed killing and at the time, I could have killed him. They take in a huge chunk of money and dispense a huge chunk of misery and death."

"That's very interesting," was all Senator Concannon could say. Before he could utter another word lunch arrived and the conversation stopped. Both ate in relative silence except for an occasional question and answer of general interest.

Not more than twenty minutes later the senator paid for the lunch and told Rose he needed to return to work. Rose asked, "Aren't you going to tell me what this is all about? Why did we have this talk? Where do I come in and why do you care about my theory?"

"No, Charlie, I'm not going to say anything more right now. You had a free lunch and we had a nice talk. I very well may get back to you and then maybe we can get into some heavy discussion. For now let's leave it at that." Concannon reached across the table and took Rose's hand, they shook and said goodbye. Rose finished his coffee and slowly left the restaurant still wondering what they hell it was all about.

As soon as he closed the door to his house he tossed his keys onto the counter and reached for the phone. He dialed and a voice came on the line stating, "Federal Bureau of Investigation. How may I help you?"

"Agent Paul Caverly, please."

"Agent Caverly speaking."

"Hey, Paul, it's Charlie. How's it hanging?"

"Good, man. What's up?"

"Listen, I need to talk to you, can we meet after work?"

"Yeah, sure, what's up?"

"Not on the phone, Paul, later. Our usual place, say about six?"

"Yeah, that's cool, see you there."

At 5:55 Charlie was sipping his scotch when Paul reached the table and shook the hand of his friend. "Hey, man. What's up?"

"Senator Concannon is what's up. Anything you can tell me?"

"Let me think. He's been around awhile, three or four terms. He's on several committees, military and crime, I think. I know he's the head of another, but damn if I can remember which one. Why, Charlie, what's up with Senator Concannon?"

Charlie filled him in on the lunch and conversation and added, "You know I don't trust any politician, never have, never will. I don't have any idea what this guy is up to and I wanted to pick your brain."

"I'll nose around and see what I can find. Maybe he wants to give you a job."

"Yeah, I'm sure the senator needs a fifty-six-year-old retired cop."

Two days later the phone rings and Paul tells Charlie that everything he can find out is good. "An honest man and very patriotic, a real flag-waver. It's said he is very frustrated the way the country is going and there's a hint that he may run for president. I haven't heard a bad word spoken about the man even from the other side of the aisle."

Charlie said, "Thanks, buddy. I owe you one," and replaced the phone on the receiver. "Isn't this interesting. Well, as usual we'll have to see how this all plays out."

Over the next week Charlie Rose for the first time in his life attended two Senate committee hearings open to the public. He had found that Concannon had two open hearings this week and he made sure he attended both. He sat in the gallery and listened intently when Concannon spoke and he liked what he heard. He was a hawk; he spoke openly and showed his frustration at several of his milk-toast colleagues. After the second hearing, he was leaving when approached by a man who said, "Mr. Rose?"

"Yes, I am."

"Senator Concannon wishes to speak with you, will you please follow me."

"Charlie, how are you?"

"Fine, Senator, and you?"

"Please sit down and let's talk for a minute, that's all the time I have, sorry. I noticed you in the gallery the other day and again today. You have an interest in the subject of the hearing?"

"No, not at all. I came here to hear you and watch you in action, that's all. I want to know everything about you. That's the way I run an investigation.

Know your victim, know your accused or suspect, know as much as you can to add it all up; and come to a common sense conclusion."

Concannon grinned and said, "That's only fair. I checked you out before I contacted you; I guess you have the same right. I hope you found what you wanted. Listen, I really do have to run. I wanted to ask if you can come to dinner this," looking at his calendar, "Wednesday night, around 6:30?"

"Yes, I can make it."

"Okay, good. We can get to some really good conversation after dinner. Listen, my wife will be out of town, so it's just you and me."

"Okay, sure, fine."

"Casual please."

After a pleasant dinner both were sipping brandy and talking about family, retirement and run-of-the mill daily routines. Senator Concannon finally said, "Okay, Charlie, let's get down to some serious discussion. The house is empty and we can talk freely and without interruption. I like your fifteen-cent theory and I want to hear more. Are you willing to talk with me or better yet join me in what I'll call a new venture?"

Charlie thought for a half-minute, formed his words and said, "You see, Senator…"

"Stop," said Concannon. "Let's keep it Carl and Charlie tonight, okay?"

"Okay, if that's what you want. Carl, I'm not sure I know what your venture is. Is it business, politics, what?"

"That's a fair question. I can give you an explanation for now, but it's only a brief one, not all the facts just yet. I have been thoroughly pissed for some time at the way our country is going. Our president is trying to get it straightened out, but it's not going too well. We are slowly but surely losing our status in the world. Some think we're already a second-rate nation. There are others, besides me, who think the same way and these are people I trust. There is not an actual group formed and we have no actual agenda on paper, but I'm working on that. The bottom line is that I may run for the presidency and if I do, what we put to paper will be my platform. This platform will be based on radical change, so radical we could become a police state for a period of time." He stopped and sipped his brandy. "Does that idea shock you, Charlie?"

"No, not really. Not much shocks me anymore, but I am surprised." He too picked up his drink and sipped, then continued, "I'm surprised that someone has the balls to think like you. What you're thinking could be just what this country needs, but I can't see it ever happening."

Carl stood, walked to the bar and refilled his drink. After a sip he said, "Well, I agree with you, it does sound far-fetched when you think of our present and past way of life and form of government. In order for us to regain what's been lost and then move foreword, something that far-fetched just may work. For tonight let's leave it at that. I want to know your thoughts. I will ask you the same question I asked ten days ago: If you were in charge and could make changes, what would you do?"

It was Charlie's turn to stand, walk to the bar and refill. After a small sip he said, "There are so many things I want to see change; I don't know where to begin. First off I'd quit the war and pull out. I'd stop all foreign aid. I told you about shooting the druggies. I'd also start shooting the wetbacks crossing our borders. I'd throw out those already here illegally. I'd get rid of welfare and throw about ninety percent of the welfare recipients off the rolls and put them to work. They could do a lot of things; clean streets, build roads and houses. I'd get rid of the civil court system where these outrageous amounts of settlements are handed out. I'd fire half the judges we have now. I'd make a maximum speed limit of fifty-five mph for everyone and a nasty penalty for violations of it. I'd make car manufacturers make engines that would only allow a vehicle to do fifty-five mph. I'd force mass transportation on people. The prison system would no longer be a hotel; they would work and work hard, chain-gang style. Shit, I could go on for hours. There are so many unfair practices like divorce laws, adoption rules, stupid shit that hurts a lot of little people. Common sense would prevail." Charlie stopped and sat down almost out of breath. "I guess I must sound like a preacher, huh?"

"No, Charlie, you sound like the man I thought you might be and I like most of what you said. Getting any of it to happen will be the real trick and it will not be easy. Look, let's do this: I'd like you to put these ideas to paper. Take a week or ten days and give it some deep thought. Oh, I guess I should first ask you if you want in. Do you think this is something you would want?"

"Carl, why me? I'm just a retired cop. There's a whole lot of people out there a lot smarter than me."

"Charlie, I'm asking you, not anyone else. I can't promise you anything. There are an awful lot of things that need to happen for this to work. I like your ideas and I want you in, but what does it mean? Look, I don't know what the future holds for this, I can only hope it works. For now just take ten days or two weeks and write it all down. Think about what's been said and decide for yourself. I'll not twist your arm. It's strictly up to you. Before we quit, I'd like to ask you one more question. The speeding thing, go into some detail, what's in your head?"

"Well, like I said I'd make the speed limit fifty-five mph nationwide. I'd have a system set up so that daily violations are inputted on a same-day basis so it would always be up-to-date. It could be manned by some of those thrown off the welfare rolls. Each time a person violates the rule, he is ticketed. First offense is $500. Second offense is $1,000 and a third offense, they lose their car. If a driver changes his name, address, buys a phony license or however he tries to get around the law, we slap his ass in jail for thirty days on the chain gang. It may take a while, but I will guarantee to stop the speeding problem. We'll save a lot of gas too. I would also make all motor vehicle regulations uniform throughout the country. All states would be uniform."

"Charlie, I love it. I can't believe you had all that on the tip of your tongue."

"Carl, when you've been dealing with shitheads for twenty-five years and seeing all the misery these shitheads cause, its always right on the tip of your tongue. It's hard to forget the carnage I've seen."

"Alright, let's call it a night. I'll call you in ten days or so and we'll see where we stand. Good night, Charlie and thank you."

"Night, Carl."

During the next ten days Charlie thought and wrote. His list of things he would change was put to paper.

WELFARE REFORM. Everyone who is capable of working will. Each case will be evaluated and possibly eighty percent will be taken off. Jobs will be made for them such as the data system for the speeding change. Body pickups will be needed for the druggie deaths. Cleaning roads, building roads, building anything that needs labor.

MOTOR VEHICLE. All states will have the same motor vehicle regulations. The speed limit will be fifty-five mph for everyone. Violators first offense is a $500 fine. Second offense, is a $1,000 fine. On the third offense, their car is confiscated. Anyone circumventing the rules in any way goes to the chain gang for thirty days of hard labor.

AUTOMOBILE MANAFACTURES will build cars that cannot exceed the fifty-five mph limit.

INCOME TAX REFORM. Everyone pays a flat tax to be determined by the financial people who know these matters. The basic premise is everyone will pay "X" percent of his income.

PRISON REFORM. All inmates will work eight hours a day. The harder the prisoner, the harder the work. The chain gang is back with guards ordered to shoot to kill anyone escaping or trying.

COURT REFORM. All court cases, criminal and civil, will be heard by a panel of three judges. Speed will be the priority. All legal maneuverings are out. Hear the facts of the case and make a decision in one day or less. Civil cases are only heard if the facts merit it. Those civil justices freed up by the caseload will help out in the criminal section. Realistic awards for civil cases.

ADOPTION REFORM. If a baby is available for adoption and a couple is available to adopt it, so be it, first come, first served. Birth mother cannot change her mind once the adoption is done.

FOREIGN AID. All aid is stopped. All money presently used for this purpose will now be used only in the U.S.A. Cases of natural disaster will be judged on the merits. Friends of our country will be the only ones considered.

MILITARY REFORM. All military units will be brought back to the U.S. All bases in foreign countries closed.

IMMIGRATION REFORM. All immigration stops. All illegals in the country will be deported unless it's in our best interest to keep them.

U.S.-CHARTERED COMPANIES. Any U.S.-chartered company will make his product in this country. No tax breaks for any company. All U.S. products get first priority for sale.

MEXICAN BORDER. Inform the Mexican government that we are closing the border to illegals and drug runners. If they can't stop the problem on their side, then we will start shooting them.

THE UNTIED NATIONS. Quit it immediately. They are a useless organization that costs us too much money. China once called us a Paper Tiger. The UN is the real Paper Tiger. Start towing all the diplomatic cars that owe New Your City so much money and then tell them to vacate the building.

WAGE BOARD. Set up a board to set standards for wages based on the worth to the country, education, etc. Dedication is a criteria to be used. Labor unions are out. The outrageous sport salaries, CEOs, lawyers, etc. are out. The best will be topped out at $100,000. Wages and prices are to work hand and hand. Free enterprise is alive, yet it needs to be fair.

PUBLIC OFFICIALS. Any public official who abuses the color of his office will be jailed or shot depending on the severity of the offense. No exceptions. The public needs to see it's fair to all in order for the changes to work.

WEAPONS. Weapons can be kept by hunters and collectors, but any person carrying a gun and not committing a crime will be jailed for five years. Any person carrying or using a gun or dangerous weapon while committing a crime gets shot on the spot.

SERVING YOUR COUNTRY. Upon graduation of high school, all males and females will enter the military service for a period of eighteen months. The only exceptions are those really physically unfit, diseased, etc. Minor sickness, such as asthma, is not an excusable reason. College classes can be taken while in the service, but nobody goes to college full-time until their service time is served, Israeli style. Anyone quitting school before graduation gets drafted immediately, if at least seventeen years of age.

SUPREME COURT. All Supreme Court justices are on sabbatical for the period of change. They can and will assist wherever needed and hear criminal cases of a higher nature. All appeals court judges will do the same and there will be no appeals. The courtroom workload could climb or decrease. As we expect, one day's trial and sentencing, the load could increase; but on the other hand with the severity of our system we may deter a lot of crime.

THE MEDIA. The media will be asked to do their part by printing and broadcasting the new rules and regulations to the public. If they don't, they will be ordered to do so. As new ideas and problems arise, changes will be necessary. The media will keep the public informed on a daily basis. Media criticism is expected and will be tolerated to a point. If their criticism hurts the good of the nation, it will cease or their publication will cease.

PRICE CONTROL BOARD. Like the Wage Control Board. Prices are out of control, such as prescription drugs, malpractice insurance, etc. Reasonable profit will be allowed, but excessive profits will stop.

LOBBIES. The practice of lobbying will cease in D.C. and all state and local offices. No longer will any legislator, governor, mayor, etc. be pressured to use or protect a product or service.

DONATIONS. Monetary donations to any political organization or individual politician are prohibited.

Charlie put his pen down and thought about what he had just written. *I think a lot more will have to be added to the list but it's a good start. Will this guy have the balls to try and go through with this? Will I? As usual, we'll see how it all goes.*

Eleven days passed and Charlie was sitting at the kitchen table paying some bills when the phone rang.

"Hey, it's Carl."

"Hi, Carl. What's up?"

"Can you make a dinner meeting tomorrow night?"

"I guess I can."

"My driver will pick you up at 5:00 p.m., is that okay?"

"Yes, fine. Is it dress or casual?"

"A step up from casual, but no jacket or tie."

At 4:58, a light blue Town Car pulled in his driveway and a middle-aged black man walked to his door.

"Mr. Rose?"

"Yes."

"I'm James, nice to meet you, sir."

"Same here, but please, no 'sir.' I'm a working stiff or used to be just like you. Would it be okay if I rode with you up front?"

"Why, I guess it would be okay. Not many folks would, but sure, it's fine."

James was humming a gospel tune while making turn after turn until Charlie got his bearings and observed they were heading west on Route 50.

"Where we heading, James?"

"All I'm allowed to say is Northern Virginia, horse country."

"Okay, that's a start."

Nearly an hour later, Charlie noticed a sign upon entering the town of Middleburg. He also noticed the class of homes had gotten much more expensive looking. He also saw several large farms, horse farms mostly. James made a right turn off 50 onto a secondary road, but Charlie didn't see a street sign or name. Another ten minutes of driving through some beautiful countryside and James turned and entered a private driveway. In the driveway another 500 yards and they came to a fence and gatehouse with a guard. Charlie immediately observed the guard was packing a semi-automatic holstered on his hip.

"Can I help you?" the guard asked politely.

James replied, "Yes, sir; I have a passenger for your dinner party, Mr. Charles Rose."

The guard walked to the passenger side and asked, "May I please see your ID?"

Charlie handed him his driver's license and the guard said, "One moment, please," and started walking away. He walked to the guardhouse, picked up a phone and talked for a very brief minute and returned to the car. Handling the driver's license over he said, "You may proceed to the main house." He stepped back and the gate opened.

James drove in about 1,000 yards and Charlie saw a two-story house that impressed him. The red-bricked house had a nice light yellow trim that fit the area perfectly. The yard and everything in sight was meticulously maintained. Charlie said to himself, *Definitely out of my league.*

James escorted him to the front door and before he could knock, it opened. Carl Concannon stood with his hand extended and said, "Good evening, Charlie. Nice to see you."

"Same here, Carl." Charlie turned to thank James and saw he had vanished.

The inside of the house was as impressive as the outside had been, even more so. As they walked towards a large open area a female who appeared to be fifty-five to sixty years of age and dressed rather smartly handed him a scotch.

"Charlie, this is our hostess, Barbara Twell."

"It's nice to meet you, Mr. Rose. I have been waiting to meet you for some time."

"Thank you, Madam Justice."

"Oh, you know me?"

"Yes, Madam Justice, I certainly do. In my previous life, I once had the honor of protecting your back, but I'm quite sure you never knew it."

She smiled and replied, "I'd like to hear all about that one day when we have the time. Please follow me to the library and we can meet the other guests."

Upon entering the room Charlie observed three men and a woman all chatting with drinks in their hands. When the group saw the three entering the room they all turned as Barbara Twell clapped her hands.

"Friends, please allow me to introduce you all to Mr. Charles Rose. This lady is Catherine Carter, assistant secretary of the treasury." They both shook hands. Turning she introduced Senator Craig Trobridge, again a handshake. "This gentleman is Congressman Sid Braverman."

Charlie went through the motions of another handshake feeling his heart racing. It felt like it was at one hundred beats a minute and a small accumulation of sweat was appearing on his brow.

"Our final guest is Mr. Steven Ames, CEO of Ames, Lane and Parker Brokerage."

Charlie turned to Carl after the last handshake and said, "I feel I may be in a little over my head here. I am very impressed with your friends, Carl."

"Well, I hope you can relax now, Charlie. I will say that those here are equally impressed with you."

"Please, everyone, let's sit and chat for a while and get to know each other better."

Everyone except Charlie did just that. Charlie was trying to figure out what all these prestigious people gathered here had to do with him and the plan that Carl had talked about. Rather than trying here and now to figure it all out he reverted to his usual, let's see how it all plays out.

After a pleasant dinner they all returned to the library and were sipping brandy or wine. Carl interrupted the leisure by saying, "Please, sit and let's get to the reason were here. Charlie, the people before you are part and parcel to my plan, the plan I vaguely outlined to you. The six of us are the nucleus of the movement we hope you will join with." The look of surprise or shock on Charlie's face must have been very evident to Carl as he said, "Yes, Charlie, we're asking you to join us."

Charlie's head was pounding, his hands were damp and his was pulse racing. He actually was terrified that he might pass out. He stood and faced the group of six and said, "You have only just met me tonight, how can you be so sure of me?"

Carl answered first by saying, "Charlie, when we first met I told you that I had been following your career with interest. I was very impressed with you and the list you wrote out and I could have told you that each of these people were equally impressed. At that time I was just the spokesman for the group. At this time, everyone here has agreed on you joining us.

"Before you give us your answer let me add a few thoughts. The ideas you put to paper and more ideas we have will be my platform when I run for the presidency. We all hope and pray that if elected, based on this platform and with the people backing us, we will change the was our government operates and return us to a world power. Each of these people has a group of peers who feel the same as we do. It's like a pyramid. Not one person here has asked what's in it for me. I know I can trust everyone here isn't seeking anything for himself, but everything for his country. We feel that you too have the same attributes. Will you join us?"

Charlie was used to making quick decisions; slow ones were usually deadly. Without much hesitation he replied, "I feel very humbled to be one of you and I hope to God I can live up to your expectations."

On the ride home Charlie kept running things over in his head. His final thought for the night was *They never said what would happen if I said no.*

Chapter 4

If you drive north on Route 3 in the state of New Hampshire you eventually will cross the border into Canada where the road becomes Route 257. If you continue north for another fifteen miles, you will enter the town of Scotstown in the province of Quebec.

Most of the residents of Scotstown knew there was a small group of Americans living just outside of the town limits. Most paid no heed to the young Americans, but there was a group of locals who had a major bitch with them. It seemed several of the men did a lot of odd jobs around the area and that didn't sit well with this group. It was taking money from them and they resented it. It was also widely considered that the young Americans were probably draft dodgers, but the locals knew they couldn't do much about it; after all, the Canadian and American authorities didn't seem to care much.

The Americans did their odd jobs, hired themselves out when they could and grew vegetables; and probably got money sent to them from home. It was further known that at least two females and two young children lived in this commune-style relationship. The building they occupied was really an old barn that was converted into living quarters. It was rented by an old couple who owned the land and could care less what the locals thought. They needed the money to subsist themselves. Living in Canada when you're retired is no easy task. They paid green American greenbacks and paid it on time.

The local police also knew of the Americans, knew they caused no problems; hence, they paid no attention to the local dissatisfaction. At least once a week, sometimes more, one or more of the Americans would go to town to buy food, fuel or whatever it was they needed. Over time they had learned what merchants were friendly towards them and that's where they spent their money.

One bright, sunny day it did not go unnoticed that three new faces had appeared in Scotstown. To those who were sharper than others it was further observed that the white Chrysler minivan had Massachusetts plates and carried two men. The third man drove a Canadian vehicle with government plates. The three men had hoped to be in town for a short period of time and did not want to raise any eyebrows, but they had just by being there. The previous evening the two Americans who just happened to be U.S. Army military police officers had met the Royal Canadian Mounted Police officer at the New Hampshire State Police barracks in Second Lake, N.H. Staff Sergeants Warren Oats and Randy Johnson met with MP Sergeant Peter McGinnis in a conference room of the barracks. Oats filled McGinnis in on what they were going to do and why. McGinnis had orders from the very top level of the mounted police that he was to give the Americans anything they wanted, within reason. They told him the Americans wanted to make an arrest and no paperwork would be needed. The arrestee was to be taken to the border and passed through with no questions asked. It was hoped that no violence would occur during the arrest, but if it did McGinnis was to minimize it.

"This is our target, Peter, Vincent Wainwright," he said, handing McGinnis a photo. "He's a white male, age twenty-two, five feet eleven inches and about 185 pounds. He is a draft dodger and we will be taking him back to the U.S."

"But why, Warren? The draft dodgers have been around for over two years and nobody cared about them before, why now?"

"I don't have a right answer for you, Peter, but I will tell you this much, all over your country this same conversation is taking place right now. We are just one team for one arrest. It's my understanding that there are hundreds of other teams doing the same thing."

"Jesus, mother of God, do you mean your government is finally doing something about this mess?"

Oats smiled, telling McGinnis, "That's just what I'm saying, but it's not for publication just yet. In a week or so I'm sure you'll be reading about the whole deal."

"What we'd like to do tomorrow is drive up to Scotstown, look over the area, locate their address and see which way the wind blows."

McGinnis nodded his head in agreement and asked, "What about the local police?"

"We'll have to fill in the local head man of our target and our intentions. If we need more help, he's our man."

The three men entered the Scotstown Police Department after breakfast and now they, along with the chief of the local police, left town in the Canadian-plated car. Chief Bruce Kibblehouse directed the car north for about a mile, turned off onto a dirt road and stopped.

Kibblehouse pointed and said, "You see that barn there? That's the place you want. I have never been inside, but I have been told it was converted into living space. The Foulks are the owners and live in the house to the left. No problem with them either, they just don't like town folks."

"What's behind the barn?" Oats asked.

Kibblehouse thought for a second and said, "Not much--a yard and some woods about thirty-five yards behind the barn."

"Do they have running water, toilet facilities?" McGinnis asked to nobody in particular.

"I have no idea," replied Kibblehouse.

McGinnis turned to Oaks and said, "Have you seen enough for now? I think I have an idea how we could get in."

Oats thought for a moment, looked at Johnson and Kibblehouse and said, "I guess we have enough for now."

Kibblehouse started the car, turning towards the road and said, "Let's get back and see what you have up your sleeve."

McGinnis then just blurted out, "What do you think would happen if I drove right up the house with my Canadian car, plates and accent and told them I was a health inspector; that we had a complaint they had no facilities and that I needed to see for myself."

Oats looked right at McGinnis smiling. "Not bad, not bad at all. What do you think, Chief, will it work around here?"

"Well, I guess it could work. See, I don't generally get involved with health stuff unless they suspect trouble. I guess it could work, nothing ventured, nothing gained."

The next morning at 9 a.m. Sergeant Oats, Johnson and McGinnis, along with Chief Kibblehouse, sat with Dale Seymour, Province of Quebec Board of Health.

McGinnis spoke first, "Dale, we need to check this place out relative to a criminal matter. The person we're looking for is this man," passing the photo to him. "It's not a dangerous matter, but then you never know. I propose that we go as a health inspection team, you and I. We've had a complaint that the barn is occupied without the proper health facilities. Once we're in, we want to look the place over, see who's there, our target especially, are there guns around, other people, kids present, whatever intel we can gain from it. Do you think you're up to this, Dale?"

Seymour, a timid-looking man of perhaps forty, didn't answer. He appeared to be thinking over what he had just heard. In fact, that's exactly what he was doing because he suddenly said, "I have several questions. First, who authorized this?"

McGinnis looked him squarely in the eye and replied, "Dale, I have direct orders from the chief officer of the RCMP, who received direct orders from our prime minister to allow this action to be taken." McGinnis reached for the telephone, picked it up and handed it to Seymour. "Dale, feel free to call the chief officer." He handed him a card, noting that it was a direct line to the chief officer's desk.

Seymour looked at the card, seemed to be forming words, but didn't say anything. He finally said, "No, I don't think that will be necessary. Do you think there is any danger for us?"

McGinnis immediately replied, "No, but you can't be sure. These people are American draft dodgers and criminals. This Wainwright fellow will be arrested is all you need to know right now; but in the very near future you'll see the whole picture and your part in it and you'll be able to talk about it then."

Seymour was a meek man, but not stupid. If you looked closely you could see the hint of a smile on his face. None present knew just what he was thinking, but Seymour did. He was thinking to himself that this could be the only time in his life he could be some sort of hero. *To myself, my wife, my children and my country. Wow, a hero.* "I do have one more question if you don't mind," Seymour added.

McGinnis nodded and Seymour asked if he would be armed. McGinnis shot a glance at Oats and said "No"; and Oats said "Yes." Then they all looked at each other.

Oats said, "You first, McGinnis."

"Well, I figure they are naive and unsuspecting. We should easily pass for a health department team, so why risk a confrontation if we can avoid it?"

Oats thought before he answered, "I agree with that, but I'm not sure I'm good with it."

"Look, Oats, we're in Canada and I'm an RCMP officer. Trust me, please."

Oats smiled and agreed, "Peter, you're right. But I do want two cars to back you up as close to the site as possible. One on each side of the barn and out of sight, but close enough to be a help if needed."

"Okay, I'll buy that, "McGinnis added.

The next morning with Seymour driving his Board of Health car, they headed towards the Foulks home. McGinnis was admiring his new ID card showing him to be an inspector of the Province of Quebec Board of Health.

Seymour observed and said, "They did a good job with the photo, don't you think?"

"Yes, they did. Remember, Dale, we address each other by our real names, you understand? It's easier and no chance to slip up. It's Dale and Peter, right?"

"Yes, I have it, but I am a bit nervous."

"Dale, relax, please, you do just what you normally would do in a situation like this. Look for health problems. Just keep your eyes and ears open and remember what we're looking for…Wainwright and weapons. Don't overdo it, just look and listen. Okay? You all right?"

Seymour breathed deeper and replied, "Yes, I'm all right."

When the doorbell rang Rene Foulks looked at his wife with surprise. Rarely did anyone call. *Maybe it was the Americans,* he thought. When he opened the door, to his surprise, there stood two men looking at him. "Yes, what do you want?"

Seymour smiled and announced, "Good morning, sir; I'm looking for Rene Foulks."

"That's me, and who are you?"

Holding his ID card up, Seymour continued, "I'm with the Province Board of Health."

Rene looked at the offered ID of both men and replied, "What do you want here?"

Seymour fell right into his job mode now and said, "We have received a complaint that your barn is occupied by humans without the proper facilities and we must see if this is true."

Rene shot right back with, "Who made this complaint?"

Seymour added smoothly, "I'm sorry, I am not allowed to answer that unless it comes to a court proceeding."

Rene exhaled with a contempt all people have for such interruptions of their lives and with, "This is all bullshit. They have just what they need and there is no health problem."

McGinnis got into the act with, "Mr. Foulks, I'm Peter McGinnis, you have seen my identification already."

Before McGinnis could continue Rene said, "I don't give a damn who you are, there's no health problem here."

McGinnis smiled at Foulks this time and added, "Mr. Foulks, why don't we just go out to the barn and let us see for ourselves. If what you say is correct, we can be in and out in two minutes and it's all over."

Foulks seemed to hesitate before saying, "Okay, let me get my coat and you'll see."

In less than ten minutes McGinnis and Seymour were out and back in the car heading for town. As soon as they were out of sight McGinnis reached under the seat and pulled out a mike and spoke to his backup cars. "We're out of the residence and heading towards town, do you both receive that?"

Oats replied "Received" and then Kibblehouse replied the same.

McGinnis sipped his coffee with a smile. "You know these kids have a good setup. They are perfectly legal, running water and all. They have an outside john which Seymour tells me is also legal in these parts."

Oats interrupted with, "Was Wainwright there?"

Seemingly giddy with the success of the operation, McGinnis put his coffee down and replied, "Yes, he was and bit suspicious at first. He asked for and looked over our ID very carefully. He asked a few technical questions and Seymour answered very smoothly and technically. He calmed down after that. He has long hair and a goatee but it's him alright. There was another guy outside chopping wood and I got a look at him, but no ID naturally. There were also three females and one small child maybe two years old. They have partitioned the place off into living quarters, a kitchen and a general sitting area. I'll diagram it later when we're done here."

"Any guns visible?" asked Kibblehouse.

"No, not that I observed. Did you see any, Dale?"

"Nothing out of the ordinary," Seymour added.

Oats then chimed in with, "Okay, let's wrap this up. Once we have the diagram we can figure out what we need to do, I'd like to grab him tomorrow and be gone."

After a quick lunch the four men sat down together. Oats stated, "Seymour is on his way with our thanks and an admonishment to keep quiet until this hits the papers. He seemed as happy as a kid in a candy store. I got the impression he really enjoyed his 'undercover operation' as he called it."

After an hour or so of discussion everyone felt confident of their plan. The same crew who had done today's operation would be enrolled again tomorrow. As there were only two doors to be covered it seemed to be a simple deal as long as nobody pulled out a weapon. It was hoped that at 5 a.m. with everyone asleep, then confused, it should be quick and successful.

At 4:45 a.m. both entry teams were in place and waiting. The regular entry door was already picked open. Oats was very good with a pick set and had the job done in less than three minutes. Oats and Johnson were to enter before the 5 a.m. entry of the second team in hopes of finding Wainwright and getting him neutralized first. Oats figured only Wainwright was wanted and had the most to lose. As both men were watching the seconds tick away toward entry, they had to freeze and hug the wall as they saw a light at the same time. It came from inside the barn. It seemed to be bouncing as if whoever was holding it was walking down a flight of stairs. In fact it was a flashlight and the holder of same was one Vincent Wainwright who was pulling on a coat as he walked towards the door. He exited the door and headed straight ahead towards the outhouse. Both men froze in both fear and anticipation. Both immediately realized where Wainwright was headed and as the fear subsided, Oats broke out in a wide grin that couldn't be mistaken for anything other than sheer joy.

Oats thought to himself, *Shit, he's making this too easy for us. He's cornered himself with virtually no chance for him to go for a gun.*

After the outhouse door opened and closed, Oats eyed Johnson and nodded to move to the outhouse. Combat-trained men always work with hand signals and this was just the right situation. Oats motioned that when the door opened they would grab him. Oats pointed to himself that he would grab Wainwright's head and hope to muffle any cry. As the door opened both men were coiled like springs ready to leap upon their prey. Before they could move, Wainwright dropped his flashlight, swore and bent over the pick it up.

As Wainwright reached to pick the light up Johnson put a 45-caliber pistol to Wainwright's ear and whispered, "I wouldn't make a sound if I were you."

Wainwright couldn't make a sound if he wanted to as Oats had his hands around Wainright's head and mouth. He froze as the cuffs were quickly applied to his wrists. Oats and Johnson pulled him to his feet and walked him to the rear of the outhouse. Johnson quickly then ran to the front main door to stop the second team from making their entry.

Oats bent down and whispered into Wainwright's ear, "Listen to me carefully, you are under arrest. We're going to enter the barn and find out the identities of everyone inside. We don't want to hurt anyone, especially the child and the women, do you understand that?"

Wainwright nodded his head in the affirmative.

"Okay good. I'm going to ask you one time and one time only. Is the other guy inside a draft dodger also?"

Wainwright's eyes bulged wildly with the sudden realization of just what was happening. He slowly closed his eyes and nodded in the affirmative.

The main door entry group were now crowded around Oats and Wainwright. Again Oats whispered into Wainwright's ear, "Now listen carefully again, here's what we're going to do next. I'm going to walk you inside very quietly and you're going to point out the other guy. We're going to arrest him also. In order that nobody gets hurt, you're going to do this right, you understand me?"

Nod yes again.

"If anyone gets hurt, it's because you did something stupid and it's all going to be on your head."

Oats now turned towards McGinnis. "You take your group after we get the second guy in custody. Be careful please, this has been too easy so far. I don't want to see it go bad now. Got it, are we all on the same page?"

Nods of yes by all.

Three minutes later all the lights in the barn were on. The scene looked like a practice session from a law enforcement training session. Two young men lay face down on the floor cuffed behind their backs. Three females looked like they were in shock.

Oats stood facing all seven occupants of the barn. All eyes were glued to his face. "Okay, now listen up," he barked. The two men were now sitting on their butts, still cuffed behind their backs. One of the females was very gently weeping. "We are military police officers from the U.S. Army," he said pointing at Johnson and himself. "The other men in this party are Canadians representing the Royal Mounted Police and the Scotstown Police. Wainwright is a draft dodger and is going back to the U.S. under arrest. You", pointing to the second young man, "I suspect are also a dodger and you will be detained until we can ascertain your positive identity and verify your status. If you are who I suspect you are, you can also tell us now and save everyone a lot of time."

The young man looked directly at Oats with tears flowing down his cheeks and uttered, "You're right, I am a draft dodger. My name is Jason Steinmetz from Brooklyn, New York."

Oats now faced the ladies and uttered, "You will each furnish Sergeant McGinnis with valid identification. If you cannot do that then you will be detained until positive ID can be made. I am not in the position to say what if any charges may or could be lodged against you, but you definitely have been aiding two criminals from justice. I am asking you to please cooperate now and let's hope this all ends right here and now." Again, turning towards the men Oats looked at Steinmetz directly and said, "Now while you ladies get out your ID, Jason and I need to talk."

From this point on it was easy as both groups of men and women seemed relieved it was all over and hoped life would return to some semblance of order. Three hours later, Oats, Johnson, Wainwright and Steinmetz crossed the border and were back in the U.S.

As Oats and his vehicle crossed the border into New Hampshire, a hundred and some miles to the west, in a working-class neighborhood deli of West Toronto, a young couple was finishing up their breakfast.

Eighteen-year-old Melissa Stanley watched as her boyfriend, soon-to-be-husband finished his coffee. "How did work go last night, honey?"

The young man looked at her as he was thinking what he wanted to say. He was still pissed at her for the argument of yesterday, the same constant argument. He was getting really tired of her question, *When are we going home?* She just didn't seem to see the problem he faced back home. Finally, he put his mug down and looked at her. "It's boring as shit to work all night in a job with no future."

Melissa immediately jumped in with, "That's right in line with our lives right now, no future here in Toronto."

"Come on, Melissa, you know damn well I want to end this shit, but what choice do I have? You want to see me go to jail?"

"No, but nobody's gone to jail yet, at least that we know of."

"I know, I know, but right now I need to sleep, let's get out of here."

Holding hands Steve and Melissa left the deli and walked out onto the sidewalk heading towards their apartment. The two men walking directly at them got Steve's attention fast and he wheeled around in the opposite direction. As they did so there were two more men of identical design facing them. Steve opened his mouth to ask just what the men wanted of them as he felt two strong hands grab him from behind and force his hands into a set of cuffs. The distinct whirl and click of the cuffs locking got Melissa's attention also. At that very moment the sheer terror of just what was happening struck both of them like a lightning strike. Both heard the dreaded words they had hoped never to hear, "Steven Jacobs, you are under arrest."

Four hours later several employees of the Toronto International Airport remarked that it was unusual, but not unheard of to see an American Air Force C141 taxiing on the tarmac. As they returned to their work, the C141 lifted off the runway and headed south. Not a single soul outside that aircraft knew that inside the plane were forty-six young American men returning to their homeland and to an adventure they never dreamed possible.

On rare occasions different agencies of the U.S. government can work together. Many DEA agents had been taken from their regular duties to effect arrests. The head of the DEA Investigations Section during a regular weekly meeting had a revelation. All the DEA agents knew that many draft dodgers were working in the drug trade. When one was caught they naturally wanted to talk to cut themselves a deal. Several dozen of the dodgers were working on the Mexican side of the border with Texas, New Mexico, Arizona and California.

Chief investigator in the Texas area, Thomas Gallagher, stood before his staff explaining what they already knew. He raised his voice slightly and said, "Here's my plan. We are sitting in the cat bird's seat on this one. We have an active case against Lamar Stevenson and Robert Needham for trafficking. With the situation being what it is, why not use this opportunity to get the Mexican Police to help us grab these two birds and shut down their business in one felt swoop. We grab two big dealers under the pretext of arresting draft dodgers. To the best of my knowledge there have been no distinct orders to only grab draft dodgers. At this point I want to call the boss and run this by him. If he buys it they can set up a meeting with the Mexican authorities. We go into Mexico, grab our two guys and when we return we ask how the government wants to deal with it. My gut feeling is once we have them home, the office won't want anything but criminal charges. The draft dodger shit will just disappear."

The drive from the home office in El Paso to Presidio is not one most people like. The DEA was used to getting to difficult locations so it wasn't hard to wrangle the Army to fly them by chopper and chalk it up to a training exercise.

Four DEA agents, U.S. Army pilot Major Jack McCauley, the sheriff of Presidio and four members of the Mexican Narcotics Police Unit sat around the large conference table in the Presidio sheriff's building.

Lieutenant Francisco Gomez of the Mexican National Police explained his orders. "I am to assist you in any way to arrest two Americans living on our side of the border in the town of Oninaja. There is to be no paperwork of any kind as long as it all goes routinely. My question is why are you arresting these men and what would cause it to be other than routine?"

Lieutenant Carl Anderson, head of the detail of DEA agents, stood saying, "That's a fair question and you have every right to know. For several years now American draft dodgers have been living on your side of the border. We didn't push it and neither did you. Our government has decided to take back our lost children and these two are lost. Furthermore, they happen to be trafficking in drugs from your country to ours. We thought this would be a good opportunity to kill two birds with one stone." Oh, maybe not a good choice of words Anderson decided. Kill was not the right way to put it, he had quickly realized.

"Look, we want to take them as routinely as possible, no violence if possible, unless we receive it first. Understood?"

Gomez looked at Anderson first and then his three colleagues. "First let me explain to my men in Spanish what you have said and confer with them. If we have any questions, then we will ask." Gomez quickly explained the situation and some bantering went on back and forth between them for a minute or so before Gomez turned to Anderson and asked, "How do you intend to effect the arrest?"

Lieutenant Anderson took out three aerial photos explaining that this was the house the Americans were living in. There was plenty of open space all around the house.

One of the Mexican officers then told Gomez that he recognized the house as one of the locations his unit had been watching. He added that the investigation was in its early stages, but they were sure the traffic was in large quantities of marijuana.

For a half-hour they all talked of different strategies to do the job.

Finally Major McCauley asked if he could add to the discussion. Everyone turned to hear him speak. "From the aerials it's apparent that I could land the chopper right there," pointing to a large open space just to the rear of the house. "Would that be of any help?"

Everyone just stared at McCauley until Anderson asked, "Are you shitting me? You would do that?"

McCauley smiled and looked into Anderson face. "Hey, I was told to assist you in any way possible. I'm not saying we should publish pictures, but if the Mexicans have no objections I don't. Hell, it's only three or four miles from the Rio Grande. We could be in and out in a few minutes."

Gomez and his men discussed the plan in Spanish and turned to Anderson nodding agreement. They all then went about working out details. The Mexican detail of four, along with three DEA agents would hit the house at 4 a.m. If all went according to Hoyle, they would effect the arrest and signal the chopper. The chopper would be sitting running on the American side of the border or flying a circle pattern awaiting a signal.

It was easy sneaking up to the house. It was dark and the neighborhood was very quiet. Three vehicles parked around the yard indicated that maybe more than the two subjects were inside. Two Mexican officers and two DEA agents huddled next to the only two doors to the house. One man at each door was holding a ramming device. Each ram-holder after seeing the door they were to open felt it was not going to be a problem, as the doors look barely usable. At exactly 4 a.m. both doors crashed into kindling wood as the teams entered the house. Shouts of DEA and police reverberated around the neighborhood, but nothing stirred and fortunately no other sounds were heard.

As Anderson and Gomez converged on the scene of the two men lying face down on the floor, they could not help but notice the naked females watching in rapt awe. Gomez motioned to the empty tequila bottles lying scattered around the floor.

Gomez smiled at Anderson. "They made it very easy for us, eh?"

Anderson smiled nodding his head. Anderson quickly changed pace adding, "Okay, let's move. We'll get these two wrapped for transport and call the angel, agreed?"

Gomez nodded his head in agreement. Three minutes later the wop-wop of the rotors was heard as the chopper came in for a landing, but Anderson noted it was surprisingly quiet as it touched down. The DEA men briskly just about threw the two cuffed men into the chopper and were quickly joined by all the DEA agents. The chopper quickly lifted off and headed east toward the U.S. border. Anderson could not contain his curiosity any longer motioning to the crew chief to take his helmet off.

The crew chief did so and asked, "What's up, sir?"

Hollering over the noise Anderson asked why the chopper was so quiet on landing.

The crew chief just smiled at him and shouted back, "Sound-suppression exhaust system. We use it a lot along the border, comes in damn handy at times."

If you were to drive a few miles north of Great Falls, Montana, on Route 15 you will find acre after acre of wheat fields. It would surprise most Americans to learn that the wheat is some of the finest grown in the world. Just off Rt.15 is the small town of Cordova. In Cordova the family Grayson is well known for its wheat ranch. The Grayson wheat acres number well over 1,400 with several hired hands to run the ranch.

The two military police officers from Fort Carlson, Colorado, and the two Montana State Police officers had collaborated on their plan for some time and felt it was a good concept. The youngest of the Montana S.P. officers was Tom Kellogg, who would drive to the Grayson ranch in an old pickup seeking work. If he were lucky enough to gain employment, he could keep an eye on the target and hopefully get close enough to make the arrest easily. Kellogg would have a very small transmitter to call for assistance when the arrest went down or call for help if the need arose.

Kellogg drove to the Grayson ranch and pulled in front of the house. The front door opened and out stepped an older woman, perhaps fifty-five to sixty years, who put her hand over her eyes to shade them from the sun while straining to see who this stranger was. Finally she said, "Hello there, what can I do for you?"

Kellogg removed his hat and replied, "I'm looking for work, ma'am, any chance you may be looking for help?"

Julia Grayson sat down on one of the porch chairs and looked at Kellogg. "I wish I could help you, son, but I've got all the help I need right now. I think maybe the Melborn ranch might need a hand; I could call them for you if you like."

Kellogg knew he had to think fast now; this was what they all had hoped wouldn't happen. He had only been in the field a year since completing the police academy, but he was bright and quick. He felt he didn't have much choice so he reached into his boots and removed his ID and handed it to Mrs. Grayson; and at the same time asking her not to raise her voice. "Mrs. Grayson, I didn't mean to deceive you, but I'm looking for this man and I needed to be careful." Handing her the picture of their target, he glanced around looking for anyone within earshot. "The man's name is Henry Biddy, might you know him?"

Julia Grayson studied the photo and quickly stated, "He works for me, but his name is Price, not Bibby."

Kellogg again looked around trying to see if anyone were near them, but nothing could be seen.

"Where is he now, ma'am?"

"Why, he went into Great Falls this morning to pick up some gear at the farm store. I think he should be back about now."

Kellogg pulled out his transmitter and called the rest of the team to notify them of the turn of events. Just a minute later all three arrived at the house.

Mrs. Grayson was more than startled at this turn of events. "God Almighty, is he dangerous?"

"No, ma'am, this is just routine when two different agencies get involved."

The four men fanned out around the yard. According to Mrs. Grayson he should pull into the driveway and go right to the main barn to unload the gear he picked up. Forty minutes later a newer model green pickup pulled in and drove right to the front door of the main barn. A blonde, young man of perhaps twenty-one or twenty-two years got out and began picking things up from the bed of the truck. He had picked up an apparently heavy item and turned to walk towards the barn when he saw a man standing right in front of him pointing a 45-caliber automatic at his chest.

Bibby just bent forward and laid the heavy item on the ground and looked at the gun asking, "What in hell is going on?"

"Bibby, you're under arrest, please place your hands behind your head now."

He was quickly cuffed and his hands placed behind him.

"Henry Bibby, we are military police officers and these two men are Montana State Police officers. I guess you know why you're under arrest, but let me inform you anyway. You're a draft dodger and your going back to face the music."

"Can I ask one thing, please?"

"Sure, go ahead."

"Could I get my gear from the crew quarters? I have several family pictures I really would like to have, plus my personal stuff."

Looks were exchanged between the military police and nods of approval were given.

"Re-cuff him in front and stay with him. Kellogg, would you handle him and Sergeant Finley will assist while we go get the vehicles?"

Everyone agreed and Bibby, Kellogg and Finley walked towards the bunkhouse. Bibby and Kellogg went inside, left the door open and Finley waited outside the door.

Bibby walked to his bed and motioned to the pack next to it. "That's it." He looked at Kellogg.

Kellogg picked it up and went through it rather quickly and felt it contained nothing harmful. He told Bibby to gather his family pictures just as Finley yelled in to ask if everything was all right. Kellogg turned his head slightly to answer and never saw Bibby take the 9 mm pistol from under his pillow. Kellogg never got a word out of this mouth as the 9 mm slug tore the side of his head apart. As quickly as the echo of the shot reached Finley, a second shot reverberated through the room and Bibby fell to the floor his face a bloody mass. Operation Roundup had taken a bloody turn.

Ocracoke Island is at the southern end of the Outer Banks of North Carolina. To get to this island you must take a short ferry ride to the northern tip of the island. From the south, it's a long ferry ride from numerous places on the mainland. Ocracoke is not a very large island, with only about forty families living there, mostly all fishermen.

Staff Sergeant Art Thompson, a twelve-year veteran of the Marine Corps military police drove the government van off the ferry gently and immediately pulled to the side of the road. He turned to his partner, Sergeant Harry Briener, corporal, USMC. They had known each other from working in the military police at Camp Lejeune and Thomspon was familiar with the N.C. area.

Thompson took out a map and spread it across the steering wheel. "May as well act like a tourist while we get our act together. From here on we dispense with the rank. I'm Art and you're Harry, you with me?"

"I'm with you"

"If we slip up with the rank, we can queer this deal real fast and I don't want to be the first detail to fail. Let's just amble into town and get the lay of the land. We ask the tourist-like questions and actually see a few of the sights. It's not very large, so let's see what's here. We know he's a fisherman, so let's show some interest in fishing. There can't be that many fishing boats out here with a twenty-two-year-old working on them."

Thomspon folded the map and put it aside. He drove forward, noting the Ocracoke Village sign pointing straight ahead.

After a quick lunch, Thompson asked the waitress how many fishing boats were available. The cute little seventeen-year-old asked, "Y'all want to fish?"

"Yes, hon, we do."

She pointed and said, "Just down the street is the main dock and all the fishing boats you want. You can take your pick."

Both men smiled and thanked her as they headed towards the door.

Several slips advertising fishing were empty. One boat was docked and two men were working on its engine. The MPs sat on a bench and began looking around.

The two men working on the boat finally turned around and Thomspon said softly, "No arrest here, they both look in their forties."

Thompson and Briener got up and began walking. Thompson noted the inlet leading out the harbor could be observed while still walking around the village, so they kept walking.

Near 3:30 p.m. Thompson saw a fishing boat coming towards the inlet. As it got closer he estimated the boat to be about thirty-three feet. As it entered the harbor, it appeared that a couple was sitting on the deck and two crewmen were working the boat. One was definitely out; he had a gray beard and was about fifty-five years old. The second crewman looked to be a mate from a distance and looked in the area of eighteen to twenty years old. Thompson and Briener causally walked to the dock the boat was apparently heading for and sat on a bench.

The couple on the deck were chatting away with the older man about the fish they caught. The old man told them that the mate would fillet the fish and they could have them fresh tonight. He was no doubt the captain, but was not easy to follow with his very pronounced Southern accent.

The talk was just chatter back and forth, while the young man took several fish to a fillet table and began his work. He did the job quickly and efficiently; and rewarded the local pelicans with the carcasses of the fish. The boy then handed the couple the fish, adding, "Got about twelve pounds of nice fresh fillets." The man took the fish and handed the young man a ten-dollar bill.

As the couple walked off the dock, the older man could be heard talking to the young man. "A good day of fishing, Jed, you did a fine job. Mom and I are proud of you, son. It won't be long before we retire and you get the boat for yourself." Both men laughed as they began cleaning the boat.

Thompson watched the young man closely and then motioned to Harry and they walked away. Once they got inside the van, they got out their target packet and studied the eight-by-ten picture. "No way, but you need to confirm it," as he passed the photo to Briener.

Briener looked at the picture for only a couple of seconds and responded, "I concur."

"Let's go check out the rest of the island. We need to find a motel for the night."

Later, as they casually finished up a flounder dinner, their waitress, Sarah, walked to the table and picked up the plates. "How 'bout another beer?"

"Good idea, two more."

As the patrons finished up their meals, Art and Harry were finishing up the last of their beer. Thompson saw Sarah walking in their direction and as one who usually makes fast decisions, he called them "gut decisions," made one.

"Any more I can do for you guys? Sarah asked, giving them her big tip smile.

"Yeah, young lady, there is. Can you sit for a minute?"

"Sure, but just a minute, I got to get this place cleaned up."

"Listen here, Sarah; I'm looking for my nephew. He disappeared last year and my sister is just about crazy over it. My friend, Harry, and I been traveling around the coast looking for him. We heard he may be working on a fishing boat."

"What's his name?"

"Well, we don't think he's using his name, see he's hiding. He got this girl pregnant and her daddy wants to kill him, that's why he left so quickly. The girl disappeared about two weeks later and everyone just knows they have to be together."

"God almighty, it could be..."

"Who, Sarah?"

"Well first tell me what he looks like."

"He's twenty-two years old, light brown hair, blue eyes, six foot and maybe 175 pounds."

"Yeah, that sounds like Sandy. That's Sandy Lyle, his wife Joan and their son, Jimmy. They live just up the road there. Well, let me see. It's the second house on Swamp Pond Road, just off Beech Road."

Thompson got hold of himself, trying to act calm and cool but suddenly thought, *She could screw this up totally.* Without another thought, he pulled out a twenty-dollar bill and handed it to Sarah, who just beamed with joy.

"Listen, Sarah, here's the deal. Harry and me are going to ease up to Sandy's house and try and get a look at him. If it's him, I want to call my sister and get her here by morning. I need for you to promise me you won't say anything about this to anyone until we can get his mom here."

"Why sure, I can do that. I won't say a word to anyone, I promise."

"Thanks, Sarah. I'm sure my sister will want to come around and thank you personally."

Sarah's eyes just sparkled with anticipation of another twenty or more.

Thompson and Briener went back to the guest house they had taken a room in. From the van they took the map and located Swamp Pond Road and Beech Road. It was only four blocks to walk, but before they set off they took their night-vision binoculars out of the van. It was dark enough that nobody should see them as they stood behind a crape myrtle tree across from the house suspected of housing their target. After fifteen minutes of checking the house, room by room, Thompson whispered to Briener to get behind the house and see what he could.

It was a good twenty minutes when Briener came back. He whispered in Thompson's ear, "Bingo. He's out back grilling some food and I'm sure it's him."

Both men went to the rear of the house, but by now the target was in what was presumed to be a kitchen. He was sitting at a table opposite a female who was also eating. It didn't take Thompson longer than ten seconds to confirm Briener's assessment, it was the target. Thompson motioned to move away and they got back onto Beech Street and started walking towards the guest house.

When they reached the guest house porch, Thompson said rather loudly, "What say we test the van out on the beach?"

"Good idea," replied Briener.

Nearly fifty yards from the gleaming ocean, Thompson turned off the ignition. "Okay, let's map out a plan." For thirty minutes they worked out plans and revised them until they were satisfied. "Okay, let's go and find the local law and get a feel for him. If we don't like him, we'll call for a Statie."

Sheriff's Deputy Cecil "Bubba" Gore was a very big man, nearly six foot seven and weighing in at 280 pounds. Thompson and Briener chatted with Gore like most tourists would until Thompson mentioned that they were Marine Corps military police.

"Holy shit, so was I. I was in the crotch and an MP also. I was stationed mostly at King's Island, Georgia, looking after those nuke subs. Damn, it's a small world."

After ten more minutes of chatting, Thompson glanced at Briener and they both nodded that they felt they could trust Gore.

"Cecil, is this a good place to talk? I mean nobody needs to hear what I want to tell you."

Gore looked surprised, but quickly regained his composure. "Well no, it's not. That dispatcher there has the biggest mouth in town."

Thomson said, "Let's take a ride on the beach in our van."

"No, my vehicle is a four-wheeler and I need to be in contact by radio. Let's take it."

After filling in Deputy Gore, he said, "That's hard to believe." Gore was just staring at Thompson with his mouth open. "I like that boy; he's a good worker, seems to be a fine family man and is a damn good father. To be all them things and a deserter, don't add up. But shit, I've heard stranger stories than this before."

Thompson let Gore's words trail off before asking him, "What can you tell us about him?"

"He worked here on one of the boats last summer. Said he was going back to college in September, but come Labor Day and he just stayed on. About a month later, I saw him with a pregnant woman. When I finally spoke to him next, he told me it was his wife. He said he liked fishing and Ocracoke so much he was staying. She had the baby in December or January."

After Thompson finished making notes, he put the pad away. "Cecil, what time does the first ferry leave the island in the morning?"

"Well, let me see," putting his massive hand to his temple. "Leaves the other side at 5:45, ten minutes to us and returns at 6:10."

"What about sunrise? What time?"

Gore reached over his visor and withdrew a folder, opened it and began reading. "Let's see, high tide, Monday, sunrise, yeah 6:27."

"Okay, here's what I think is a plan."

In the early morning, parked just one house west of their target, the three men were sipping coffee. Thompson noted it was just about 5:30 when he saw a light go on in the house. "Shit, an early riser," said Art.

"Not really," added Gore. "All fishermen usually get up about this time. They don't even eat or make coffee, just grab the lunch pail the wife made up the night before and head to their boat. They usually sail at sunrise."

Thompson said, "Wait a minute, I have an idea. Instead of going in the house and raising a ruckus, let's take him as he leaves the house, outside. Cecil, you ask him to get in your car, that you need to ask him something. Once he's in the car, we come up, take him and it's all over. With no paperwork, we can be on that ferry before anyone is the wiser."

"That's all well and good for you, Sarge, but remember I got to do some paperwork on him."

"No, Cecil, you don't. Here, read this," handing him the presidential document.

As Cecil read, he said, "Holy Jesus, I ain't never seen one of these before. Are you sure he's just a deserter?"

"Cecil if you have any doubts or feel uncomfortable with that, you call your sheriff and verify what we said."

"No, I don't think I need to do that. I seen your credentials and paperwork, I know you ain't shitting me."

"Okay, Cecil, just a couple of things more. You need to keep this quiet about this until you see in the papers about more arrests. You can then say anything you want, okay?"

"Well, that's not a problem for me, but what about his wife? She's gonna be looking for him."

"Well, you have a good point here, Cecil. She knows he skipped out on the military, so she shouldn't be shocked over his arrest. Tell you what, give us a half-hour start and then you tell her the story. Maybe you can help her out by calling her family if she wants. Okay?"

"Yeah, okay."

"Here he comes, Cecil, move up," as both Thompson and Briener moved away into the shadows.

"Hey, Sandy, need to talk to you a minute."

No sooner had Sandy closed the car door then Thompson and Briener were all over it. Both men had drawn guns and said, "Mr. Radison, you are under arrest for desertion. You will not say a word or utter a sound or I'll crack your head open."

Radison sat wide-eyed as Briener opened the door and got him out of the car. Tears were streaming down his face as his hands were cuffed behind his back. When he saw he was being shackled at the ankles, he sobbed audibly. It was all over in less than two minutes.

After thanking Cecil for helping his wife, Radison was driven away. He finally found the courage to ask if Cecil would really help his wife.

Thompson assured him Cecil would and told him the plans they had discussed. In less than fifteen minutes they were on the ferry and off the island heading north on Rt. 12. They had a six-hour drive ahead of them to Camp Lejeune.

Chapter 5

The White House press secretary, John Brundage, stood at the podium in the press briefing room. The noise was rather loud and definitely not appropriate. It sounded like a children's playground rather then the briefing room. Brundage glanced at his watch and said silently, "It's time." He looked out at the assembly of press and lifted his hand up, palm out. It took a minute, but they complied, knowing that being quiet was the only way they were going to get what they wanted.

"Ladies and gentlemen, please listen carefully," he began. "We have a set of ground rules for this briefing and there will be no deviation, I repeat no deviation. This will not be the usual press briefing, as you may have already guessed. The president has promised all day that he will give the country a brief statement and he will. Please listen to what he tells you and write it down as there will be no questions and answers."

The roar became deafening with reporters shouting out and waving hands. Brundage just smiled and remained calm. He was loving every second of it. Seeing all the pain-in-the-ass reporters begging all the time was tiring and getting old. Just watching them being put into place was most enjoyable to him. They always acted this way; they felt it was their right to get what they wanted. It was about change and he loved it.

Brundage held up his hands and after several seconds they began to calm down. Picking up the mike this time, "People, please listen to me for a moment. The president is waiting for a signal to enter, but he will not do so until we have the rules laid out and you all calm down." The room immediately quieted. "As I was saying, there will be no questions and answers. The president will tell you what he has to say and leave once he's done. When you hear what he has to say, we hope you'll understand more. If there is anyone who cannot abide by these rules, now is the time for him to leave, for good."

Stunned silence pervaded the room. Never before had there been rules like these, never. The silence indicated to Brundage that now was the time and he nodded to a Secret Service agent who opened a door. The president walked in and took the podium.

A smiling President Barringer told all to be seated and they did. "Six days ago I authorized the arrest of every draft resistor we knew of. With the approval of neighboring countries such as Canada and Mexico, members of every branch of the U.S. armed forces, law enforcement agencies and many other government agencies, we began rounding up those who have evaded the draft laws of our country.

"At this time we know that 12,362 have been taken into custody in the US, Canada and Mexico. Most have been moved by military transport to the Marine Recruit Depot, Parris Island, South Carolina. A note about Parris Island: Please save yourself the time and expense of going there, the area is closed down. It is a restricted area for three miles in every direction. The airways about the island are restricted space as are the waters around the island. The Coast Guard is patrolling both air and sea.

"In the next forty-eight hours I will address the nation via our usual means, TV, radio and the paper media. At that time I hope to be more specific with details and will add more information as to what our plans are for those arrested.

"A word of warning, any member of the press corps who badgers anyone from my staff will have their credentials suspended. Any member of the White House staff who talks with the press about anything related to this matter will be leaving government employment immediately. I presume that's clear to everyone." The president turned and walked off the podium leaving a completely stunned press corps.

After Charlie Rose stepped from the shower, he was half-heartedly drying himself. His brain was going a mile a minute thinking about the press conference he had just watched. Carl had said the president was a good man who was trying to get things straightened out. It had taken a large amount of balls to do what he did and he was going to catch a large amount of flack over it. The ringing of the phone brought Charlie back to reality. He picked it up and before he could complete "hello" the caller asked, "Charlie?"

"Yes."

"It's Carl. No time to talk right now nor would I want to over the phone. We need to meet tonight, is that a problem?"

"No, sir."

"Good. Do you think you can find the place we last met?"

"Yes, sir, I think so."

"Good, because I need the car to take me from where I am. Be there by 6 p.m. Okay?"

"Yes, sir, that's fine."

Finding Barbara Twell's home was not a problem. Charlie had kept a good eye on where he was taken and made it without mishap. He stopped at Twell's guard house at exactly 5:50 and handed the guard his ID. At 5:55 he had a scotch in his hand. Five of the group was already present and from what he could hear all engaged in chit-chat relative to the day's events. The entire U.S. and no doubt much of the world was either applauding or condemning the president.

Just after six Senator Concannon arrived and Barbara Twell stood to speak. "I've taken the liberty to have a small dinner buffet prepared. We will have it here in the great room. It will be quick and easy and that will give us more time for the task at hand."

In less than an hour the group had finished dinner and were sipping after-dinner drinks. Carl looked at everyone and felt confident he had their attention. "Okay, folks, we all know what has taken place. What we need to do is to pool our intelligence to see if we've missed anything. For my part I will tell you this. All day my best sources have told me absolutely nothing. It seems the president has a very tight lid on this and if anyone knows anything they are afraid to speak. Usually in D.C. that's a total impossibility, but it's true here. Has anyone gotten anything other then what we all heard from the president?"

Not a single hand went up. "Well, I guess we're all in the same boat. Being on several military committees, I tried to use that to get some input, but got nothing. What I heard only confirms what the president said about security measures. I will add this here and now, I have always liked our president and I know he wants to do what's best, but I never in my wildest dreams thought he would do this. It's a very bold move and in retrospect, a very good one indeed. I like it. Does anyone care to make comment?"

Barbara Twell spoke right up, "I agree it's bold, imaginative and I like it to some degree, but I've put a lot of thought into it and suspect it's going to be challenged in court on several different issues. The word impeachment has been flying around the court all day. I foresee a long and protracted court battle."

"Barbara, I agree," the senator added. "I've heard the ACLU is already gearing up for the fight. What we need to do is see where we fit in now and what course of action do we take, if any. Do we continue working towards our previous goal? Do we want to see how the dust settles? Do we back the president? There are a lot of options here."

For an hour or more the group talked. Comments, opinions and banter flew around the room. The general consensus seemed to be to wait and see what the president had to say in his speech. At this point the group seemed to quiet down and not much was being said.

Carl looked directly at Charlie. "Charlie, is there something wrong? You have barely spoken tonight."

"Not a thing, sir. I'm thinking politics is not my ballpark, but it is yours. You all have a much better insight on this thing."

"You sell yourself short, my boy. You have very good instincts and I want to hear what is in your head."

Charlie was somewhat ill at ease being in the spotlight on this matter. It had happened many times before on the job, testifying in court gets you right up there in the spotlight. But if you have your act together and know your job, it's real easy. It makes you hard and you lose your shyness rather quickly.

Taking a small sip of his scotch, he looked at Carl and asked, "How well do you know the president? I mean are you friends?"

"Well, in the political offices we hold, no, I don't see him often. We are friendly and outside of politics, we know each other rather well. We have spent time together before. Why, what are you thinking?"

"Well, sir, I have spent the entire day mulling this over. Just know this is not off the top of my head. If I was sitting in your shoes, and I'm not, I would want to sit down with the president before his speech to the nation. In the short time I have known you, Senator, I think I have a good part of you figured out. You want this country to turn around, to be what it was and more. I think your aspirations for the presidency are not for personal reasons, but are for the nation's best interest.

"Having said all that, I would tell the president just what you and this group's goal was and is. I'd throw in with him. Let him tell the nation what he and we want to do. Let him ask the nation for a mandate to suspend the Constitution temporarily and until he and we can begin to fix these problems.

"If he is going to face impeachment, he may as well go for the whole ball of wax. If the people back him and want change, good. If they disagree and impeach him, it's over for us too. The whole idea is to get it done all in one fell swoop."

It seemed like an eternity before anyone could or would speak. Senator Concannon finally uttered, "Well, I'll be a son of a bitch."

"I'm sorry, Senator, but that's how I feel."

"Charlie, you don't ever have to say you're sorry to me or us. I think your idea has a lot of merit and we all need to talk this over, now."

The discussion went on for ninety minutes. Concannon finally put a stop to it by asking for a vote. "Before we vote, let me add this. I'm really excited by this idea and I have no ego problem here. I don't need to be president. As long as the job gets done, I'm happy." The vote was 7–0 in favor of throwing in with the president.

As Charlie was getting ready to leave, he held back to say goodbye to Carl, who was on the phone. He was talking with the president's chief of staff, Max Wobser. "Max, I understand and I can appreciate it, but you have to explain to him it's imperative we speak before he writes his speech. I'll come right now, 6 a.m. or whenever he can spare fifteen minutes. You better tell him that fifteen minutes could get longer once he hears what I have to say. Okay, get back to me soon."

Carl Concannon had been to the White House many times, but could not remember being there at 5:45 a.m. Max Wobser was pouring coffee when he entered the Oval Office.

"Max, thanks much for this. I'm sure you're going to find this a very interesting scenario."

"Carl, you and the president go back a long way; you don't owe me any thanks. He wanted to see you, but his time is really very limited, he's barely sleeping."

"I can appreciate that, Max, I understand the time limitations."

Concannon had no sooner sipped some of his coffee when the door to the Oval Office opened and in walked the president. Concannon stood and he shook hands with the president.

"Good morning, Mr. President."

"A good morning to you, Carl, but please, for this conversation here now, let's keep it Jim and Carl."

"Yes, Mr. President, I mean Jim."

"Carl, while I pour my coffee you'd better get into what you have to say, twenty minutes isn't much time. I have a briefing with the Joint Chiefs in twenty minutes," the president said, stirred his coffee and opened his hands for Carl to speak.

"Jim, I have for the past year been planning to run for the presidency. I have a very close group of six others who have been meeting, talking and planning. The basic premises was/is to change the way our government operates and try to turn it around. We, our country, are being laughed at and many feel we are becoming a third-rate country. My platform was to be run on the merits of completely changing the way we do business. We were/are going to try and suspend the Constitution in order to achieve those goals. Our intention was to ask the people of the nation if they were as fed up as we were and if so to give us the green light. If we got our way, we'd start by killing drug dealers on the spot of their violations, reform welfare by taking ninety percent of recipients off the roles and putting them to work. Reforming the court system by getting rid of all the bullshit that holds up proceedings, getting rid of lame judges, one-day trials, no appeals. Change the archaic adoption laws, have wage and price controls, do away with outrageous salaries and costs. There are many more, but I think you get the picture." Concannon tried to read the president; he looked right into his eyes, but to no avail.

The president stared back and asked, "Is there more?"

"Yes, Jim, there is, but what you did three days ago with the draft dodgers was a stroke of genius. My group and almost everyone I know applauded you. You now are about to explain yourself to the nation and you can no doubt expect to get a lot of flack and the threat of impeachment, but I'm sure you know that and expect it. After many hours of discussion, we, myself and the group have decided to step aside and let you run with this, if you so choose. After what you have started, why not just keep going and incorporate our ideas into your plans."

The president was staring out the window at his roses. He said not one word for a minute or more. "What happens if I say no to your idea?"

"We will continue as planned and I will run for the presidency. If elected I will do the things stated here"

"You're willing to forsake a run for the presidency?"

"Jim, I never wanted to be president. I have no ego problem either. What I want is for the best interest of the country, that was/is, always will be my motivation. I think I will be glad to pass the torch to you and not have to put up with all the bullshit you have to live with."

"Carl, for as long as I've known you, you have always been a honest man, who always spoke the truth and I know what you have said today is just that and your right on with the bullshit too. It's taken its toll on me. When I made the decision to go ahead with the draft dodgers plan I knew I was a one-term president. I also have the country's best interest in mind. Between those two facts I thought what the hell, what's the worst that can happen. If it works, we can move forward and change things for the better of the country. If the opposite happens, I get impeached, but I will go to my grave knowing I gave it my all."

The door opened and both men looked at Max. "Mr. President, it's 6:50."

"Okay, Max, in a minute."

Both men stood and the president extended his hand. "Carl, let me digest all this. You know the timetable. I'm supposed to speak tomorrow night at 8 p.m., so we really don't have much time. I will decide before the day is over. Please keep your people on alert. If I agree to this I will want to meet with your people here tonight. I'd like to see and hear from them, get a feel for them. Please give Max a number where you can be reached at all times. Thank you, Carl, for being the man you are and for being a good citizen. I am proud to be both your friend and a fellow American. Most of all thank you for your trust in me."

As the president walked into the War Room he eyed Henry Lloyd. His nod was immediately understood and Lloyd stood and walked to the president. The president lowered his head and whispered in Lloyd's ear, "Go to the Oval Office and play the tape. I had an early visitor and I want you to hear it. Go over it and make notes. When I get done here I'll be in and we can discuss it."

Forty minutes later the president and secretary of state were face to face in the Oval Office. "What do you think of Carl and his plan?"

"Mr. President, it's one hell of a bold plan and very refreshing to hear from another hawk like myself; we think alike. I basically like what I heard, but would like to hear more details."

"You will tonight, I'll set it up for 8 p.m. here, you and me and Carl and his group. I like what he said and apparently so do you, so let's get to the whole package. We do it here to get the privacy plus get it all on tape, just in case it's not on the up-and-up. One more thing, there are six besides

Concannon. I want the Secret Service to listen in to the introductions only to get the names and backgrounds of those we don't know. As fast as they can, I want whatever they can find on them. They have my permission to interrupt the meeting to get me what they find."

The introductions went well. Most of the group was known to the president or Secretary of State Lloyd, to some extent. The two members they didn't know were Charlie Rose and Steven Ames. The president made sure he asked the right questions of them to allow the Secret Service to get working on backgrounds.

"Senator Concannon, I suggest we start out with the matter of suspending our Constitution," the president calmly stated. "How did you or do you suppose to get that done?"

Concannon looked to Barbara Twell, who took the cue and spoke. "Maybe a Supreme Court justice should answer that, Mr. President. Sir, back in the time of President F. D. Roosevelt's term, a precedent was set stating that in time of national crisis the president had the power to suspend the Constitution for the survival of, and/or the good of the nation. It was never used, but it's there. It is the opinion of our group that the best way to achieve the same result would be to ask the nation for a mandate. In that respect, you'd only be doing what the people have asked. If our polls are correct and we feel they are, the majority of the nation will approve. Those same polls show a group or groups will seek to impeach you."

Unbeknownst to each other, the president and Henry Lloyd were thinking that these people have their shit together. They even have polls. The good thing was that they weren't dealing with amateurs.

With a pause in the action Carl took the lead again. "Mr. President, I'd like you to hear from Charlie Rose. As I've told you, he is a retired D.C. detective and the author of many of our ideas. He is our man in the street. He spent twenty-five years dealing with the problems on a daily basis. We," spreading his arms to show everyone in the room, "come from a different world. We know of the problems, but he has lived them in the trenches and better understands them."

Charlie had been sitting back listening and watching somewhat awestruck at the surroundings. For all his prowess in his field, this was definitely out of his league. He had been feeling much more at ease with his group, but this was the top of the line. He was committed to the group and their ideas, so with a slight smile of fear figured, *What the hell, I'm free of the job, what can they possibly do to me?*

Looking directly at the president, Charlie launched himself into his discourse. The drug problem and his fifteen-cent theory were outlined in complete detail. He told of the idea of the war in Asia, the United Nations, motor vehicle reform, welfare, adoption, auto manufacturers, income tax, prisons, the courts, military, the Mexican border, prices and wage controls and public officials. Each heading was explained in detail on how the group would seek to reform or change it completely. His presentation was so passionate and detailed that nobody ever noticed a Secret Service agent enter the office and hand the president a piece of paper. On that paper were a quick background on both Rose and Ames.

Charlie had stopped speaking as the president was reading. The president looked up and said, "You don't have to stop on my account, Mr. Rose."

"Well, sir, I'm finished. I really have only touched each topic and haven't gotten into the meat of each subject. That would take some time."

"That's fine, Mr. Rose, but I do have a question for you. Why is it that you and your group, of course, think you're so uniquely qualified to make these suggestions?"

Senator Concannon jumped into the conversations. "As I've said..." but with a wave of his hand the president cut him off.

"I asked Mr. Rose the question and I would like him to answer it."

Charlie took in a breath thinking and reasoning. *Why am I here? Shit, I knew I was in over my head, now how do I get out of it? Just tell him the truth, it's always worked before. Tell him why you feel so strongly. The truth shall set you free or kick you in the ass, so Mama used to say.*

"Mr. President, the only thing in this world that I feel uniquely qualified in is police work. This group reached out to me and I'm glad they did because I strongly believe in the same things they do. My thoughts come from working in the streets of the city, day in day out. When you do that you see firsthand the horror, filth, deprivation and every word in your vocabulary to describe life. What drugs have done to this world is beyond anyone's imagination. The death, disease, killings, the crime all are eroding our way of life. Those that sell drugs need killing. I know what you may be thinking. I have been called everything from Hitler to Stalin to the devil himself for this idea. You start killing them off and in time, a year or so, you will see one hell of a reduction in crime and death. The little guy in the street is beyond fed up. He could care less about the law, taxes, or who's running for president. His only ambition is to stay alive and have something in his belly. Outside of the city and the circumstances change little. They have a home, a job, save some money, but they too are fed up with other things in their lives. The politicians in this country are perceived to all be crooks. Each one is working for his own best interest and financial gain."

"Why do people feel that way?" asked the president.

"When you see candidates spending millions of dollars and in many cases their own money to get elected, you have to ask why. You can't BS the average Joe that they are doing it for the good of their country. Lawyers in this country are like sharks swimming around waiting for someone to fall in so they can take a bite out of him. Who are these politicians we speak of? Lawyers, for the most part. Who makes the laws of this land? Lawyers turned politicians. Who hears arguments over the laws these lawyers turned politicians make? The Supreme Court, who are what? Lawyers. The people don't trust lawyers or politicians or you, Mr. President."

That brought a slight gasp from someone.

"I'm sorry, Mr. President, if any of this offends you, but I'm trying to tell you just how it is, right from the hip with no punches pulled."

"Mr. Rose," asked the president, "may I call you Charles or Charlie?"

"Yes, sir, you may."

"Charlie, I don't doubt you one bit, but my popularity is unimportant at this time. You have made some very startling comments or accusations, I'll admit. The ordinary man in me says you speak the truth as much as the lawyer politician in me hates to hear it. Can I presume the rest of your ideas are similar to what you have started already?"

"Sir, I believe they all intertwine in a way. It's my belief that in today's world we lack common sense. Some court decisions handed down are enough to make one gag. Why does a flag burner have that right? Because of the Constitution? Wrong. Not good common sense. A mother gives up her baby for adoption. The baby and its new parents get settled into life and the birth mother changes her mind and wants the baby back. We give it to her, wrong. Common sense is the whole underlying thing here." Charlie stopped and the entire room was silent.

The president looked at Henry Lloyd for an indication of his thoughts and felt he saw interest. "Ladies and gentlemen, will you give Secretary Lloyd and me and few minutes alone?"

When the group had exited and the door closed, the president asked, "What's your gut telling you, Henry?"

Without hesitation Lloyd said, "I like what they say. It's bold and imaginative, but fraught with legal problems, to say nothing of the impeachment problems."

"To hell with all that, Henry, if we can get the Constitution suspended that ends all the legal problems and possibly the impeachment idea too. The only problem I foresee is selling it to the public. They are the ones who will make this go forward or stop. What do you think of the members of the group?"

"Mr. President, I think Concannon is one standup guy and he carries a lot of clout. The others are good people, but I don't know too much about some of them. The cop, Rose, is something else. Straightforward with no agenda, it seems, other than being super patriotic. I hope we can get some background on him quickly."

The president handed Lloyd the sheet the Secret Service had provided saying, "We already have what we need. It indicates he is one hundred percent clean with an outstanding record with Metro P.D. and he is very well thought of in police circles. We'll go deeper into his background for our own protection, but it may be a waste of time. For now, do you agree or not to join forces with them?"

"Yes, sir, I think so, but are you comfortable with the idea?"

"Yes, I am. I think it's a very good idea. Let's run with it."

When the group returned and was seated the president walked to his bar. "Would anyone care for a drink?" he asked. All declined. He looked directly at the group and said, "We agree to join forces with your group. I am truly delighted to be around such a fine group of Americans. What I would like each one of you to do is to go home or your office and make a tape recording for me. Blab your heart out about all the subjects covered here. Tell me your innermost thoughts on what you want changed, why and what those changes would do. Nothing long-winded, please, just what, why and how. Have your tape in my office by 8 a.m. As you know, I am due to make a speech tomorrow night at 8 p.m., so we don't have much time. Is there any question in anyone's mind?" No one spoke and with that everyone rose and headed for the door.

Chapter 6

"Good evening. As you all know, several days ago I authorized the arrest of all draft dodgers or resistors. These people deserted us in a time of need. Many generations before them fought and died for the right to have us free. These measures were long overdue. A word on what has happened to those taken into custody.

"As I speak, those arrestees are being classified in several categories. All will receive some military training, but only a portion will be trained as fighting men. Some will be given non-combat training, such as medicine, motor transport and various others. The military training, that being the initial training, will have to be spread out as Parris Island cannot handle that large a number.

"We expect these men to perform as a military unit just as the generations before them have. Those who complete their military training and time in service, which is two years, will be honorably discharged with no mention of resisting the draft. Those who fail the training, refuse to train or attempt to run away will serve two years in prison and have a record over their head for the rest of their lives.

"Please listen very carefully to what I am about to tell you and think before you reach any conclusion. When our forefathers decided to fight the British to gain our independence, it shocked people around the world. Not since that decision has any president told our nation what I am about to say to you.

"For many reasons I will later explain, I am asking you for a mandate to suspend our Constitution for a short period of time. We as a nation are heading in a terrible direction. Many of us have been talking of change, but with our system it's nearly impossible. Partisan politics and special interest groups are handcuffing any change. We have been laughed at for our stance on draft resistors. Some of our closest allies have told me that we are the laughing stock of the world. Our enemies can't believe how fortunate they are and how stupid we are. You, the average American, are fed up with the system yet you can't change it. You throw out one party and the new party comes in and does the same as the party you just threw out.

"You need to think of the direction we have taken the past five to ten years. Think about some of the terrible decisions that have been made by politicians, the courts and like government agencies. Getting into the present war, adoptions and allowing illegals to continually flood our country.

"I expect the Constitutional suspension would last a year or two, hopefully a year. We will base changes, all changes, on common sense. If that doesn't seem to be right, we modify it until it is right. For example, we could ask those in a particular industry or service and those who use that service for their input.

"The vote on the Constitution issue needs to be quick and simple. I want the vote to be taken within thirty days and to make it very simple. You vote either yes or no on the issue. We are not going to debate this thing because as I have stated, we debate things to death and nothing get done. Common sense. To those members of the boards of elections, please don't start with you need more time? Get off your duffs, roll out the machines and ask one simple question. Here we will get into step one of the changes.

"The drug/crime area is the first problem we attack, and I mean attack. Very quickly a schedule of the worst drugs and quantities will be published. All dealers caught selling drugs will be shot on the spot of the violation. Shocking isn't it? You're damn right it is, but so is what drugs are doing to our country both in the loss of lives and the cost in crime. Users in possession over the prescribed limits will also be shot. Many of them sell to friends to support their own habit. There may be bodies all over but I can promise you this, in a year or so you will see a very large decrease in crime and other related problems. We will lose a number of our population but as the author of this idea told me, 'nobody's going to miss them.' These dealers have been killing people for a very long time and causing unbelievable misery with their deeds. It's payback time.

"We intend to bring all our military home and close all overseas bases. We can expect to save at least five to ten billion dollars in the first year alone. The plan is to take that money and use it domestically. We'll start using that money to create jobs, add some to teacher's salaries, building roads and other infrastructure that are decaying. This money will be used in a common-sense way, not by political port barrel legislation.

"Another substantial amount of money will be saved because we will no longer be doling out foreign aid. Neither of these moves is going to sit well with many nations on the receiving end, but this is how we intend to radically change the way our government works. We can't worry what other countries think about us, we have problems and we have to solve our problems first, not theirs.

"We will immediately launch a system that will affect each of you. Many will applaud and many scream. The national speed limit will be fifty-five mph, no exceptions. First-time violators will be fined $500, second time $1,000, and the third time you will have your vehicle confiscated. An automated system will be used to update violations within hours of the violation. Many of those taken off the welfare rolls will be trained on this system. Many of the former welfare recipients will also be working on body pickup for all the drug dealers we shoot.

"Remember some of the horror stories in the area of adoption proceedings? A baby is placed with a family who grows a bond with the baby and at some point the birth mother wants to baby back. Wrong, no common sense. It's not going to happen again, common sense will prevail.

"We hope to reduce the welfare rolls by eighty percent. We expect to put these people to work in some areas I've already mentioned, but in many other areas of need. Common sense tells us that we need to stop the vicious cycle of welfare.

"All states will have a uniform set of motor vehicle rules and regulations. You will drive in any state of the union and have the same regulations. Oh, I forgot to mention the fourth penalty in the speeding area. If after the third violation, you lost your vehicle and you are caught speeding or circumventions the rules, you automatically quality for thirty days on the chain gang.

"Auto manufacturers will only make engines that attain the speed of fifty-five mph. Any alterations to obtain more speed will get you a free thirty-day vacation on the chain gang.

"Income tax will be changed to a flat tax. Everyone, without exception, will pay a percentage of his income. The paperwork should be easy from now on. Probably one page.

"Prison reform. All court cases will be heard by a panel of three judges. Speed will be the priority. No legal maneuvering, just state the facts and reach a verdict. Civil cases will only get to the hearing level if the facts merit it.

"All immigration stops immediately. All illegals will be deported unless it's in our best interest to keep them.

"All U.S.-chartered companies will produce its product or service in the United States. All U.S.-made products and service will get first priority for sale. No tax breaks for any company for any reason"

"We will inform the Mexican government that if it cannot or will not stop the illegal immigration problem, then we will start to shoot those sneaking into our county.

"We will cease being a member of the United Nations. It is one useless organization and it costs us too much money. The Chinese once called the United States a paper tiger. Well, that is just what the U.N. is, the real paper tiger, all bark and no bite. The City of New York will start towing in all those diplomatic-plated cars that owe so much money for traffic violations. The U.N. building will be vacated; we don't want them here.

"Wage controls. Wages will be based on the worth to your country. Labor unions are history. The outrageous salaries paid to CEOs, sports figures, attorneys and the like will stop. Free enterprise will be alive and well, but its needs to be fair.

"Public officials. Starting from me on down to the lowest level, no official is exempt from this; any official who abuses his office will be shot. No exceptions. The public has every right to a fair system for all for these changes to work.

"Weapons can be owned by hunters and collectors, with some new guidelines. Illegal possession of a weapon without committing a crime will get you five years. Any person committing a crime while in possession of a weapon will be shot on the spot.

"The Supreme Court will be on a sabbatical for the period of this change. They will assist wherever needed in criminal courts. All appeals courts justices will do likewise, as there will be no appeals. We expect the harshness of this new system to decrease much of the crime now committed.

"Service to one's country. The Israelis have a wonderful system that we will be adopting. All children upon reaching the age of eighteen, graduating high school or quitting school will enter the military for training. The mandatory period is eighteen months.

"The media will be publishing all the rules and regulations. If they fail to or refuse to, they will be ordered to do so or close up shop. As new rules or ideas arise this will be the quickest way for the public to hear. Media criticism is expected and will be tolerated to a degree. If their criticism hurts the public good, the publication will cease to exist.

"Price controls will go hand in hand with wage controls. The present prices of items such as prescription drugs, court awards, etc. are outrageous. Reasonable profit is fine, but gouging is not.

"Lobbies. The lobby industry is a dead industry. Lobbying is no longer legal on any level. As I said earlier, special interest groups are a thing of the past. All groups need to have equal representation.

"Monetary donations to any and all political parties or persons will be prohibited.

"My fellow Americans, these are just some of the major areas we want to change, surely not all. It's going to take time to get to all and we will if you, and only you give me the approval. Oh, it's out of order, but with all I have had to say it's not surprising. I forgot to say that we hope that within a year or two we can eliminate the draft and go to an all-volunteer army. With our youth going through an eighteen-month period of service, some may find a career.

"For some time, as your president, I have been very uneasy with our country and its direction. A group of people, who you will soon meet, came to me only yesterday. This group is led by a man who was going to run for the presidency and had been working on many of these changes I've mentioned tonight. After we began rounding up the draft dodgers this group decided that in the best interest of the country to join forces with me to change the direction we're headed. They felt, and I reluctantly agree, that we're becoming a third-rate nation.

"I know the controversy that lies ahead. I have heard and ask myself constantly the same questions you and others will raise. Impeachment will blear out loudly. I can't stop that, but I'm not afraid of it either. If you want to live in a free nation, free to walk the streets at night, not afraid to let your children out of the house, tired of the senseless killings, the theft, the danger on our highways, then you need to think this issue over. We have a very bad habit in this country, debate. There will be none on my part. If you want to be a part of our new country, then this is your chance. I assure you, we are not going to be a socialist state, a Communist state or any other state. We are going to be a United States of America. God bless and good night."

Chapter 7

The president and secretary of state were both reading the headlines from various newspapers. Secretary Lloyd laughed softly gaining the presidents attention. "What, Henry?"

"The *New York Times* says 'Hitler Is Alive' and goes on to say that you must because mad as no sane man will support you."

"Well, Henry, just listen to the *Washington Post*. Their headline is 'Big Brother Is Watching' and says I'm creating a police state. According to the news reports I've seen this morning, I'll be impeached before a vote can be taken, the ACLU is going to file suit against me before the sun sets, the religious right is going to see me in hell and every foreign country who receives aid from us is hollering mad. I've heard I'm an isolationist and we should expect trade sanctions against us immediately."

"Mr. President, I'm just surprised your phone isn't ringing off the hook."

"It would be, but I told Marge and Max to take all calls and log them. Every caller is being told I am not available to anyone today as I have a tremendously full schedule, which I have. Has everyone been notified and are they here?"

"Yes, sir, in twenty minutes as you asked. The full cabinet, key personnel from your office and Senator Concannon's crew of seven."

"Good, Henry, we're going to need everyone to pull together to get this done on time."

As the president walked into the White House cafeteria, everyone stood. "Please be seated," stated the president. "I'm sorry we have to use the café for this, but we don't have the proper space for this amount of people anywhere except here." There were a few mumbles here and there, but it was generally quiet from most. Glancing at the faces of the audience, the president thought he could see each person's facial expression and he wondered what they thought of him and his plan.

"Good morning to you all. I know that many, if not all had to cancel plans and appointments to answer my beck and call and I apologize to each of you for that inconvenience. That will be the last apology you hear from me on the matter. From this point on, it's full bore to finish this project or to finish me.

"Regardless of your personal feelings of this plan, I expect each of you to do my bidding. If you can't do this, get up and leave now. If you leave, go straight to your office, pack up your personal property and keep on going. You are with me or against me. Is there anyone who wishes to leave?" Heads turned every which way to look, but not a soul got up.

The president smiled. "Okay, let's get going. Each of you will be working on a dual plan for the next couple of weeks. The biggest issue is getting the vote done. From setting up the ballot, a simple yes or no, to getting people out to vote, to making sure the polling places are up and running. I want no electioneering, no forcing anyone to vote yes or no. In between doing that, you need to be thinking and writing about what I said needs to change; and what you think needs to change and how to do it.

"Chief of Staff Max Wobser will lead the White House group and Henry Lloyd will be the leader of the cabinet members and anyone else we need. Each of those men will assign tasks that are needed and you will handle that task or what is asked of you. The main job is to get the vote done by the end of the month. The mandate I am asking for is the number one priority of each and every one of us. Your present job is secondary or omitted for the next month. As I said, when you are not engaged in the vote process, you are to be working on the major changes in our system. I don't care how wild your thoughts are, put them to paper and let me be the judge.

"Before we go any further, I need to introduce some folks. Senator Concannon, will you stand up?" As he stood, the president smiled at him while lightly clapping his hands. "For those who don't know him, this is the good Senator Carl Concannon. Carl will you in turn introduce each of your team."

"Yes, sir," came the ready reply from the senator. He turned toward his team and smiled as the president had. "Please stand as I call your name. Congressman Sid Braverman, Senator Craig Trowbridge, Assistant

Secretary of the Treasury Catherine Carter, Supreme Court Justice Barbara Twell, Steven Ames, CEO of Parker, Lane and Ames Brokerage, and lastly Charles Rose, retired detective, Washington Metro Police Department."

"Thank you, Senator. This group of citizens before you is the authors of much of what I have spoken on during my TV statement. These wonderful Americans have been working on doing just what I am asking our nation to allow me, us, to do. The good Senator had planned on running for the presidency based on these ideas of change. He has dropped those plans to join forces with me, for which I am extremely grateful. Each of these seven men and women are truly patriots and I salute them." A mild clap began and rolled on louder and louder until the president had to hold up his hands asking for quiet. "Thank you for that, it is well deserved. By the way, the senator and his committee will be here in the White House for the next couple of weeks or longer to work on the same tasks that you will.

"In the next twenty-four hours, Max and Henry will call upon some fifty-one people. Each of the fifty-one will be assigned a state, including D.C. That person's job will be to see that his assigned state has just what is needed for the vote. In doing that particular chore, should anyone try to impede your progress, you are to threaten him or her with replacement within eight hours. If he still doesn't budge, you are to get Henry and Max involved and have him replaced. Henry and Max will assist in any way needed to push people to get this job done on time. There is no doubt in my mind that you will run into problems and you must be at your best to overcome them. If Senator Concannon and I read the American public correctly, we will have a lot of supporters. As in every job of this magnitude, we will have those for and those against us.

"You know the mandate I asked for. Now I am giving each of you a mandate. Go out and get the job done and help to get our country back to where it belongs."

"Gentlemen, please be seated and quiet down." The Democratic Speaker of the House, Richard Malatesta pleaded. "The party has asked us to look into impeachment proceedings and that why this committee has been so hastily formed. As head of the committee, I will speak first. Each of you will have your opportunity to speak your mind.

"As a lifelong Democrat I think this is a perfect opportunity to nail the president to the cross. I don't foresee much of a problem getting him impeached and making the Republicans the laughing stock of the nation.

What he is asking for is lunacy. He has to be insane to even think in the terms he is." Several heads nodded in apparent approval and several just stared at the Speaker.

One by one the next five members of the committee agreed with the Speaker. The seventh and last member was Gordon Hobbis Sr., a snow-white-haired Floridian, who had represented Florida for the past seven terms. Hobbis was a straight talker, a hard drinker and a true American patriot. Many a time, he had crossed party lines to vote with his heart and for what was best for his country. In doing so he had made enemies within the party and he was shocked that he had been called upon to be on this committee. It was now his chance to speak and unlike the other members, he stood.

"Mr. Speaker, with all due respect, just what has the president done to warrant impeachment? He hasn't committed a crime. He has not violated any rule or role of his office. He has merely asked the American people for a mandate. He has that right and the people have the right to vote yes or no. A lot of people may not like what he's asking, but they can say no and stop him right there. We are at war, undeclared or not and the Constitution says the president can ask for a mandate and he has. My last point is this, I have the feeling that you're asking for impeachment purely for political gain." As Hobbis sat, six faces now looked directly at him. Most seemed troubled, but at what?

Malatesta was furious and it showed. "I would expect that kind of talk from you, Hobbis, always the maverick. To answer your question, yes, it is party motivation I have in mind. I feel we can make hay from this and improve our party status at the same time. What Barringer has proposed is barbarous. It will never fly. If he is willing to make an ass of himself and his party, then we should oblige him and do just that."

"Mr. Speaker, I can understand your party motivation, but not once have you said anything about what may be good for the country," Hobbis replied to the Speaker.

"Are you saying you agree with him?" Malatesta retorted.

A smiling Hobbis again stood. "Mr. Speaker, much of what he said is true. We are on the verge of becoming a third-rate country. We are doing a great many things that are not good. We need change and he may be right in his thinking."

Malatesta was like a dragon, breathing fire and smoke. When he had calmed himself down he turned to the members of the committee looking for support, but didn't see what he had hoped for. "Do each of you gentleman agree with Hobbis?"

Congressman Bob Bradbury, the ranking member present spoke. "Mr. Speaker, I for one don't disagree with Mr. Hobbis. I have reservations about a lot of what's been said, but I agree we need change badly. As for the impeachment, I do agree with Mr. Hobbis. I can see no reason for such a proceeding. He has done nothing to warrant such action. I am also a lifelong Democrat and will always be, but right now I can see no reason for this charge, a very serious charge. If I had to vote right now, it would be in favor of what the president is asking for."

The silence was deafening. For another forty minutes the other members of the committee made comment.

After the committee meeting had broken up, the Speaker of the Democratic Party sat contemplating just how he as going to tell the national committee head that his committee vote was 5-2 in favor of no impeachment proceedings.

Parris Island in the dead of summer is akin to hell. It is hot, humid and a terrible place to be if you have to physically exert yourself. In winter it's a rather pleasant place to be, weather wise. If you are a Marine Corps recruit it's never a pleasant place to be. The draft resistors were spread out all over P.I. as room was at a premium. They had been told nothing of what was going on, typical of a recruit depot. For the present, they were told they could not leave the squad bay or talk to anyone including their squad mates. A few had already been screamed at and even smacked around when the screaming didn't work. One drill instructor informed them to think of themselves as slaves.

Word around the Marine personnel was that the commanding general, Gregory Humbolt, had refused to address the resistors. Colonel Ned Mier, the assistant commanding officer, was supposed to meet and speak, but the logistics were being worked out. Due to the large number of men involved, the speech had to be outside, on the grinder. A speaker system was being set up so everyone could hear.

As Colonel Mier exited his staff car, he stood looking over the assembly of bodies. He had never seen so many men on P.I. before and wondered how so many could be properly trained the Marine Corps way. He walked to the steps of the stage eyeballing Sergeant Major Kennedy, who stood at the microphone looking at the colonel for a sign. He then spoke into the mike.

"Attention, attention, you civilian scum. The next man I see move his lips, I will personally beat the shit out of him. Now listen up."

Col. Mier reached for the mike and looked again at the huge assembly. "Can everyone hear me, those in the back?" Several DI's in the rear gave the thumbs-up signal. "My name is Colonel Mier. I am the assistant commanding officer of this depot. The commanding general has refused to address you and if I could, I would also refuse. A good Marine does what he is told, so here I am. I hope someday you too will follow your orders, exactly as they are given to you.

"By fleeing your country and obligation to serve same, you have become an outcast to our society. The only people in the world who have love for you are your immediate family and I'm sure some of them aren't too proud of you. The choice you made to run from your obligation is the reason you're in your present situation. This is the one chance you get to change that. You will be trained by Marine Corps drill instructors. You will receive the same training that a volunteer Marine receives. Not one thing will be different, except if you fail and I'll get to that later. You have pissed off your government, its people and it's your move." He turned and walked towards the steps and stopped, turned around and walked back to the mike. "I forgot to inform you of your rights. You have none. While you were hiding out in Canada or Mexico, your government, with citizen approval passed a few laws to authorize your arrest and detention. For deserting your country, you have been found guilty with no appeal. Your sentence is to retrain your brain and body. If you do it our way, we will teach you to fight for your country and hopefully survive. If you survive, you get a full pardon and an honorable discharge. Those who fail will go to prison for two years. That record will hang around your neck for the rest of your life. Another change is that prison is no longer a country club. You will work your ass off on a chain gang at hard labor. It's your choice." He turned again and walked down the steps and into his car.

Sergeant Major Kennedy took the mike and repeated his first message. "Shut up, assholes. There are three ways you can leave this island. The first is in a pine box, which happens to be my choice for you. The second way is as a prisoner, which is my second choice. The third is in a uniform to fight for your country. I pray to General Chesty Puller that it's not in a Marine uniform. I don't think any of your bastards deserve to be here on these hallowed grounds, let alone in a Marine uniform. The entire Marine staff of P.I. will do its best to see you leave in one of the first two choices.

"As you were driven onto this island, you passed through the only gate or road. This island is surrounded by water, marsh, swamp, quicksand, gators, sharks, snakes and all manner of death. I will gladly draw a map for anyone who wishes to challenge your surroundings. For every fifteen who try, only one will make it to the mainland. If you make it and are not shot in the process, you will be awarded the option of the two year prison sentence.

"Normally we have eighteen to twenty percent of recruits fail training. We encourage those who don't want to succeed to run, go over the hill. You will be guarded night and day and I'm sure a few of you will still try. For those who die trying, we will just write you off the rolls and forget you. We will not risk anyone to retrieve your body, it's gator bait. If you should make it to main side, the brig chasers have been given permission to shoot to kill. We are at war and when a man in the military leaves his post its called desertion and we kill deserters.

"You are in for the worst twelve weeks of your life. You have no idea what hell is in store for you. Hundreds of thousands of men have gone through this same training before you. You can make it if you want to, but it's going to be rough. This is your one and only chance to change the bad decision you made when you ran. Personally, I think you're getting more than you deserve."

One hundred and fifty young men stood at attention. Most were white, with a sprinkling of blacks and Hispanics. Each moved his eyeballs toward the four DI's who entered the squad bay. A sudden scream by one of the four sent chills down the spines of many.

"You keep those fuckin' eyeballs straight ahead you; asshole, you hear?"

"Yes," came as a feeble reply.

"You shithead, you answer loud and clear, 'Sir, yes sir,' you hear me, you dumb fuck?"

"Sir, yes sir."

"Louder, you female bitch, this ain't high school."

"Sir, yes sir."

"I am Senior Drill Instructor Gunnery Sergeant Robert Flack. The three Marines with me are Staff Sergeant David Williams, Sergeant James Claudell and Sergeant James McDaniel. We are your mother and father for the next twelve weeks, or less. This will be the last time you will hear me speak in a calm civil tone. Because you are an unusual group of shitheads, more educated, I'm speaking to you in a more human manner, but don't judge me by what I say now, I'm going to be your worst enemy for the next twelve weeks.

"We have been training Marines for a long time, very successfully. We will attempt to train you in the same manner, but with a few exceptions. Regular volunteer recruits who can't make the cut are kicked out with medical or general discharges. In your case, you can easily die in training or while escaping. If you don't die, you can get two years in prison. You can also do what you're told, push yourself to the extreme limit, excel and become a what? I dread calling you Marines, I loathe it. According to my orders, that's what you can be if you so desire. We'll see what happens.

"You will be training six days a week, plus. Sundays are normally a nothing day, but I don't think that's going to happen. From 0500 hrs to 2000 hrs, you will be running, marching, exercising and doing all the things you may hate. Normally we tell recruits nothing, we keep them in the dark. You are a different class of asshole so I'm giving you just the basics.

"You are 150 in this platoon. It's going to be a little tight until we lose some bodies. We normally start around 130 and reduce to 80 or 85. I think we'll lose some rather quickly. We lose recruits many ways. They have found all sorts of ways to kill themselves, escape and fail. In your case nobody gives a shit if you live or die, except yourself.

"You will have no contact with the outside world, none. Each of your families has been notified that you have been arrested and detained here. They have been informed they will not be told anything about you until you finish your training or die. The last item is this. We know all the tricks of the trade. You break our rules and you will pay dearly. Go to sick call or to the hospital; when they let you out, you go right back to another platoon just starting and begin all over again. For once in your life stand up and be a man." Gunny Flack walked out and the shit hit the fan.

"Hit the deck, hit the deck, you stupid shit heads." One hundred and fifty men struggled to get to the foot of their racks and get to attention. The racks are actually metal bunk beds but in the naval service there are called racks. The vocabulary was going to be tough to get used to what with all the other things being thrown at them all at once.

Jim Radison's head was swimming. The floor was a deck, the doorway was a hatch and the wall a bulkhead. Christ, you'd think we were on a ship.

"Once again, kiddies," shouted Sergeant McDaniel, "when I say racks, you jump in and lay at attention and stay at attention until I cut the lights. You hear me girls?"

"Yes, sir," came the 150 strong replies.

McDaniel walked up to a terrified young man. "What's your name, asshole?"

"Sir, Private Lane, sir."

A vicious punch from nowhere dropped Lane to the deck. He groaned and his breathing was rapid.

"When I ask a question, the whole platoon answers. Your lips never moved, Lane. You all better learn what teamwork is. Everyone does the same; everyone…Hit the deck and give me twenty-five pushups, now."

All 150 dropped and awaited the order to start. "One, two, three," shouted McDaniel. "God damn, you girls are sloppy. I guess you never learned to do pushups what with being in school and drinking and fooling around with the girls and running away too." After twenty-five poorly preformed pushups McDaniel called them to attention as Gunny Flack entered the squad bay.

He walked up and down the squad bay staring at the faces of his platoon. Those faces showed anger, sweat, confusion and fear. One face appeared to Flack as having a smirk to it. He stopped in front of the man and asked, "What's your name, idiot?"

"Sir, Private Fabio," but not to the volume Flack desired.

Flack threw a strong open-handed slap across Fabio's face, immediately raising a white, then red print that was very visible. After the immediate surprise ended, Flack saw the hate in the eyes of Fabio.

"Go ahead, asshole, make your move, take a swing at me."

Fabio, sweating profusely, eyed the DI, but never moved.

"Wise choice, asshole." Flack continued his stroll around the squad bay and gave a nod to McDaniel as he left.

McDaniel turned back to the platoon and said, "Listen up. Fire watch is mandatory. Four privates a night will work in two-hour watches, starting with the first man to my right and then around the entire squad bay. You walk the squad bay, head and stairs with a flashlight. Your duty is of a watchman. You will wake up the duty DI if you observe anything of a danger. Danger means a fire, someone sick and needing first aid. Five minutes before your two hours are up, you wake your relief. He takes over the flashlight and the watches, any questions?"

"Sir, no sir."

"Sleeping on watch is one step below desertion. You get caught sleeping on watch and I guarantee you'll do brig time. Hit the rack."

Bodies flew in all directions, some bumping into each other. McDaniel suppressed a smile; it's the same with every group. They need to learn each other's moves. As he walked out he flipped the light out and walked to the DI's hatchway.

Bodies could be heard moving from position to position, trying to get comfortable. When you're scared to death, sweating and pissed to the max, it's not easy to get comfortable.

Jim Radison closed his eyes, trying to blot out his surroundings. *What in hell have I got myself into? Can I do this? Is it worth it? God, I miss Joan and Jimmy. What have I done to them? I hope she's at her family's or mine, she needs help right now. They must all be confused about this.* The desperate need for sleep took away all his thoughts and he drifted off to a deep sleep.

It seemed like he was asleep only a minute when he awoke to screams. "Fire, fire, get out of the rack." As he opened his eyes, the light was terribly bright, but all he saw were bodies flying out of the racks. He jumped to the deck and followed the herd outside. As the platoon lined up at the curb in front of the barracks, they stood at attention while McDaniel counted heads. The H-shaped building held four platoons and all four were standing at attention in the street. Standing there in their skivvies and barefooted, they were a sight to see, but nobody was laughing.

The South Carolina night air was on the cool side, in the mid forties. Not unusually cold for the time of the year, but damn cold when you're half asleep and without clothes or shoes. Radison was unsure what time it was, as watches were not allowed, but did it really matter? Twelve weeks is a long time for this type of harassment.

At exactly 0459, Sergeant McDaniel stood at the hatch of Platoon #344's squad bay. His swagger stick tucked under his armpit as he counted down to 0500. He flicked on the lights, then walked to the G.I. can and removed its lid. He dropped the lid to the deck with a loud crash and proceeded to run his swagger stick around the cans interior. The circular motion makes one hell of a racket.

McDaniel shouted, "Up, up, get out of those racks. Hit the deck, you idiots." Sleepy faces fell to the deck and stood until all 150 bodies were at attention in front of their racks.

"You have fifteen minutes in the head. At 0515 you will commence field day. You will fill buckets with soap and water, scrub the deck, swab it and make sure the area is entirely clean. Temporary squad leaders will assign the tasks, who does what. That head better sparkle, get to it."

One hundred fifty men needed to use the head and be done in fifteen minutes. Most thought, *He has to be nuts, it can't be done.* To use the toilet, brush teeth and shave, get into gym shorts, tee shirts and sneakers in fifteen minutes takes some getting used to. Coordination and teamwork begins here.

Most of the first week is a Chinese fire drill or what the Marine Corps refers to as a "cluster fuck." One hundred fifty men very early in the morning trying to work together are funny, but it will cause many a disagreement.

At 0600 Sergeant Flack and McDaniel appear at the hatch. Both men walk the area and head looking at the results of the field day, while the platoon stands at attention. Flack barks out discrepancies while McDaniel writes them down. Small puddles of water, mop strings at the rack legs or footlockers, dust on a window sill or locker top. It's easy to find such things.

"You pussies must never have cleaned anything in your life. I wonder if you clean your asses as badly as this squad bay. Well, we'll change that tonight." Flack reached out and smacked a recruit who nearly hit the deck. Flack bent over screaming at the private, "You keep them eyeballs straight ahead asshole or I'll knock your head off."

0615 and Platoon 344 stands at attention in the street. Sergeants Flack and McDaniel exit the barracks dressed exactly as the recruits except for their campaign hats. Flack calls, "Forward, march," and the platoon marches forward. A minute later comes the order, quick time, and the platoon moves forward at a running pace. After a mile of running the platoon is brought to a halt. Flack turns to the rear to watch as the stranglers are trying to catch up.

"You sorry asses," Flack screamed.

Thirty-seven of one hundred fifty could not run a mile and the senior DI was as mad as a hornet. McDaniel was taking down the names of the thirty-seven who failed the run.

Upon returning to the barracks at 0645, Flack addresses them once more. "You sorry asses are a disgrace to yourselves, your country and the Marine Corps. I guess the first time you ran away, you drove; you damn sure didn't run. The thirty-seven who didn't keep up have one week to make it or they go to the fat man's platoon. There you will lose the weight you need to and get into the proper shape to do what you need to do. You are then reassigned to a new platoon and start over again at day one. Your motivation is to push yourself to the max or you start over again. You have fifteen minutes to change into fatigues and line up for chow at 0700."

At 0702 the platoon lines up in front of the chow hall.

"Listen up, idiots," barks Sergeant Flack. "You will line up on the sidewalk leading to the hatch, bellybutton to asshole. Those eyeballs better be straight in front of you and be square on the back of the skull in front of you and no where else, you hear?"

"Sir, yes sir."

After lining up Flack continued with educating his platoon. "You have fifteen minutes in the chow hall, to eat and be out at the curb. You are not to speak to anyone in the mess hall unless it's another drill instructor. If you see a prisoner with a brig chaser, you better not get between them or you will wind up eating with them as a prisoner. You hear me, idiots?"

"Sir, yes sir."

"When you exit the chow hall and line up you may see other platoons smoking. You will not, until you earn it."

As the platoon passes through the mess hall, Flack and Sergeant Claudell watch that each man took what was offered and did not open his mouth. Each man then takes coffee, milk or water and sits at tables designated by Sergeant Flack. Watching other platoons is the best education a recruit can get. They see that the first served were the first out to grab a cigarette. That, at the time seemed unfair but the DI's knew that it all worked out fairly in the end because the two lines of the squad entered the chow hall differently each meal.

At the fourteen-minute mark, Claudell shouted, "Platoon 344, you have one minute left." The last two men eating pushed what was left on their trays into their mouths and ran to get rid of the trays and leave.

They marched back to the barracks and fell out. Twenty minutes of looking over what they were issued and trying to learn what 782 gear went on the web belt and how it went on. 782 gear consists of a canteen, cartridge case and bayonet. The web belt is about three to four inches wide with grommet holes everywhere to attach the gear to the belt.

At 0800 Sergeant Claudell shouts, "Fall out." The platoon marches to the dispensary. Caudell shouts out, "Remove your jackets and do as the corpsman says."

The platoon passes through a line of corpsman on both sides shooting some type of shots into each arm. One corpsman shouts, "Relax, God damn it, relax."

Caudell moves to the scene and watches. As the corpsman injects Private Jones again, the injected liquid squirts out again. Caudell yanks Jones from the line and says to the corpsman, "Give me that syringe." Caudell shouts at Jones for him to relax. "I'll make you my personal pincushion, if you don't." Caudell punches the syringe into Jones time and time again. "There, asshole, you have my initials to remember me." Jones glances at his arm to see a perfect "C" with blood dripping down his arm. Caudell and several corpsmen are laughing, but none of Platoon 344 is.

0900 marching on the grinder. The first week of marching is hilarious for anyone observing, but not those marching. The platoon is broken up into thirteen-man squads. The mere basics take a week of listening to, just to get a handle on. The DI's cadence call is an art on his part, but a bitch on the listener. Hearing each command sung to a cadence takes constant diligence. Let your mind wander for a second and you can march off on your own. In that first week many will turn right when the command is left and turn to the rear when commanded to face forward. While on the grinder the DI's will scream, shout, demean and finally punch you for your errors, but after duty is over, they will laugh and howl over the antics observed on the grinder.

The entire morning is consumed with marching. To the recruit and anyone not familiar with what is being done, it seems asinine. In twelve weeks of boot camp, a recruit may march as much as one hundred hours. What the recruit never realizes is that he is learning to listen to commands without any thought to what that command is and to do it as a team. Little does he realize at this time that listening to the command and reacting to it may one day save his life.

After midday chow, Sergeant Flack calls the squad to attention in the squad bay. He walks around the squad bay twice and appears to be making mental notes. He finally stops and overturns the G.I. can and sits on it. "At rest," he bellows, "grab the deck and get close to me. For squad cohesiveness we need a squad chain of command. I make the decisions on who gets what and does what. You do the job well and you can be rewarded. The recruit commander, squad leaders and guide-on usually get a promotion to PFC at graduation. This is how the Marine Corps promotes its people, do a good job and time in grade, and you get a promotion. The recruit commander is the top dog and does my bidding. He oversees the squad leaders and does what is needed to keep good order. The squad leader is in charge of a squad of thirteen men. He will assign jobs such as field day and work details. The guide-on carries the platoon colors and is my house mouse. The house mouse is my mouthpiece. If he says to stand on your head, that means I told him to tell you. If he gets crazy and says anything I didn't tell him to say, I'll beat his ass to a pulp and he loses his job. These jobs are another way for me and the other DI's to see where leadership potential is. You can't refuse any position, I choose, but you sure can lose it fast enough.

Wainwright, front and center. You are the recruit platoon commander."

"Sir, yes sir."

"Radison, Palmer, Norris, Ketchum, and Fischer are squad leaders. Fabio, you are guide-on and house mouse."

After evening chow, Sergeant Williams calls the platoon to attention. "Okay, girls, here is your evening entertainment. Sergeant Flack was very unhappy with your field day this morning, so you're going to do it again and get it right this time. Every time you fuck it up, you get to do it again. Twice a day is not cool so do it the right way and end the bullshit. Wainwright, keep one squad out of the field day. After the barracks is done and I inspect it, everyone hits the showers. After that the squad you choose will field day it and I will inspect it. Do the job right the first time and you may have an hour and a half to work on your gear before lights out. If you get that free time, I suggest you get together in small groups and help each other out. Those who have the grasp of it, teach the others how to lay out their gear in their foot lockers and stand-up lockers. There is an inspection of both and they better be right."

Lights out at 2200 came without anything unusual. One hundred forty-nine bodies were asleep in minutes, the cumulative effect of seventeen hours takes its toll. Only one man couldn't get to sleep, he was the fire watch.

The president looked up from his reading as Max and Henry entered the Oval Office. "Fix yourself some coffee if you like," he offered. "I'm just reading today's papers. It seems I'm still the nutcase or savior of the country depending who writes the article. The overseas stories are more negative than positive. The countries that relied on our military help are very upset about losing our backing. The usual and expected comments from Russia, China, North Korea and a surprising Germany are saying it's a good thing that we withdraw our military and mind our own business. It's going to be very interesting to see who starts pushing who over there.   "How are we doing here?"

Secretary of State Lloyd spoke first. "We have agreed on the wording of the ballot and sent it to all fifty states. It reads, "shall we do as the president has asked and allow our Constitution to be suspended for a period of one year and a maximum of two years? Yes or no."

"Sounds fine to me, simple and to the point," replied President Barringer. "What else?"

Max Wobser looked to his notebook. "Not much feedback yet. A couple of states via their governor's office say they could have a problem with the costs and time frame. We have informed them, very politely, that they will comply or else. Henry and I are both wondering just what that 'or else' could be?"

The president smiled. "I have a few thoughts on the subject. If it gets to that, you let me know and I'll get to that governor in question. Anything else?"

Lloyd spoke up, "Yes, sir. I have a report that the ACLU has asked the Supreme Court to hear arguments ASAP on the constitutionality of your mandate request."

The president looked at both men awaiting further comment and when none came he asked, "Have you run it by Barbara Twell and asked her opinion?"

Henry replied, "Yes, sir, I have. She feels you're on solid ground with the Constitution, but with the magnitude of the mandate that the members of the court may think it merits an open forum."

The president stood and walked to his garden window. "Well, if she feels we're okay on the Constitution, then I agree that letting that court hear arguments may be a good thing for us. They could hear all the arguments and rule it okay and end the legal issues right there. The people would or should feel fine with the legality of the question. With the legal question out of the way, we only have to deal with the moral right. I, for one, like the odds."

The intercom buzz was not what the president wanted to hear. Marge knew not to disturb him unless it was really important, so it must be. "Yes, Marge?"

"Mr. President, I have the governor of Michigan, Governor Peterson, on the phone. He has a major problem and wants to speak with you immediately. Sir, he has told me of his problem and I think you need to hear it."

"Pete, this is Jim Barringer, what's up?"

"Mr. President, about thirty minutes ago, at least fifteen armed men took control over the sheriff's office in Lansing and are holding at least twenty-six to thirty people hostage, including the sheriff. I just got off the phone with the leader of the group. He calls himself General Curtis of the Michigan Militia. We've known about this group for several years, but they have never done anything illegal that we know of. So far they have just been a lot of talk, until today. They are against your proposal and intentions and demanding to speak to you."

"Do you think they will harm any of the hostages, Governor?"

"I really don't know, sir, as I've said we haven't had any trouble with them before."

"Okay, give me the phone number and I'll do some quick thinking before

I call. General Curtis, this is President Barringer speaking, how can we resolve this matter?"

"Well, I'll tell you what we want. We are peace-loving people, mostly farmers. We have never liked big government and always thought it would come to this one day. You and your cronies are going to try and take over the country and become dictators. That's why we formed our militia ten years ago. We have plenty of arms and ammunition and are going to fight to the death."

"General, I guess you don't quite understand what it is I'm trying to do. As peace-loving people, I'm sure you're fed up with the drug and crime problems, the fear and unsafe feeling everyone has. I want to start killing off this vermin and return the streets to the peace-loving people. I want to stop sending our money all over the world to nations that don't care about us and our problems. I want to bring our military home to stay. I want to end all the injustices in our system and do what's right. I want common sense to prevail over the nation. I don't want to run your life; I want to make it better."

"Sure you do," Curtis interrupted, "you want to take our guns."

"General," the president continued, "I don't want to take guns from you or from any other law-abiding citizens. I want to take the guns from criminals and people who will use them to rob and kill. I don't agree with a group like yours being armed and being like an army, and I never will. If you and your group do as you have for the past ten years, I have no problem with that. It's the criminal element I need to wipe out."

The president hoped he was getting to this man and continued on. "General, what you're doing isn't helping our country or your state. You need to rethink what you're doing. I suggest you lay down your weapons and end this right now."

"If we do, will you guarantee that no charges will be made against us?"

"No, sir, I can't promise you that. What you have done is a state and local problem right now. It's going to be up to them, not me. I will promise you this. If you stop this right now, I promise that there will be no federal charges made. I will let it remain a local problem."

"Well, I'm going to have to talk with the other members about this."

"General Curtis, as you might expect, I'm up to my ears in problems here trying to get this mandate on the road. I hope you can deal with Governor Peterson from here on. He's a fair man, work it out with him."

The president hung the phone up, walked to the bar and poured three fingers of scotch and downed it in one gulp. He looked right at Henry and Max. "There are more crazies out there than we know of. Come to think, if Peterson doesn't kill them off, maybe we can use them later to kill off some of the drug people."

"Mr. President…" Max stood up.

"Relax, Max, I'm trying to make light of a bad situation. Marge, please get me Governor Peterson on the phone."

"Pete, it's Barringer. Look, he doesn't sound like a crazy, but he is misguided. Based on your comments of his past, I'm presuming he's harmless. I don't discount what he gotten himself into now, but I think he may be more talk than action. I told him to lay his arms down now and I would not push for any federal charges. We'd leave it local, but I don't see how you can just let it go. I'm leaving it up to you to do what you have to do locally, naturally we'd assist you in anyway you ask or need, but generally it's yours."

"Welcome to the Think Tank, Mr. President."

"Thank you, Carl, how's it going?"

"Well, sir, Charlie Rose and I right now are working on some suggestions. As a matter of fact, I'd like to bounce this off you and get your reaction, if you don't mind."

"Go ahead, I'm all ears."

"Well, Charlie was talking that every year that the P.D. couldn't get a pay raise it seemed the topic of conversation always turned to the Congress and Senate. Their bitch was that the pay raises and perks those politicians got far outweighed every field and occupation. The pay raises were bad enough but the perks they got for the rest of their lives…"

The president was smiling and trying to stifle it at the same time.

Concannon saw the smile and said, "You remember your Senate days, don't you?"

"Yes I do. Pay raises were always a bone of contention, yet the voice of moderation always lost. The reality of it is, we need to do what's best for the country and us. Everyone voiced concern, but voted in favor of the raises."

"Well, sir, we're trying to find ways to repeal some of those raises."

"Carl, I can appreciate what you're saying, it really would be good for the everyday Joe, but after the suspension when we go back to a regular life of government, I'm afraid they will go right back to those raises."

"Yes, sir, I think you're right, but it would send a huge message to the people and both the House and Senate."

The phone rang and Charlie picked it up. He said, "Yes," looked at the president and handed him the phone.

President Barringer took the phone and answered, "Yes?" He listened to the caller for perhaps two minutes and finally asked, "Is there anything we can do for you, Pete? Okay, if you need anything call. Thanks for the update."

The president sat down and filled in both Senator Concanon and Charlie Rose. "That call was Governor Peterson. He just told me that apparently General Curtis was telling his men they needed to give up. One of his own men took exception and shot and killed the general. Curtis' son then shot and killed the shooter. The rest of the group has surrendered with no other injuries."

Chapter 8

"All rise." The packed courtroom arose and the members of the Supreme Court paraded in and took their seats. Chief Justice Robert Holm raised his gavel and slammed it down stating, "The Supreme Court of the United States of America is now in session."

Chief Justice Holm awaited a slight murmur of activity to die down and spoke. "Those attorneys present and wishing to be heard have been given a written response to the question at hand. This court has publicly stated that we see no Constitutional objection to the president's request for a public mandate. Having said that, we all understand the magnitude of what the president has asked. Because of that unusually high degree of uncertainty, we are offering those present a chance to speak to this court on why they feel as they do. I warn you, do not bring up the Constitutional issue, we have made our decision on that issue and we will not visit there again. Mr. Wilbur Coleman, representing the ACLU, you have the floor and please remember your time limitations."

Mr. Coleman stood to speak. He was a staunch anti-government advocate and had been since childhood. That fact is understandable when you consider since childhood he had heard the ranting and ravings of his father, against the same government. Like father like son, many said. Even before Wilbur finished law school he had been accepted by the ACLU as a rising star. Coleman had argued several cases before this court, but none larger in scope than this.

"Mr. Chief Justice, ladies and gentleman of the court, thank you for allowing me to address this court. I am sorry that Justice Twell is not present; I would have liked to address her on this issue."

"Mr. Colman," Chief Justice Holm interrupted, "Justice Twell felt she needed to recuse herself as she was too close to the issue, and I agree with her determination. Please go on."

"Ladies and gentleman, I am personally appalled at the proposal of our president and terribly disappointed at this court for agreeing with him."

"Mr. Coleman," the chief justice interrupted, "don't put words in this court's mouth. We never said we agreed with the president, we merely stated we saw no Constitutional issue with his request. This court has no obligation to you or anyone else to be heard on this issue. We are here to allow you to voice your opinion on the matter and we're not obliged to do so. Do you understand?"

"Yes, sir, I do. You are handcuffing me and my freedom of speech. You have already suspended my Constitutional rights."

"Mr. Coleman," boomed the chief justice, "please sit down."

"Sir? I am just beginning."

"Mr. Coleman, sit down while I speak with the other members of the court. Ten-minute recess."

Twenty minutes passed before the justices reseated themselves. Chief Justice Holm asked for Mr. Coleman and the three others slated to speak to approach the center bench. When the four were lined up in from of Holm, he asked, "Is it the intention of you to stand before this court and tell us how appalled you are? Do you wish to say that what our president has asked for is unprecedented? That no time in the history of this nation has such a request been considered? Do you feel our president is attempting to become a dictator and that our society will become a police state? Are those the subjects you gentleman wish to speak of? Well, I am going to ask you individually if any of you have anything concrete to add to my list. Mr. Coleman?"

"Basically you have covered it except for the moral issue."

"Mr. Buchanan?"

"Yes, sir, what you have stated covers most of it."

"Mr. Day?"

"The same for me, sir."

"Mr. Guzman?"

"The same for me, sir."

"You may all be seated. It is this court's opinion that you four are wasting this court's time and your own. Do you think for one minute that the members of this court haven't been asking these same questions for the last three weeks? We have and will probably do so again. We have ruled on the Constitutional issue, period. End of report. You have no right to come into this court and state we have suppressed your Constitutional rights, it's just not true. In one week the people will vote and they will make that decision. The arguments are mute and this court is adjourned."

"Mr. President, have you heard?" Max Wobser was entering the Oval Office with a large smile on his face. "It's all over the networks. The court has adjourned and refused any arguments."

"Yes, Max, I see it. I'm not sure why, but I really don't care. It's another hurdle out of the way, anything else?"

"Yes, we're having some trouble with Governor Grady of Washington State and Bessemer of Wisconsin. They are both giving us grief over the election and their opposition to it."

"Get me both on the line, together on a three-way hookup."

"Gentlemen, I don't know what your problem is, but I need to tell you a few things. Of fifty states, only you two are causing trouble. Our polls show this mandate question is 60-40 in favor. I don't see how it can fail. Now, your voters have the same opportunity to vote that every other citizen has. If you deny them that right, I'll have you both out of office and you know damn well I can and will do just that. I have no desire for absolute power, but if I get the mandate I will have unprecedented power and the first thing I will do is to remove you both from office. Now get off your politically-motivated asses and get the election process done, you both hear me?"

Governor Grady quietly said "Yes" but Bessemer did not respond. The president harshly added, "Chuck, what's your problem?"

"Well, I feel that what you're asking is way beyond the guidelines of decency."

"Chuck, I'll tell you what. You have just twenty-four hours to get your ass in gear or you'll pay a dear price for your personal pride. If you don't move in those twenty-four hours, I guarantee you'll be coming down with a very serious ailment that will require complete bed rest and your eventual retirement from the political ring. Do you hear me, Chuck?"

"Yes, sir, I do."

Platoon 344 was at ease in front of the chow hall, the smoking lamp was lit. Those that smoked did so and those that didn't just stood around glad for the few minutes of idle time. As the ranks filled, time ticked. In three minutes Sergeant Flack returned and called them to attention.

Sergeant McDaniel observed an open spot in the ranks. "Who's missing from the ranks there?" he called.

The reply back was, "Sir, Private Moore, sir."

"I'll beat his ass into the ground," he mumbled as he walked back into the chow hall to search for Private Moore. In two minutes he returned and reported to Sergeant Flack that Moore was nowhere to be seen.

Once back at the barracks, Sergeant Flack notified the company commander, Lieutenant Miller, that Private Moore was absent. Flack had no sooner hung up the phone when it rang. Lieutenant Miller quickly stated that a man, apparently a recruit, was observed climbing the water tower. Twenty minutes later, all four platoons of the company stood at attention within 150 yards of the water tower. This tower supplied all the drinking water for the island and stood near 180 feet.

Sergeant Flack put the platoon at ease and called Moore's squad leader to front and center. Private Gallo responded and stood in front of Flack. "Here, take these binoculars and tell me if it's Moore," handing the glasses to Gallo.

Gallo took about fifteen seconds before turning to Flack replying, "It's him, sir."

"Back in ranks," Flack ordered.

Several of the brass had arrived and huddled nearby. Flack approached them, saluted and spoke with them for a minute. He then walked toward the tower, bullhorn in hand. "Moore, can you hear me? Get down here you idiot, now."

Private Moore did not move nor give any sign of life. Flack continued to talk to Moore for another five minutes. He finally gave up and returned to the brass, and then returned to the platoon.

"Sir, Private Gallo requests permission to speak with the drill instructor."

"Speak," shouted Flack.

"Sir, I can get him down. I'll climb up and guide him down. I'm not afraid of heights."

"No," shouted Flack. "He got himself up there and he'll get himself down, one way or another." Flack told Sgt .McDaniel to march the platoon back and resume the training schedule and he would stay on scene. McDaniel turned the platoon and was not seventy-five feet when everyone could hear the dreadful scream and a dull thud. It didn't take a rocket scientist to know what had taken place. McDaniel halted the platoon and addressed them. "Private

Moore took the easy way out. He'll be on his way home tomorrow, anyone care to join him? We have now lost seventeen men, sixteen to the fat man platoon and now Moore to the Grim Reaper. We have nine weeks to get rid of another thirty-five or so. Speak up, clowns, I'll show you how to climb the ladder to success."

"This is one sorry-ass waste of time; this deck ain't dirty one bit."

"Shut up, Martinez, you'll get our ass in a sling."

"Aw, cool it man, the DI's never fuck with us when we're doing field day, they might get water on those pretty shoes. Hey man, I saw a couple of guys marching on the grinder wearing gloves, what with that?"

"You know, Martinez, for a city spic you don't know jack shit." Romero, looking right at Martinez knew he had hit a nerve.

"Why you call me a spic, you one too."

"Yeah and it's okay to call one spic to another spic where I come from."

"Where you come from?"

"San Antonio, Texas. Why?"

Martinez continued scrubbing. "You know why those guys had gloves on?"

Romero smiled. "They got caught choking their chicken."

Martinez stopped scrubbing and looked at Romero. "What the fuck you talking about. Who got a chicken?"

Romero had to bite his lip to keep from laughing out loud. "He was beating his meat, asshole."

"Oh, why didn't you say that."

Romero continued, "You see the guy marching all by himself with the guard?"

"Yeah, I seen him, why? What's up with that?"

"That guy's going out on a psycho discharge."

Martinez quickly spoke up, "You mean you get out being a psycho? I could?"

"No, not us. Remember they told us if we fail we get prison for two years?"

"Yeah, I remember. I'd like to get out of this place."

"Martinez, you ain't getting out unless it's after they train you."

"Well, I'm thinking of going out through the swamp or river. You want to go with me, Romero?"

Romero smiled again. "Martinez, you're stupid, I'm not. If that swamp doesn't suck you in, the gators or sharks will. You're stupid."

Their squad leader, Gallo, spoke up. "You guys get caught shooting the shit and I'll swear I never heard you."

Both looked at Gallo. Martinez asked Gallo, "You know why those guys were wearing gloves?"

Gallo chuckled. "Yeah, I know. They were beating their meat, why?"

"Romero just told me, I didn't know."

"Well," added Gallo, "it's a wonder they could with all the salt peter they put in the food."

Both men looked at Gallo. Martinez said, "What kind of peter?"

"Salt peter," said Gallo. "It keeps your sex drive down and under control. I know I haven't had a hard-on since I got here, you?"

Both replied "No."

"See," Gallo offered, "it works. Come on now, get to work and finish this up."

All Romero and Martinez could ask, over and over was, "I wonder why they call it salt peter."

President Barringer stood watching the rain fall. *Sure is one lousy day,* he thought. *Joan used to say, what a wonderful day this was, a gift from Mother Nature to us. God, I miss her so much. Jimmy too. This is the same kind of day when he got hit. I hope he didn't suffer.*

He could feel the tears welling up in his eyes when he heard a voice, "Mr. President?" As he turned, he saw Max standing in front of him. "You okay, sir?"

"Yes, just passing thoughts rearing up again. I wonder if it ever stops."

"Anything I can do for you, sir?"

"No, thanks, only time will help."

"Yes, sir, Henry is waiting."

"Okay, bring him in and let's get to it."

"Where do we stand, are we all ready?" The president looked at Henry.

"Yes, sir, we've done all we can, its up to the voters now. In less than forty-eight hours we'll know."

The president was aware that he was drifting off, his mind wandering. He turned to the two men and said, "Any late problems?"

"No, sir, not one thing. As I said, everything is in place and we're waiting for the polling places to open at 0700 tomorrow."

Max cleared his throat. "You are aware, are you not, that you're still taking a beating overseas? I just finished a story out of Paris saying you're going to get beat."

President Barringer smiled, added quietly, "Well, they all of people know a lot about defeat, don't they?" All three laughed at that. When he stopped laughing, the president said, "You know, I've seen so much good and bad press that I don't give a damn what they think or say. All I care about right now is the American people and how they vote."

At six the next morning, the president was sipping coffee at his desk. He was reading the overnight drafts from around the world, his "briefs," that's what everyone called them. A quiet tapping got his attention.

The door opened a couple of inches and Bill Tyson peaked in. As the head of the president's Secret Service detail, Tyson was a frequent visitor to the Oval Office. Come on in, Bill. Want coffee?"

"No, sir, had some. Mr. President, as usual, we'll be taking you to vote today, but I need to bring you up-to-date first."

"Why, Bill, is there a change from the previous times?"

"Yes, sir, there is. We'll be going to a different polling place via a different route."

"Why?"

"Well, sir, I don't want to alarm you, but we're working on a rumor and there is some credibility to it. If we can solve it, you'll be the first to know, but for now, we've got to tighten up when you leave the building."

At 8:55 a.m. the president was escorted to Marine One, his helicopter waiting on the White House lawn. Once airborne, Bill Tyson sat down next to the president. "Here's the plan, sir. We're going to Richmond. We'll land at a small airport outside the city. No press. Nobody is expecting us. You vote, we leave and you're back in an hour. After we're back, your press staff issues a release and a video showing you voting. The explanation will be that you want to be seen in a different polling station and Richmond was pulled out of a hat as a location. Sound okay to you, sir?"

"Yes, it's fine, but I would like some further explanation on what this is all about."

"Fair enough, sir. We got hold of a rumor about three days ago that several foreign nations had put out a hit on you."

"What, are you serious?"

"Yes, sir, this is no joke. These countries are recipients of a large amount of foreign aid and they don't want to lose it. According to what we know to this point is that they have pooled ten million dollars to have you killed. Supposedly organized crime families were offered it and none would touch it. Somehow, a person high up on the food chain got hold of it and is running with it. He supposedly is not a big fan of yours."

The president looked startled, but asked, "Do you have an identity of his man?"

"Yes, sir, we're checking it all out now."

"Bill, I don't want to pick your brain right now, but I need to know that this person is not a member of my cabinet."

"No, sir, he is an elected official, but at this point we're still doing a lot of work on this and I'd hate to say who it is in case he's not involved, you understand, sir?"

"Yes, Bill, what you're doing is fine. It's all in your hands."

All day the president's staff and Senator Concannon's staff watched and waited. They had assembled in the White House café again with a large-screen television set along with a bank of telephones. The kitchen staff worked all day also, preparing food and serving this unique group.

In the Oval Office, Secretary of State Lloyd, Chief of Staff Wobser, Senator Concannon and Charlie Rose sat with the president. "How's the vote going, Henry?" asked the president.

"Well, sir, the major networks are all saying we hold about a five percent lead. The fact that we have to wait for the West Coast to catch up, in about three hours, should give us a good idea."

"Any problems?"

"Nothing worth mentioning," replied Max. "A few technical glitches that we've already mentioned, but nothing more. You've seen the protestors marching in several cities but it isn't a problem."

The president stood. "I think I'm going to my quarters. I need to call my sister and then I think I'll take a nap. Let's meet here again about 5:30, okay? We'll go over the results to that point and around six join everybody in the café and have dinner with them. We can all watch the results together. Damn, I know what I forgot. How do we stand on tomorrow? I mean if we win the mandate are we ready to proceed?"

Henry Lloyd spoke up first. "Yes, sir, we're ready. Every item on the list has been worded and approved, as you know. The list of changes and explanations is the same that has been furnished to each state via the governor's office. They have instructions that if we win the mandate, these changes go into effect at midnight tonight. The staff that we appointed to represent each state will be or already is at each state governor's office to see that the changes are implemented and to answer questions that may arise. He or she will be in direct contact with us if it's necessary."

Max added, "Naturally these same items have been published in every possible publication for the past three weeks. Every voter should just about have them memorized by now."

"That was a Charlie Rose idea and a good one at that," added Concannon. "Giving every voter the complete opportunity to see and study each proposal was a splendid idea. No voter could possibly not know what he's voting on."

At 5:33 the president walked into the Oval Office to find his staff all present. As he sat, Max asked, "How's your sister doing, sir?"

"Fine thanks. The surgery took a lot out of her, but she sounded very cheerful. She's worried that she can't get out to vote. I informed her of the provision on absentees and she said she had forgotten that. I guess her mind's not too sharp either. Well, where are we?"

"The latest projections are that we should win by a seven- to eight-percent margin," replied Henry Lloyd. "It's still a possibility that the West Coast vote could change things, but it's not expected. This vote is the highest ever voter turnout in history. The number yet to vote is minuscule."

Everyone was smiling and excited, everyone that is except President Barringer. He sat for the moment, not saying a word. Finally he said, "I don't know if I'm glad or sad. It's what we have all worked so hard for, yet I also know or think I know what's ahead of us. I very much look forward to the changes that will improve our way of life, but at the same time I'm asking an awful lot of our police forces. To kill any amount of human beings is going to be awfully hard on them, even though some of the scum deserve it." He hesitated a long time, as though mulling over his thoughts. He finally added, "I guess I have secured a page or two in the history books."

As the president and his staff entered the café, the applause and cheers became ear splitting. The hoots and hollers finally died down. The president worked his way to the middle of the crowd, so everyone could hear. He raised both hands and said, "It appears that your hard work is about to pay off. It's not quite official, but it looks awfully good. I thank each and every one of you for your efforts; I won't forget it.

"Before we sit and break bread together, I would appreciate it if you all would join me in a prayer." The entire group stood, joined hands and became silent. "God in Heaven, the God of all religions, I implore you to help us. We are about to embark on a new path, in the hope of righting a lot of wrongs. We are heading into a new direction as a nation and we surely need your guidance. Please give us the strength to make the right decisions and follow the proper path, for the sake of the entire nation. Please forgive those who have to carry out my orders for I know you cannot forgive the taking of a life. The commandment 'thou shall not kill' has to be put aside in order to eliminate a horrible plague that has fallen on us. May you have mercy on our souls?"

At 7:46 p.m. the large screen broadcasting the results showed a "flash alert." The cameras went to Walter Cronkite. "Ladies and gentleman, CBS, NBC, ABC and the Associated Press have concluded that the mandate vote has been approved by a margin of 58 to 42 percent in favor." His voice faded into the noise of the room. Everyone was shouting, slapping backs and kissing, yet the president sat with his eyes closed. Nobody had a clue to his thoughts, as he prayed that the Lord would forgive those he was ordering to kill.

It was 11:28 p.m. when the president turned off his light next to his bed. The thought that today had been one very unique and historical day crossed his mind. The phone rang and changed that thought. "Yes?"

"Mr. President, its Bill Tyson. I really am sorry to bother you, but could I have one minute? I'm right outside your quarters, sir."

"Sure, Bill, come on in."

"Mr. President, I'm not sure that what I have to tell you is going to make you sleep any better."

"Well let's find out, Bill, what is it?"

"Today, we put in place a very complex system of observing your usual polling place. The tip was that a sniper was going to take a shot at you as you entered or left the polling place. One of the spotters in a high-altitude helo spotted what turned out to be a sniper lying on a rooftop, with a sniper rifle set up. We have been talking to him for the better part of the day. All I can confirm is that he is a David Zurawski, a mercenary and former military. He's not saying much." Tyson looked at his watch. "In about thirty-one minutes, a whole new set of rules go into effect and I expect he might be more apt to speak to us. I honestly think given that he can and would be shot, I expect him to cooperate. I will have a more complete story for you in the morning. Good night, sir."

"Thank you, Bill, good luck to you."

After turning off the light again, the president's thoughts drifted in various directions. The past month had been a very hard one and even the news on the plot to kill him didn't stop his body from going into a dead sleep within minutes.

At 7 a.m. President Barringer had just finished his first cup of coffee when Bill Tyson tapped on the door. "May I come in, sir?"

"Sure, Bill, coffee?"

"No, sir, it may keep me awake. I've been at this all night and hope to grab a few hours' sleep after I fill you in. First, let me say that we have three men in custody and we don't expect anyone else to surface. I'll start at the beginning for clarity.

"Ten different countries who have been receiving foreign aid each put up one million dollars for a total of ten million. In return for their money, ours really, your life would be taken in the hopes that the U.S. would return to status quo and they would get their foreign aid money again. As a side note, for six of the ten countries we have ongoing investigations in reference to that country's president or prime minister stealing aid money for themselves.

"The hit was on the open market and the organized crime families all turned it down. Somehow a member of a family put a call in to the senator from Rhode Island, William Miller, who is not a very big fan of yours. He gets his chief of staff, who just happens to be his brother-in-law, to use as a go-between. Miller was in the Army and formed a friendship with a man who just happened to be a sniper named Dave Zurawski. They were buds and Miller knew Zurawski was into mercenary work. The brother-in-law offers $500,000 to Zurawski and he accepts. The brother-in-law was supposed to offer a million, but at the last minute decided to only offer a half mil and keep the other half for himself. The old 'honor among thieves.'

"Zurawski caved in when he was informed that he would be immediately shot, ASAP. His story is that he really didn't know if he could pull the trigger on you, but he wanted the 500 G's. He has about one and a half million tucked away in Spain and with the 500 G's he was going to retire in Spain with two mil in the bank. I did have to cut a deal with him. He is smart enough to know that we needed him and his confession. He figured without him, we had nothing and he was right. For his cooperation I agree to allow him to get to Spain, but renounce his U.S. citizenship. Naturally he's not going to see any of the money.

"We picked up Miller's brother-in-law and when he heard what we had and that if he didn't cooperate we would shoot him, he sang the song and gave us Miller. We arrested Miller here in town and he screamed something fierce. We got him into the interrogation room and laid out the plot, he broke quickly. He's begging you for his life. He says the ten mil was never given to him, but he did get one mil upfront for expenses."

The president stood and walked to his favorite window and stood there thinking. He finally said, "I thought I had heard just about everything in my lifetime, but this is certainly a new one. To think an elected senator of my own country could be that hateful and greedy to boot. The whole story turns my stomach. Well, I have a lot to do today so we'll have to put him aside for now. Lock him up somewhere. Have the AG charge him and we'll send it to the court ASAP. Under the new rules, it shouldn't take a week before they shoot him."

Chapter 9

Lieutenant John Ducey was a twenty-four-year veteran of the Washington Metro Police Department. Seventeen of those years were spent in the narcotics division. As the number two man in the division, it was his responsibility to set up and carry out raids and today's was not much different, except for one little nuance. Today was the day that the new rules went into play, kill the dealer or possessor of quantity.

Being reasonably intelligent and very street smart, he knew it was best to let his young bucks break in doors and do whatever heavy work was required. He rarely entered a scene until the all-clear was called. Like him, his men were also intelligent, street smart, young, strong and willing to do what the job required.

Like all veterans, he had seen the death, destruction and misery that were the end result of the drug world. The staggering amount of crime committed just to purchase drugs was beyond the comprehension of most. He knew deep down in his soul all the justification needed to kill these slime balls was present and justified, but the nagging question, could he? Pulling the trigger on a perp who had a gun aimed in your direction was a no-brainier, but that same perp without a gun and no defense would make it different, if not difficult. Ducey personally had not killed before. Yes, he shot one man but he lived. He thought about that. *I really have no regrets about shooting him, I'd do it again. Are the 'kids', as he called them, thinking the same as I am? We had better talk about this and get it out in the open because someone is going to have to be first.*

As Lieutenant Ducey entered the room he heard, "Hey, Loo, it's nice you could join us." Everyone got a chuckle out of this usual greeting.

Ducey looked at Detective Steve Marinaro who had shouted the welcome and said, "You are buying the beer and pizza tonight, remember that." Everyone joined in the laughing and cheering for the lieutenant.

"Okay, guys, let's get serious. We have about thirty minutes before push off so let's go over it once more. 726 Foster Ave., a two story tenement. Our guys are on the first floor, all of it. The second floor is used for office space, female entertainment and gambling. One door in front, one in the rear. We think there's a door leading to the roof. At exactly 6:45 a.m., the door busters hit the front and back doors. Four men rush in and secure the first floor and four more follow up and rush the second floor. One man stationed at each door and he will remain there throughout the raid. His secondary job is to watch for bodies and junk coming out the windows. One man, plus a sniper on the roof next door. Does every man here know his assignment?" Nods of yes all around. "Are there any questions?" No questions.

"Okay, good. Now we all know the new wrinkle in our job. Speaking for myself only, I have given it a lot of thought. We have all said it a million times; I wish I could kill this shithead. Well, the talk is over. Each of us knows that we all will have to take some lives, each and every one of us. You need to know this and be aware that if you don't kill today, you will tomorrow. If anyone has any doubts he can do it, now is the time to speak up. I know the macho shit and not wanting to look bad in front of your peers, but you have to forget that shit and speak up."

Detective Tom Bachman raised his hand. "Tom?"

"Loo, what if it's me and I freeze up?"

"Tommy, you got the same training and lectures we all got. You know you have two choices. I think many will hesitate, but in the end you shoot or be replaced in the unit. I personally have justified it by telling myself to remember all the dead and missing I've seen because of drugs. We have a new weapon and I intend to use it. Each of you have to make your own decision, but you don't have much time to decide. P.S. today's the first time for this so the bad guys may think it's all been a bunch of bullshit and PR. We are going to shoot first and it's going to get rough. After today they are going to get wiser, so we've got to change our tactics. We'll start using some military takeouts and takeouts with surprise. If we don't or can't, we will lose some of our own."

Dealing drugs is usually a nighttime activity. The sellers are selling, using, drinking, partying or screwing themselves to death. At 6:45 a.m., they have usually just gotten into bed. Having been heavily engaged in their trade all night, they are exhausted and it is the perfect time to hit them. Their reflexes are slow or non-existent. At 0645, right on time, the front and rear doors of 726 Foster Avenue ceased to exist. Eight highly armed, trained and eager officers stormed the first floor and were quickly followed by four more to take the second floor. One gunshot was heard. Lieutenant Ducey broke his rule and rushed into the apartment. Just as he entered, he heard what he most wanted, "Clear," followed by another from the second floor. Ducey hollered, "Leaders report to me." Detectives Marinaro and Chuck Finnerty found Ducey and reported.

Marinaro stated, "We have two males on the first floor, one wounded in the shoulder. He was told to freeze, reached under his pillow and was shot by myself."

Ducey turned to Finnerty. "One male and one female on the second floor."

Ducey added, "You two check to see if the roof and basement were used and are all clear."

Ducey turned towards the male and female handcuffed, marching down the stairs and seated them on the floor with the other two males. The wounded male was holding a towel to his shoulder and moaning.

Several minutes lapsed until Marinaro and Finnerty returned and reported to Ducey that the basement and roof were clear, with nothing to add. Ducey heard the search team say they had found a half kilo of coke, fifty to seventy-five bindles of heroin and about five pounds of grass.

Ducey was making notes in his pad on what type of drug and quantity, when he stopped and said, "I want ID on all four now." He was quickly handed three sets of identification by Finnerty. "What about the fourth?"

"Says he has none. He claims his name is Charles Joseph Levi, 3/10/46."

After Ducey copied all the data on identification, he handed the list to Detective Marinaro and told him, "Call it in to headquarters and get the rap sheet ASAP."

Ducey walked to the four prisoners and told them who he as was. The bleeding man kept asking for a doctor and Ducey lied to him, "In time. Who owns this place or rents it?" Nothing. "Which one is Washington?"

"I am, why? Why you ask who owns or rents this place when you know it's me?"

"I wanted to see if you were going to play it straight or not."

"Fuck you, cop, I never been honest with cops, never will either."

Ducey was thinking quickly. "Stand up, Washington." He struggled, but finally got to his feet. Ducey took out his .357 and aimed it at Washington's head. Ducey looked at him and said, "Do you read the newspapers? Do you know we can shoot you on the spot?"

Washington stared at him and said, "Fuck you, pig."

Ducey did his best to remain calm, but inside the turmoil was building. Once again he addressed Washington. "One question. One answer; or your dead. Who's your supplier?"

Washington laughed and said, "You can't shoot me, whitey," as Ducey pulled the trigger.

The noise of a 357-caliber handgun going off is staggering to the ears, especially in an enclosed room. It can't be explained in words, it has to be felt. The occupants of the room never heard the shot. They were stupefied by what had occurred. It seemed like a long time before anyone reacted to what had occurred, when they finally did, it was because the noise had finally caught up to the brain and their ears began to hurt. The blood and sinew from Washington's head shot was all over them and it was not a very nice feeling.

Detective Finnerty was the first to react. He reached for and grabbed the wounded man, Charles Levi. Ducey looked at Finnerty, as he put his three-inch detective special to Levi's temple. Ducey asked Levi where the junk was bought. Levi looked at Ducey and at Washington and pointed to the third man. "He gets it, that's all I know. He brings it here; me, Washington and her sell it."

"You better be telling me the truth." Ducey nodded to Marinaro to get the third man to his feet. "What's your name?"

"Samuel Coates."

"Well, Sam, it seems you're the main man here."

"Not true, I don't know anything about this shit."

Ducey turned to Finnerty. "Shoot him," pointing at Levi. Finnerty pointed at Levi's head and fired. Just like the first shot, everyone in the room was or appeared stunned. It seemed like a movie, not real, yet two bloodily bodies lay on the floor.

The female began crying, "You gonna kill us all?"

Ducey turned to her. "That depends on what you have to say."

She tried to stand but it took Finnerty to help her to her feet. "I don't know nothing. I come here to sell shit on the street. He," pointing to Coates, "gives me a little for myself and screws me too."

"Stand Coates up," ordered Ducey. Ducey walked right up to Coates face and said, "You got something to tell me?"

Coates cooed, "Don't know nothing."

Ducey eyes Marinaro and pointed to the woman. The look on Marinaro's face was pained, his eyes pleading with Ducey. Ducey pointed to the woman again and said, "Do it, Steve, now."

Marinaro reached down to his ankle holster and removed his three-inch special. He slowly walked to the woman, pointed at the back of her head and fired. She barely hit the floor when Marinaro fled the room and could be heard wrenching his guts out.

Coates was now visibly shaken. He looked wildly at Ducey, then Finnerty and back again. Ducey again looked Coates in the eye and said, "For the last time, are you going to tell me where you buy or do you want to join your friends?"

Coates was shaking and a bead a sweat trickled down his nose. "What do I get if I tells you?"

"If your info is good, real good, you may get life, but that's no promise. You don't have a choice, if you don't tell me, your dead. If you do, you have to see what I'll do, but either way you got one choice and only one choice."

Coates was uncuffed and handed a yellow pad and pen. He wrote for nearly ten minutes as Ducey told him want info he wanted. When he finished, Ducey took the pad and read it. Ducey turned and headed for the door. He stopped outside and told Det. Ken Brown to shoot Coates. As Ducey reached for his car door, he heard a single gunshot from the apartment.

The police vehicles and the gunshots from the apartment had roused the neighborhood and thirty to forty people were milling around across the street. A newspaper reporter and photographer were also milling around and begging for info.

Ducey called to Sergeant Mike Sullivan, the area supervisor. "Mike, do me a favor, will you. Get my guys to pull the bodies outside and lay them out on the sidewalk."

"Sure, Loo, but are you sure you want them on the sidewalk?"

"Yes, I do. I want the whole neighborhood to see what's happened here, and I want that reporter and photographer to ask questions and take pictures. I want the whole city to see what the new rules are. When that's all done, call for the body snatchers."

Lieutenant Ducey put his coffee mug down and watched as the squad entered the meeting room. He studied those who did the shooting the day before, looking for a sign and saw none. After everyone was seated, he asked, "Did everyone sleep okay? Better yet, did anyone not sleep okay?" No response. "Okay, I know, I'm pushing, but I'm worried that one or more of you has a problem with yesterday's events. I can't be anymore open than that." Again, no response. "I take that to mean we can go on with business.

"Let's critique the op. Anyone have anything to say, pro or con?"

Steve Marinaro spoke up. "Boss, the female was sort of a surprise. I mean, yeah, we all know they sell too, but I mean the killing part."

"Steve, we can't be biased with anyone, male, female, white, black or even a kid. Speaking of kids, what happens when we get a ten- or twelve-year-old selling?" Ducey paused, he knew he'd hit a nerve, in fact it had hit him as well.

"Shit, I'm not whacking a kid like I saw yesterday, I won't do it." Det. DeVito was looking from face to face for support. Every man in the unit was wondering to himself, if he could.

Ducey looked directly at DeVito. "Ben, I hope we don't run into this problem, but I'm telling you right now, you do not pull the trigger and someone else will; and you'll be doing another job. The presidential mandate committee states that all sellers and possessors of quantity be shot on the spot. It does not say at what age. You, DeVito and all the rest of you better give it some thought. You all know damn well that we have many teenage sellers.

"I take it that we all feel the unit did its job and we have no further complaints? Okay. In today's papers there are several stories of other cities that made headlines yesterday. At least ten major cities conducted raids and the body county is already over one hundred dead. We can conclude from that, that the word is out and we will no doubt start getting a lot of return fire from our targets. I also think that from here on, we may have to think of some new tactics. If I were in their shoes I damn sure would station lookouts around their dens for early warning protection. We need to start thinking, all of us, how to get this job done in new ways."

Ducey saw Det. Sid Pennington raise his hand. "What's on your mind, Sid?"

"Loo, last night some of us went out and hoisted a few and talked over the raid. We had a hunch we were in a new kind of war and felt exactly like your comment on new tactics. As a group, we thought why not an assassination squad. We use our undercover guys as we always have to make the buys. We photo the buy as evidence and to ID the seller. We then use a sniper team to blow him away. Secondly, we know many of the big dealers who we can't get the proper evidence on. Under the new rules, why not just whack him whenever we can. The way we see it, this is now a war and all's fair in love and war."

Ducey was surprise and tried to hide it. He perceived it was going to get nasty but he didn't think it would happen so quickly. "Sid, for now I want to think on your ideas. At worst, I'll take it upstairs and see what reaction I get."

In the following twenty-four hours, Lieutenant Ducey and his squad set about laying the groundwork for an assassination squad. It all seemed rather simple and closely followed the outline Det. Pennington laid out. The team would consist of four or five men. A sniper and a spotter, plus two or three lookouts. Undercover agents would make a week's worth of buys while being filmed. Once the buys were completed the teams would fan out, set up positions and do the dirty deed. It was hoped that all the shooting could be completed as close together as possible, for once the word got out of the shootings, the game would be over quickly. A photo of the target would have to be positively identified by both the sniper and the spotter before a kill could be made. In less than twenty-four hours, the word from above came back and Ducey had his squad assembled.

"Okay, guys, the old man has approved the A squad. His main concern is that we don't go too far out. You need to hear his words verbatim."

Ducey lifted several papers from his desk and began to read. "'If you kill or wound a wrong man, you're going to answer for it. If you attempt in any way to settle old grievances, you're going to swing. I approve the A squad and its method of action and I will take the heat, if any, for it. I will back you one hundred percent, but if you start to stray off target or settle grudges, you'll be in a world of shit, so help me.'"

Ducey put the paperwork down and asked, "Are there any questions? Are you all clear on what the old man said? No questions? None, okay. For the past eighteen hours I have had the girls going through the files, compiling a list of candidates. I want you all to start going over the lists and make sure its all current. I don't want to whack a guy who was dealing five years ago and is clean now. By current, I mean in the past six months. When that's done, we'll sit down and make a plan."

Det. Ken Brown was lying prone on his stomach. His scoped sniper rifle lay on a sandbag pointed out into space. He lay there thinking back, about how all this came about. His time in the Marine Corps sniper team was a good time. He shot at least once a day, but it was at paper targets or moving silhouettes of a man. Being peacetime, he never made a kill. Since joining the P.D. all his practice was at paper, but that was all coming to an end. He was here to kill a man for the first time in his life. *Am I going to be able to do this? I know this clown is a first-class dirt bag but he is still an American.* Thankfully this kind of self-doubt ended when his spotter said, "Ken, there he is. See him. He's talking to some guy in the green car? I make this ID one hundred percent positive."

Brown moved his rifle into place, focused in on the target and then glanced at the photo and back to the target. After doing that twice, he told his spotter, "I confirm this target one hundred percent."

Charlie "Goodstuff" Logan was doing his thing. He had a new batch of smack and was doing a brisk business. He was also talking to himself. *Two damn weeks of new laws and here I am still doing business. Cops are a lot of bullshit.* He glanced up to the roof of apartments across the street for a second time. Something looked out of place, but he couldn't see what.

"Hey, honey, got something for me?"

He turned to see Gloria-somebody smiling at him and he suddenly remembered her. He had screwed her a couple of times for a dime bag. "What you need, girl?"

She extended a twenty-dollar bill towards him and said, "Gimme my stuff." He handed her two dime bags and she disappeared as quickly as she had appeared. "Shit, man, this is easy. Just stand here and rake it in."

A white Chevy Corvair pulled up and as Logan raised his eyes to see who it was, a .223 slug passed through his heart. Before he reached the ground, the sniper, his spotter and the backup were moving. In the same hour that Goodstuff Logan entered oblivion, fourteen other street sellers joined him. It was a good start for the A squad.

Saleem "The Lord" Taylor had a dream. He was going to Africa and set himself up as the lord of his land. He would buy up as much land as he could and have as many people as his land could bear to serve him. He wanted to start out as the lord of his kingdom and work his way up to higher status. For the past four years Saleem had been saving his money to fulfill his dream. At last check he had nearly twenty-two million dollars stashed away in offshore accounts to pay for his dream.

The money kept rolling in and anyone who did not cooperate with his enterprise, disappeared. At times they were found, but barely recognizable. The Lord was one of the largest drug dealers in the D.C. area. For three years the Metro PD had tried to put him out of business but always failed. The Lord was not only a savage businessman, but a smart drug dealer. He set things up, told his underlings when and where, gave them the money needed to make the purchases of his stock and had it distributed to all the sellers. He never saw any drugs, touched any or had direct contact with most of the world.

The Metro narcotics division had a man who wanted to hand the Lord to them on a silver platter. Menu Ugilac, a native of Kenya, was an insider of the Lord's business enterprise. He had asked for Lieutenant Ducey, walked into his office and sat. Ducey looked at the man and recognized him from the files on the Lord's organization.

"Do you have your passport or any photo ID?" asked Ducey. Uglac smiled, reached into his jacket pocket and produced his Kenyan passport. Ducey looked it over and passed it back. "I have your name as Kipjae, is that correct?"

"Yes, it is my nickname."

"Okay, Kipjae, what is it you want?"

"I have what I think you call a proposition. I need to go back to Kenya and until you can get me there, I also will need protection. In return, I will give you the Lord on a golden platter."

Ducey smiled knowing it was supposed to be a silver platter, but why bother? "Why would you do this?" asked Ducey.

Kipjae stroked his chin softly and said, "I am in what is it called a bad situation. To be very truthful, I was fucking the Lord's girl. I found out today that he knows and is planning to kill me. You give me what I want and in return I will write out his entire organization, the layout of his house in Arlington Heights and the banks he has his money deposited in offshore. Your part of the bargain is to protect me until you can get me on a plane home."

Ducey was trying to contain himself. He was thinking that he has a golden opportunity sitting before him or a pile of bullshit. "Would you like something to drink, coffee or cold drink?"

"No, nothing."

"Okay, wait here. I need to talk to my boss."

Less than ten minutes passed when Ducey returned. "You got a deal, if and only if your info is good. If you're bullshitting me, you may never leave this building alive."

In the next twelve hours, Kipjae laid out a perfect organization chart of the drug business, a detailed drawing of the Lord's home and grounds and a complete list of banks as he had promised.

Lieutenant Ducey walked into the meeting room and told the entire squad to be quiet. He filled them in on what he had picked up and what he planned. "As we speak, the military is doing a flyover of the property and will have for us a detailed blowup of the house and grounds. Once we have the pictures in our hands, I want to see if we can get the A squad into a good shooting position and send the Lord to his Maker. While we wait for the pics, I want you all to get the sniper spotter guys out for some shooting practice. The figure this informer gave me was that we could probably shoot from 800 to 1,000 yards. Go practice at those distances."

The following morning the squad assembled again. In front of the room, were several blowup photos of the Lord's home and grounds. "Snipers, look these over now. It appears to me that we can get two different angles for a shot. Our guy says that every Saturday afternoon the Lord hosts a backyard BBQ and is very much present. He loves to speak with everyone present and sort of hold court. We have less than forty-eight hours to plan, position and be in place."

At noon on Saturday, two snipers with spotters were in position. The four men were dressed in military camo, black faced and in shooting position. One was up in a tree. The night before, the teams had quietly picked out the tree and climbed same and found or made the proper shooting and spotter positions. Now all they could do was wait.

Prior to entering the trees, the two teams had sat with Lieutenant Ducey to talk over the plan. Ducey's first question was "Are you both confidant you can make a killing shot at this range?"

Both snipers replied, "Affirm, Loo. We had a ten for ten yesterday at this range and up to 1,100 yards."

"Good. We agree that once positive ID is made, one or both can take the shot. No contest here, guys. I want one shot and done. Whoever is positive and set, goes. There's going to be a lot of targets out there, but I don't give a shit about anyone but the Lord. We straight on that?"

"Yes, sir."

"Did you both shoot with your suppressors on yesterday?"

"Yes."

"Okay, go to work."

At 2:29 p.m. the Lord made his entrance to the huge patio surrounding the pool area. For thirty minutes he moved around shaking hands and talking to his guests. At 3:03 p.m. he finally sat in the overstuffed lounge chair he liked to call his throne. At 3:05 p.m. the Lord pitched forward and fell to the deck floor. As his bodyguards quickly rolled him over they saw a neat hole in his chest and a large amount of blood staining his white linen jacket. The Lord had gone to his just reward.

Lieutenant John Ducey was staring out the window of his office. The events of the past weeks were flowing through his head. *What have we become? A squad of assassins and cold-blooded killers? We are that, but look at what we have accomplished over the past couple of weeks. We've taken out four major dealers, thirty-eight street-level dealers and one gigantic dealer. We haven't lost a man and the junkies are going nuts for lack of supply. If we...* the ringing of the phone stopped his thought.

"Lieutenant Ducey, Narcotics."

"Duce, this is Chief Morganthall. Listen closely. The White House has asked for someone from the department to brief some top level brass, possibly the president himself tomorrow around 1300. You have the best knowledge of what's been done and what's needed, so you go. Any questions?"

"No, sir." As he replaced the phone in its cradle, he wondered out loud, "I hope this isn't a stop order or ass chewing."

Ducey sat outside the Oval Office contemplating what may happen. The Secret Service agent he asked had been no help. They had taken his weapon and given him a pass to hang around his neck. As he looked over the pass, he observed the Secret Service agent at the Oval Office door watching him. The agent half smiled and asked him if this was his first time in the Oval Office.

"Yes, it is."

"I know who you are, Lieutenant, and let me assure you, he's a nice guy and he'll quickly put you at ease. He's one of us and we'd all do anything for him. As an added bonus, an old pal of yours will be in there to back you, Charlie Rose."

"No shit?"

"Yes, sir, he's become a regular around here for the past couple of months. Nice guy too."

Ten minutes later, Ducey was walked in to the Oval Office. The Secret Service agent introduced Ducey and left. The president walked to Ducey and extended his hand. "Please let me introduce you to the crowd. This is Secretary of State Henry Lloyd, my chief of staff, Max Wobser, Senator Concannon and retired P.D. Detective Charlie Rose, whom I'm told you know very well."

"Yes, sir, I sure do." They shook hands.

"Welcome, John," said Rose. "You have been doing one helluva job and I'm very proud to say you're my friend."

Ducey, not one to take to compliments, turned to the president and said, "Sir, if this man is one of your advisors, I would say you've got one of the best."

"Alright," said the president, "let's sit and get to business. I would like you to fill us in on just what is taking place on the street and in your department."

After rattling off a list of numbers and facts, the president stopped him. "Lieutenant, those figures impress a lot of people, but I'm not one of them. Please, in simple language, your thoughts."

Ducey remembered what the Secret Service agent had said outside the door, *He's one of us.* "Mr. President, we're knocking their socks off. We have taken out four major dealers and one gigantic dealer and thirty-nine street dealers. The supply on the street is drying up at an alarming rate. If the feds can keep the stuff from coming into the country, the total supply will be exhausted in a couple of weeks.

"We are seeing an increased incidence of break-ins of pharmacies, armed robbery of pharmacies and doctor's offices. We have kept the local legal distributors notified and warned them to arm themselves. We suspect truck hijacking could be next. They now have an armed guard on every delivery truck and the hospitals have done the same. The problem is the doctor's offices. There are so many of them and an armed guard can get expensive. With the lack of drug supply, the rehab clinics have waiting lists. The heavy-hitters are getting their fixes via the methadone clinics.

"Physiologically my unit is okay. A few of us, most of us, have lost sleep over the way we get rid of the junkies and dealers, but we're dealing with it. I've made it mandatory that each man see the department psychiatrist every ten to fourteen days, including myself."

The president seemed pleased. "That was a very good summation you presented us. I want you to take back to your unit my heartfelt praise of them and the thanks of the people of this city. I also want to ask you what your feelings are on this methadone business."

"Sir, I personally hate the idea. I'm not a physician, but I don't think we're doing these people a favor by giving them free drugs. If they can get the real thing, they will and then go right back to their regular habit. Methadone is only keeping these people from getting cleaned up. I know junkies that have been getting free doses for three to five years. Keeping them addicted isn't helping them to get straight."

"Very good, Lieutenant, thank you. Anyone have any questions of the lieutenant?"

"Yes, sir," spoke up Charlie Rose. "John, have you been getting everything you need to do this job?"

"We have. It's been very surprising in that respect. The druggies naturally don't think too highly of us and we're careful in their neighborhoods with our patrols. No single officer's on patrol ever, everyone is doubled up. We had anticipated that they would attack some symbol of the police authority, but so far they are only interested in getting a new supply."

"That's good, John, thanks."

The president rose, extended his hand and said again, "Lieutenant, I'm very proud of you and your men, if there is anything you need, just ask."

"Are you shitting me--he passed? I'll be a whore in church. Set up another test with another operator right away. I'll make a call and probably be on my way in ten minutes. I'll call you back in one hour and I want an answer by then." Lieutenant Ducey immediately looked for the card Charlie Rose had given him. He dialed and waited.

"Charlie Rose speaking."

"Charlie, it's Ducey. I got something very hot and I need some very high-level advice. You got some time for me right away?"

"Yeah, John, come right over. Report in at the gate shack and I'll have a Secret Service agent escort you right to me."

Thirty-five minutes passed until Ducey and Rose were face to face. "Charlie, you ain't gonna believe this shit, I swear."

Rose stared at his friend, put his hands out, palms up and said, "Try me."

"Yesterday this guy walks into the station and asks for you. He says he used to provide you with info on occasion. His name is Marvin Sneed. You remember him?"

"I certainly do, he was a good source with good info, but a user."

"Well he still is," added Ducey, "probably on the heavy side too. He says he and his girl have been surviving on methadone, but it's not doing the job. They need a lot of medical help, but can't get it. He tells me that he knows of a guy very high in the DEA who's dealing. We put him on a polygraph this morning and he passed. I ordered a repeat test with another operator and I need to use the phone now to get the results."

Rose pointed to a phone and said, "Hit three first and the number."

Ducey dialed, got his man and asked, "What do you have for me? Jesus, yeah thanks." He faced Rose. "This guy's legit, he passed again."

"Okay, where are we? Well, he says on two or three occasions a friend of his got a kilo from the deputy director of the DEA, Kevin Lowitz. This friend introduces him to Lowitz and they did a couple of kilos a few times. Now that he's strung out and hurting real bad, he wants to give us Lowitz in return for the medical help for he and his girl, along with a new identity."

"Jesus H. Christ, I can't, rather I hate to believe this," muttered Rose.

"Yeah, I know, I felt the same way but two polygraphs don't lie," Ducey added. "Charlie, I have no problem taking this guy down, in fact I'd love it. The son of a bitch is going to make one helluva bad name for all us, but we need to do him. I figured we had to bounce this off of someone, who?"

Rose didn't hesitate, "The president, that's who." He reached for the phone, dialed and waited. "Marge, this is Charlie Rose. I'd like to see the president as quickly as possibly. Okay, I'll wait." He put he phone down and said it will be a few minutes.

Eleven minutes later, Rose and Ducey were in front of the president and repeated their story. "The greedy bastard has to be in it for the money," said the president. He stood, walked to his bar and poured a couple of inches of his favorite scotch and downed it. "You want one?" he offered. "No, sir," came replies from both. "I said from Day One that no one person is untouchable from me on down and I damn sure meant it." He turned and faced both men. "You two do what you have to do, take him down. One thing. I'd like to have him alive if possible. A public execution would be a stain on law enforcement, I know, but it will do wonders to show the rules apply to both the everyday Joe and government officials."

Chapter 10

Colonel Ned Mier, assistant commanding officer of the Marine Corps Recruit Depot, Parris Island, sat at the head of the table. To his left sat Sergeant Major Jim Kennedy and around the table were four captains who led the four battalions of recruits.

"General Humbolt has asked me to sit with you and see how the training cycle is going. It goes without saying that this cycle is unique, actually like none we've ever had. The general thinks that after four weeks of the cycle, you should have some idea of just what we have. Understand that what you say here is off the cuff, nobody is going to be held accountable for anything said. We need to get a feel from you just how the program is going."

Captain Richard Napolitan spoke. "Sir, the four of us got together earlier in the week and discussed this matter, as we were asked. I drew the short straw and will be the spokesman for the four. We have reached a consensus and all four agree on the following:

1. On average each platoon has been whittled down to approximately one hundred twenty recruits. We expect to lose another twenty by cycle's end.

2. These men seem to be much more intelligent than the average volunteers. Many have one to four years of college.

3. They are trainable and most are doing well, or as well as can be expected.

4. Unless we are very much off course, we foresee that most will complete the training cycle.

5. For morale purposes, we suggest that each recruit be allowed to write and receive one letter a week. A question does arise on this as to if the letters can and should be censored.

6. A very large question raised by most Marine personnel is, if they become combat trained, will we be able to trust them. There are questions about what will happen when they are given live ammo to qualify. Our suggestion would be to have one man per recruit standing behind him all at times on the live fire range.

7. What happens when they do graduate and go on the Infantry Training Regiment? Confinement there is not going to be as easy as it is here.

"Those are our thoughts at this time, sir."

"That's fine, Captain, I appreciate your time, efforts and candor. The general, Sergeant Major Kennedy and I have been tossing around some ideas ourselves. The general thought you should hear it and think about it. One of many proposals is that every man from me and Sergeant Major Kennedy on down who is involved in the training cycle continues on with them to ITR and to combat. How do you feel about that statement?"

The four captains seemed caught off guard. Each man had his own thoughts, but the question needed more time to answer. Captain Napolitan spoke up first. "Colonel, I think it's too early to answer that. I personally need some time to think that over. I can foresee some good and some bad in the question, but the bottom line is that I go where the Marine Corps sends me."

"Do you three agree with Captain Napolitan's answer?" asked the colonel. All three agreed they needed time to think about it. "Well, gentlemen, for now that's all we have. We plan to do this again in four weeks or sooner if the need arises. For the last four weeks of the cycle, we meet as much as weekly."

Platoon 344 stood at rigid attention, each man lined up in front of his bunk. Sergeant Flack walked the barracks, up and down three times. He looked at the rifle rack and rifles, windowsills, a foot locker, but with no pattern. He finally stopped at the center of the squad bay and called them to parade rest. He then changed that to 'at rest.' "You girls at each end of the squad bay move in and crowd around me.

"If you ladies ever get to be Marines, you will learn that you follow orders regardless of your own desires. Whether you like it or not, you do as you're told. Today I have orders to follow that I don't like. The brass feels that for morale purposes, you should be allowed to send and receive one letter a week. You will not be allowed to seal the envelope, as the letters will be censored. I still have the last word on this and if you fuck up I will stop the privilege.

"You have completed four weeks of the twelve cycle of training. You have a lot to learn and the training is going to get harder starting today. You have been learning the book stuff, now you're going to start on the meat of the matter. Your rifle training will double. Dry-firing and breathing exercises need to be fine-tuned. Your physical training will also double up. Physical contact will be the order of the day. You better understand, I am not going to make life easy for you. You better stand tall and get the job done. Prison waits for the failures, killing you is a possibility and we need to cull down another eleven to thirteen bodies.

"In three weeks we march out to the rifle range for a week. That week is vital to you and the Corps. You fail to qualify with your rifle and you're out. You are being trained to fight and you can't fight if you can't shoot. Back to your bunk area. Stand at attention. Tomorrow, maybe after study hour, you will be allowed to write a letter. Sergeant Williams is the duty DI and he will give you an address to use. Just remember what I said. It's easy to lose this privilege and if you doubt me, try."

Right after chow the next morning, the platoon fell out to the side of the barracks. Recruits spread out and each man practiced what he had been taught. Sight alignment, breathing and trigger squeeze. Sergeant Flack walked between men constantly reminding them, "Take aim at the target, take in a full breath, and let half of it out, all the time adding pressure to the trigger squeeze. When the rifle fires, it should be a surprise to you. If it startles you, you did it right."

Each man was doing what he had been told but by rote. Most were really daydreaming of what they were going to say in their letter. *How do I tell someone what it's like? They wouldn't believe it. I guess the main thing is to tell the folks, wife, girlfriend or whoever was the receiver of the letter, that I'm alive and doing okay. Not happy, but alive.*

Jim Radison wanted to tell his wife how much he loved and missed her along with their son, Jimmy. He missed them terribly and was sure they felt the same. He concluded it would be best not to say much about what he was going through, better nobody knows.

128

At 2100 hours, Sergeant Williams did in fact allow them to write a letter. "You assholes remember this, you tell whoever you're writing to, no pictures sent to you. No writing on the envelopes with shit like SWAK or perfume. You can receive no packages in any shape or form. No cookies, no pogey bait, no nothing. If you do get a package, you won't like the result. You can lose your letter writing and you may get the entire package jammed down your throat. You hear me, idiots?"

"Yes, sir, loud and clear."

Around the White House, the term "Top Dogs" was used with admiration. Several who were not picked to be one of the top dogs had some negative comments but those were only spoken to another negative speaker. The Top Dogs were assembled in the Oval Office, as they usually were on Monday mornings.

President Barringer, Chief of Staff Wobser, Secretary of State Lloyd, Senator Concannon and Charlie Rose. They were the Top Dogs. Each Monday morning at 0800, they meet to discuss what had occurred the past week and what may be needed in the week to come.

When everyone was settled, the president spoke. "Yesterday, Henry and I had some visitors. The matter is of international consequence, but I feel you all should know about it. This matter is not to be mentioned outside this room.

"Very quietly, the representatives of Germany, Korea and Japan slipped into the White House on a quiet Sunday morning, without notice, I might add. What was discussed was the fear that these three nations have of Russia and her intentions. Their speculation is just what does Russian have in mind for these countries. Each country fears that Russia may attack them. That fear and our stated intentions of minding our own business has them very worried that we would, in fact, stand by and watch them be taken over. I gave them my word that we would not stand by and watch if they were attacked. I now need to say that publicly. I intend to do that this week. First, I must have a face-to-face with the Russian president or his representative. I then will make a national speech giving the American people knowledge of this fact and to update them on changes taking place at home. I would like an update on the changes, your suggestions on past practices and new ideas."

Senator Concannon had been chosen to be the speaker for the group. Each week the group meets prior to meeting with the president to get their ducks in a row and select a speaker of the week. Any member could still speak at any given time, he if chose. Concannon uncovered a chalkboard used to list items for discussion.

"Number one for today is adoption. We discussed it last week and found out that with the easing of rules and regulations and the use of common sense, the applications for adoptions are up some fifty-five percent. We intend to watch closely, to see just what happens to those applications and when it happens.

"Number two is an unusual call from the Coast Guard in Key West, Florida. They had two high-speed boats in their possession for smuggling cocaine. The question was just what were they to do with foreign nationals who had violated the drug possession rule. The men operating the boats were Colombians and the weight was in kilos. Mr. President, would you care to take it from here?"

"Yes, I guess I should. Without any thought, I answered that the rule applies to anyone caught; it did not say anything else. No mention was ever made to age, color, nationality, etc. I personally called the captain of the guard boat and informed him of just that. Just after we hung up, the four men were executed on the grounds of the C.G. station, Key West. By the way, I would like to see this story given to the press." The president nodded towards Concannon, indicating he was through.

"Number three. We are seeing many stories in the newspapers, magazines and TV in reference to chain gangs. It seems the public is taking to the idea in a big way and a lot of work is being accomplished to boot.

"Number four. The gun dealers are crying the blues. Their comment is that they are way off in sales, permits are hard to get and they are being forced out of business. Along the same lines, the auto manufacturers are also crying that the new mandate on engine size and speed is going to ruin them. Anyone have comments?"

"Yes," said the president. "If we get any direct inquiry from either group, the answer is, live with it. There will be no changes in those areas."

"Number five. A glitch has come up in the agricultural area. The local-grown-U.S.-products-sold-first part. Leave it up to an ingenious businessman to get around the rule. It seems that a distributor of foreign produce asked his employees to take the foreign produce out of the shipping boxes and put them in U.S. product boxes. One of the employees didn't like the idea and tipped off the local authorities. In court, the owner of the business was found guilty and given five years at hard labor. As a side note, this court case took exactly sixty-eight minutes from beginning to end."

"That, too, should be put out to the press for public consumption," the president added.

"Number six. The border patrol issue has heated up. They have been shooting warning shots for the past ten days. It seemed to have deterred some to turn back, but it's not working overall. They want to know what the next step is."

"The Mexican government is screaming about everything we do on the border," said Henry Lloyd. "I have just had a long talk with the powers-to-be in Mexico. I told him that the past week was a trial run and his government had to do more to stop the illegals on his end. He says they are working at it, but cannot do any more unless we fund the effort. The president told me to inform them they had ten more days to get it fixed or the bodies would begin to pile up. We need to wait now to see who does what."

"Mr. President, that concludes what we have right now. We are still working on some smaller issues and we hope that we can report on them next week."

"Thank you," the president said. "I want you all to know how much I appreciate your help in these matters. You all know that this can't be done by any one man. It takes the combined effort of talented people such as yourselves.

"Now on another matter. This is another item that you don't need to know, but I feel you should. It's part and parcel to the whole theme and I want you to hear what's taken place. As usual, what's said here remains here. In fact let's not have to mention this again, it should go without saying.

"On Thursday afternoon, I had a visitor; none other than the secretary general of the U.N. himself. The conversation was so good; I thought you ought to have the pleasure to hearing it first hand. I brought it along." His hand reached for the recorder on his desk and he switched it on.

"Good afternoon, Mr. President, it's nice of you to find time for me."

"I have been rather busy, Mr. Secretary, but I can always find time for you."

"Getting right to the point, Mr. President, I hope you've had the good sense to reconsider your statement on the U.N. Most all the members of the U.N. feel you have made a grave mistake and a very serious breach of political etiquette. There is no reason why the American people should not be represented in the world community. You may only be in office for a short time, but you're taking your county out of the world's most important organization for peace. If you forgo your membership now, your country may not be accepted when your next president comes to office. Would you reconsider?"

"Mr. Secretary, you have wasted your time coming here. I should have you thrown out, but I'll be a gentleman and explain to you once more. A very large amount of your membership fees come to you from the U.S. For that outrageous price, we get very little. We get stonewalled constantly. We get shut out of key committees. We get shit on. You all talk, and talk and talk. That's all you do, talk. You're afraid to take any action on really important issues.

"Every time some rogue nation breaks the rules, you talk. Most every man assigned to the U.N. in New York City shits all over that city, its people and police. They break every rule in the book and you look the other way. You will now see just how to survive without the U.S. to shit on. Find yourself another sucker to fund your folly. Why not ask Russia? The Communist Block countries will gladly help, if you let them take over first. Mr. Secretary, these are my final words to the U.N., you have ninety days to clear out of New York, forever. Goodbye, sir."

President Barringer turned the machine off. A smile crossed his lips, it was unmistakable. "I have waited sometime to say those words and I feel damn good having said it, especially to that pompous ass."

In the early spring, Parris Island gets warmer and the critters get to stirring. Rarely did one see anything really dangerous such as snakes; they avoided the recruit areas because of the activity. The flying critters were another matter. In the real summer, May through October, when it really gets unbearable hot, it seems the mosquitoes could attack and kill a grown man. The recruit's only salvation was the spray truck that made a daily or nightly trip around the barracks areas with its deadly cargo of DDT. At least it made sleeping in the barracks bearable. Outside was another story. In summer, the intense sun will keep the skeeters at bay, but it did not bother the sand fleas. The Parris Island sand flea is a legend; nothing kills it except a direct hard slap. They attack at will and being nearly invisible, they usually succeed.

Platoon 344 was lined up in front of the chow hall. As one platoon clears the hall, another files in to eat. Platoon 344 waited at attention. It just so happens the sand fleas were looking for dinner also. Private Reinhart had his eyeballs trained directly on the neck of the man in front of him when the flea decided to bite Reinhart. Without a conscious thought, Reinhart slapped his neck and killed the flea. He had no idea what wrath he had brought on himself and the platoon until he heard Sergeant Caudell screaming at the top of his lungs.

Sergeant Caudell had a clear view of the killing and went into a rage. He ran to Reinhart screaming, "You son of a bitch, you stupid son of a bitch, you killed that sand flea." Every man in the platoon was biting his lip to keep from laughing, yet each man held it in knowing what the consequences were to laugh.

"Why did you kill that sand flea, Private, why?"

"Sir, he was biting me."

"You dumb shit, fall out." Reinhart stepped from the ranks. Caudell screamed, "Find that sand flea, now." Reinhardt reached to check his neck and collar area but found nothing. He dropped to the ground and started searching for the dead critter, to no avail. Caudell pointed to two men. "You and you, help him."

With all three on hands and knees searching, in no time did the bell ring and Private Reinhardt said, "Sir, I have the flea."

Caudell screamed, "You put him in a safe place on your body until after chow." Reinhart acted out the fantasy of putting the dead sand flea into his pocket before reentering the ranks.

After chow, the platoon marched towards their barracks, but when they got to the point where they normally stopped, they continued marching. When Sergeant Caudell finally called the platoon to a halt, they were facing an area they had never seen before. Caudell stood in front of the platoon and spoke.

"This swamp," pointing behind him, "is called Ribbon Creek. A few years ago, several recruits drowned in this creek. Remember what you see here because the next time you see this creek, you may be about to enter it."

"The ten shovel-like tools you see are called entrenching tools. Private Reinhart and his squad will dig a grave for the sand flea he killed. Third Squad, fall out and start digging. I want a grave three feet by three feet by four feet deep, now dig." When the grave was dug, Caudell threw a wooden matchbox towards the recruits and said, "Bury that poor sand flea in that box and after you bury him, Private Reinhart will say a few words over the grave."

Once the box was buried, Reinhart said, "Lord, please accept the return of one of your creations. He died by my hand, for which I am truly sorry, Amen." The burial detail got back into ranks.

Sergeant Caudell stared at the gravesite and barked, "Platoon at ease. Form up around me. Reinhart, you're not the first and not the last to do this.

What you all need to know is when Reinhart slapped that sand flea, he killed most of you, maybe all. You need to learn to block out these annoyances that occur in life because if you don't, you're going to die very quickly. In combat, especially close combat, when you can see the eyes of your enemy, you can't afford to let anything distract you. Even if a snake curls up on you, you have to control yourself and not make a sound.

"First Squad, get over the edge of the marsh there and hide yourselves good. Second Squad, march route-step past them and stop when I tell you." When the second squad came abreast of the first, Caudell said, "Stop."

"Now both squads are looking for each other and stalking slowly and quietly. Now Reinhart slaps his neck to kill a sand flea. Either one or the other squads is dead, depending on who reacts fastest. See what a slap can do? Blank it out, live with the discomfort and you may live to go home."

Superior Court Judge Martha Hannon rapped her gavel and said, "This court is back in session. Before I sentence the defendant, his attorney, Mr. Chinn wishes to be heard. This is out of the ordinary, but due to the severity of the case; I am going to allow it. Mr. Chinn."

"Thank you, Your Honor. Firstly, I am asking you to throw this case out. I have had only one week to prepare a defense for my client, nowhere near enough time. Second, this case was heard in one day and I didn't have the proper time to present, cross and re-cross those that testified. Third, this court has circumvented all case law and not allowed time for an adequate defense. I could go on and on. This isn't American justice; it's uncivilized. What this court has done, I will appeal to the ends of the earth and I request sentencing be delayed until those appeals are heard. The last thing I would like to add is that I do not appreciate the smirk on the prosecutor's face. I feel Your Honor has a smile also."

"Mr. Chinn, I will address your issues in the order you brought them up. First, I will not throw this matter out. You have had as much time as allowed by our new rules. That answers number two. Number three, I have not circumvented any case law and have allowed time for an adequate defense minus a lot of wasted time. You have no right of appeal. Mr. Chinn, have you been living on another planet for the past weeks? We are all under new rules and procedures and we all have to adapt. Lastly, if the prosecution and I were grinning, I apologize, if true, it's not very professional.

"This matter is not at all funny, but what your client has done is no laughing matter either. In fact, what he did is beyond belief for any American.

Your client is no ordinary man, he is a senator, elected by the people of his state, to represent them in Washington.

"The testimony we heard today is very simple and quite clear. Your client, his brother-in-law and the man ultimately hired to kill the president, have all signed confessions to their parts in this conspiracy, yet we're all here because they wanted to pled not guilty. They were afraid of the consequences of a sentence. Each of these men acted out of sheer greed, with Mr. Miller being the greediest.

"We are now here at this very late hour of 7:18 p.m. to sentence two men after having been found guilty of all charges against them. As I said before, Mr. Zurawski is in federal custody and I have no control of him or his circumstances.

"Mr. William Miller and Mr. Arthur Schilling, please rise. You have been found guilty of the charges of conspiracy to murder the president of the United States. It is the order of this court that you will be put to death within the next forty-eight hours. It has been requested by the president that your sentence be carried out in a public forum and I agree. Bailiffs, please take these two away." Some very low sobs could be heard from someone in the gallery, but no more sobbing then from the two men being led away.

The bailiffs quickly cleared the courtroom. Once that was accomplished, a group of new faces began to filter into the room. When all were seated, Judge Hannon returned and assumed her seat on the bench.

"We are here to sentence a Mr. .Kevin Lowitz who has been found guilty of trafficking in narcotics. Due to circumstances, Lowitz was not put to death as he was not found in possession of the contraband. He has asked to address the court and I am allowing it. Mr. Lowitz, you may now speak."

Lowitz stood, obviously very nervous, if not terrified. He was in handcuffs and leg irons which made moving around hard. "Your Honor, can these be taken off?" referring to the confining chain and cuffs.

"Absolutely not, please begin."

"I am or was a senior official in the DEA and have made a lot of enemies in the course of this job. I find it very difficult to believe that the court is not taking the word of such an official who has a perfect record of public service over the word of a bunch of drug addicts and pushers. This is one huge setup and this court can't see that. I swear that I am wholly innocent of these charges and demand an in-depth investigation."

Judge Hannon looked as if she were going to explode. Her face clearly red and if you were close you could see the veins popping in her neck and temple areas. She understood her physical condition and did everything in her power to calm down.

"Mr. Lowitz, you did in fact have an exemplary record of service and that is exactly why I find it so hard for me to accept what you've done to yourself and your country. All day yesterday, this court heard testimony showing how you ruined your life and career. God only knows how many other lives you ruined with the drugs you sold.

"You confessed to what you did, yet you beg for your life by saying you were set up. The court heard from a man who testified he sold you between thirty and thirty-five kilos of cocaine over two years. We heard how you then resold these kilos to drug dealers and reaped a huge profit for yourself. If it could get any worse, it was you who made it so. You were in a trusted and respected position, entrusted by the United States to do a job and you didn't do that. You took an oath to stop drug trafficking, yet that's exactly what you did, out of greed.

"Mr. Lowitz, under the new rules we live by today, you should have been shot when you were arrested, but for the fact you did not have any drugs in your possession at that time. You have been found guilty of trafficking narcotics and in another forty-eight hours you will forfeit your life. Not more than thirty minutes ago, I sentenced two men to be shot for conspiracy to murder our president. Sir, you will join those two men and be executed in a public forum. I will not say 'may God have mercy on your soul'; you do not deserve any mercy."

Recruit training at Parris Island runs in twelve-week cycles. In that cycle something can and usually will go wrong. In this case, it is too many recruits using too few facilities, hence you have a problem. To eliminate these problems, a platoon or several platoons may be put on a workweek. Workweek can be mess duty, cleaning any number of things from inside to outside. Anything that needs manpower can and will be done by recruits.

Platoon 344 got an unusual assignment for workweek. They were going to pull targets on the rifle range. Usually several platoons will be firing and several pulling targets and they will switch. No explanation was given, just do it. From the recruit's side, it's a break, pure heaven. No DI hanging around your neck, you work in an undershirt, there's plenty of time for breaks and the recruits can BS with each other. The range juts out towards the Broad River and Port Royal Sound. Across the sound and slightly south is Hilton Head Island, a barrier island with few inhabitants.

The 30-caliber rifle bullets are fired at paper targets and pass through the target and into the river. It's a perfect backstop for the lead. The recruits are given instruction and told how to mark the targets. Once a target is hit, it's pulled down, a marker put into the hole, a long handled marker put up to show where the hit was and how much it scored. A complete miss and Maggie's drawers are shown. Maggie's drawers is nothing but a red flag. A loudspeaker system lets the recruits know when to put the targets up and when to expect firing.

One range instructor is located in the butts to watch over the operation and he really could care less what the recruits do other than the job at hand. The recruits learn to love this job as they can talk and goof off without any drill instructors getting upset. As long as they do the job assigned, the range officer in the butts looks the other way.

On the second day of target pulling, a mechanical or electrical malfunction occurred and the recruits were told to relax, which they gladly did. It was warm and all were working in their tee shirts, enjoying the sun. Jim Radison and Vinny Wainwright were talking about where they were from and families when Romero asked Radison what was out in the river.

"What do you mean out in the water?" Romero pointed at fins slicing through the surface of the river and disappearing and reappearing. Radison laughed. "That is what's keeping you from jumping into the water and escaping. Those are shark fins, Romero."

"You shittin' me?"

"No, watch them, you see them moving around and going under the water and then coming back up near the surface."

"Holy shit," Romero said. "I figured those fuckers were giving me a BS story about sharks. But why are they in a river? I thought sharks lived in the ocean."

Radison pointed east. "The river looks to be ending at the mouth of the ocean, maybe four miles or so. They're probably after food."

Everyone laughed when Martinez said, "I wonder if they eat lead."

The four men sat waiting to go back to work. "You gonna fight, Wainwright?" asked Romero.

Vinny looked at him. "I don't know; I have mixed feelings. I didn't ask to go into the military and I didn't want to fight, that's why I went to Canada. Since I've been here, I've been thinking and I'm wondering if it's an obligation we all have. You know, to fight for your country. I lost two uncles in WWII. My mom and dad always told me they did it so I could be free.

When I ran away I felt guilty, but I didn't want to fight or die. Like I said, I have mixed feelings."

"What about you, why did you run?"

Martinez spoke up first. "I come from New York City. I'm a Latino with not much education. The guys in my neighborhood told me we were just bodies to take the lead and get killed first. Somebody said we was cannon fodder, but I didn't know what that meant."

Romano nodded his head yes. "Right on, bro. We're just Puerto Ricans who don't believe in war, unless it's a gang war. What about you Radison, why'd you run?"

"I had a wife with a baby on the way. We talked it over and decided to go. I was doing what I wanted when they got me. I was fishing on the Outer Banks; commercial fishing and I loved it. We lived on Ocracoke Island and we had a great time. I didn't want to be away from my wife and son but here I am, away from them anyway. On top of that, I don't think my folks or in-laws are too happy with us. The funny thing is I have had sometime to think about all this and wonder what I'd do if I could do it all over again."

"You gonna fight?" Martinez asked.

"Yes, I am."

Romero quickly asked, "Why?"

"The same reasons Wainwright said. First, for my son. I owe him his freedom. Second, and it's going to make you laugh considering where we are and why; the DI's are a bunch of sadists, but they have struck a patriotic nerve. A lot of good men have died so we could be a free nation. I never gave that much thought before I ran, but I have since my kid was born. I will fight for him and my country."

Martinez said, "You know I was bullshitting with Palmer in the Fourth Squad. He said, 'Fuck all of them,' he ain't fighting. The first chance he gets, he's going to run away from all this shit. Another guy heard him and said, 'You better make sure you do it when nobody's got live ammo or you're gonna get it in the back as you run.'" None of the four said a word. They were all lost in their own thoughts or guilt. That thought process didn't last long when the order was given to stand by for live fire.

The Marine Corps base at Quantico, Virginia, is not much of a drive from D.C. The main gate on this day was guarded by an unusually large number of MP's. Today was the day that would go down in the annals of history, a day that the United States was going to publicly execute three men and televise it nationally. The press had been given a reasonable number of passes, but those who didn't receive one were still trying. A group of protestors were marching back and forth, holding placards with various sayings: "Impeach the president," "Killers" and so forth.

At the rifle range, all was ready for the execution. Three posts had been placed into the ground, each protruding six feet above the ground. The posts had been planted right in front of the rifle butts, so that the background would absorb the lead. Ten Marines had been picked for the firing squad from a pool of volunteers numbering in the hundreds. The only qualification was that the Marine had to be an expert with the rifle. The public had been informed that there were over three hundred thirty volunteers for the firing squad. The word around the base had been that these bastards deserved to die and I'd be glad to do the killing.

Every major network was represented with a TV camera and operator, a commentator and a photographer for stills. Many radio stations were also on hand. The big surprise was that there were twenty-four foreign countries also present. The execution was going to get worldwide coverage.

At exactly 9 a.m., a truck drove to the area where the posts were located and stopped. Nine MP's removed the cuffed and shackled men from the truck. Each man was led to a post and his body attached to the post by a rope. Most were watching and never saw the ten-man Marine firing squad march up and take a position.

Colonel John McVigh stepped up to a microphone and said, "Attention to orders.

1. Mr. Kevin Lowitz, you have been found guilty by a court of this nation, in that you did traffic in narcotics. Your sentence is death by firing squad.

2. Mr. William Miller, you have been found guilty by a court of this nation, in that you did conspire to assassinate the president of the United States of America. Your sentence is death by firing squad.

3. Mr. Arthur Schilling you have been found guilty by a court of this nation, in that you did conspire to assassinate the president of the United States of America. Your sentence is death by firing squad."

Colonel McVigh did an about-face and nodded to the three MP's standing astride the prisoners. Each then placed a hood over the head of the prisoner. As this was being done, another truck pulled up to the scene and a major exited the truck walked to Colonel McVigh and saluted. He handed the colonel a piece of paper, did an about-face and walked to the truck. He ordered two MP's to unload another prisoner. The fourth prisoner was walked to the spot next to those tied to posts.

Colonel McVigh said over the speaker system, "Another prisoner has been added to the execution. Mr. Robert Forsight, you have been found guilty by a court of this nation, in that by using the color of your office, as a police officer, did force sexual contact on a female and your sentence is death by firing squad." McVigh nodded and the MP's put a hood over Forsight's head. Both MP's retreated and picked up rifles and joined the firing squad.

A lieutenant who headed the firing squad stood in front of the squad and spoke softly to them. "Due to the change in numbers, you will count off by three's. Each three will fire at one prisoner. First three fire at the prisoner on the right. Second three the next to the last on the right. Third three the prisoner second from the left and the fourth three the prisoner on the left. Are there any doubts in anyone's mind regarding your target?" No reply. He then ordered the squad to stand by. "Ready." All raised their rifles. "Aim." All took aim at their target. "Fire," immediately followed. The silence was unbelievable. They only thing that could be heard was a commentator talking towards a camera, saying "They actually did it."

Chapter 11

It was Monday and the Top Dogs were at it again. This was the sixth get-together in as many weeks. Secretary of State Lloyd and Senator Carl Concannon were fixing coffee awaiting the others to arrive. They each took their seat just as Chief of Staff Max Wobser arrived. He said to both, "Marge just told me that the girls in the White House don't like the name 'Top Dogs,' so they have decided that they will refer to our group as the Fab Five." They were chuckling when President Barringer and Charlie Rose walked in from different doors.

"What's so funny?" asked the president

Wobser replied, "Marge told me that the females in the White House didn't like the Top Dogs title so they renamed us. We are now the Fab Five for the female population only."

"I'm glad they have covered that crisis. Okay, let's get to work. I've got a tight schedule."

Charlie Rose stood, uncovered the chalkboard and said, "Good morning, Mr. President.

"Item #1. The question of the flag- and draft-card burners. A great many of us and the general populace are getting tired of seeing this type of disrespect. Under the Common Sense Doctrine, it is felt that these types of actions deserve punishment. The recommendation is taking away their citizenship and deporting them, or putting them in jail. Questions arise, who goes where and who will accept them? Second question, how much jail time should be given?"

It seemed Rose was finished with his statement, so the president spoke up. "I have some strong feelings on the matter. I regret it's taken so long to address it, but I'm glad its time has come. My personal feelings are that if that person is a naturalized citizen, send him back to where he came from. If it's a U.S. born, give them a choice. Be deported and lose your citizenship or go to jail for one year. That said, I would first warn the nation via our usual channels of communication. After ten days, if someone violates the rule, carry out the punishment. Any comment from you?" Nobody said a word. "Okay, end of discussion. Go on, Charlie."

"Item #2. In Golden, Colorado, the state police stopped fifteen members of the Hell's Angels. The fifteen were riding cycles with three more in a rental-type truck following. It's well-known in law enforcement circles that the Angels usually will have a van following the riders. It's their parts department and armory. It is rumored that on one occasion, the van carried a mounted 50-caliber machine gun just behind the doors. Before this stop was made, the CSP used very good sense, coordinated it well and got the proper strength together before the stop. The cycles were clean with the exception of one idiot with a small amount of grass and a switch-blade knife. He'll do five years for being an idiot. The van was another story. It contained twelve handguns and two carbines. The three in the truck will also do five years, but the bikers go free because they didn't have possession of any weapons. I think everyone saw the story in the papers.

"Item #3. The Mexican border. The Mexican government hasn't stopped didley. The flow of illegals continues. Do we go ahead with our threat?"

The president didn't immediately say a word. He finally said, "I don't see any other way to handle it. We must stop this activity and we must do as we have threatened. Anybody disagree?"

Henry Lloyd spoke up. "The president knows my feelings on this matter and it's time you all hear it. I am not against this, but I am worried about world opinion and Amnesty International is going to rip us a new ass once the killings start."

"And my comment was to him, they are ripping us now, so what's new? I'm not about to change my mind, unless you can convince me." No further comment came, so the president said, "On to number four."

"Item #4. The High School to Military Transition Program. The board that was formed to handle this has some problems. The protocol and paperwork is in print, but the facilities to train these people are lacking. It seems that the military is jammed with the fighting of a war and training the dodgers. We

142

need to remember that the Marines have the big load, but all branches are lending men and supplies to assist them. The military viewpoint is, for now, find a way to put this off. In our discussions, we have come up with an alternative. Our suggestion is to look at setting up an ROTC-type organization where at a minimum they get started on the basics of military life. If you approve, sir, we will pass this on to the Transitional Board to run with."

The president said, "It seems like a good alternative, why not."

"Item #5 and the last. The Wage and Price Control Board is having a time with just about everyone. As we all expected, everyone wants prices to go down, but nobody wants to see their salary go the same way. The professionals are the biggest complainers; pro athletes being on top of the list. They said they will not play. Doctors are a mixed group, some saying they are amenable to the change, but the big-buck guys are screaming."

The president stood and walked to his garden-view window. It was a cloudy, but warm day and he longed to be able to drop all these problems and go play a round of golf. *How long has it been since I played? I fear it's going to be a long time before I do again.*

"Well," the president said, "I'll tell you just how I feel about them. Let the pro athletics teams stay home and not play. Once they are not drawing those big salaries and they have nothing to do, I'm sure they will be happy to play for a hundred thousand a year. The doctors, who don't feel they can live on one hundred grand, may face jail. They could ply their trade on the inmates and do it for free. We all knew going in this was bound to happen. My suggestion is to tell the Wage and Price Board to stick to the program. At the same time, tell the pro's what their options are. Is that all we have?"

Rose looked to the group and back to the president. "Yes, sir."

"Well then, let me fill you in on a new development. As you all know or suspect, we have people undercover just about everywhere. I wouldn't be surprised if that Hell's Angels deal wasn't because of someone inside. Yesterday I was informed that there are some rumbling from some militia groups. I was told that the information is sketchy at best. For now, all we can do is wait and see, but I thought you ought to be aware of it."

Before he could say another word, his phone light began blinking and then buzzed. He picked it up. "Yes, Marge." He didn't say a word for thirty or forty-five seconds, then said. "Thanks, Marge." He looked at the Top Dogs and finally said, "You want to talk about coincidence. The National Guard armory in Albany, New York, was broken into overnight. It seems Guard policy is not to man the armories overnight, which by the way, will end today. The items taken were weapons and ammo, mostly rifles, nothing heavy. That's all we have for now, the Army is investigating and I'm sure a lot of other agencies are going to get involved. I will order all armories that contain weapons to be manned overnight starting immediately. Better yet, on a twenty-four-hour basis."

Twenty-four hours passed when the president called Secretary of State Lloyd to join him. "Henry, we have a problem brewing. Another Guard armory was hit, this one in Hartford, Connecticut. More rifles and ammo were taken along with about fifty frag grenades. We have no intelligence, we have nothing."

Lloyd asked, "I thought you ordered all armories to be manned on a twenty-four-hour basis?"

"Yes, I did, but I didn't ask for details. I'll let the Army handle that. I'm concerned with all this, Henry. I'm truly afraid what these nuts can do. We are using all the resources we have to get a line on them but so far, nothing."

At 4:36 a.m., the duty Secret Service agent on duty knocked on the president's bedroom door. He opened it slightly and said, "Mr. President, I need to speak with you."

"Come on in," answered the president.

"Mr. President, Mr. Wobser and Senator Concannon are waiting for you in your office. They say they need to speak with you immediately. They said it was something to do with a National Guard armory."

The president didn't bother to dress, just put a robe over his pajamas and began to walk to the Oval Office. As he entered the office, Wobser handed him a cup of coffee. "Thanks, Max." He took a sip of the coffee, sat down and said, "What's happened?"

Henry Lloyd said, "Around 3 a.m., an armory just west of Boston was taken over by an unknown number of men. That particular armory is a tank depot. It appears that two Guardsmen were on duty, no word on either of them. The story is a third Guardsman was going in early to relieve one of the men for some reason. As he got to the armory, he saw strangers attempting to start the tanks within the gates. He watched for a short time and saw they were unknown to him. He immediately called the local police and then his commanding officer. The armory was completely surrounded and is in lockdown mode. No communications from in or out so far."

The president stood, walked to the coffee pot and refilled his cup. "That's it, nothing more?"

"No, sir, that's all."

"Do me a favor, Max, get on the phone and get me the person in charge at the scene. I want up-to-date info."

Twenty minutes passed before the phone rang. "Yes. Who is this?"

"Sir, this is Colonel Frank Fitzpatrick, the CO of the Guard in the Boston area. We have nothing from the intruders nor can we get anyone to answer the phone. We have several snipers scoping the compound, but it's to dark to see much. They do see men attempting to start the tanks. My concern is that if they do start them, they could ram the gates and attempt to get away. On the other hand, they can't get very far, considering the top speed of a tank. They could not outrun anybody especially in the city. The nearest large patch of woods is probably thirty miles."

"Colonel," the president interrupted, "I have some questions. Do you have any idea what's happened to your men?"

"No, sir, we don't."

"Next question. Is there ammo in those tanks?"

"Not in the tanks, sir, but in a vault there are practice shells with a very low yield."

"Can they get into the vault?"

"No, sir, not unless they blow it or cut it open. The only two keys to the vault are in my possession and my executive's."

"Last question. Do you have a weapon that can stop them if they should break out?"

"Yes, sir, I have two antitank guns set up for that purpose."

"Colonel, if they break out, kill them. I don't want them to leave with a tank, do you understand?"

"Yes, I most certainly do."

"By the way, Colonel, who is in charge of the scene there?"

"Well, sir, because it's a military installation, the state police are letting us handle it with them as backup. They tell me that if anything spills out into the street, they will take over."

"Colonel, I would suggest to the state police that if a tank gets out to the street, they don't have antitank guns, but you do."

"That I will, sir."

"Very well then, keep me informed if anything new develops and especially about your two men. Just remember, they do not leave with a tank."

In the following hour, the president conferred with the Joint Chiefs, the FBI and the CIA over the situation. He politely listened to their opinions and advice but made no decision. At 7 a.m. he hadn't received any new information so he put in a call to Colonel Fitzpatrick.

He asked, "What's going on up there?"

"Sir, we had to wait for daylight to really get a good view. The sniper has told us that he can see what he believes to be two bodies in the yard. He can't get a good look until daylight. I sent one of my men to join the sniper; once its light he can make a positive ID. I am now waiting for him to make an ID of the bodies."

"By the way, Colonel, are you close to any residential areas?"

"Mr. President, we have a barrier of open land about one hundred yards around the property. The nearest property is commercial. Why, sir?"

"Colonel, if it hasn't been done already, I would suggest the area around the armory be evacuated."

"Sir, I'm not sure I understand what you're driving at."

"Colonel, if your men are in fact dead, I intend to level that armory with all occupants. The most practical way to do that may be by aircraft. I don't care about the men inside if they have killed your men, they will die also. You following me, Colonel?"

"I sure am, sir."

"One other thing, Colonel. Get hold of the design plans for the armory and have them in your hands. If the operation has to be by land forces, they will want them."

"Will do, sir."

"You let me know the minute you get any confirmation, you hear?"

"Yes, sir, will do."

The president called for the chairman of the Joint Chiefs. General Harmon arrived quickly and the two spoke over coffee. "General, if the two Guardsman are dead, it is my intention to level that Armory possibly with an air strike. I know this is your area of expertise, but I want those bastards on a stake, dead. Do you have suggestions, General?"

"Yes, sir. The staff has discussed it and we have several plans. Our preference is to use a unit of Special Forces to take out the bad guys. They can be inserted in several different ways, kill all the occupants and probably preserve the armory or at least most of it."

The president walked to his window. He was thinking, *I ought to call it the thinking window.*

He stared out at the early morning sunrise. It promised to be a nice day. *It's not going to be such a nice day in Boston, is it? The families of the two Guardsmen must be frantic with worry.* He turned to General Harmon.

"General, I guess it's best that the decision is left up to you and the military. I did tell Colonel Fitzpatrick to evacuate a half-mile area around the armory in case we bomb it. The minute I get a confirmation that those men are dead, you get a go signal. Are we are on the same page?"

"Yes, sir, we are."

"Okay, General, I'll call you the minute I know."

General Harmon turned and reached for the door when the phone rang. "Hold it a minute, General." The president picked up the phone and listened. "I see, yes, Colonel. I am sorry and please express my condolences to their families. I am turning over the operation to General Harmon and the Joint Chiefs. He will decide on the operation and I'm sure he will be in touch with you soon." As he hung the phone up, he looked at Harmon. "The two Guardsmen are dead. You do what's needed and do so without regard to the lives of the men in the armory. Either way, they are dead men."

"Colonel Fitzpatrick, I understand you're the CO here. As a courtesy I'd like to fill you in on the operation. Thank you, Major Orlando. This is Colonel Meo of the Massachusetts State Police. He is my counterpart."

Major Orlando had the armory plans in his hand and spread them out over the hood of a jeep. "Our recon and yours indicates that at least four possibly, six bad guys occupy the area. Here is our plan. Two helo gun ships will fire small-caliber rockets at the interior of the compound to do whatever damage they can without hitting the tanks. The rocket explosions will divert enough attention that the main force should gain some advantage. They will blow the main gate when they hear the first rocket explosion. The gun ships will machine gun any movement only up until the main force gains entry. Concussion grenades will be used throughout the building area to minimize damage yet get the job done. If we do the job right, it should all be over in less than five minutes. Do either of you have any questions?"

Col. Fitzpatrick asked, "Do your orders say to kill off the men inside?"

"Colonel, my orders are to get the job done without regard to the lives of the intruders. If we get lucky and have a survivor, it could provide some intel into who these people are and why they are fighting against their own government. Anything else?"

Colonel Meo asked, "When do you intend to hit them?"

Major Orlando looked at the sun and then his watch. "I would say about 1630 or 1700 hours. That sun should hide one of the gun ships. It will look right into their faces, which is an advantage for us. It is now 1404 and I have some work to do." He saluted both colonels and left.

Just before 1600, a helo arrived and made several passes over and around the armory. It then hovered on the east side of the compound for several minutes. It took no ground fire from the complex, yet it did get their attention, which was exactly what was hoped for. The desired effect was that the occupants of the armory were so worried about the gun ships that they would not and did not see two men scurry to the main gate and place explosive charges where needed. They completed their work quickly and withdrew trailing a wire as they ran.

At 1633, the unmistakable womp, womp, womp of the helicopter was heard. The two ships, on different sides of the compound, slowed to a hover. Everyone on the outside could see the eighteen-man assault force moving toward the gate. Nobody heard the rifle shot that took out one of the bad guys because of the noise from the choppers. Only seconds later did Major Orlando learn that a sniper had taken out a man running to see what the helo was doing.

The main action began with each gunship firing four rockets into the compound. Almost simultaneously a large explosion took out the gate and a series of gunshots could be heard. The gunshots ceased in less than forty-five seconds and then several dull thuds from the buildings. Several more shots rang out, then silence. Total action time was three minutes and forty-five seconds. Major Orlando was informed by the squad leader that all the shooting was over, but his men were conducting a sweep of the compound to make sure all the bad guys were dead.

Orlando ran to the main gate and slowly entered. He was met by a captain who reported that seven bodies had been found, plus the two dead Guardsmen. He was informed that one of the intruders stated that he was a member of the New England Militia and he wanted to know why they were being killed as they were both fighting for our country. He died without saying another word, but it was obvious not everyone liked our new form of government.

Orlando Lewis walked towards the waiting van with a grin on his face a mile wide. He sat in the passenger seat as the driver, Travis Grant, stared at him. "What in hell got you all smiling, you get laid?"

Orlando turned to face Grant and reached into his pocket and brought out a City of Chicago payroll check. "That's why I'm smiling. I have not got a check for working in nearly ten years and it sure feels good."

"What in hell you been doing for ten years?" Travis asked.

"Welfare mostly. Made a couple of bucks now and then doing odd jobs, but mostly it was welfare. It sure is funny, 'cause I got used to that welfare stuff, but it feels mighty nice to work and earn it. I feel like a man again. Just the other day, my woman came home from work with her first paycheck and she told me the same thing. I didn't understand then, but I do now."

"What your wife do?"

"They got her putting stuff into a machine they call a data center. She got more education than me. She said she puts all the stuff from tickets the cops write for speeding and stuff. She be real happy working and doing that tech something stuff. I didn't understand the word she used but it's tech-something-olgy. We was talking the other night about our jobs and we both got the same talk from the consul or guy about breaking the welfare cycle. We won't tell anyone, but that guy is right. My grand-daddy and my daddy and us all on welfare. If we don't work and change, our kids be on welfare too. Tween us now, we making more money than we ever got from welfare and we both feel good about working. She even say something about going back to school and getting a GED, but I don't remember what that means."

"Where we going, Travis?"

"We got a pickup over on Hooper near 10th. The cops killed another street pusher."

"Man, that's about eight this week, ain't it? Them cops got no problem killing the brothers, do they?"

"Yeah, but they killin' white guys too. And if the truth be said, we ain't sorry for any of the drug pushers getting killed are we?"

"No, you right. They fuck up more blacks every day they sell that shit."

Field day was now a time that the members of Platoon 344 looked forward to. It was the only real time they could talk. Between the pace of training and the fact that the DI's were on their backs constantly, they just didn't have any time to bullshit. Nobody realizes it at the time, but it's a lack of social life, the need to interact with their peers that Radison, Martinez and Romano made sure they scrubbed together, so they could soothe the need to socialize.

Romero was humming a popular tune when Martinez said, "I ain't heard any music since we got here, you know. I miss the shit out of the movies and the radio. I remember my grandmother saying, 'You don't miss the things you got until you don't got them anymore.' She sure was right about that. A nice cold beer and a pizza and after that getting laid."

"Man, shut the fuck up. I don't want to hear about that shit, 'cause I can't have it," said Romero. "I been alright about it until you opened your mouth up."

Radison smiled at them, himself thinking about his wife and son. Romero asked, "When do we do the PX thing again? I need some stuff."

Martinez added, "Me too. I wish we could buy what we wanted. That shit with the DI telling us what we can and can't buy is bullshit. Man I sure would like to sneak in a candy bar."

Radison said, "It's pogey bait, not candy."

"Yeah, I know," smiled Martinez. "Man, I'm making eighty-six bucks a month and I can't spend it the way I want. They don't even give us the money. The DI said we buy our stuff on credit and they take it out of our pay, but where's the rest?"

"We get it when we graduate, don't you remember?"

"Man, I want my money now."

Radison asked him, "If you had it in your pocket now, what could you spend it on?"

Martinez looked at Radison. "You're right, I can't spend it anywhere, can I?"

Radison was daydreaming of his family while scrubbing rote-like, in a circle. Wainright walked up behind him and asked, "Radison, you okay?"

"Yeah, I'm fine, just thinking. When I was fishing, it was hard work and I was in good shape. After doing all this PT we get, I realize that I'm now in great shape and I like it."

Wainright added, "Yeah, I know. This last week, when they increased the PT, it was a bitch, but I liked the challenge. The more they throw at us, the better I like it."

Romero entered the conversation. "Yeah, that telephone pole is a bitch. The first day we picked it up; I didn't think we could move it around like that. It takes every man to do his part or we drop it."

Wainright said, "You just hit the nail on the head. That's exactly what they're trying to get us to do, work together as a team. One guy fucks up and we all fail. Remember that sand flea? Same thing."

After chow, the platoon fell out in PT uniforms. The red shorts and yellow shirt with the USMC emblazoned across the chest stood out and was sporty.

It was one of the few possessions a recruit had that said they were part of the Marine Corps. When they arrived at the PT area, they fell out and into a classroom setting. The class today was pugil sticks. The stick was about two inches in diameter, five feet long and at each end, a boxing-glove-like device, less the thumb. Recruits are teamed up by size and weight. A pair was chosen. They are helmeted and told to beat the hell out of each other. The only area not to be hit was the head, but in the heat of the fight, the head got its share of hits. Rarely is there any serious injury, but your body will tell you about it for days.

The platoon moved on to the telephone poles. They are thirty to forty-five feet long, twelve to eighteen inches thick and probably weigh 800 to 1,000 pounds. That weight depended on if they were dry or wet. Each squad handles its own pole, shifting it from side to side, overhead or wherever the DI calls for it. In the end, you're asked to run with it for a very short distance, the end result usually being failure.

The platoon then run for a short time to limber up. They run to another area where the strength test will be given. Men are paired off again. One man is tested and the other assists him. Sit-ups are first, doing at many as you can in one minute. Push-ups are next, same timing. Pull-ups are last and hardest. It takes a lot of strength to pull yourself up again and again. No time limit, but you do as many as you can. Ten is very good.

With no real rest, the platoon moves to the obstacle course. The OC is like a giant playground for adults. It takes strength, agility and good timing to run the course. You climb, use ropes and go in and out of obstacles. You're timed from beginning to end. It's fun if you're not tired, but a recruit at PI is always tired.

To work out the kinks and sore muscles, the platoon runs back to the barracks. All this is done daily to get ready for the strength test that will come after the rifle range. Every recruit must pass the minimum requirements to graduate.

After a shower and change into fatigues, the recruits are off to the grinder for two hours of marching. It seems there is no end to marching. Each and every recruit asks the same question: "Am I going to combat or marching in a parade?" The marching part is about as boring as one could imagine. In order to get through it you need to learn to listen to the commands and at the same time daydream. It's the only was to keep your sanity.

Private Reinhart liked airplanes. He kept his sanity by watching the jets from nearby Marine Corps Air Station Beaufort. Most days the planes were all over the skies and Reinhart watched them with great interest. He had learned the art of listening to the DI's commands and watching the planes without missing a step. It made the hours and hours on the grinder possible. On this particular morning after the rigorous PT, he was more tired than usual.

He was watching a flight of four F8U's in their landing pattern when he suddenly realized he was alone, not a soul around him anywhere. He stopped marching, did an about-face, only to see Sergeant Flack some twenty-five yards away watching him. Flack walked up to him, face to face, like DI's like to do. Reinhart knew he was in a world of hurt when Sergeant Flack said, very quietly and without emotion, "Why don't you go to the barracks, put your rifle away and sit on your footlocker and relax." Flack did an about-face and returned to the platoon as Reinhart marched to the barracks and did as he was told.

Sergeant Flack arrived at the barracks some ten minutes later and told Reinhart to go into the shower area. Flack hit Reinhart with a flurry of punches, but not with the power he possessed. It took all the willpower Reinhart could muster to not punch back. The only dignity that Reinhart could muster was not to hit the deck. He refused to fall. After surviving the barrage of blows, Reinhart stood tall as Flack said, "You do that again and I'll put you in the hospital next time. You concentrate on nothing but me, you understand?"

"Sir, yes sir."

The rest of the day was spent on rifle practice, breathing, sight alignment and trigger squeeze. Then first aid class, Marine Corps history and studying the Corps Manual. Along with the rifle qualification and strength test, there would be testing on first aid, Marine Corps history and numerous questions from the Marine Corps Manual. One item in the manual is a compete set of rules that apply only to standing watch or guard duty. An analogy could be made that it was much like exams at a college.

An integral part of the Marine Corps Boot Camp is guard duty. Like everything else that is taught, guard duty in the military is an everyday detail and in combat, a life and death situation. The DI's spend a couple of days on this aspect of training, but in the end it's the recruit's newness to military life that will cause him problems. Many a recruit has been smacked around and worse, for screwing up on guard duty. The NCO's know this and usually joke about it. Some have fun with the recruits and some go to extremes.

A very unauthorized tradition at Parris Island is for the off duty DI's, usually the single men, to mess with the recruit's mind, after having a few too many at the club. It was usually a bet that started it and they would then head to the area where the recruits always had guard duty, the warehouse section of the depot.

As part of the training, the recruit walks a guard post; and like any other training, it's on-the-job. The average civilian could never understand military guard duty; it's complex, yet simple. There are a plethora of regulations that go with guard duty; they are called general orders.

Sergeant Caudell of 344 was just the man for this task. While in the club having a few beers with his friend, Sergeant Jim Leddy, he hatched the idea to harass a recruit. Caudell was single a long time. His wife left him years before after he was busted for drinking and being late for duty, for the umpteenth time. He was an excellent Marine, but when drinking, a non-conformer. Leddy wasn't much different. He was single and busted once for drinking and taking a swing at an officer. He also was a fine Marine, when not drinking.

On this occasion, Leddy bet Caudell ten dollars that he couldn't get a recruit that frustrated on guard duty that he wouldn't call for the corporal of the guard.

The two men approached the warehouse area and Leddy picked out a recruit as the target. Caudell slowly walked directly at the guard and at a distance of thirty yards. The recruit yelled, "Halt, who goes there." Caudell's reply was, "The King of Siam." As a recruit that has only recently been taken from the only life he has ever known, thrown into a setting that is completely alien to him, beat on, scared to death; he is now hit with a problem he can't comprehend. Never was he told that a situation like this could arise. His rifle is useless as it's unloaded and he can't remember his general orders out of frustration.

Sergeant Caudell is far from falling down drunk, just somewhat shaky on his feet. He approaches the recruit. "Relax, recruit, I'm Sergeant Flipper. I'm checking up on you. What is your first general order?"

"Sir, my first general order is to take charge of this post and all government property in view."

"Very good, Private. Why then when you challenged me and I gave you a stupid answer, did you not call for the corporal of the guard?"

"Sir, I…I panicked and forgot."

"I hope that if we ever serve together in combat and you're on guard duty, you don't panic again, it could cost us both our lives. You understand that?"

"Yes, sir."

"I tell you what I'm gonna do. If you promise me you will study your general orders, I promise I won't tell anyone about this. We got us a deal?"

"Sir, yes sir."

Caudell wobbled away and found Leddy behind a building, watching. "Gimme ten bucks, as he held out his hand. Leddy handed him the money and asked, "How in hell do you do this and get away with it?"

"Shit, I done this a dozen times before. It's a good way to make money from suckers like you. Those recruits are shit-scared and will agree to anything. It's all in the way you handle it, my boy, all experience." The two wobbled away towards their quarters.

"The weekly meeting of the Top Dogs/Fab Five is now in session." An unusual, but welcomed sense of humor from a beleaguered president. Everyone grinned at his opening. "You may now proceed with the dog and pony show."

Chief of Staff Max Wobser was speaker of the week. He uncovered the chalkboard and said, "Item #1. It appears that the American public is happier with you this month than last, Mr. President. Your approval rating is up two points to sixty-four percent. The group's reaction to that number indicates to us that the people like the changes that are taking place.

"Item #2. In a follow-up to the adoption applications, we have found that not only has a large increase occurred in applications, but a much higher approval of those applications. The figure given was seventy percent approval of the applicants. It was also noted that a large increase in approvals for mixed marriage adoptions. To the Adoption Board and us, it seems like a win-win situation.

"Item #3. The death rate from motor vehicle accidents is down five percent over the past two months. The Department of Transportation feels it's due to the reduced speed limit. They also report that summons for speeding maybe peaking, but the confiscation process is starting to climb. In a cross-related stat, the chain gang population is rising and we're all hoping this area will improve as the adoption situation did.

"Item #4. Every agency and committee working on changes report the paperwork, notifications and confusing areas are decreasing or disappearing.

"Item #5. The training process in Parris Island seems to be progressing normally. The rate of failures is on par with that of volunteers. Of the 3,000 or so in training, they have jailed less than one hundred men for various infractions or failures.

"Mr. President, that's all we have. It appears that the program is running smoothly."

"Thank you, Max, I hope you're right. I don't have anything at this time, anybody else? Okay then, it's a wrap."

As everyone stood, Wobser said, "Mr. President, do you have time for Henry and I on a political matter?"

After Concannon and Rose were gone, Wobser said, "Mr. President, you are nearing your two-and-a-half-year anniversary in office. This is the normal time that the planning starts for reelection. We need to begin planning strategy."

"My God, has it been two-plus years already? It seems like it was just yesterday we moved in, yet an awful lot has happened in two years." He stood, walked past the bar and to his window. He saw the first blooms of the season were showing in the flower garden. Summer was just around the corner.

He turned and faced his two friends and sighed. "I guess this is as good a time as any to tell you both, I don't intend to run for a second term. We have an awful lot to do in the year or eighteen months it's going to take to get this program running and completed. That is my only objective. I intend to announce that fact when it's feasible and I had hoped to tell the public that the Constitution suspension was over.

"I can see a conflict in that now. The party needs to know who the candidate is, and if it's not going to be me, they need to be finding a candidate. Obviously I can't make both announcements at once. I owe it to the party and their candidate to make that announcement soon. We'll have to get going on a speech informing the public that I am devoting my complete energies to the changes and not the election.

"I seem to remember that when we decided to go ahead with the plan I indicated that I would only be a one-term president. I intend to live with that. I'm asking you both not to try and change my mind. My wife and son have been very heavy on my mind of late and I need a change in life style. My daughter and grandchildren are calling me and I intend to devote a lot more time to them. I have a few other things on my mind, but retirement is the number one issue. You two confer with the party and get the writers working. I will give the speech when you tell me its time."

At this time in boot training, the end-of-the-day routine is predictable. At 2100 hours the platoon was given an hour free time to write a letter, work on their gear or to just read the Marine Corps Manual. At 2155 the duty DI would call the platoon to attention. He would then stroll towards one end of the squad bay and then down the other end. He would do an eyeball inspection of each man looking for problem cuts, signs of infection, skin problems, powdered feet and clean underwear. He would stop at anytime and look at something or ask a question then move on. After inspection he would holler "hit the rack" and turn the lights out.

On one particular night Sergeant McDaniel was the duty DI and he walked into the squad bay at 2100 hours dragging a chair. He sat at the hatch opening and called the platoon to him. "Gather around me. In two weeks you will be starting final field. The physical part you know about, you have been training for it since the first day. Do what you have been doing the past two weeks and you'll have no problems.

"The part we need to stress here is the field marching phase. You know you will be competing against every platoon in the regiment and will be judged by the team of senior NCOs and officers. What you don't know is that we drill instructors feel you have the potential to win the competition.

"We are so confident that we have bet a very large sum of money on you. Normally the DI's always bet each other that their platoon will win, but this time we have bet the house on you. What this means is that you have to go out there on that grinder and listen and react without any faults. You win that competition and your last week here can be real pleasant. You loose and it could be real bad. It's all in your hands.

"After you leave here you're going to Lejeune for another five weeks and then onto Nam. I spent combat time in Korea, so I thought I might give you some advice. You have been trained to react to commands and in combat that's when that reaction will save your life. You may hear a command to hit the deck, do it without thinking. You hesitate and you could be dead.

"The Asian mind is a lot different than ours. They have little regard for life and are not afraid of death. They are raised to be honor-bound to their gods and their chairman. If ordered to lie on the ground in from of a moving tank, they do it without question. If you hesitate to kill him, don't think for a second he'll return the favor, he won't.

"I would suggest you avoid the Asian women. They carry a lot of VD and have a tendency to kill foreign white men, especially those fighting in their country.

"The first time you kill is the hardest. You may feel bad for a short time, but you'll get over it quickly. After the first, it's easy. I still remember my first and it seems I always will. My squad was out on a patrol up near the Chosin Reservoir. It was as cold as a witch's tit. We saw some smoke and crept up on it to check it out. Turned out to be four gooks cooking some rice over a nice warm fire. We shot them and pulled their bodies away from the fire. We sat down around the fire and ate the rice. I couldn't eat, but after that I would every time. Life goes on for the living."

McDaniel glanced at his watch and said, "You have five minutes to get ready for lights out." He got up, took his chair and left. Five minutes later he returned and began the ritual inspection. He was nearly finished when he suddenly stopped.

Each rack had that man's 782 gear hanging from the end of the rack in a standard position. McDaniel reached for the web belt and held it in his hands. He pulled the bayonet from the scabbard and then returned it. He then unclipped the scabbard from the belt and held it high in the air as if he was looking at something. At least six men facing this scene were biting their lips to keep from laughing. The man next to Sergeant McDaniel, Private Spence had an erection and it was bulging out his underwear. Those same six men sucked in a big gulp of air as McDaniel reached up to replace the scabbard and in a split second struck downward and smacked the scabbard broadside across Spence's penis. Spence went to the deck screaming in pain and everyone who saw it nearly did the same. With a smirk on his face, McDaniel walked to the wall switch, yelled, "Hit the sack," and turned off the lights. As he returned to his quarters and shut the hatch door, four men reached Spence and lifted him into his rack. He limped for a couple of days after that.

Chapter 12

Platoon 344 had eight weeks under their belts. The slightest bit of a salty attitude was beginning to show. It was not an unusual occurrence and the DI's knew exactly how to handle it. The platoon was pushed to near exhaustion. The men were quizzed into embarrassment, exercised above and beyond what each man thought he was capable of. The salty attitude disappeared quickly.

The ninth week of training was very much anticipated. It meant a lot of things new. The first was a chance to prove they could shoot, the mainstay of a Marine. It also meant they were beginning the last month of recruit training and that meant getting out of Parris Island. Lastly, the march to the range meant they were ready for a new level of training. They were to march route-step nearly all the way, through a wooded area of the island. They were going to finally act like Marines and carry their rifles and a full field pack.

On the day of the march, Sergeant Flack addressed them before leaving the barracks area. "We will march route-step most of the way out. The formation will be two files, right and left sides of the road. This will be your first taste of what Marines do, so you can and should expect anything. Don't think of this as a stroll in the woods because you should expect to be attacked at any time. You must react to the situation and do so as a unit."

The march to the range was only about four miles, so after nothing happened after the first two miles, they all began to relax. At about the three-mile mark, Sergeant Flack screamed, "Air raid, air raid, take cover." To the surprise of Sergeant Flack, Williams and Caudell, the recruits acted quickly and calmly by departing the road and blending into the surrounding foliage. After the recruits were in the prone position, they looked towards the road and got the surprise of their lives. Two groups of three men were acting out a scene from a bad play. Two men were on all fours while the third man kneeled on their backs. He pointed his arms straight into the air and began pumping them forward and backward imitating an ack-ack gun. Each time he pumped his arms, he shouted out, "bam, bam, bam." Every recruit except the six men acting as anti-aircraft guns were laughing and trying not to be hysterical about it. Even the DI's were smiling, but in a very controlled manner. Once the attack was deemed over and everyone was back on the road marching, it took all their willpower to refrain from laughing. The final mile of the march proved to be a pleasant stroll.

The rest of the day was spent in an outdoor school conducted by the range instructors. Like an old, tired tune, the importance of the basics was stressed. Sight picture, breathing and trigger squeeze. The range instructor then briefed them on the order of events through the coming week. "Four days of schooling and live-fire practice, followed by the fifth day with actual qualification. That will occur regardless of the weather. Sun, wind, rain or whatever the clouds bring, you will shoot on Friday."

Monday at 0500, started a new and exciting week for 344. It started off no different than any other with a two-mile run, some PT and field day of the barracks. After chow was when the fun began.

The platoon was broken down by squads. Each squad was led by a range instructor, his assistant and the DI. There was a difference today, but only regular Marines were aware of it. A horde of regular Marines were present, definitely not a usual situation. These men were to be stationed one on one with each recruit in possession of live ammo. At this point, no regular Marine trusted any of the recruits and every precaution was being taken.

A range master is in overall charge of the entire rifle range. He, and only he, makes decisions. His voice would become familiar in a hurry. He would call out, "Ready on the right, ready on the left, all ready on the firing line." You watch your targets and when your target popped up, you fire. For now, he stood in front of the platoons who were to shoot and said to one recruit, "What is that weapon you're holding?"

"Sir, this is a Garand, 30-caliber, gas-operated, semi-automatic shoulder weapon."

"That's good; you know what you're using. You will be going through a dry-fire exercise this morning. Each platoon will get exact instructions from his instructor. You will first be shown how to load the eight-round clip and assume the firing position. You will then go through your normal procedure as though you had live ammo. You will simulate firing off-hand from one hundred yards. You will then simulate firing from the prone position. This distance is all gravy. It the easiest and you should clean up here with all fives.

"You will then go to the 300-yard line and shoot from the sitting position. Again, you should be near perfect here. After that it's the 500-yard line for prone shooting. This afternoon you will do exactly what you do this morning, but with live ammo. Today you may miss a few shots while you zero-in your weapon, but very few. Your instructor will help you zero-in your weapon using elevation and windage as needed. You will remember your dope by writing it down in your shooting book. This all may sound slightly complicated, but by the end of the week it will become second nature. Alright, go to it."

The entire morning they practiced. The hardest part was getting used to putting in the clip and letting the bolt slide forward to chamber a round without getting your thumb caught in the receiver section.

After chow, the afternoon fun began. The recruits were no different than the thousands before them. Half were eager for the challenge and the other half terrified. Being terrified did not help the learning process. The first shot fired is as exciting as the first time you have sex. When that first round goes off you experience a host of thoughts all at the same time; the shock of the recoil into your shoulder, the sound of the explosion and the unbelievable desire to know what you hit. You feel like you have a bowling ball stuck in your throat while waiting for that target to pop up showing your score.

That first score is a tremendous physiological mark on each man; it can make or break a man for the week. A bull's-eye will bring a well done and a lift to the psyche, where a miss will bring a mild scorn and harsh words that you did something wrong. The man who continues to score is praised and coached to get the best out of him. The man who has trouble is coached and schooled one on one and everything possible is done to get him corrected. Ninety-five percent of the time he will learn, correct his mistakes and qualify on Friday.

Overall, about three to five percent of recruits don't qualify, and in this case, those who don't qualify won't go to jail as they were told, but rather will be used in a non-combat situation. It takes three men in non-combat roles to back one man in actual combat. At the end of the day, 344 was shoulder-sore, but excited and happy. Almost all would sleep the sleep of the satisfied this night.

On Tuesday, the platoon followed the same procedure they had on Monday, except they fired from the 500-yard line. This is the distance that scares the hell out of everyone. When you lie in the prone position and site in from five hundred yards, you have to wonder how in hell can you possibly hit such a small target. A recruit cannot comprehend that a rifle bullet is somewhat like an artillery shell. It's fired from a weapon and the projectile is lobbed to its target.

On a rifle, it's done with elevation, just as it is for the artillery weapon. At 500 yards, you may be aiming at the target but with the added elevation you are actually aiming a foot over the intended target. When you fire, the projectile flies out to its apex and then falls. If you have done it all the right way, it will fall right into the bull's eye. On qualification day, it's not unusual for seventy percent of those firing to score a possible from five hundred yards.

By the end of the second day, most of 344 were feeling good about the range. A few were having problems and they were being coached one on one to get them through. At sack time, Sergeant McDaniel was tucking them in when he called out, "Private Larrison front and center."

Larrison stood before McDaniel, "Private Larrison reporting, sir."

"I understand you have the first fire watch, is that correct?"

"Sir, yes sir."

"Get your weapon."

Larrison retrieved his rifle from the rifle rack and returned to McDaniels. "Port arms," ordered McDaniel. As Larrison stood at Port Arms, McDaniel ripped the weapon from him. After inspecting the weapon, McDaniel leaned forward and said to Larrison, "Put your thumb in the receiver." When he did so, McDaniel's let the bolt slide forward, but gently. "You will keep your thumb in there for the two-hour period of your watch, do you understand?"

"Sir, yes sir."

"If I step out of my house and your thumb is out, I'll have you in the brig before you can whistle Dixie, you got me?"

"Sir, yes sir."

McDaniel hollered, "Hit the rack." After the light was out and men were settling in, a soft laugh could be heard over Larrison's plight while others sympathized with him. He had all sorts of problems with his thumb and getting it out after loading a clip. He now had two hours to think about his problem.

Wednesday proved to be the best day of the week for most. The day started at the grenade range. Each man was put into a large hole with a wood wall that was supposed to represent an over sized foxhole in combat conditions. An instructor worked one on one with each man showing him the fundamentals of throwing a grenade. Each man threw one, which made a loud pop rather than an explosion. While this was going on, another third of the platoon was firing a Browning automatic rifle. Each man was allowed one short burst. The final third were firing a 50-caliber machine gun, again a short burst by each man. The platoon was shifted around until all were given the three phases.

After chow the platoon was marched to the chemical and biological weapons area where they received two hours of instruction on chemical and biological weapons. After the two hours of schooling, the range instructor led them to the tear gas house which was no more than a metal-sided shed. "Each of you will be shown how to put on and wear a gas mask. In that pile you will pick one out and try it on. My staff and your DI's will assist you to get a good fit by adjusting the straps. Once everyone is masked, you will be led into the gas chamber and told to take your masks off. Don't try to hold your breath, you're going to stay in there until you suck in a goodly amount of tear gas. It will not hurt you, but it will make your eyes tear, you will cough and some will get sick to their stomach."

The first squad was led in and gas was already present. They were told to see if the masks were working and all stood in a group. Sgt Caudell yelled and motioned to them all to take the masks off. Those who were slow to obey had them ripped off by Caudell. Each man reacted normally, fear, but no panic. After a full minute, they were let out and as they exited all fell to the ground choking, gasping and with tears flowing down their faces. The next squad did not like what it was seeing, but didn't have much choice. By the time the last squad was in the chamber, the first was feeling normal. Only four men had thrown up, but they too were returning to normal.

As they marched away from the area, Radisson, Martinez and Romano were all thinking the same thing, *I wonder if the others liked it as much as I did?* They all were excited about what had taken place this day and eager to get to field day to talk it over and compare notes and to share his excitement with his friends.

Romero especially needed to talk as he was having trouble and was worried about the dope on his rifle. He was taught that each click of windage or elevation would move the hit on his target one inch. His range instructor had told him on a windy day you may have to add four or more clicks to the dope. He couldn't understand that and he was afraid to ask and seem stupid. He knew his friends would set him straight.

Thursday, day four of firing. Sergeant Flack had the platoon seated in one of the school sheds so the range instructor could address them. The instructor was a buck sergeant from Texas and you needed to listen closely to what he said or you would miss the meaning because of his drawl. "Okay, ladies, y'all gonna shoot a dress rehearsal today. We gonna have y'all shoot the same as if they were qualifying day. You get fifty rounds that count five points each. You throw one round and you lost five points, so you best be careful. Minimum qualification score is 190 and max is 250. Here on the board y'all can see how the score you shoot relates to your shooting badge:

190 to 210 marksmen

211 to 229 sharp shooter

230 to 245 expert

246 to 250 distinguished expert

"The one big thing I want to remind you is that you must see your target. By that I mean look for your number first and the target second. You could shoot a possible and if it's on somebody else's target, you're shit-out-of-luck. You have been schooled and reschooled. We done all we can, it's now up to you. You do just like you been trained and you'll do fine."

He looked at Sergeant Flack, who then stood and faced the platoon. "As Sergeant Hale has noted, there's nothing more we can do for you now. From what I've seen from my past platoons, you should have no problem. Remember your schooling and what training you have gotten and you'll all qualify. If you do fail to qualify, you fail the training altogether."

He would not tell them that it had already been decided that if they did not qualify they would not go to jail. Everyone was afraid to tell them before they shot because a smart man could deduce that if he intentionally did not qualify, he could get himself out of combat. The range staff was concerned about eight men, less than the usual amount in the volunteer units.

As the platoon moved to the firing line, it was a sight to behold; fifty identical targets with the exception of a number in front and below the target. In the excitement, more than one would fire on the wrong target. First up was ten rounds from the off-hand position. You stood, rifle locked in position by its carrying straps made into a sling and your own strength. You had two minutes to fire all ten rounds. Every man in the platoon was now sure why a man was stationed behind him. After the live-fire, each man had to pick up his brass and hand it to that man behind him who counted it and logged it on a sheet.

Radison had correctly stated that they were probably there to make sure no live rounds left the firing line. In the past a recruit had taken a live round and blew his brains out and one recruit tried to do the same to his DI .

Stage two was at 200 yards. It consisted of firing ten rounds from the kneeling position. He would also fire ten rounds from the sitting position, but that would be rapid fire, within a thirty-second time limit.

Stage three was at 300 yards, prone position and rapid fire.

Stage four was at the 500-yard line. This is the yardage that scares the recruits the most. The difference from 100 yards to 500 seems like shooting at an elephant and then a sparrow. The requirement was ten rounds, prone position, and slow fire. If you do as you were trained and keep your wits about you, it was entirely possible to hit all ten shots in the bull, a possible. It seemed hard; it looked hard, but in reality wasn't.

After chow, the platoon was given the evening off, a true rarity. They were told they could write their weekly letter, read or practice rifle positions, but they were to do it without talking. Naturally, that never happened. Radison, Romaro, Marteniz and Reinhart were all grouped together in a corner, whispering to each other.

"How'd you do, Radison?"

"I shot a 221."

"Jesus, that's great," Romero said. "I only got a 195, but I'm not gonna bitch, it's better than I thought I could do. Martinez, what did you do?"

"Two-oh-one," he said.

"You don't seem too happy about it," Reinhart added.

"No, I'm not. I'm still having trouble with the fucking clip and the bolt. I damn near got my thumb caught again."

"How did you do, Reinhart?" Radison asked.

"Okay, I shot a 214. For a guy who never saw a weapon close up before, I think I did okay. I'm sure I can do better, but I'm happy with that. I just hope the weather keeps up for one more day. We haven't had the pleasure of shooting in the wind or rain and I don't want to start tomorrow."

On day five, they got their wish. It was exactly as day four with only a moderate breeze. Everyone was told to add one click of right windage to their dope to compensate. At the end of the morning, it was a near carbon copy of day four. Of the 109 men in the platoon, only four did not quality. The Marine Corps considers that a victory; the four men who failed to qualify didn't agree.

After chow, the platoon hiked back to main side, this time without the air raid. Most of the platoon felt they were Marines now and were full of themselves. The four non-qualifiers were thinking only of their humiliation and the desire to run away as far as they could. Each was terrified that the threat of jail hung over their head.

Once back in their own barracks, they set about cleaning clothes and getting their gear back in shape. At 1600 hours, Sergeant Flack usually secured for the day. Being the senior DI had its perks. He only had duty on days and never stayed overnight, that was the junior DI's duty.

Sergeant Flack strolled into the wash rack area and called the platoon to attention. "At rest, gather on me. Listen up. Larrison, Harris, Peppler and Sincaric all failed to qualify on the range. You four need to know you fucked up. You did not do what you had been trained to do for whatever reason. The brass has decided that if you finish up the next three weeks and graduate, you will be assigned to a non-combat unit and not be jailed." Several reserved yells could be heard from the platoon, which Flack let go. For the very first time, Flack seemed to have a heart after all.

"Okay, settle down. After the range, recruits seem to get salty but I'm here to tell you, you're not salty. You're a different breed, but you will toe the line. You fuck with me and the next three weeks could be the most miserable in your training. You should all know by now that I am capable of making your lives miserable and I will do it if you push. The next three weeks will be the most hectic of all twelve. We still have to finish up tailoring your uniforms; you need to start graduation practice. We have a march to Elliott's Beach and overnight bivouac and a whole bunch of little things. You are not Marines yet, maybe in three weeks, but not now. You do what we say for these three weeks and make your life easier for you and everyone around you. Get back to what you're doing."

As Flack was leaving, many quick conversations took place among the members of 344. Not one man in the platoon wanted to be his friend, yet for the first time in nine weeks; it seems that Flack acted like a human being to them and it was a good feeling.

The Top Dogs/Fab Five were meeting for the ninth straight Monday. The group were all having coffee and chatting when President Barringer entered and immediately apologized to everyone for being late. "I was on the phone with the German chancellor. He was crying about the economy of his country being hurt by the withdrawal of our troops. I tried telling him that the economy of the U.S. comes first in our minds, but I'm afraid it went over his head. Every head of state calls telling me of their problems, but not one believes we can have problems too."

Senator Concannon stood and uncovered the chalkboard. "Mr. President, the way things are going, there's a very good chance we may be able to have our weekly sessions on demand only. We have only two items to discuss.

"Item #1. The edict that U.S.-chartered companies produce their goods in the U.S. is being ignored. All the companies that this applies to are saying it's going to take time to work it all out. Their argument is that you can't close a plant down in Mexico and set it back up in the U.S. without a lot of planning.

"The feedback we're getting is that what they are doing is stalling. The idea is that in a short period of time, the Constitution will be back in place and all these changes won't apply anymore. If that does happen, they go about their business as usual without ever having to produce in the U.S. We cannot find one single incidence of a U.S. company making plans to make the move implied by the changes.

"In our group discussion on the matter, we feel the issue should be turned over to the proper agency for some input and recommendations. Our only idea was that we would put a short time period in place to make the move. If it doesn't happen then, we should impose a very high tariff on that product. In effect it would make that product too high-priced to make it worthwhile."

Without hesitation the president began speaking. "Well, Carl, we in the political field had an idea this was going to happen. Off the top of my head, I'd say your plan sounds good; easy and to the point. The whole problem here is that once the suspension is lifted and we go back to our normal form of government and I'm out of office, what really is going to happen? Will all the changes go by the wayside? Will some be kept and others discarded? Nobody knows and I'm sure that big business is hoping we go back to business as usual.

"Another point to be made is the presidential candidate. If big business or any business has the money and clout to back a man who will run the country without keeping the changes, then the presidency will be bought. If we can find a candidate who we know will keep the changes in place or at least most of them, then he's the man we must back.

"This is the argument you must take back to the party and let them see just how important their choice is. Another unknown is, will the people like or dislike the changes so much, that they will have any influence? It's always been just a political decision but things could change depending on the feelings of the people."

"Item #2. We have been contacted by a local law firm seeking some help for the lobbyists who no longer have jobs. It is their feelings that since the government put them out of existence, they should have the opportunity to be retrained and at government expense."

The president could not hold back his laughter. 'That's pretty good. In our old system they probably would have sued us and won. Unless your group feels differently, I would give them my three-word answer, get a job."

"That, Mr. President, is all we have. Things are going well, few if any problems and as I said, we're wondering if we need to meet every week or just on demand."

"It's not a bad idea, Carl, but I have an item to bring up and it may mean some new work for the group. I believe that you, Henry and I have discussed this before. Politics in this county is beginning to look like a circus. I'm referring to the election process. We start two years before the actual election and spend a scandalous amount of money in that time. The need to raise that much money is part of the problem. This is the area where lobbies and favor donations are a danger. We all had too much electioneering at parties and in backrooms. We know that ambassadorships have been bought, as long as the price of the contribution was high enough. That was a major reason we outlawed lobbies and forbade campaign contributions. Toss it around and look into the feasibility of such a measure, okay?"

"Will do, sir."

Colonel Mier, Sergeant Major Kennedy and the four battalion captains were discussing the training cycle, as they had been every four weeks. Captain Napolitan was again speaking for the group of captains. "Sir, in the matter of the personnel here, following these men through ITR and into combat, is a bone of contention. The DI's involved are very much against this proposal. They feel that the method used to break these men and then mold them into Marines is sometimes brutal.

"We all know what takes place and we all look the other way because we know the method works. They are also aware that many recruits never forget the treatment they received here, some for years. The DI's think if they continued on with these men, they would be targeted and possibly killed by their own men. We are all well-versed with pushy second lieutenants who have been shot in the back once in combat.

"Another thought is that these DI's are uniquely well trained. It would be a loss to the Marine Corps to put them into a different situation. We have many young sergeants who can lead in combat; we don't have that many well trained DI's hanging around."

Colonel Mier looked at Sergeant Major Kennedy and asked, "What's your feeling Top?"

"I think they have a genuine concern, but I also think the second point is more important than the first. Good DI's don't fall off trees."

"Okay, I see some merit in this and I'll take it to the general and see how he feels. How is the cycle going, Captain?"

"Very well, sir, they have finished up on the range and the failure rate was two percent lower than volunteers. All they have left is the strength test, final field and some minor things. Essentially they have passed and I must add with a very good record. At this point, we can see nothing to change our minds."

Charlie Rose was reading some reports on wage and price problems. He wondered if this area was ever going to work itself out. Having spent nearly twenty-seven years as a police officer, you see just about everything that man can do to man. He didn't think there was much left that could surprise him, yet he was wondering if this was one of those times.

In his brain, half of the world was greedy and the other half questionable. Most every professional group was willing to work with the system and take salary reductions in stride. In reality, prices were going down so why not salaries? The exception was the professional on the top of the scale, athletes and very highly paid physicians. *How do you make these people understand the concept? Is the president right? Let them not play ball, let them find out how the rest of the world lives.* He continued to read when the phone rang.

"Hello, Charlie Rose."

"Charlie, this is Marge. The president would like a word with you if you have time."

"Of course, I always have time for the president. Be right there."

"Come in, Charlie, how are you?"

"Fine, sir, thank you."

"I've been looking around for a golfer and your name came up."

"Me? Mr. President, I played maybe once a week or did until all this came into my life. I'm just a hacker."

"Well, Charlie, I'm not much more. When I had time, I was a seventeen handicap, what about you?"

"I was a fifteen, sir."

"Listen, my doctor wants me to get out and play once a week. My weight is climbing and the lack of exercise is showing. How about joining me in the morning? I'd like to play nine holes and walk. You up to that?"

"Not a problem, sir."

"One of my Secret Service people will pick you up at 6:30 a.m., is that okay?"

"Not problem, sir."

The next morning when Charlie got into the Secret Service van, he immediately asked, "Where are we playing?"

"Mr. Rose, you're playing at Congressional County Club."

"Hey, none of that Mr. Rose shit. I was a cop and you're sort of a cop and we have common ground. Charlie, please."

"Okay, Charlie, I'm Bob."

"Well, Bob, how's all this work? This is my first time playing with a president and I'm a bit confused."

"Don't sweat it, Charlie. The course is closed when the president plays, any president. The members know it and expect it, as it only happens infrequently. They don't mind; they get bragging rights by telling their friends that they play at the same course as the president. It's only nine holes today, so you'll be done in two hours. We need to close the course for security. You can't imagine how many agents will be around the course doing what we do. We're all glad to see him going out and getting some exercise; he needs the diversion."

Charlie never in his life had played at such a nice facility. The lack of activity struck him also. Nobody was around the course except black suits. After hitting their tee shots, the two men strolled down the fairway towards their ball. The second shot and putting-out was routine and completed without much conversation. The third hole was a par five and after the tee shot, they began to talk.

The president asked Charlie, "Tell me about yourself."

"Well, sir, I was born and raised in Jersey City, New Jersey. After high school, I joined the Marines and saw some action in Korea. After the Marines, I just migrated to the D.C. area, got into the P.D. and began my career. A lot of schooling, training and on-the-job learning. Retired after twenty-seven years. That's about all."

"Never married?"

"Yes, I was, but it didn't last. Working shifts, not being home at night, missing important dates because you're working, it added up very quickly to disaster. Fortunately we didn't have kids and the break was clean. Let me hit this shot, Mr. President. See any yardage markers?"

"Says here it's 240 yards." They continued towards the green after hitting their second shots. "You haven't asked anything about me," stated the president.

"Well, to be perfectly honest, I didn't think I had the right to."

"If these were ordinary times I would agree with you, but they're not. You need to realize we are far from ordinary people. We are both doing things that will have a tremendous impact on the county and possibly the world. Have you ever thought of that?"

"No, sir, not really. I thought I was helping my country, but never did I think of it on a world-wide basis."

"Well, we are. You will not repeat anything we discuss, by the way. This is between you and me. I have already decided not to run for another term, this is my one and only hurrah. I plan on devoting the next two years to getting these changes in place and not any thing else. After my term is up, I plan on doing nothing but spending time with my daughter and grandchildren. They are all I have left and I need to spend a lot of time being their father and grandfather.

"This is what I want you to think about. In the next two years I hope to play golf once a week for physical and mental health reasons. I like you, Charlie, you're my kind of man. I'd like you to be my golfing partner for those two years and after I'm out of office."

Charlie had to stop and he looked at the president. "Mr. President, I have devoted the past five months to you and your ideas. I like you and would do anything you ask of me. I can't think of any man I'd rather play golf with and be your friend to. I'm truly humbled by your offer."

"Don't be humble, Charlie, I put my pants on just like you do."

Charlie didn't play very well after that conversation. He could not keep his mind on golf. He was completely blown away that this man, the president of the United States of America wanted him to be his friend. *Are the guys in the P.D. going to go ape-shit over this bit of news.*

Chapter 13

Half of the platoon was lined up at the post exchange for their last haircut. The other half were in the tailor shop getting their final uniform fitting. Some of the men were thinking to themselves about all the gear they were getting, among the many, Martinez and Romero. While the tailors did their measuring and fitting, Romero began to contemplate exactly what he was getting. So many clothes had been issued when he first got here, such as work and dress shoes, underwear, socks, green winter uniform, khaki summer uniform, a raincoat, an overcoat, three different hats and work uniforms. He had been daydreaming about it all when the tailor told him he was done. He never moved.

Sergeant Caudell grabbed him by the neck and pulled him aside. "What's with you, Romero? You falling asleep?"

"Sir, no sir."

"Well get your ass out of here."

Trouble was the last thing Romero wanted at this point in time, so he got back into ranks and tried to keep his mind alert. *Christ, this is more clothes than I ever owned in my life. The guys at home ain't gonna believe this.*

The platoon reversed positions and when everyone completed both tasks, it was back to the barracks, grab your rifle and two solid hours on the grinder. After ten weeks of constant drilling, the men of 344 felt pretty confident of their marching ability. They all knew they had better be good or they would hear it from Flack. They had been warned that a lot of money was bet between DI's.

Final field was one of the last major steps to graduation. The strength test and obstacle course were all part of the steps to the finish line. At final field the platoon went through their stuff, the marching portion. The officer staff and senior enlisted men were judges and judge they did. Points off for the slightest infraction would cost several platoons the opportunity to win the marching competition. The top three platoons were given much praise for winning, second and third.

Mucho dinero was wagered on this event and the losers were not happy campers. In fact, a lot of money was bet on various aspects of the final field. It was not uncommon to bet on an individual who stood out at any stage of training such as the rifle range or pull-ups. Each DI had a man they believed excelled in some aspect of training and he would not hesitate to brag about him and eventually bet on him. A very good bet was a recruit who could do one hundred good pushups on time.

After noon chow, the platoon fell out and settled on the ground, around the barracks. A predetermined list of gear was required of each man to place into his field pack. Actually, they had so little to take for an overnight bivouac that the DI's had to have them pack water bottles or sand to get the weight up to the forty pounds they wanted each man to carry. After the packing lesson, the platoon set off for Elliott's Beach.

The march was about the same distance as the rifle range had been. The route-step march was done with every man expecting another air raid, but it never happened. The march was uneventful except for a couple of men ahead of Private Wolfson, who heard him humming a tune that none could identify. They made note to ask him later.

The platoon arrived at Elliott's Beach at 1500 hours and found it was certainly not the Riviera. It was in fact a beach, but on the river. It did possess a grove of trees that was ideal for camping or a bivouac.

All four DI's then began their lessons. The platoon was divided among the four men who began the process of setting up an overnight area. The first thing to do was to stack rifles. Sergeant Flack gathered the platoon around him. "Listen up," he barked. "The stacking swivel just forward of your hand grip is just what its name implies; it's used to stack rifles. Two men face each another. Engage the swivel and twist against each other, like so. Then these two will lean their rifles against the stack of others and form a sort of tee pee. This is what the fighters of old did, in the colonial times and even later.

"The Manual says this is what you'll do and so you will. I'm here to tell you that you'd better keep it in your hands in combat. In Korea I even kept it in my hands when I took a crap. You sleep with it; everything you do is with your weapon. Stacking is for peacetime. When some prick is trying to kill you all the time, you don't want your rifle anywhere but in your hands.

"Each man was issued a poncho or shelter half. You have worn it over yourself in the rain and tonight you're going to attach it to another man's to form a tent of sorts. Some call it a pup tent, but you'll love it when it rains. It's not anything you would want to sleep in when it's cold, but it will keep you somewhat out of the rain."

Lister bags appeared from somewhere. They were shown how to fill them, add the iodine tables and hang them. "Make sure you pick a sturdy tree limb to hang it from. It will be your only source of water."

Hemp rope was laid out and surrounded the entire encampment. "Anybody know why we do this?"

Private Cox raised his hand and Flack nodded to him. "To keep snakes away."

This brought some snickers, but Flack quickly added, "You assholes laugh, Cox is right. No snake will ever cross a rope and nobody knows why. Seeing as how we're in a nice warm Southern climate, we are loaded with rattlers, copperheads and moccasins. If the rope offends you, sleep outside it, but don't call on anyone if you wind up sleeping with a snake tonight."

Two squads were told to dig with their entrenching tools a trench one foot wide, two feet deep and ten feet long. When it was completed, Flack said, "This is a slit trench or an outhouse. This is what the Corps wants you to use in the field. In real life, you're always moving, so no trenches. Here we will not use it either. This island is too small and over the years of trenching, has caused some environmental damage to the river. We have built a small shithouse to use over there," he pointed.

"The next thing is to start to gather as much firewood as you can find. You won't be cold, but that fire will sure protect your ass, being here in mosquito heaven. It's the only way you can keep them at bay. Pick up some wet stuff also. Once the fire is hot, the wet stuff will smoke and burn slowly and the skeeters don't like smoke. When you're out picking up wood, watch your ass. Look first then reach. I wasn't kidding about the snakes.

"After firewood, you can chow down on your C rations. If anyone wants to try hot coffee or chocolate, we can do that too. Now listen up very closely. You may talk to each other in subdued tones, just above a whisper. The minute I can hear you, it's too loud and I will cut off all talking. Take what you can get and be happy with it."

The men of 344 set about searching for wood, no easy task when for years, every recruit that passed though Parris Island did the exact same thing. Reinhart walked to Wolfson and asked, "Hey, Wolf, what was that you were humming on the march?"

Wolfson was surprised that anyone would want to know but answered him. "'Ghost Riders in the Sky,' why?"

"I never heard it before and it has a nice sound."

"Yes it does, it was one of my favorites in college and I used it in the final recital."

"Your what?"

"A recital, I had to play a bunch of music for an audience in order to graduate with a music degree."

"No shit?"

"No shit."

The men of 344 were really feeling salty. They felt they were Marines. They understood the rules and everyone spoke in a whisper. A few of the men such as Radison, Martinez and Reinhart were together. Cox came over and sat with them also. Each man was in the process of opening his C rations. Radison had franks and beans and ate them without a word. Many traded with each other, as they did not like the main courses. There was enough to survive on and if you got hungry enough, you would eat anything.

After chow, the fires were lit and everyone was just sitting around relaxing. Wolfson walked past the group and Romero called to him to stop. "What's up, Romero?"

"Hey, man, I heard to you talking about that tune and I got it running in my head. Can you give me the words to it?"

"Yeah, no problem. I been thinking about it all afternoon and I think I'm gonna try to put the Marine Corps Hymn to it. I think it will be a knockout. The ghost riders are about cattle men rounding up cattle and the words aren't important, the tune is. So let's put the tune to the hymn."

From the Halls of Montezuma to the shores of Trip..o..li, we will fight our country's battles in the air on land and on sea...

First to fight for right and freedom and to keep our honor clean, we are proud to claim the title of, The United States Marinesssss...

It didn't take long for the other members of 344 to hear and gather around the group singing. In no time the newcomers added their voices to the group and it didn't take long for Sgt Flack to hear it all. As he approached the group, he asked, "What are you doing to my hymn? You are fucking with an honored tradition. What is that tune?"

"'Ghost Riders in the Sky,' sir."

Wolfson felt it was his idea and responsibility so he stood up and said, "It's my fault, sir. I'm sorry."

Flack looked at Wolfson and said, "Boy, I gotta tell you that a lot a Marines are gonna kick your ass if they hear you doing this to their hymn. I would like to hear it please." Not everyone sang, but enough to make it pleasant. Flack added as he walked away, "After tonight I would not sing it again, I'm warning you." As he walked back to his area, he couldn't help humming the tune and thinking he liked it.

The men of 344 slept fitfully this night. Although they all knew the fire watch was awake and watching, each had a fear the rope was not foolproof. Each and every man thought he would be snake-bitten. Nobody was bitten and in the morning they made hot coffee or chocolate, packed up and policed up the area before marching back to main side. It was a lark, a different experience, but it was a falsehood they had seen. In the months ahead, in real combat, the bivouac would not be so easy. A snake bite would be the least of their worries.

Colonel Ned Mier, the assistant commanding officer of Parris Island Recruit Depot called the meeting to order. "The man to my right is Captain Richard Napolitan and he speaks for the recruit battalion commanders. The man to my left is Sergeant Major Jim Kennedy, the senior enlisted man on the island. Your turn, Colonel Brunt."

"Thank you, sir. My name is Colonel Harry Brunt, assistant CO Camp Lejeune, representing General Donald Sweeney. The gentleman next to me is Major Joseph Lowery, my executive officer."

"Thank you, Colonel Brunt. The reason we're here today, is to allow Col. Brunt and Major Lowery to pick our brains in reference to the recruit class we are training. In less than three weeks they will graduate and be transferred to Lejeune for ITR. Please allow me to start off by giving you an overview.

"All in all, we are pleasantly surprised at the progress of the group. They were nowhere near the problem we anticipated. In general, they are more educated than the volunteers are and have adapted well. The rate of loss is about two percent, which is lower than normal. Reasons for failure are pretty standard. The fact that we had two suicides from the total amount we are training should tell you something of their mental state. That said, we have to move on to the fact that they have been well protected by the topography of the island. The opportunity for escape is self-evident, but an area of concern once they go on to Lejeune."

Mier turned to Napolitan and asked, "Would you like to add anything?"

"No, sir, I think you've covered it."

Col. Mier then looked at the sergeant major and asked the same question.

"Yes, sir, I would like to make a few comments. When the president was here to visit, I had the honor to speak with him privately. He asked me for an enlisted man's opinion of what we had and I told him the truth. He asked me if I was ready to release them as Marines and my answer was, Nondum Fidelis. Translated from the Latin, it means, 'Not Yet Faithful.'

"My orders, as of now, are to proceed to Lejeune and then into combat with these boys. I have no fear of that, but I will be sleeping with one eye open until I can be assured they are Semper-Fi. My only suggestion is that the colonel may want to speak with some of the DI's to get their perspective."

Colonel Brunt thanked his counterparts and further added, "It's good to speak with those who were on the ground floor. I think from what I've seen in the past days that you all have done a fine job with these men. I was not sure what to expect, but from looking over the troops so far, they look no different than any other recruits I've seen.

"Getting back to the problem at hand, Lejeune has a much different land setup. Our main gate is always guarded with military police. We have a state highway running right through the base. It can be manned with MP's and usually is, but that may have to be a stronger force. You see, civilians drive through day and night. It would be very easy for a civilian to use that road and pick up a man who was deserting. A lot of our base perimeter is not fenced; it's never been needed." Colonel Brunt stopped and looked at his counterparts. "Any thoughts?"

Sergeant Major Kennedy raised his hand. "May I, sir?"

"Sure, go ahead Top."

"Colonel, I don't think it's going to be a problem. I will be there to help out, but it's my gut that tells me there's not going to be much in the way of desertions. If we talk to these people and lay out the drill, I think they will adapt well. If we get more than one desertion, then I think we can revisit the subject. What I perceive is a problem in their personal lives.

"None have had any contact with their families except for a letter a week. Can we, should we keep them from a family visit? A few of these men have wives and children. Do we have the right to deprive them of seeing each other? We all know where they are going. They need contact with family because a lot of them aren't coming back."

Colonel Brunt had the look on his face of a child who had been caught looking at a girly magazine. "Jesus Christ, I never thought of that. All I could think about was security and training."

Mier looked at Brunt with sympathy in his heart. "Harry, you and your general get the leaking bag of shit real soon. I think you have some serious thinking to do. May I make a suggestion? Send a transport down and fly the Top back to Lejeune for couple of days. We can spare him for a time."

"Excellent idea. You have any objections to that, Top?"

"Sir, I go where the Marine Corps tells me to."

Dear Mom and Dad,

I hope this finds you both in good health. I'm doing great, yes great. I can't believe how I've adjusted to this new life but I have. I am in peak condition physically and mentally, I'm in good spirits. I miss my freedom to do as I want and naturally miss my music very much. Overall I'm a new person.

I hope you have found it in your hearts by now to forgive me for the mistake of running away. At the time I thought it was the best thing to do, but now I realize it was the wrong decision. Dad always told me that we learn by our mistakes and it's true. I have a whole new perspective on life. The Marine Corps has made a man of your son.

We were told just today that our families will be informed (I hope by now) that they will be allowed to attend our graduation next week. I know it's a trip but I hope you can make it. We need to rekindle our family life. If you come, I hope you can bring Jennifer along. I miss her terribly. It is my intention to ask her to marry me, but not until I see what my immediate future holds. If I have to go overseas, I will wait until I return. By the way, I hope the letter from the Corps lets you know where you can stay. They are allowing the family to visit graduation day and the day before. The week after, we move to Camp Lejeune in North Carolina for five weeks of infantry training. The scuttle-butt (talk) here is after a week there; we will be allowed some freedom to move around and begin more family visits.

You may find it surprising to learn that you didn't waste your money sending me to college. I am using my music background in some small way. I have changed the music to the Marine Corps Hymn, much to the chagrin of my drill instructors. They really think it's cool, but hate the idea of me messing with their beloved hymn. I have also become mesmerized by the cadence we march by. It's like another language, in that it's singing, yodeling and with the rhythm of gospel all rolled into one. It's truly a gift very few of the DI's have but those who do, make it sound unbelievable. If you can come to graduation, pay attention to it, it's earthy and very much like American gospel.

I have to run now, a lot to do before graduation. Please let Jen know of these plans and plead with her to come along, but only if you do. Please let my grandparents know that I'm safe and back to being a true American. As I said, I made a terrible mistake, but I'm ready to fight for my country. All my regards to the Wolfson clan.

Love you all,
Jules

The president and his chief of staff, Max Wobser were working on routine paperwork in the Oval Office when Senator Carl Concannon entered the office.

"Good morning, Mr. President, and to you, Max."

"Good morning to you too, coffee's hot."

"No thanks, sir. I thought I should bring to your attention that there are certain rumblings of discontent."

"Oh, by whom?"

"Some members of both Houses who feel they have been pushed aside and cannot do what they were elected to do."

"And they have just come to that conclusion?"

"No, sir, but they are starting to talk of doing something about it."

The president stood and walked to his favorite window, peered out for a second and turned. "Carl, let me tell you exactly how I feel about both Houses. Before I do, you must understand I don't really give a shit anymore about their feelings or party unity. I have harbored this feeling in me for years and now is as good a time as any to let it out. Our form of government is probably the best in the world, yet it needs help. Congress and the Senate don't represent the people, it represents itself. All they do is talk and play partisan politics. Every once in a while they will pass some legislation and give the people something to bitch and moan about. The most important part of the Senate and Congress is there for one reason, themselves.

"A poor or common man can't run for office, he can't afford it. Ninety-nine percent of our elected officials are wealthy people, some filthy rich. The reason they are here is to become richer and more influential. They have made themselves a retirement system that's the envy of the world. Not a single one will every have to work again, if he or she so chooses. Many will step into jobs of importance just because they were members of the Senate or Congress. They will join corporations or get a professorship that will only enhance their already outrages retirement.

"We all know of the assets these people have already, but we all look the other way. We always can find one or two men in each House who truly wants to help this country and its people, but they are only a handful and are quickly pushed aside.

"Now having said all that hateful diatribe, I will admit I have no idea how to fix or change it. I really do have some ideas but I know I'll never get to try them. What I've already done is precedent-setting; I don't think I'm going to get another chance for another change."

Carl Concannon stared at the president. He needed time to digest what he'd just heard and decide if he wanted to answer. Finally he muttered, "I guess I'm just shocked to actually hear it said. I have thought along the same lines, but never uttered it out loud."

"It's sort of shocking to hear isn't it?" replied the president.

"Yes, sir, it certainly is."

"Well, Carl, if you stay in politics, maybe in time you can work on changing it all."

"Change is awfully hard to come by, Mr. President. Just the other day Charlie Rose and I were talking about changes and he told me this story. It seems a lot of thought was being put into consolidation by certain men in the police field. Consolidation could save taxpayers an unbelievable amount of money.

"Let's say you have a county that has eighty different police departments serving it. Each has a chief and the high-ranking staff associated with it. Each has to buy the equipment to keep it running. Now if you could consolidate into one department you can have the buying power of a whole county and the cost saving can run into the millions. Instead of eighty different departments buying cars, weapons, equipment and even everyday supplies, you could have one central purchaser, with a lot of buying power.

"You now have one central head issuing orders that cover the whole county instead of eighty different heads issuing orders for one small area. Only an idiot would not see the benefit of consolidation, yet it hasn't happened because eighty police chiefs and eighty mayors don't want to lose their fiefdom. It makes all the sense in the world yet it will never happen unless it is mandated by a higher authority who has the balls to make that decision."

The three men were mute. They looked at each other yet nobody said a word. Finally Max said, "What a depressing conversation."

The president agreed. "Do me a favor, Max, call Charlie and ask him if he's free. I need to get out of here and get some fresh air. Maybe if I can smack a ball it will be better than smacking my head up against a wall."

"Stand at rest." Sergeant Flack looked over his platoon and quickly realized that the group of young and dumb kids were now men. He and his junior DI's were proud of what they had produced. They turned out to be as good as any he had ever had. Considering how they started out, they could be the best he'd ever seen. He wasn't ready to tell them all this, but he would make it a point to do so before they all entered into combat.

"Listen up," he barked. "In two days you get to strut your stuff and get that globe and anchor pinned on. What you need to know is this. After graduation, you will be turned loose with you families. You all will have the freedom to roam the island, wherever you like. I hope at this point you all realize your past is past and you need to earn trust.

"I trust you, but I don't make the rules. If anyone tries to run away, he could be shot and anyone assisting him also. What I can add is that in two days you will be called Marines. You have been accepted by us, but you need to prove yourselves to the rest of the Corps and the world. Until you do that, they will be suspicious of you. Once you finish up here, you go to Lejeune. More freedom awaits you there but still not one hundred percent.

"Back to here and now. You can enter and use the PX or snack bar facility on this island with your families or friends. This also applies to those whose family can't visit. Mess hall #3 will function as a dining area for you and your visitors to use for lunch and dinner. The PX and snack bar is not very big, so I'd suggest you eat at the mess hall. If your family brings you food, you can always go to Elliott's Beach picnic area.

"For those who families will not be here I offer the following. If you are twenty-one years of age you can enter and drink at the Depot Slop Chute, but I need to caution you to be careful. It would be a damn shame to see you get a snoot-full and get into trouble after all you've been through.

"Last item. I know nothing of the rules at Lejeune. When we get there, we'll find out." The faces quickly made Flack realize he never told them. "Okay, settle down. I never told you, but the plan at this time is for some of the brass, the Sergeant major and all the DI's who trained you to go with you to Lejeune and then into combat." The mumbling from the platoon was getting loud.

Flack again shouted, "Knock it off. You better remember this. I've said it twice already and this is the last time. Your bad time is still not over. The only Marines who trust you are we who have trained you. The rest of the Corps is going to be very suspicious of you, so get used to it. You must earn their trust. If one man turns tail and runs, it's going to make it even harder for all of you to be trusted."

The presidential helicopter touched down on the grinder. General Humbolt, Colonel Mier and Sergeant Major Kennedy walked toward the aircraft and waited until the president exited. They saluted him and General Humbolt said, "Welcome to Parris Island, sir."

"Thank you, General, it was nice of you to invite me, after all this is a very special graduation. I'm honored to be part of it."

"Mr. President, we've done some historical work and found that you're the very first President to ever visit the island."

"Is that good or bad, General?"

"Good question, Mr. President. Sir, let me introduce my exec, Colonel Mier and the top enlisted man, Sergeant Major Kennedy."

"Nice to meet you again, I remember you both."

"We hope you'll join us at the officer's club for lunch, sir."

"Lead on, General."

After lunch the president was given a tour of the island, the facilities and the general breakdown of just what is accomplished in the depot. The president asked the general what the schedule looked like. His staff knew, but he didn't.

"Sir, tonight we'll have a dinner at the O club with wives in attendance. Tomorrow at 1000 hours the graduation and your speech."

"Well, General, it seems we have time before dinner. I would like to talk with a group of these recruits privately, is that possible?"

"Mr. President, I don't see any reason why you can't. If you'll just step over here. You see that wall? It lists every platoon graduating tomorrow. You pick a number and the rest is easy."

The president's motorcade stopped in front of the barracks, not unnoticed by Sergeant Flack. "Holy shit," uttered Flack, "I don't believe this shit." Flack met the president, general and the rest of the following at his barracks hatch. After the introductions, the president turned to the general and said, "I want to go in alone, nobody else." The Secret Service agent leaned in and whispered into the president's ear. The president frowned and said, "Only my Secret Service agents go in with me."

Flack called the platoon to attention. The president walked in and Flack walked out. The Secret Service agent closed the doors as the president said, "Please, men, be at ease. Come closer so we can talk without shouting." The men of 344 were as surprised as anyone on the island.

"Gentleman, I would like to say how very proud I am of all you've accomplished in the last three months. I know your life for the past twelve weeks has not been what you expected, but I'm told you have done well. I'm looking forward to your graduation tomorrow and I hope to hear good things of you in the future. Is there anyone who wishes to ask anything of me? What you say will remain here; you have no fear of recrimination."

"Sir, I am Private Reinhart. Don't you think the method you chose to arrest us was a little illegal?"

"Well, Private Reinhart, before the mandate, yes, it would have been. That's one of the reasons I asked for the mandate. I wish you would remember that what you did, running away, was just as illegal at the time."

"Sir, I am Private Romero. I didn't ask for this and I don't want to fight or die. You didn't give me a choice. You're asking me to possibly die while you sit safe in Washington. Just what sacrifices are you going to make for the war?"

"Private Romero, that's a good question and I have an answer for you. My sacrifice has already been made. My son James went to Nam twenty-three months ago and thirty-nine days into his stay, he was killed in action. That was my sacrifice and it aches in me every day and every waking minute."

The poorly educated Romero was truly touched and offered his sincere condolences to the president and his family.

The president sat down in a chair quickly provided by one agent; he was clearly shaken. "I'd like you all to know something. My heart aches for my son and all over the country other fathers, mothers and sisters and brothers ache with me. All of us have lost loved ones. Since the American Revolution, right up until today, families have lost loved ones. Every man who has given his life for his country wanted to live, just like you do. They wanted to get an education, get married and have children, see those kids grow up and then retire, but they paid the ultimate price so you and I could be here today and talking freely. Freedom is not cheap; it's very expensive. You're supposed to be a bright group. If you weren't free in the first place, you could have never run away. Gentleman, I hope from the bottom of my heart, that each and every one of you lives to return home and live the American dream."

The next morning at 1000 hours, the president addressed the graduates.

"Good morning, recruits, or is it time now to call you Marines. The ceremony I witnessed this morning was truly impressive. You looked like the best of our American youth and in fact, you are. You started out on the wrong foot, like a child who had lost his way. I acted like a parent and grabbed you by the nap of the neck and dragged you screaming and kicking back into the family. Over the past twelve weeks, you have proved to a great many people that you are the best your country has, but you still must prove it to the world.

"General Humbolt has told me that your next step is to spend time in advanced infantry training up in North Carolina. That is your next trial. Complete that training as you have done here and for your reward we're going to send you to fight for your country. I sincerely hope and pray that each and every one of you gets back to his family. The ultimate reward will be to say you fought and defended your country and your misstep will be forgotten. I promise you, no record will exist of your original choice.

"Yesterday I had a very nice chat with Platoon 344. A member of that platoon asked me what sacrifice I was going to make for the war effort. He felt he was being asked to possibly give his life for his country while I was safe back here. My answer to his question was that I have given my son, James, my only son to the war effort. In order to preserve freedom, we all must be willing to make sacrifices. I wish you all God speed and I will pray for your safe return." As the president left the podium, it was evident to all close enough to see, that the president had tears in his eyes and down his cheeks.

A brunch was scheduled at the O club for the president, after which he would leave the island. In the middle of eating, the president turned to General Humbolt and asked, "Where is your sergeant major today?"

"Mr. President, he is my right-hand man, but this is the officer's club and he's an enlisted man."

"Yes, yes I see, the military caste system. Would you please have him available after we eat, I'd like to chat with him."

After lunch the president was leaving the club when he spotted Sergeant Major Kennedy standing aside waiting for him. He approached Kennedy, shook his hand and said, "Walk with me." The two men strolled around the O club grounds, everyone was watching and wondering what was being said.

"So many I have spoken with have given me his opinion except you, Sergeant Major. I would like to hear yours."

"Mr. President, these men are as ready as we can make them here. We've done everything we could and naturally they need more training, but I don't see a problem. We have culled out the bad apples, but a few always get through. Hopefully we'll find them and get rid of them. For the most part, I would fight beside them; in fact that's the plan. I don't fear their backbone, but I still have a touch of doubt deep inside. As I told you on your first visit, it can be best summed up in two words, Nondum Fidelis."

"Yes, I remember, 'Not Yet Faithful.' An impressive thought."

As the president was preparing to get aboard his chopper, he was saying his goodbyes to General Humbolt. "I appreciate the fine job you all did here and I truly hope these men set a good example of the Marine Corps tradition. I also want to say that Sergeant Major Kennedy is quite an intelligent man."

"Well, Mr. President, he should know Latin, he holds a master's degree in it." As the president took his first step towards the chopper door, he stopped, turned around and said to General Humbolt, "Don't let anything happen to that man. He is a very valuable asset and I just may steal him from you."

Chapter 14

As President Barringer got out of bed, he thought to himself that he may as well do some reading and not waste the whole night. Not being able to sleep didn't happen very often, but with so much going on, *My head is just running in nine different directions.*

He turned on the light, got a glass of milk from his portable fridge and sat in his recliner. He reached for a small pile of unopened letters and ripped open the first. It was typed, short and unsigned.

"Mr. President, I would like to express my admiration for you and for what you have done and are doing for our country. I not only admire, but applaud you. I have many colleagues who feel as I do. Unfortunately we are cowards. You see, sir, we are elected officials from various states that have been put out of work by your mandate. I don't really mind it, I can see why it's justified. Because of party politics, I must remain anonymous, for obvious reasons. Sir, you're doing the right thing, but the pressure exerted on us by upper-level politicians is tremendous and I'm not one of the rich elected officials. I must feed my family, so I must abide by the partisan politics. If you get feeling lonely, regale in the fact that you're doing a wonderful job. My hope is that one day I may stand up in public and praise your name and your legacy."

The president put the note back into the envelope and wiped a small tear from his eye. *You poor S.O.B., I know just how you feel. I can well remember when I was new in the game and the pressure exerted by the party bosses. What a system. Is it really the system or is it because each man does not want to fail in his public life? What would have happened if I had stood my ground when I was young, would I have gotten any further? Would I be here today to do what I've done? Oh well, we have no crystal ball so why agonize over it.* He reached for another envelope.

"Dear Mr. President. I am a thirty-eight-year-old mother of two. The two children are brand new to me and my husband and for that we need to thank you. We had been turned down several times because of my husband's health problems. His problem is not fatal, only debilitating, yet the adoption agency said he could not be a good father. Thanks to you and your mandated rule changes he is now a father of a boy and girl who just happen to be brother and sister. You have made four people very happy and we are proud to say you're our president. I just wish I could give you the biggest hug. It is our opinion that you have done more for the country in the past six months than any president has done in the last fifty years. If you run again, I'm positive you will win in a landslide victory. God bless you."

As he returned the letter to its envelope he thought to himself, *That almost makes it all worth the effort and that's only one family.* He picked up another and began reading.

"It had been my intention to write you a nasty letter about you thinking yourself as a god. My nineteen-year-old son has been a car nut since I can remember. Being a car nut also includes being a speed freak. If you haven't guessed by now, he got three speeding tickets and finally lost his car. He had a fortune in that car. Well because of your new laws, I had to drive him everywhere, including back and forth to work. It's been a real hardship on me and I guess that's why I was going to rip you. Something happened between my son losing his car and this letter and that something is this. A truly good friend lost her child in a car accident. Her son was a speed nut also and now he's dead. My boy may not be the best in the world, but he's all I have and I love him very much. I still have my son and it's thanks to you that I do. You have done a good service to this mother and for that I need to thank you."

Another in the plus column. With those good thoughts in my head, I think it's time to hit the hay. He did and slept the sleep of the happy parent and leader.

The first thing the president did in the morning was to give the three letters to Max. "Please start a file, name it my last speech and put these in it."

As he sat at his desk he heard a voice, "Mr. President?" Marge was peeking into the Oval Office door.

"Good morning, Marge."

"Sir, Admiral Needham is here and requests to speak with you."

"Okay, let him in."

"Mr. President, thank you for seeing me."

"No problem, Boomer, always glad to chat with you. What's up?"

"Well, sir, we have been working a situation with DEA in Colombia. They have people buried within the cartels and we receive a steady stream of information. About a week ago, the insiders notified DEA that a very large shipment of coke was going to be loaded on a freighter. No destination was known. We later got word that the ship was the *Lima Star*. It was in the process of being loaded and would put to sea within twenty-four hours.

"We monitored it and when it was about eighty miles east of Cuba, a Coast Guard cutter intercepted it. They hailed the ship repeatedly with no response back. The Coast Guard said the freighter was a coastal type about 485 feet long. It was further noted that the ship had two five-inch guns mounted, one on its bow and one on its stern. A tarp on the upper deck appears to be some sort of weapon; we think it's possibly a missile launcher. We have an aircraft in the area and a sub nearby and we intend to board that ship or sink it. I wanted you to be aware of the situation first, just in case it might cause international consequences."

"Well, Boomer, this does present some problems, doesn't it? How much time do we have?"

"Well, sir, if they keep their heading east, out to sea, only a couple of hours. Any other direction gives us unlimited time."

"Okay, let me put in a call to the president of Colombia and I'll get back to you as quickly as possible."

"Mr. President, hello, sir. How are you? Good, I'm glad to hear that. Well, we have a problem that I need to discuss with you. The ship *Lima Star* took on a cargo in Cartagena. A good portion of that cargo is cocaine. We have hailed this ship several times about eighty miles east of Cuba. It refuses to respond to our hail. It is also showing two five-inch guns on its deck and a covered device on its upper deck that my people feel could be a missile launcher. It is our intention to either board that ship or sink it. Before we act, I wish to inform you in the best spirit of our cooperation and trust. Yes, Estaban, it's very good information. That's fine; I'll wait for your call."

Thirty-five minutes later the president called Admiral Needham back.

"Boomer, I've just hung up with the president of Colombia. Bottom line is that he's hearing two different stories. The people he trusts tell him they believe the whole scenario. He also has people telling him we're lying. He says for us to go ahead and do what we have to do. You have my permission to proceed with your plans."

Admiral Needham did exactly what he had to. A flash message went out to the Coast Guard Cutter *Diligence* and U.S. Navy submarine *Yellowfin*. "Stand off out of the five-inch gun range. Coordinate with the *Yellowfin*. Radio the *Lima Star* to stand to and fire a shot across her bow."

To the *Yellowfin* commanding officer, "Have a firing solution ready to go. If the *Lima Star* fires on the *Diligence*, fire and blow her out of the water. Be advised the *Lima* possibly has a missile system on deck covered by a tarp."

On the bridge of the Cutter *Diligence*, Commander Bill Wannstedt called, "Comm."

"Comm, sir."

"Radio *Yellowfin*, we' ready,"

"Comm, sir."

"Go Comm."

"*Yellowfin* is ready, sir."

"Lieutenant Grysko, put a shot across her bow on my command. *Lima Star*, this is the United States Coast Guard Cutter *Diligence*." He repeated his call three times, without a response. He then said, "Fire, Mr. Pennington." The five-inch deck gun barked and a splash of water appeared in front of the *Lima Star*. The *Diligence* turned 180 degrees and left the *Lima Star's* firing range.

"Muzzle flashes reported," the officer of the deck shouted. Wannstedt ordered all watches to report any flashes observed and to monitor the tarped area on the upper deck.

"Radio *Yellowfin* we're being fired on."

From the time the *Yellowfin* fired its MK 25 torpedo, to the time it hit the waterline of the ship, was only seventeen seconds. Because of the fear that the *Lima Star* could launch a missile at the *Diligence*, the skipper of the *Yellowfin* had decided a close-in shot was best. The concussion would be harder on his ship, but it was worth the risk considering the consequences of a missile hitting the *Diligence*. If the *Lima Star* wanted to launch a missile it would have had to be awfully fast. The torpedo hit the small freighter and nearly broke it in two; it was a mortal shot. In less than nine minutes, the *Lima Star* disappeared beneath the waves.

Hector Mirabella sipped his rum and hoped his blood pressure would drop. His good friend and doctor had warned him about drinking any alcohol, but he needed it right now. He was pissed to the max. As he sipped, he thought of possible solutions to his problem. He had more problems than solutions. He picked up the phone and dialed a number. He left a short message. "Call the directors to a meeting tonight at six."

Hector greeted his guests with his usual smiles and warm gracious manner. Each guest returned the gracious warmth of the host. Each knew that trouble had to be brewing. Hector rarely called for meetings; he didn't want them to be seen together. So there had to be a major problem. Hector's business sense knew the less they were seen together the better. As the second largest cocaine cartel in Columbia, Hector was security conscious and rightfully so. One small slip and the business and all its partners could be gone.

For an hour Hector and his guests dined on a beef supper and drank heartily. After supper, the five men retired to the main living room area and all took seats. Hector toasted to renewed business. "As we are all aware, the U.S. has put a very severe crimp in our business. In fact, our sales in the U.S. are down seventy-eight percent."

The four guests were visibly shaken by this number. "That much?" one groaned.

"Yes, that much. The reason for this quickly called meeting is even worse news. Our latest shipment now sits at the bottom of the ocean ninety-eight miles east of Cuba, thanks to the U.S. Navy." With this news the guests began running off at the mouth to each other in wild excitement.

"Calm down, be still," intoned Hector. "We all know that in this business you incur losses, it's part of the trade. This particular loss is harder to accept due to the losses in the States before the shipment."

One guest asked, "What is the amount of our loss here?"

"Between the cargo and the ship, seventy-five million dollars. We can expect another couple of million if we compensate the crew's families as we usually do. For the last couple of months, I have had a couple of people in the States looking at solutions to this problem. They report to me that the majority of the people in America support the president and are happy with what he is doing there. We can always find dissidents and greedy people who can assist us, but the question is what do we do to stop our losses.

"We can attempt to kill the president of the U.S. but if we succeed, at what price. If it got back that we were behind his assassination, there would be no stopping them and our own army from destroying us. If we go ahead with an assassination, it has to be so clean that we are not involved in any way. The second problem is finding another way to get our product to market, if we have a market. The usual dealers in the States are terrified. So many have been killed off that the rest are afraid to sell what they have."

Someone asked, "Do you have a plan, Hector?"

"Not so much of a plan, more of a thought. It seems to me that we have to not only get rid of the president, but the whole plan he has laid out. What we need is to find a viable presidential candidate, back him and hope he wins. If he wins, we get back to business as usual. I am thinking that if we can get close to the best candidate, infuse much money into his campaign and see that he wins, then we own him.

"Naturally he cannot know it's our money until after he wins. We would hold two threats against him. One that we backed him financially and two, we will kill his family if he refuses. It will be a tricky thing I propose and it could fail as easily as not. It will not be cheap, but much cheaper than what we have just lost. I suggest we think about this for a while and mull over possibilities. We will meet here in one week and take this matter up again."

The men of Platoon 344 were but a small part of the 900 men assembled on the parade field at Camp Lejeune. Each platoon felt its loss of independence; their own little world was no longer little. For the first time they were now part of a far larger group and insignificant.

"Good morning, Marines. I am General Donald Sweeney, the commanding officer of Camp Lejeune. The other officers and men here are the assistant CO, Colonel Harry Brunt, Major Joseph Lowery, the training officer, and Sergeant Major Kennedy who has been your senior enlisted man in Parris Island. We would like to welcome you to Camp Lejeune. We have a very ambitious training schedule for you and at the same time get you used to being a Marine.

"You have proven yourselves worthy to be called Marines and that's the first step. The past is the past and we hope we don't have to revisit there, but it is cogent to your status. This is not P.I. We don't have the same physical boundaries. We do have the ocean to our east, but that's all. We have a main gate and three other gates. We also have a state highway running right through our camp, so you will be seeing a lot of civilian vehicles around. That highway is used night and day unless we have to shut it down for tank or artillery firing.

"We have no expectations that any of you will go AWOL or desert, but in all honestly it will be hard to stop you if that's your intent. Be aware that the same rules apply to you here that did so in Parris Island, you run and the risk of being shot or there is jail for two years. I want to think that will not come into play. I feel, based on what I've seen and heard, that all that is behind you. Regardless of my feelings, your freedom will not be the same as the regular volunteers. After the first week, you will have family visits. Naturally you will not be allowed off base and I hope that's a temporary rule. At some point in time, I hope to allow you all the very same liberty all Marines deserve, but that's up to you. You have to prove yourselves yet again. You earned the trust of your trainers in P.I., now you have to show us you belong. It's a sad fact, but it's true.   It is my profound hope that in five weeks I will again be addressing you, wishing you Godspeed in your new endeavors, all nine hundred of you." He turned and nodded to Major Lowery, who stepped forward.

"I am Major Lowery and I am your training officer here at Camp Lejeune. The program is called ITR which stands for Infantry Training Regiment. Our sole purpose is to train you in the basics of infantry fighting. You will learn at the squad level, but you will see how that interacts with the platoon, company and Regiment on up to Division. You will train on machine guns, BAR's, more rifle training and shooting, grenade use, bazooka use, anti-tank guns, artillery support and close air support. You will also use flame throwers and learn camouflage and how to survive off the land, map reading and any and all conceivable tactics that will insure the completion of your task.

I would like to add another thought on top of what General Sweeney has said. Think of this step of your training as the step from high school to college. No longer will someone lead your around by the nose and hold your hand. You are Marines and grown men. We will train you, but nobody's going to hold your hand. We will be doing our part and so must you. The bottom line is this, you have the basics; we now will add the main ingredient. Together they will save your life and every other mans life if you do as we teach you. One little mistake can cost you your life and the lives of everyone around you. This afternoon you will be issued all the gear you need, get organized with records and paperwork and get assigned your NCO's. Tomorrow we start training."

Secret Service Agent Edward Garvey was living a life that was completely alien to him, but one that a lot of men would give anything for. He was living in a condo with a beautiful go-go dancer. In fact, the young lady was an FBI field agent from Seattle who had some dancing background. The lady was Karen Wilson and she was working with Garvey for the good of the country, yet neither of their respective agencies knew it.

Garvey had agreed to it only after his wife did. He had been informed that he was picked for the assignment and why only he was considered. He was not only a good candidate; but the only candidate. He was good-looking, young enough and on the presidential protection detail. Everyone involved agreed that this would be a ninety-day maximum detail.

When Garvey arrived at the Kit Kat Club, he was greeted by smoke, loud leering cheers and the sight of his partner gyrating around a brass pole. He immediately felt pity for Karen. It was one thing to work a hard detail, but another to bare your body and have a bunch of drunks and junkies leering at you. He sat down and had a beer placed before him, all the time watching the unruly crowd. A cute red-headed waitress stopped by his table and asked if he needed a refill. He said no and as she left, she dropped a small piece of paper on the table. Garvey took a few sips of his beer and after an appropriate amount of time picked up the paper. The note said, "Mr. Paterno is outside in a white Cad. He wishes to speak to you; now."

Garvey took a few more sips, got up and slowly walked to the door. He knew who Paterno was and had no fear of seeing him. He saw the white Caddie with two goons standing nearby. He walked to the car and one of the goons pointed to the door. He opened it and got in. Frank Paterno was the spitting imagine of the picture he had been given. The play-acting began because you never knew who may be bugged.

"Listen, my friend, you owe me one hundred grand and I want it. An acquaintance has work to offer you. He has assured me that you will be well-paid and that means I will too. Are you interested?"

"I'm always interested in getting rid of my debts. I guess I really don't have much choice do I?"

"Someone will contact you soon. He will ask you if you are Felix and you will answer, yes."

"Sounds easy enough."

"Goodbye, Felix."

Garvey returned to the club and waited for Karen to finish up. They left together and returned to the condo. Garvey picked up the phone and dialed a number. "I'd like to order a pie, large with sausage and peppers delivered to 448A Grove Lane, Alexandria." After hanging up he scribed a note and placed in his pocket with a twenty-dollar bill. Thirty-five minutes later, a delivery person brought the pie and Garvey handed him the twenty and the note. He then turned on the TV, loud enough, as each grabbed a piece of the pie. Garvey then whispered in Karen's ear explaining what had taken place at the Kit Kat Club.

The next morning Garvey entered the White House as usual. He reported in at 7 a.m. and at 7:15 was in an unmarked room with his superiors. He went over the scenario from the night before.

"Okay, Ed, this may be what we've been waiting for. We have a pair of very mildly tinted sunglasses. You will wear them constantly and if asked why, you answer, 'it's a mild eye strain.' In each bow of the glasses is a listening device. I dare you or anyone to see it. It's been manufactured perfectly. Once you leave this office, you will be wearing the glasses outside all the time and inside whenever not on duty. From this time on, a truck will be not far from you and constantly recording everything you say or is said to you. Remember it's recording everything you say so be discreet and watch what you say and to whom."

The following day after work, Garvey stopped at his regular food store to pick up some items. Upon returning to his car, he saw a young man standing in the area of his car. He was rounding up shopping carts, but now just standing still. "Hey, man, are you Felix?"

"Why yes, I am."

He pointed and said, "See that green VW? Go take a ride with the man behind the wheel."

The driver was a young Spanish-looking man who didn't say a word as they drove away. After a five-minute drive, he pulled into a local A&P store and parked in the lot.

"Listen to me, Mr. Garvey. You have yourself a very big problem and so do my employers. What they want to do is to kill your president and they want you to help to get them close enough to accomplish that."

Garvey didn't miss a beat. "You're crazy as hell, you can't kill the president, it's impossible and I won't be a part of any attempt to."

"Mr. Garvey, you owe Paterno a hundred grand and that figure is growing every day with interest. If you don't come up with 100 G's real soon, you're going to have a serious accident. We know you have no means to come up with that amount, so use your head. Here is our deal. We will place one million dollars in any overseas bank you choose before the killing. Once the job is done we will put another million in the same account. As a bonus, we will pay off Paterno and your debt is gone. Mr. Garvey, you have forty-eight hours to think this offer over. I personally think you'd be crazy to pass up this opportunity."

Garvey got out of the VW, taking note of the plate number. As Garvey walked to his car, the VW drove off; having no idea that he had obtained an iron-tight tail. Not only was a car following him, but a helicopter was flying overhead and recording the car's every move.

Two days passed. Garvey stopped to pick up his dry cleaning and when he left the store saw the green VW parked next to his. He placed his dry cleaning in his car and then got into the VW.

"Hey, Felix, how you doing today?"

Garvey didn't say a word.

"Okay, Felix, what is your answer? We got a deal or not?"

"If I say yes, do I get the details?"

"No, you don't need to know, nor do you want to. If we're successful, you're going to be under a great deal of pressure. A polygraph test is definite, you know that. The less you know the better. We'll plan it all; you will give us the details we ask for. On the day we do it, we'll need you to get us into the White House or wherever we do it. After that, you're out of it. What is your answer?"

"I'll do it."

"Good choice, Mr. Garvey. We'll be in touch."

Days passed and Garvey and his superiors began to wonder if the plan was off or did the group suspect Garvey was not a rogue agent. After the sixth day, Garvey was returning home from work. As he exited his car, he saw the green VW parked across the street. He walked to it and got in.

"Hey, Mr. Felix, how you doin'?"

"Okay, what s up?"

"Well, the big day's coming up. Next Tuesday your president is going to meet with some representatives of the Organization of South and Central American Countries. This bag has two handguns in it. You will find a good place to put them, where our man has access to it. You find out what room they are going to meet and hide the guns where he can get them."

"Well, that's a good plan and I think I can handle it, but I think it would be a good idea if I knew your man. I could be assigned to that meeting and I think if I knew who he was I could avoid watching him. Also, I'm supposed to watch each person and kill anyone who threatens first. If you can't tell me, then I may have to call in sick."

"No, we want you there. With you present, you take suspicion off yourself. Let me think a minute."

Garvey was also thinking, about how to get this guy to agree with him. In the end he figured he had said enough, maybe too much.

"Okay, I guess you could be a help. Here's the deal. On the morning of the meeting, we will kidnap the Colombian representative. Our man will take his place and he looks just like his twin brother. He has been trained just for this job and expects to get out afterwards. You got all that?"

"Yes, I do but I think you're bullshitting me or you're dreaming. That guy has little or no chance of escaping."

"Well, we'll see about that, it's not your concern. You got the bank and account for me?"

Garvey handed him a piece of paper with the bank info on it.

"The day before, you check with the bank and see what your balance is. You do your part and the next day check the bank again."

"And what about me if there's not two mil in the bank?"

"Felix, you're dealing with very professional men. They won't fuck with you, I promise."

"Yeah, your promise and twenty-five cents will get me a cup of coffee."

"Man, have some faith in your partners."

"Good morning, Mr. President."

"Good morning, Bill, and to you too, Mr. Garvey. Two men from my protection team must mean it's important."

"Yes, sir, it is. That's why we're here," added Tyson. "After the last attempt on your life, we did a brainstorming session and thought there could well be another attempt. We went about setting up a scenario that a Secret Service agent on the presidential detail was in trouble in his personal life.

"We and the agent both agreed to the length of the period where his own wife would leave him for several months. Agent Garvey's wife left him to live with her family. We made it well known that the reason was a marriage crisis. We set Ed up with a live-in go-go dancer, who just happens to be an FBI agent with the Seattle office. At the same time, we had a major crime figure on the hook who specializes in gambling activities. This man agreed to the story that this agent was into him for $100,000.

"The whole scenario was leaked out to the right people at the right time. We went so far as to insert into his personnel file a report that Garvey was under investigation for various personal problems. With all this in place, if there was someone reaching out for a person to get close, that this agent could likely be that insider. While waiting, we worked on several other scenarios."

195

The president interrupted and looked at Garvey. "Young man, you have certainly put a lot on the line for me. I would like for you and your wife and children to know that you are and will be in my thoughts and prayers. From the bottom of my heart, I truly thank you and your family for your sacrifices."

"Three weeks ago Garvey was approached by our gambling boss and asked if he was interested in making a good amount of money. He strongly implied that Garvey would do it. Two days later he was contacted. This contact told him he was needed to get someone inside and help them kill you. The offer was two million dollars in an overseas account and payment of his gambling debt. This man was immediately tailed, his identification very quickly learned. The tail was easy and it appears he does not fear Garvey is anything other than a rouge Agent. We traced him back to none other than Estaban Garcia in Colombia.

"Garvey was contacted again and given two handguns to hide in the White House. Next week you are scheduled to host a get together for members of the Organization of South and Central American Countries. The Colombian representative will be kidnapped that morning and a replacement will take his place. This new man supposedly is a spitting imagine of the original man. He is the hit man.

"That's the entire story, sir. We are on top of it and will take this guy out before anything can happen. What I think you need to know is this is as far as I and the Service can go. We are hoping you and the CIA can go further and nail Garcia and his organization."

President Barringer entered the room and asked everyone to be seated. He looked to each seat to make sure those in attendance were who he wanted. Ralph Springstead, his secretary of defense, Robert Kilgore, director of the FBI, Chairman of the Joint Chiefs General Robert Harmon and Murray Palmer, the director of the CIA. He was satisfied and said, "What have you come up with?"

Murray Palmer spoke up, "Mr. President, we have gone over several options and have settled on a plan we expect to be perfect. Our scientists have been working on a system of guided bombs. This is how it works. A team on the ground aims a light called a laser at the intended target. A high-altitude aircraft coordinates with this team on the ground via radio. On signal the aircraft releases a high explosive bomb and it homes in on the target via this laser light. The tests have been highly successful and they feel it's ready for actual use. This system can be used without anyone knowing a plane is even in the air. The best part of the plan is that it can be done when you have a person or group in the target area. Let's say we have a group of ten we want to take out. The ground team monitors the target and makes sure all the intended are in the building before the bomb is released. Depending on how close you have your aircraft, the target could be bombed in minutes."

The president looked around gathering his thoughts. "Have any of you actually seen any of these tests?"

"Yes, sir," offered General Harmon. "Director Palmer and I have."

"You both saw it personally and the test went as drawn up?"

"Yes, sir, that's correct."

"Fine. For now I'd like you to get your team up to speed. The area of concern is naturally Colombia. Get your people in place but they can do nothing until I give the order, are we clear?"

"Yes, sir, we are clear."

"Mr. President? Yes, hello, it's James Barringer. Yes, you're right, two calls in such a short time. Yes, it went well, thanks to your help. Now, sir, I have another problem. In fact, we have one together. I would like to send my secretary of state, Henry Lloyd, down to met with you, face to face. Yes, sir, that's fine. Yes, a safe place is very necessary. Nobody but yourself should hear what he has to tell you. I will call you back as soon as we can set it up. I'll let you know his arrival time. Thank you, Mr. President."

In less than five hours, Henry Lloyd was en route to Colombia aboard an Air Force jet. His job was easy. The president of Colombia had a much more difficult one. In less than twelve hours, Lloyd would be back in Washington with an answer.

For two straight days, a crew worked on the phone lines in the foothills of San Anofre. The area was the home of many very wealthy Colombians. Anofre overlooked the Caribbean Sea and was not far from the seaport of Cartagena. The four-man crew worked from a green box van with the logo of Telepfona National adorned to each side. Two of the men were doing legitimate phone work while the other two stayed inside the van working on some very expensive electronics gear.

The object of their work was a very large home in the foothills not more than a half-mile away. The two men in the truck looked Colombian, young and good-looking, but in fact were Americans belonging to the U.S. Army Electronics Command. Their Spanish was flawless. Even the two legitimate men working on the lines thought them Colombians. They were told the two men in the truck were working on a new type of equipment that could detect flaws in the phone lines.

A group of men were ushered into the White House after having been checked out by security. Each had been required to identify himself by showing their membership cards indicating them members of the Organization of South Americans Countries. Each then passed through a metal detector. They were offered coffee, juice and Danish from a large buffet table and then seated around a large conference table. Roberto Salazar approached a Secret Service agent. They shook hands while introducing themselves.

After they shook hands, Salazar put his hand into his pocket and it remained there. The agent pointed toward a bathroom that was signed "VIP restroom." Salazar entered the restroom and went to the urinal and did what he had to do. When finished, he put his hand into his pocket and retrieved the key the Secret Service agent had placed in his hand during the handshake. He walked to the locked closet door marked "Janitorial Supplies."

Salazar reached into the closet and removed a shoebox-size package. He removed two handguns and checked each was properly loaded and had one round in the chamber. He placed both weapons in his waistband and walked out of the restroom. He walked towards the conference room when from nowhere four Secret Service agents grabbed him and restrained his hands, cuffed him and left the area very quickly and quietly. Not one person from the conference room saw anything of the arrest.

Within five minutes of Salazar's arrest, a radio signal went out saying the field goal was blocked. That message was received by a U.S. Navy carrier in the Caribbean Sea about one hundred miles off the coast of Panama. Twelve minutes later, an F4 Phantom launched from the carrier. Every sailor on the flight deck had observed civilians working around the F4 and the odd-shaped weapon that hung from its underbelly. All they could see was that the bomb was marked in red with the letters HE, for high explosive.

In a matter of minutes, the specially equipped F4 was cruising at 55,000 feet, higher than any South American radar could reach. Thirteen minutes into its flight, the pilot sent a radio message out saying, "Caribbean blue." Seconds later he heard a reply saying, "Caribbean blue, tried and true." Two minutes and thirty seconds later, the large house overlooking the town of San Anofre erupted into a gigantic ball of fire and smoke that was heard and seen for miles.

In the basement of the White House, the president and those who knew of this operation waited to hear a report from Colombia. While waiting, General Harmon asked the president, "How did you ever get the Colombians to agree to the plan?"

"General, his answer was simple. He said nobody will ever really know what happened and that Colombia was a much better country without this band of killers."

"Well good for him, at least we know we have at least one honest citizen in Colombia," added the general.

A man appeared in the room, walked to CIA Director Palmer and handed him a piece of paper. Palmer read it and then handed it to the president. "Gentlemen, this is a message from our on-ground unit. We confirm that all five members of the cartel were in the home at the time of the hit. The destruction was complete and it's doubtful anyone could have possibly survived. They had to leave the area quickly for obvious reasons."

Chapter 15

"Good evening from the White House. I'm Bob Nyberg reporting for NBC. This much-anticipated news briefing is nearly ready to start. The buzz word around Washington has been about what the president is going to say tonight. Many feel it's going to be about the present system of changes. Some feel it's going to be about ending that system of changes and returning to our Constitutional protection. A very few feel it will be a political announcement about what the presidents future plans are.

"Some insiders have been hinting that the president will not run for reelection. Since the president received approval for the suspension of our Constitution and all his changes have gone into effect, he may feel his work is done. It's also a fact that anyone on the inside will be fired or worse if caught leaking anything to the press.

"Finally there is that story out of Chicago. That story asks the question, is he the second coming of Christ or the second coming of Hitler? It's a good question to a lot of people, but the bigger question is why was it allowed to be published?

"In our present system, any negative news that is not good for the general public is banned from being printed, yet the government allowed this story to be printed and published. Why? That question is on everyone's lips. Hopefully we will get all the answers in just a few minutes. In fact I can see the president's press secretary approaching the podium."

"Ladies and gentleman, the president of the United States of America."

President Barringer walked to the podium, put some papers down and said, "Good evening and please be seated.

"I have several topics to cover this evening. The first is the status of our draft resistors. These young men have completed their basic training at Parris Island. If you know a Marine ask him what that training was like. It is no picnic by any stretch and only the best complete the training. I am happy to report that the best have completed that training and are presently in Camp Lejeune, North Carolina, for further training. The Marine Corps is happy with these men as a group and so am I. I met with many of them during their training at Parris Island. Both the Marine Corps and I agree that they have done a good job and we see no problem with them fighting for our country. I pray for their safe return

"Topic two is in the area of changes to our system. We have a new item to add to our list. Rape and child molestation are a growing problem. We put this problem to the courts, the American Medical Association and the religious community to review and comment.

"The overall question was the penalty for those offenses. Death and castration were the two sentences most often mentioned. After due deliberation, the mentioned groups agreed on castration. As a result, conviction for either offense will mean that offender is castrated along with any jail sentence incurred. This ruling commences immediately.

"A second change is in the making. In my many years in politics, I've seen numerous problems in the intelligence area. By intelligence I mean not only about foreign countries, but intelligence of a domestic nature. There is even a lot of intelligence gathering in law enforcement. It has become very apparent that these agencies are not sharing this intelligence with each other. Presently all data that is collected is put into categories and filed for use at the right time or need. So much data is collected that much of it is forgotten over time. Data-storage technology is still in its infancy, but we're working on that problem. Right now storage units are large and expensive. Once they become less expensive and smaller, all intelligence agencies will be so equipped. All intelligence will be put into one pot, so to speak and all agencies will share its use.

"I recently put all intelligence agencies on notice that they will supply one man from each agency to set new standards for sharing. We presently have several agencies that have very large egos and like to see that their agency alone gets the credit. That is going to stop. Any agency who withholds intelligence will have its director fired. I will not tolerate ego problems.

"The reason I am telling you about this intelligence problem is that I want you, the American public, to see that changes not only affect you, but reach right up to the top of the government ladder. It's not only the everyday Joe, but the directors of our largest government agencies who also are getting changes put upon them. If you remember, I said on Day One that no one from me on down is above changes. It's for our entire good not just one segment of the population.

"Topic three is foreign base closing. Many of you have been after me to come up with some figures. The number crunchers have come up with some figures, but I'd rather report it in another way. Based on the figures given me, it seems that what we saved by closing all foreign bases and withdrawing our troops, we can replace about twenty-five percent of our infrastructure every five years. That means in twenty years our total road, rail and air systems can be replaced. Starting in the twenty-first year we could anticipate a ten to fifteen percent reduction in income taxes. This is all predicated on the premises that whoever is in charge of our government allows this to go that long. If the minute I am out of office, the new president reverts back to the old system of foreign bases, then this all will have been a waste of time.

"That brings me to the final point of tonight's speech. In our political system, the candidate for the presidency must be known as far in advance as possible. My personal thoughts on this are that all that time is needed to rip him apart and to dull the brain of the public with four years of pre-election nonsense. If I had my way, the process would start and finish in six months and not a day longer. As we all know, that is not my decision, but that still leaves the political parties needing to know who their candidate is. I will not seek re-election under any circumstances. That ends any and all conversation on the subject. I will not answer any questions on the subject until I am out of office.

"On the international scene you and the whole world need to know that some of our former allies have a lot of questions regarding their safety. Without mincing any words, we and the Soviet Union are the big cheeses of the world. When we withdrew our bases from Europe and Asia, I said we were going to mind our own business. Some countries in the world fear that the Soviet Union has an eye on them and without our help they would be overrun and taken over. Well, you should know that I have informed them and the Soviet Union that we would not allow that to happen. We wish to be left alone to solve some of our domestic problems, but we could never stand by and do nothing if the Communist bloc invaded.

"First question, Jan," as the president pointed to Jan Kilgore of the *Phoenix Sun.*

"Mr. President, don't you think that castration is rather a harsh sentence?"

"No, Jan, I don't. Rape and child molestation are terrible crimes. If it were up to me, I'd kill them, that's harsh."

The president then pointed to Dave Williams of the *Portland Review*. "Mr. President, in an article written by Jerry Breedlove of the *Chicago Times*, he asks the question, is our president the second coming of Christ or Hitler? Under our present system, isn't it against the best interest of the public to publish this story? Why did you allow it?"

"Dave, that article is a good one and we all know the general public has that exact question on their minds. The public has the right to their opinion and I have mine. I would like to point out a few things relative to that story. I am neither Christ nor Hitler. I am nowhere near either of them. I am a simple man who just happens to be the president of the United States right now. This country has problems and it's my intention to change or correct as many as I can while in office.

"You have to either like what I've done or not, but here are some facts to help everyone make up their minds. These are indisputable figures and only a small portion of results, both pro and con.

1. Death by auto down 42 percent. Jail time due to motor vehicle violations up 125 percent.

2. Adoptions up 155 percent. Mixed-race adoptions up 168 percent.

3. All crime down 300 percent. Killings by police up 3,000 percent.

4. Unemployment down 48 percent. Most new jobs are minimum paying.

5. Drug-related crime down 279 percent. Armed robberies of doctors, pharmacies and hospitals up 400 percent.

6. Chain gangs are cleaning up the American landscape. One hundred twenty-five percent increase in minor crime arrests.

"In closing, let me say this; one reason I will not run again is because I am in the middle of the battle of my life. We are in the middle of an unheard-of change in our system and way of life and it is my intention to use all of my strength to see it through in my time left in office. I have tunnel vision; I see nothing but the results of the changes. I have neither time nor inclination for anything else.

"To prove to you that I will no longer be a politician, listen to my next sentences. What I am about to say is political suicide, but it's right from my heart. We have some very good people in our political system. Bright, energetic and honest. The problem is we have a much larger group who are in it for their own self-interests. Right now I am in a major battle, as I've said. Someone else needs to fight this new battle. Whoever he is, he is in for the fight of his life. Trying to change the political system that should work for the best interest of the people and not his own self-interest is going to be an awesome task. I wish that person godspeed. Good night, I will answer no further questions."

"That was one hellava hit Mr. P. You really got your ass into that shot."

"Thank you, Charlie, I did hit it well didn't I?"

"Yes, sir, you sure did." As they walked towards their balls, President Barrigner watched the dew rolling off his golf shoes. The grass clippings and the dew formed some intriguing designs.

"Charlie, why is it you have so much trouble calling me Jim? We agreed it was permissible out here on the course, didn't we?"

"Yes, sir, but I have a problem calling you anything but Mr. P. I not only respect you, but I respect the office as well. I'm just a retired cop, why should I have any right to call you something other than the title you hold?"

"You still feel out of your league, don't you?"

"Yes, sir, I do. I know my place, this is all temporary. I have no right to be with the president, his staff, Senators and Congressmen and members of the Supreme Court, and all those high-ranking military men, wow. I'm just a plain old guy who is in an Alice in Wonderland situation for a short time."

"Charlie, you don't give yourself enough credit. You have been an enormous help in the past months. I appreciate your honestly and plain thinking, you're a breath of fresh air."

After putting out, they began walking to the next tee. The president asked, "Charlie, when you were with the P.D., did you get to work much with the FBI?"

"Well, I don't think I could say a lot, but I did work with them on many a case. I guess I talked with one FBI person every week or two. Can I ask why?"

"Yes, you can. I'd like your thoughts on them."

Charlie smiled. "You're referring to your speech last night?"

"Yes, in a way. What is your opinion of the cooperation you got from them?"

"Well, I got cooperation, if it suited them. They never did a thing for me unless it served their purpose. Because I was in D.C., I got a lot more from them than a P.D. would in Nebraska. They have much more to worry about here in D.C., so they needed us to help out. The thing that pissed us off the most was their arrogance. They always felt they were the gods of the law enforcement world. Only they knew everything, they were the best, the only ones capable. If we asked for help on a case, the caveat was from the beginning, we issue all press releases. When they issued the press release it always said, 'The FBI with the assistance of...' Their ego is unbelievably large.

"Now having said that you should know that I was very friendly with one agent whom I like and respect. He would tell me on the QT that his bosses laid out the rules of press releases and he had no choice. He personally disliked it, but he had his back to the wall on the issue. Overall, I would say that no local cop has anything good to say about the FBI. In fact, in some police circles they were known at the Fumbling Bureau of Investigation."

When it appeared Charlie was done on the subject the president asked, "What about the CIA, you ever deal with them?"

"Yes, but very rarely. If it's possible, they are even worse than the FBI when it comes to egos. They have a patent set of lines when you ask them questions. 'I can't answer that, national security,' or 'You don't have the need to know.' We always joked that they felt we were lower than whale shit and that's at the bottom of the ocean."

After hitting an eight iron to the green, he said, "That's about the same story I've heard from a lot of people. I truly hope we can change all that. Compartmentalizing intelligence is dangerous and someday may bite us on the ass."

Friday night is the end of the workweek at Camp Lejeune for everybody, except those who have the weekend duty. A military camp is much like a city and some services are required all day every day. Every unit is comprised of four sections for duty purposes. Each section will have the duty for a seven-day period. You can plan then to have no liberty for one week every month and no free time for the same period. This system includes officers also.

The officer of the day is a twenty-four-hour job each day, 365 days a year. From the top to the bottom, each man has a job if he has the duty. On a Marine base civilians are but a small minority of help. They usually handled public services such as sewer treatment, water department and public works; everything else is done by Marines. That included guard duty, barracks NCO's, clean-up crews, mess duty and whatever one can imagine that is needed to keep a city running.

Depending on how close it is to payday, most enlisted personnel were off-base by Friday at 1700 hours. Few enlisted men were in the enlisted club on Friday night. Three sections were on liberty and the fourth had the duty. For the men of training company A through K, the draft dodgers, the E club was one of the few places they wanted to be. There are plenty of recreational services, but the E club at night was the place to be, other than a movie.

One group of Marines having a few beers was the men of Platoon 344. Many of the trainees at Lejeune had bonded with their fellow members of the Parris Island platoon. Tonight Radison, Wainwright, Cox, Martinez and Romero were all around one table. Jim Radison was the happiest of those men. He had received the best news possible. In his hands he held a memo that had been given to him at muster this morning. Romero asked him if he would read it to them again.

"To all married men or fathers of children in the Training Companies A thru K. It is the opinion of General D. Sweeney and his staff that the men of the aforementioned companies are progressing very normally. It is time for the next step in our adaptation of the regular Marine Corps life. The next step will be granting liberty to those married men and or fathers of children regardless of marriage. Liberty is granted to such men from 1700 Friday 4May until 1800 6May.

"A list of all off-base motels and hotels is available for your families to make proper reservations. You will be required to furnish Sergeant Major Kennedy with proof of marriage and birth certificate of children in order to quality for liberty. You will be forbidden to leave the City of Jacksonville, N.C. while on liberty. Everyone from General Sweeney down to Sergeant Major Kennedy want to inform you that the single men are hoping your conduct will be honorable as men and Marines. They are awaiting liberty and you are the forerunner to their liberty. By order of Brig. D. Sweeney."

"Son of a bitch," was all Romero could say. He finally added, "You lucky bastard."

"Yes, I am," added Radison. Jim felt bad that only he at the table was getting the liberty. "Hey, look at it this way, in another week or so you'll all get it and we'll all be happy."

"I'll drink to that," shouted Wainwright.

Cox asked, "Did you call your old lady yet, Jim?"

"Yeah, right after lunch. She's really excited. I miss them both so much. She says Jim Jr. is growing so fast that I won't recognize him."

Wainwright looked at Radison and said, "Enjoy your family, Jim, it's not long before we will be leaving here and we all know where we're going."

Radison calmly added, "Yeah, I know."

"Well, well, isn't this nice. All the draft dodgers hanging out together."

Everyone turned to the direction of the voice. Three young men at the next table were staring at them. They were in civilian clothes so you couldn't tell anything about them. They had to be junior men to be in the club, so it wasn't like they could be much higher in rank.

Martinez turned and said, "What is that supposed to mean?"

The young Marine stood and walked towards their table. "What I meant was that it's hard to understand why the C.O. would give you cowards anything, let alone liberty."

Martinez jumped into the face of the man, "Who the fuck are you calling a coward?"

"You motherfucker, you."

Everyone had jumped up and grabbed both men to keep them apart. The young big mouth continued on.

"You think we're going to trust you in combat? Shit no. I won't fight anywhere near your kind. You got no right being called Marines, you should be called cowards."

From nowhere came the words loud and clear, "Jergens, shut your mouth or I'll shut it for you."

Gunnery Sergeant Larry Laws stood five feet eleven inches and 205. A barrel of a man with the closest cropped hair you're going to see on any Marine. As he walked up he parted the two tables of men.

Laws stood face to face with Pfc. Jergens and said, "First, you will apologize to them, and second, you welcome them to our house and then sit your ass down and be quiet."

Jergens had a horrified look on his face. "Gunny, I can't, it would be a damn lie to say it."

Laws moved so close to Jergens' face that they could both see beads of sweat beading up on their foreheads. "You will do as I say or I'll have you in front of the first sergeant on Monday morning first thing."

Jergens looked into the face of the E club manager and knew he was in a bad place. *I guess I'm going to have to lose this one, but there will be another time,* he thought. He looked at the group in front of him and said, "I'm sorry about this. Welcome to Camp Lejeune."

Laws didn't like the sincerity in the apology, but let it go. "Now you will leave my club. You are banned from here for thirty days. You understand?"

"Yes, Gunny." He turned and left with his two friends.

Gunny Laws turned to the trainees and said, "Sit down." He grabbed a chair and pulled it up to their table. "My bartender told me he saw all this and how it all happened. I've got no beef with you all. You're going to run into this again and you better understand it. If you let a bunch of big mouths suck you into a fight, you're going down with them; it's not worth it.

"We are all Marines, regardless of how we came here, but some are going to constantly remind you of how unhappy they are about the path you took. Take my word on this. You're going to have to suck up a lot of bullshit from some people. You stick to learning your jobs, it's worth your life to be good at what you're going to do. I recently got back from Nam and it's no vacation. You learn how to stay alive and don't worry about the assholes of the world."

On Monday morning, the section leaders did their thing with muster. They took a head count to make sure every man was present or accounted for. Whatever information that needed to be passed on was done so at muster. Every member of Platoon 334 was in C Company. C stood for Charlie and was referred to as such. When all the daily bullshit was done with, Charlie's CO stood and addressed the company.

"We are scheduled to be working with the tanks today and we will, but first we will be marching to the parade field." He said no more. As the company was marching towards the parade field, the usual few men were whispering. This time the conversation was on why they were going to the parade field when they were supposed to be training on the tank range. A few scenarios were spoken of; the top being the possibility of the married man liberty was a bust.

Romero was heard to say, "If those bastards ruin my chance of liberty, I'm going to kill someone."

When all eleven companies were assembled on the parade field and at attention, General Donald Sweeney, the base commander, stepped forward to a miked podium. He nodded to his assistant C.O., who called them to stand at ease.

"Good morning, Marines. I have a brief statement to make. I have good news and bad. The good news is that every married man or father who had weekend liberty returned. They were given some slack and they did what was right. That is a giant step forward for all of you. The bad news is that two men have deserted. A Pvt .Vernon Vargas of Able Company was captured in a wooded section near Onslow Beach. He is presently in the brig and I assume he will be transferred to prison. The second man, a Private Daniel Fabio of Charlie Company, was found at the Jacksonville Airport. He ran from the MP's who then fired on him as prescribed by orders. His wounds proved fatal."

General Sweeney paused to allow his words to sink in. When 1,800 men are assembled and a Marine Corps general is addressing them, it is expected that silence would be in order. With this kind of news, General Sweeney expected to hear a murmur but heard nothing. *Was it the shock of hearing two men deserted and one was dead? Did they think it couldn't happen? Did they think the MP's wouldn't shoot?*

"You have taken a big step forward, but unfortunately you have also taken one step back. I will tell you my point of view right now. Two men out of a little over 1,800 is not a bad number. If it were up to me and its not, I would favor giving you all weekend liberty based on what the married men did over the weekend. I have faith in you. We all know it's not my call. Now we wait to see what happens next."

For the men of 344, it was a hard day to keep up with the training. When working around moving tanks, its best to keep very alert. But it was on their minds that their house mouse was dead. Many mourned the man yet some hated the thought of what he did to them and the possible consequences to come.

At the same time, General Sweeney and Sergeant Major Kennedy were on a Marine transport plane heading north. They were in fact heading to Washington, D.C., at the request of the president, commandant and Joint Chiefs. Sweeney and Kennedy were, in fact, on the hot seat. They had to explain what happened and why. General Sweeney knew in his head that he was going to stick with his convictions. He felt it was time to trust in these men and in order to do that they needed to get something in return, liberty.

After morning muster on Wednesday the men of Companies A thru K found themselves once again on the parade field. The speaker today was Sergeant Major Kennedy.

"General Sweeney and I have just returned from Washington. We were called by the president, commandant and Joint Chiefs of Staff. We spent Monday evening and most of Tuesday talking about you. The big topic was what took place over the weekend. Nobody was very happy over the two deserters, but the positives were good. General Sweeney did one hell of a job convincing them that you are good and deserve better. He won and so did you. He convinced them to trust you and treat you like all other Marines. This coming weekend you will all be allowed liberty." Shouts and cheers went up, a serious breech of military courtesy, yet no one moved to stop the troops their joy.

After they quieted down, Sergeant Major Kennedy continued. "The true test of your integrity is now up to you. You as a group either make or break it. T here is another thing you all need to know. General Sweeney has gone way out on a limb for you. His entire career is on the line over this. By the way, mine is too. You fail and the general and I are both out looking for work."

On Monday morning muster, all but two men were present, but they were accounted for. One was hit by a car and in the base hospital. The second man got drunk and the local police picked him up for drunk and disorderly. The men of Companies A thru K had taken the test and passed, with one small blemish. General Sweeney felt very satisfied that he had made the right decision. He trusted the men and they had rewarded him. Both Sweeney and Kennedy had joked to those closest to them that they were a bit worried about finding new careers.

Chapter 16

Friday's noon chow was never a great treat. The main item on the menu was cold cuts which the troops affectionately called "horse cock." That was the reason most ate in the snack bar. Radison was in the chow hall eating because it was free, so to speak. He too would have loved to be eating in the PX snack bar, but he was saving all his money, money that was needed for his wife and son to visit him. As he was eating he suddenly looked up and saw Wainwright coming his way. He sat across from Radison and both exchanged hellos.

"Hey, Rad, a bunch of us are going into town tonight to celebrate our first liberty. We're going to rent a motel room and just relax and enjoy our freedom. We want you to come with us. It's me, Cox, Gallo and we hope you. Martinez, Romero, Palmer and Ketchum are going to be in a second room. You want to go with us?"

"Thanks, Vin, but I gotta save my bread. My wife needs it to visit; we don't have much."

"Yeah, I can understand that."

"I wish we could help you out, but we got some plans. None of us been laid in so long, we don't know if we can remember how to do it."

Radison, who had a visit from his wife just the week before, knew what that was like, but keep quiet about it.

"I can't imagine what jail time would be like, at least we have some freedom to move around, be outside and at least have some type of life. I don't think I could hack that."

"Amen to that, brother."

"Vinny, keep your nose clean and you won't have to worry about jail."

Vinny didn't answer and Radison noticed he had stopped eating and was just staring out into space.

"What's up, Vinny, you okay?"

"Well, I had a thought when you said jail. If I went to jail for two years, I would come out alive."

"What are you saying, Vin?"

"What I'm saying is we're going to Nam and there's a good chance we ain't coming back. The odds are not good on this one. If I went to jail I know, I'd survive and get out and have the rest of my life."

"Vinny, you got to stop this horse-shit. I have to agree that the odds are not the best for surviving, but you need to think about some other things."

"Like what?"

"First thing is in jail you're going to be used as a sex kitten; that, my friend, is a known fact. When and if you get out, you have a life-long record. Any chance of getting a decent job is finished. Over time, I think it would eat you up and you would regret the decision not to fight."

Wainwright looked to be deep in thought and Radison got the impression Vinny was on the verge of tears.

"Vin, you okay."

"Yeah."

"Jim, are you scared?"

"You mean about Nam? You're damned right I am. I know we're being trained, got the best equipment and good leaders, but those people we're going to fight want to kill us. For me, the thought of never seeing my wife and son again is hard to take. My mom and dad were really pissed when we ran away. We're at a point now that we at least talk to each other. The bottom line is that I have no one to blame, but myself. I made the wrong decision and here I am. I intend to do the honorable thing and if I don't come back at least my son will think good of me and I'll have set a good example for him."

Three hours later Charlie Company was on a break. They had been learning about close air support, a specialty of the Marine Corps. As they waited for a new aircraft run from Cherry Point, some hitch developed and a break was called. Radison was taking a drink from his canteen when Vinny dropped down next to him.

"Hey, Vin, how's the war going?"

"We're at intermission, so I went to the head and got me some popcorn."

"Sure you did."

"You know, Jim, the talk we had at chow? I've been doing some thinking about what you said."

"And what did you conclude, my son?"

"You're right, it would be a bitch to live with that the rest of my life. I already have some alcohol problems in my family. I could see me falling right into the bottle to block it all out."

"Vinny, you got a lot upstairs, use it. I like the way you reason things out."

"Thanks, Jim, I owe you. I'm still scared though."

"Yeah Vinny, so am I."

"You sure you don't want to go with us this weekend."

"No, thanks."

"Well, I for one am really looking forward to getting my ashes hauled a couple of times."

Radison looked at him. "You're going to do what?"

"Don't fisherman read?"

"I admit that over the last couple of years I haven't had much time to read, what's that got to do with ashes?"

"In the book *The Sand Pebbles*, the main character is a sailor in China during the Boxer Rebellion. When he goes out on liberty he says he's going to get his ashes hauled, that means getting laid."

"I didn't read the book, but I don't see the connection. Vinny, enjoy your liberty and use a rubber."

"Sergeant Major Kennedy reporting as ordered, sir."

"At ease, Sergeant Major." General Donald Sweeney liked the sergeant major, but could not allow his fondness for the man to interfere with proper military etiquette. He truly liked this man, enlisted or not, he was a Marine's Marine. "You and I should not be having this conversation, you know that. Your immediate superior should be saying this, for this one time, I am going to violate military courtesy, but it will not happen again.

"You have done an outstanding job and I admire you for that. You and I have gotten one very big job completed or nearly so. I want you to understand that I have nothing but good things to say about you."

"Thank you, sir, but that sounds like you have more to say and it may not be good."

"No, no, not at all. What I want is for you to reconsider your request to go with these men to Nam. I have too much respect for you to actually ask it.

GERALD RUBIN

Besides that, you got to the president first and his yes would obviously override my no. What I'm saying to you is that I consider you a very valuable asset to the Marine Corps and I want you to promise me you'll watch your ass over there."

"That, sir, I promise."

"What we need to do is talk about the staffing situation. When the commandant refused to allow the drill instructors to go with the men, it was for a good reason. They are too valuable to the Corps doing what they do. The brass in D.C. has decided to send these men as a unit replacement. They will replace two battalions, but the officers and NCO's will stay on and take over the replacements.

"Your job will be as liaison between them and our men. I don't think it's going to be a very pleasant task for you either. If they think like some others do, they aren't going to trust our men very much. It's going to be up to you to change that way of thinking once you're in Nam."

"I hope it's not that much of a problem, General. I understand what you're saying and I have a good grasp on the situation."

"Good, is there anything else we need to discuss?"

"Yes, sir, there is. We normally see a lot of PFC stripes handed out after this phase of training. Will that still be the case?"

"I don't see why not, I would surmise many should be PFC's; and for those who made it out of P.I., maybe a lance corporal or two. That is normal procedure, is it not?"

"Yes, sir, it is. I was asking because we're not in the usual situation here. My second question is about the logistics of when this group ships out and the possibility of them getting some leave before they go."

"Good thought. I'll get my personnel people working on it, ask some questions and get back to you. I would suggest that you also take some leave and spend it with your family."

"Yes, sir, that is exactly what I have in mind."

The Monday morning muster was completed. Everyone in Charlie Company was anxious to get to chow and discuss the weekend liberty when Captain Jerry Marvel stepped in front of the company. As the company executive officer, Captain Marvel was like a father figure since his arrival at Lejeune. He was a very proud officer and a good exec. He was hard, considerate, funny and always seemed to care very much for the men.

The company did not know any better; they really didn't know how the officer/enlisted man situation worked. Line officers were very strict and hard on the men. They enjoyed the strict system, almost like a caste system. The officers will do almost anything to properly train and help the enlisted men to survive, but there was no closeness or friendship between them and the enlisted men. If an officer and an enlisted man liked each other and had something in common; it could not be, they could not fraternize. It wasn't quite as bad as the Japanese officer/enlisted man system. In Japan the common soldier was cannon fodder. Their officers could care less about them. The Marine officer cared, but from a distance.

Captain Jerry Marvel was a different breed of Marine officer. First, he was a Marine aviator and aviators treat their men vastly different. The aviator sits in the saddle of a very expensive aircraft. It may be a jet fighter, attack aircraft, a prop plane, transport or helicopter. The people who put that saddle there and maintain it is the enlisted man. The aviator feels that he needs to treat the enlisted men like a human being if they are going to keep that aircraft flying safely. There is a bond of trust between these two groups of men and that bond is worth your life.

A good example is the story of the Marine major who was having a mid-life crisis. He didn't realize it, but because of his situation, he drove his men like slaves and treated them very badly. The major was flying an F8U single-seat attack aircraft. His crew chief is the last and only one to help the pilot into the cockpit, attach all his lines and pull the safety pin on his ejection seat. He shows the pilot the safety pin and the last thing he does is help the pilot adjust his harness and make sure it's tight. Once the canopy is closed, the pilot is responsible for the aircraft.

On this day the major was flying to another air station on a training mission. Upon landing, he parks in the visiting aircraft line. A man attaches a ladder to the plane, the canopy opens and the man assists the pilot out of the cockpit. As the major got out of the aircraft, the enlisted man saw something that made his blood run cold.

"Major," he called.

The pilot turned around to see what he wanted.

"Sir, I think you need to see this."

The pilot wears a harness around his body. His parachute attaches to this harness. When a pilot is leaving the cockpit and plans to return soon he usually leaves the harness in the seat with the parachute attached. What he saw was that the harness was wired to the ejection seat, meaning that if he had ejected, it would have been impossible to open his parachute. He, the parachute and the seat would have gone to the ground together. Thankfully he didn't have to eject, but his crew chief did not fare as well. He was charged with attempted murder and went to prison. The major became a changed man. The moral being, don't bite the hand that feeds you.

Captain Jerry Marvel was a helicopter pilot and a damn good one at that. On his first tour in Nam, he took several hits to his body. After several surgeries he was getting back to normal, but not quite all the way. He was at Lejeune because he was bored and volunteered to help out. The assignment was temporary, but it was important to both he and the Marine Corps.

Charlie Company was called to attention. Captain Marvel said, "At ease and listen up, ladies. Grab a seat on the grass. Can everyone hear me? I have some info to pass on and please hold your questions. Squad leaders, you will be getting some paperwork when we're done and you can answer most of those questions. If you can't, get back to me with the question.

"The week coming up is your last here. Starting at 0600 hours Tuesday through 1700 hours Thursday, you will live in the field and go through a live-fire exercise. This exercise will have opposing forces using blank ammo. Tank, artillery and air cover will be firing live ammo. There will be extensive use of small arms fire. This will be the completion of your training here. The rest of today will be used to complete a wide assortment of paperwork, medical call for shots and a host of things you don't want to know about. One item you need to put some thought into is that you need to pick a next of kin, to be notified in case. You will be given a form will to state who you wish to receive your life insurance, if the need arises.

"Gentleman, quiet down. This is all SOP for going overseas and into combat, I've done it twice, it's no big deal. What doesn't get done today gets done Friday and when you hear what's on tap you won't want to waste time Friday doing paperwork. On Friday, every man who is presently a private is promoted to private first class. Hold it down. Every man who is now a private first class is promoted to lance corporal. For Christ sake will you guys hold it down, I know you're happy, but I've got more.

"Each of you is responsible to get your fatigue emblems and cloth chevrons sewn on your uniforms. This is not an easy task when you have 1,800 men getting promoted, so you will have that chore completed by the time you return from your fifteen-day leave." Captain Marvel could only smile as the men went nuts.

It seemed everyone was yelling and dancing around like a bunch of children. He figured he could not control their jubilation and he didn't even try. It took the squad leaders two or three minutes to get everyone calmed down so he could continue.

"The personnel section is presently working on orders for promotion and leave. If everything goes as planned your leave will commence at 1800 hours on Friday. Because of the large numbers we're working with, we will have personnel to assist you with travel arrangements. Normally it is your job to make travel arrangements, but because of the short notice, we're helping out. I would suggest that those traveling long distances may want to call home and ask for help with the cost of plane tickets. You all know where you're headed and you will only have fifteen days of leave, so time is of the essence.

"Last item on the agenda. There is a list posted on the barracks bulletin board that recommends certain personnel for Officers Candidate School. I have not seen it myself, so don't ask me any questions about it. Read it, if your name is on the list, do whatever it tells you to do. Squad leaders will check the board for copies of today's instructions and to further assist you in helping your squad. You need to know where to be with your squad and at what time. On your feet. Squads, attention. Dismissed."

Radison and Wainwright both being squad leaders went to the board to get their schedule. It was a chaotic situation, so much so that they had to call order to get everyone away from the bulletin board. After the squad leaders got their schedules, they told the squads to go to the board by squads.

After writing out his schedule, Radisson returned to his squad's area and told them to quiet down. "Listen up, people. In exactly ten minutes we need to be at building 3103 for shots we need to ship out. Be outside in five minutes, we march in six."

Soon-to-be Lance Corporal Radison stood in front of his squad counting heads. He had four minutes to get to building 3103 and he didn't intend to be late. He called out, "Squad, attention. Left face." As he turned himself, and called forward march he caught site of the sergeant major watching. When the squad arrived at sick bay, Kennedy was again watching.

Radison's curiosity was aroused and some fear was also present. *Why is he watching us? Did we or I do something wrong? I wish I could ask him.* When the squad finished getting four shots each, they formed up. Just as Radison was going to call the squad to attention, Sergeant Major Kennedy walked towards him. He thought to himself, *Oh shit, here it comes.*

"Lance Corporal Radison," he called out.

"Sergeant Major, can I help you?"

"I just wanted to congratulate you on your selection to OCS."

"Sir? I don't understand."

"Did you see the list on the board?"

"No, sir, I didn't have the time. All I wanted was my squad's time and assignments."

"Well, son, then let me be the first to inform you and your squad. You have been recommended to attend Officers Candidate School."

Radison was numb, he felt he could neither move nor speak. He heard some squad members congratulating him, but he could not comprehend it. Finally he got hold of himself. He smiled and said, "Thank you, Sergeant Major, very much."

"Don't thank me, you earned it yourself. If you make it, be a good Marine first and a good officer second."

Jim Radison stood reading the bulletin board and the Marine Corps order, still not sure why he had been chosen.

"Congratulations." He turned to the voice and replied, "Same to you, Vinny."

Wainwright had a large smile on his face and it infected Radison to break out into one also.

"I guess we should both be proud, seeing that we're the only two in Charlie to make it."

"Yeah, I guess."

"You call home yet?"

"Yes I did, got my wife after chow. Man, is she one happy lady. How about you, get a call in?"

"Yeah, I called my family and my girl. When I got caught in Canada, my girl was with me. We talked about getting married, but never got to it. She asked me today on the phone if we could get married when I got home."

"What did you say?"

"I told her I didn't think it was a very smart idea. I didn't want to get into the Viet Nam shit on the phone, but we ain't going to no picnic. When I get there we'll talk about it. She has to understand that she could become a very young widow."

The World Airways jet lifted from the runway of Marine Corps Station Cherry Point, N.C., and headed out over the ocean. For the first hour of the flight, it was quiet, too quiet. It actually seemed like a funeral procession inside the plane. In fact, something had died, it was not a life; it was a way of life. Charlie Company and Platoon 344 in particular were leaving the only world they had every known. They were intelligent enough to realize the war they were headed to was going to be pure hell. It was anticipated that one third of them would be making the return trip in a body bag. Each man had his own thoughts, but each shared the common thought, *Will I be coming home alive and with all my body part in place?*

Jim Radison was sitting next to Luis Martinez, but he was not paying any attention to him. Instead Radison was just staring out the window of the plane and he had a smile across his face as he relived the past fifteen days. He had returned to his in-laws' home in the western hills of Maryland. His wife Joan and son, Jim Jr., were staying with her family. It was a joyous reunion. He had spent a long weekend with them at Lejeune, but this was the first he had seen his in-laws since he and Joan ran from the draft nearly two years before.

It turned out to be a double surprise when he saw his mother, father, sister and brother there also. He had been making progress with them via the mail, but he hadn't expected to see them so quickly. He relived that awkward moment when he embraced them for the first time in two years. They all cried together.

The two families all sat around talking over a BBQ lunch each asking him question after question about his travels and especially Parris Island. He explained it all as best he could, leaving out many parts that he felt they couldn't handle or understand. He told them of his selection to Officers Candidate School and Joan immediately asked if that meant he would be going to school first. He remembered the color drain from her face when he told her Nam came first. It didn't take but a second before Joan started crying and he was holding her. That all led to his mother crying and his father had to hold on to her. Jim had no experience lying to his wife, but he had to tell her something. "Joan, it's going to be all right, I can feel it. After the year and I'm back home, we can talk it over and decide if I should stay in the Corps or not. The time will pass quickly and before you know it, I'll be home."

He surely didn't feel that way now as he gazed out at the blue sky and white cotton clouds. *What in hell else could I have told her?* The two weeks passed all too quickly, including a lot of "I'm sorry," "I forgive you." Hatchets were buried, but it all wasn't peaches and cream. Many of the town folks where he lived didn't want anything to do with him. He understood they had a right to their viewpoint and he just let it pass. In the blink of an eye the time was gone and he was on his way to hell.

"Hey, man, you been staring out that window a long time, you okay?"

"Yeah, Martinez, I'm okay, just remembering the past fifteen days."

"You had a good time?"

"Sure as hell did. You?"

"No."

"What's that mean?"

"You remember I told you about my gang? They called me a flag-waver. All they do is dope, rob people, rape and steal anything they can. They don't give a shit about nothing but themselves; it was really bad, man. One guy got me so mad I wanted to kill him, but I remember how they play. If I made a move on him, they would all jump me and probably kill me. All I could do was walk away from them. They was all I ever had and I walked away. I mean I got family, but the gang was family too.

"I took a week, saw all my family and headed back to Lejeune early. I turned in my leave papers a week early. They didn't know what to do with me so they said keep my bunk area clean and do whatever I wanted. I spent some time at the beach, did some fishing, but just fucked off all week."

"I'm sorry to hear that, Luis, I really am."

"Well fuck them; I don't need them no more. I got you and Charlie Company, you're my family now."

"You hear anything about Simpson, Rad?"

"All I know is what you do. He never made it back from leave."

"I bet they know and ain't telling us."

"They probably shot him like they did the Mouse and are afraid to tell us. Shit, you and the sergeant major are tight, ask him."

"We'll see what happens if I bump into him."

Another hour passed and Radison finally got up and walked to the head. As he was returning he and the sergeant major made eye contact and Radison thought, *What the hell, I'll ask him.* He approached the sergeant major, but before he could say a word the sergeant major asked, "How was your leave?"

"Real good, Sergeant Major. What about you?"

"Pretty good. It was awfully hard on my two daughters; they haven't seen me go off to war before. My wife did when I left for Korea. It's hard on the family, always was and always will be."

"Sergeant Major, I need to ask you something. The guys are all talking and I'm hearing all sorts of different stories about Simpson. One story even has the MP's shooting him like the Mouse."

The sergeant major felt about the way he looked. He was in an awkward situation. After a minute he said, "What the hell, you're going to hear it soon enough anyway. Simpson killed a guy in a bar fight and the civilian authorities are holding him on a murder charge. The Corps is trying to get more details, but I got the feeling there really isn't much more to the story."

"Is it okay to tell the guys, so we can end the bullshit stories?"

"Yeah, why not. I'll say I had to tell you to end the speculation."

"Thanks, Sergeant Major, I appreciate it."

The big jet touched down at DaNang Air Base as every man that could pressed his face against a window. What little they could see was unbelievable. It seemed like every type of airplane and helicopter ever made was at DaNang. What they couldn't see was hundreds of planes scattered around the air base, because every day the VC would lob mortar shells into the air base. That became very obvious as the local work gangs were filling in craters as far as the eye could see. Once the aircraft came to a stop, it took several minutes for the drive-up ramp to be brought to the plane and the doors opened. It had quickly warmed up inside the plane, but once the doors were opened the oppressive heat and humidity overpowered everyone.

As Charlie Company began off-loading, Martinez looked back at Radison, sweat forming on his brow. He looked directly into Radison's eyes and said, "I guess we landed right in the middle of hell, Jim boy." Radison, too nervous to speak, just shook his head.

Walking down the ramp Radison noticed the hustle and bustle of a huge airport. It reminded him of Kennedy Airport in New York. He had once seen his parents off on a trip and it looked just like Kennedy, except for all the olive-drab color on everything and everywhere. Planes were talking off, landing, taxing, being pulled and being pushed. People were everywhere, both military and civilian. He wondered how they knew who the civilians were.

Within an hour, Charlie Company was inside a series of Quonset huts. There were overhead fans turning, but the heat was intense. In a short time a second lieutenant, who looked about eighteen, walked into the hut. Someone called them to attention. As a newly minted second lieutenant, he smiled and said, "At ease. I am Lieutenant William Brown and if you are as smart as I'm told you are you'll notice you are forty men to a hut. You are a platoon of Charlie Company and another platoon is right next door. In fact, you are both Platoon 334 from Parris Island. It was designed this way, keeping you all together.

"I am your platoon leader and the sergeant standing next to me is Staff

Sergeant John Ogden, the assistant platoon leader. We have you set up into three squads of thirteen men. The one odd man will be a replacement if and when needed. The three squad leaders are Radison, Wainwright and Cox, all lance corporals.

"Don't unpack anything; you'll be leaving here tonight. You're going to fly to the ancient city of Hue, pronounced 'Way.' From Hue we will be transported east to a location to be named. We will be joining a regiment that is interdicting supply lines coming in from Laos. We leave after evening chow and fly to Hue, via C130. We can't go right now because the VC shoots down too many planes in the daylight, hence the night flight.

"For now stretch out those legs, but stay within one hundred yards of the hut. Look around and learn where the bomb shelters are, you're going to need them sooner than you can imagine. At any time of the day or night the VC will deliver their daily correspondence in the way of mortars. Their fire is usually very effective because of the sappers they employ inside our fence. If you should see a native worker who seems to be pacing off yardage, grab his ass and hold him, he's probably working for the VC.

"After noon chow you'll be getting an indoctrination talk about the country, its people, customs and a whole bunch of things you don't need know, but have to listen to. Pay close attention to the part about the customs of the people and the VD lecture, both are important to you. After evening chow, we'll saddle up at 1800 and by 2100 we should be on the ground in Hue. That's all I have for you now but Sergeant Ogden will speak with you and get your squads organized."

Lieutenant Brown left the hut and Ogden called the squad leaders to him. He motioned for them to follow him outside the hut. They found a shady spot behind the hut and sat. Ogden produced four slightly chilled beers. "Welcome to Viet Nam."

As they sipped the beer, Ogden eyeballed the three squad leaders. He put his beer aside and said, "Look, I don't know any of you, but from what the sergeant major tells me you are capable leaders. He told me Radison and Wainwright were picked for OCS, so you must have something on the ball.

"I realize you're all new to the Marine Corps, but you have been schooled enough about the chain of command to know that Lieutenant Brown gives me orders, I pass them on to you and you pass them on to your squad. You handle your squad and if there's something you can't handle, you call me. From day one at Parris Island, some sergeant screamed at you and you should have obeyed instantly. This is truly the place to do that.

"If you hear a command shouted at you, obey it fast and ask questions later. I have been in combat and I know things and sense things you can't imagine. The jungles are loaded with trip wires, attached to the deadliest things man has ever invented. 'Freeze' is a word we will be using daily. You and the squad need to learn that freeze means just that, you don't move a single muscle. Disregard it and you will die. Pound that into your people, it's a number one priority here. We will talk a lot more, but for now that's it, any questions?"

Radison asked, "Can we pick the members of our squad?"

"Why not, you know them better than I do." Ogden took a matchbook out, turned his back and took three matches from it. He turned to the three squad leaders and extended his hand towards them. "Longest picks first, shortest last."

Radison's luck was good; he got to pick first. As Sergeant Ogden walked away, Radison began mulling over his picks. He knew he wanted Martinez, Romero, Gallo, Ketchum and Palmer. They were the beginning of the new first squad of Charlie Company.

At 1800 hours Charlie Company marched to the parking area of the field and stopped near a C130 transport. It was getting dark, but there was enough light to see what each man didn't want to see. Standing to the side of the aircraft it was impossible to miss the forty or so patches to the skin of the plane. Each patch was not larger than three inches square. It was very obvious that each of those patches represented a bullet hole.

Standing at rest it didn't take Martinez long to ask, "Hey, Sarge," looking towards Ogden, "are they bullet holes?"

"Yep." Ogden turned to his charges and said, "Listen up. These birds take a lot of ground fire when they land. Takeoff is easy, but landing is a different story. It's a lot slower and steady and it makes it a good target. They try for hot landings, but many times they can't due to the terrain. Hue is a hot LZ so when I tell you to place your helmets and sit on them, do it. We take a lot of belly hits and the helmet could save your family jewels."

The looks between the men were obvious. The realization that danger was just around the corner hit everyone hard.

The flight to Hue was bumpy, cool and lacked any excitement. If any shots were fired at the plane, nobody knew it. It was also obvious to Lieutenant Brown and Sergeant Ogden that the men were scared. There was no talking among them and chalk-white faces were very apparent. Once out of the plane, the platoon was hurried to waiting six-bys and loaded up quickly. As the trucks began to roll, mortars began to fall nearby. The trucks zigzagged as they left the landing site as fast as they could.

Radison had observed that when they landed and unloaded, the plane keep its engines running. He wondered about it at the time and now he understood why as the plane roared into the sky and disappeared into the night sky. As he returned to the present, Radison looked right into the eyes of Romero. He looked calm, yet he had a wild and excited look in his eyes.

"Luis, you okay?"

"Yeah, yeah, man, I'm okay. It didn't take long for the bastards to welcome us did it? You scared, Jim?"

"Yes, Luis, very scared."

"Jim, did you see them bags lined up on the side of the plane?"

"No, what are you talking about?"

"I saw forty or fifty bags lined up near that plane we came in on. I think maybe they were body bags."

"I don't know, Luis, I didn't see them."

Radison knew Luis was probably right, but he didn't want to further excite him by admitting he was probably right.

"You know what, Jim. For the first time I'm thinking this was a mistake coming here. We ain't been in this country ten minutes and those fuckers are trying to kill us."

"Luis, cool it, just what the hell did you expect, a party? This is what war is about, killing each other. The last one standing is the winner."

"Shit, two years in jail may be a better deal; at least nobody would try to kill me."

Radison smiled. "Luis, I wouldn't bet on that. You know guys who did time, they get knifed all the time and you know it."

After a thirty-minute ride, the trucks stopped and then proceeded past a sentry and stopped again. Everyone got off and lined up for a head count. In the distance Radison saw the sergeant major talking to a captain. Shortly the word was passed they would be staying the night. "Don't unpack any gear, we stay just one night."

The following morning after a hot breakfast of shit-on-a-shingle, toast and coffee, the squads reloaded on the trucks and went off in convoy-style heading east. A voice asked, "Anyone know where we're going?"

Radison answered, "Everyone on the truck has the same question."

Martinez always looked to Radison to answer his questions. He knew Radison was smart and now he had an in with the sergeant major. *Well, he will probably get pissed at me,* he thought, *but fuck it.* "Hey, Radison," he called, "did the sergeant major tell you where we're going?"

"Yes, he did." Now the entire squad was staring at him. "He said we're going to a replacement center for further assignment."

Some asked, "What's a replacement center?"

Radison thought for a second and said, "The easiest way I can think of to explain it is that it's like a warehouse filled with parts. When a part is needed, they ship it out to whoever requested it. We are those parts now."

Martinez was staring at Radison again. Radison saw it, but decided to wait for him to ask. Finally Martinez blurted out, "You mean when some outfit gets a shit load of guys killed, we go and replace them."

"Yes, that's about right."

The entire squad was silent.

Two hours and twenty minutes later the trucks stopped and everyone got off. After riding a six-by for two and a half hours through hot sun, humidity and drenching rain, it was good to get on firm ground and stretch. Everyone was soaking wet from the rain and sweat and were told to get used to it, it would be the same every day.

The replacement center looked like something right out of an old cowboy movie; lots of wooden buildings and a series of planks on the ground leading from one building to the next, like a boardwalk. Behind the buildings were an array of tents and something that looked like a half-building half-tent. Men were walking around in all sorts of dress, including many naked from the waist up.

Charlie Company was assigned to an area of the tent-wood structures someone called a hooch. Word was passed down to get organized, stow all gear and standby. Sergeant Ogden showed up some ninety minutes later and called the squad to him.

"Here's the skinny for now. We'll probably be here at least a week getting weapons and doing some training with them. We need to get comfortable in our new home. We'll have some lecture-type talks on weather, local animals and snakes, and the local population. That's all I have for now.

"Squad leaders, you better start to check each man's gear in your squad. Anything metal will be checked frequently; in this climate it will rust overnight. Once you get your weapon, you better clean them daily, or when you need it most, it could fail because of rust and neglect. One last thing, you can write home, but you can't mention where you are except Nam, period. No details. Your mail will be censored so don't try anything stupid. You will be given a return address to use, but get used to the idea that you may not get mail for weeks at a time. It takes time to catch up with you when you're moving around. Welcome to sunny Viet Nam."

Chapter 17

Jim Radison looked up and saw it was still raining. "Shit, does it ever stop?" It was more a statement then a question. Nobody answered his question. His three bunk mates were doing their own thing, writing a letter, reading a book and sleeping. He looked again to his weapon, checking for rust and applying a light coat of oil. As he reassembled the rifle Sergeant Ogden opened the flap of the hooch and entered.

"Hey, Sarge, what's up?"

Ogden entered, his hand extended holding a beer. "Want one?"

"Yeah, but I wish it were cold."

"Keep wishing, Radison, one day it will be."

"Sarge, I been thinking. If I got some good waterproof material and kept my rifle covered would it keep the moisture out?"

"It might, but when the shit hits the fan and you need it, it's going to take time to unwrap it and you don't have much time. Do like we all do, keep it clean, but keep it close. Everything going okay with the squad?"

"Yeah, but we're all getting kind of antsy. We all feel the same; we need to see action and how we react to it. None of us have ever shot at a human before nor have we been shot at. What's it like?"

"The part where you shoot isn't hard. After you do it once you won't think about it again, it will come naturally. The part where you get shot at ain't so nice. My first time, I shit myself."

"You're kidding, right?"

"No, I'm not. I was so scared I didn't even know it until after the fight. I wasn't the only one or the last. People react differently to it. I've seen men cry, shit themselves, scream, and run. You name it, I've seen it. Very few men react calmly to being shot at, damn few. After a few times the fear won't be as bad, but it never leaves you, there's always some degree of fear. But that's not bad because fear keeps you alive. Those who have no fear usually die quickly."

Jim was silent for a time, thinking about what was said. He said out loud, "I wonder how I'll react. I hope I don't make a fool of myself.

"I have a question. When we learned to shoot at P.I. and Lejeune, they taught us that combat dope was 200 yards. Here they had us zero-in at one hundred yards."

"Good question, but it should have been already answered. Were you asleep?"

"I don't think so; the whole squad asked me the same question, that's why I'm asking you."

"I'll look into why you weren't informed, but for you and your squad the answer is simple. Most of the shooting will be in the jungle. Hell, most of it will be less than twenty-five yards. The bastards pop out of the ground when you pass them. The minimum dope for a Garand is one hundred yards, that's why that number is used. Anything else?"

"What about us going out on a patrol? Any idea when we can start to fight?"

"No. I been asking the lieutenant the same question and he's been asking his boss, but we don't get an answer. Anything else?"

"No, Sarge, thanks."

Dear Joan,

First I need to tell you how much I miss you and Jimmy. I truly love you both so much it hurts. The distance between us only makes it worse. Tell Jimmy that I have been working on some things for him. I already have a VC flag and I'm working on a helmet. I'll send them home to him.

We have been in-country for thirty-one days now and have not fired a shot at the enemy. We got our rifles and do a lot of training with them, to zero-in, etc, but all we do is carry them around and keep them clean. We had a week of lectures on the country, its people, snakes, weather and what ever else you can think of. In the last ten days we have actually gone out on a couple of missions. That means we guarded a convoy of ammo trucks up to the front lines and hauled back wounded. One man did fire a shot, at a snake. I guess this is good news to you, but it doesn't sit well with us. We have spent a lot of time in the last six months training and we want to do our share. We're all hoping it comes soon.

I can't say much about the country because I haven't seen much of it. It rains day and night, it's humid and not a very nice place to be. I guess if you never knew anything different it's okay. I'm not anywhere near the sea so I can't talk with the fishermen. I was hoping I could talk with them and see how they fish, for what and compare it with what we do at home.

It's getting dark and we can't have any lights on at night so I'll close for today. Will write again in a day or two.

My love to you both. Jim.

"Can I help you, Sergeant Major?"

"Yes, you can. I'd like to see Col. McCaffrey if I can."

"Your name and outfit?"

"Kennedy, I'm the liaison for the Marine Corps specials, as they are fondly called by the regulars."

"Okay, Sergeant Major, give me a minute."

Kennedy sat and began observing the setting of the regiment's HQ. It was like any other office you'd see in the military. Junior enlisted men typing, answering phones and looking busy. A few officers wandering around trying to look busy. *Christ, I could never work in an office, it's bad enough the time I have to spend in one now.*

"Sergeant Major, the colonel will see you."

Kennedy followed the lance corporal clerk to the office of Colonel James McCaffrey. He was actually a lieutenant colonel, but they all liked to be called colonel. He was a rather younger man about forty-five years old with a pleasant smile. He was in camo fatigues like everyone else. McCaffrey stood and extended his hand to shake. "Sergeant Major, I apologize for not seeing you sooner but I've been down in Saigon for the past ten days and I'm trying to get caught up."

"No sweat, Colonel, I'll try not to take up too much of your time."

"I have to admit, Sergeant Major, that I haven't had the time to go over records of your men, but then I really don't need to do it, do I? I have seen your service record and it's quite impressive. Several of my officers here have either served with you or know of you. I welcome you to our little part of Viet Nam."

"Thanks very much, sir. I hope I and the four companies can help you out."

"Well, with the pleasantries out of the way, what can I do for you, Sergeant Major? Something specific on your mind?"

"Yes, sir, there is. My kids have been here for five weeks and haven't fired a shot at the enemy. We're all wondering when we will see action."

Col. McCaffrey stood and walked to a coffee pot sitting on a table. "Like a cup?"

"No, sir, thank you."

He poured some for himself and sipped it as he looked directly at the sergeant major. He knew he couldn't bullshit him so he decided on the direct approach. He sat down, put the cup on his desk and said, "No bullshit, we speak the truth to each other."

Kennedy replied, "I don't work any other way, sir."

"Good. The regiment doesn't trust your men and are afraid to let them anywhere near the front. In order for me to keep the peace I have to keep your people away from the fighting or I'll have a rebellion on my hands."

Kennedy was pissed, but he knew he had to keep his cool. He took his time and tried to think clearly about his options. "Colonel, this isn't the first opposition to these men, we've seen it before. After being informed that they will be part of the Marine Corps there were no further discussion, it's been okay. Up to now everyone who has come into contact with them has nothing but good things to say."

"I'm glad to hear all that, but I've got a whole regiment that's totally against the idea."

"Sir, are you against the idea also?"

"I don't favor it. I have spoken with my officer corps and they are against it. They tell me the enlisted men are against it. So where do we go from here?"

"Well, Colonel, I'm hoping our little talk would convince you to change your mind about all this. All it takes is for you to order them into combat and it's done. Let them prove themselves."

"Sergeant Major, let me think on our talk and see what my staff thinks."

"That's all I can ask for, sir." As Kennedy walked out of the regimental offices his head was spinning. *I could have or should have expected this, but I didn't. Problem is, I'm too close to this group. How would I feel if I was one of the present group and had no contact with them? Would I too be afraid to fight with them? All I can do now is wait and see what the colonel does next. I still have my two trump cards left, but I'd hate to use them unless I have to.*

"PFC Perkins reporting as ordered."

Sergeant Major Kennedy looked up and tried to get a feel for the Marine standing before him. Perkins was a six-footer with blond hair with a tinge of red and a face full of freckles. *Obviously a West-coaster,* thought Kennedy. The problem Kennedy knew was Perkins' aversion to the Marine Corps way of life.

"At ease, Perkins." Kennedy gave some thought about just what he wanted to say, but just couldn't get a feel for Perkins at the moment. The man was here because he couldn't fit in with the rest of his unit and was constantly gambling. He needed to know more about this man, so he asked, "It appears you're not happy, and can you tell me why?"

Perkins broke out into a broad smile. "Sergeant Major, are you kidding me? I didn't ask for this. From the day when I was arrested, right up to this minute, I have been pushed into everything the Marine Corps wants, not once what I want. I admit I ran from the draft and I would do it again. Right now I'm trying to figure out a way to survive all this and get back home alive and with all my parts."

"Perkins, we want the same thing for you, but you don't want to do what you're obliged to do first? You owe your country two years and you're not going anywhere until those two years are up. In the meantime, I need to know what's with all your gambling."

"Sergeant Major, I like to gamble and I'm good at it. Actually the Marine Corps got me started at it and all I'm doing is following up on it."

"That you need to explain to me, Perkins."

"Well, I'm a distinguished expert with the rifle. In Parris Island the DI's would get together and put rifle matches on between recruits. They bet on their man and my DI's won a nice piece of change. They even had me shoot against an instructor."

"Did you win?"

"Yes, sir, I sure did. Our DI's never told us how much they won, but we were told they bet big on our Final Field. Once we got to Lejeune and had some free time, a card game would start up and I got in and did rather well. Since I got here, we play a couple of times a week if we can."

"What about you bragging about putting a mouthful of water in the bore of your squad leader's rifle?"

"I guess someone has a very big mouth if you heard about it."

"It's your big mouth that's responsible for me hearing it. Tell me about it, please."

"My squad leader in P.I. was a real ball-buster, especially towards me. He loved the power he had over the squad. He kept pissing me off and there was nothing I could do about it. One night I was on fire watch and I stopped to get a drink of water and got the idea. I took a mouthful of water and spit it down the bore of his rifle. When we fell out the next morning for inspection, the DI saw rust all over his rifle and went crazy. He lost his squad leader position and I loved it."

Sergeant Major Kennedy was really steaming, but kept his demeanor. He raised the tone of his voice some and said, "Tell me about your famous apple verse."

Perkins seemed quite upset at the question and squirmed and shifted from one foot to the other. "Well...well, it's just something I thought was funny at the time."

"Well make me laugh, tell me about it."

Perkins did not answer.

"Perkins, I am not asking anymore, I'm ordering you."

"My expression is eat the apple and fuck the Corps."

"My advice to you is this. You better learn how to adapt to your unit and this Marine Corps. You have a year here and nearly another year back home. You better learn how to blend in and you better learn real fast."

"Sergeant Major, I will try, but you have to understand, I am what I am and you are what you are."

"Private Perkins, I have spent nearly twenty years in the Corps and I can guess you can only imagine how much I love it. I can think of a lot of things I'd like to do to you, but I can't lower myself to your level. This much I will tell you, you will never ever have the chance to get any profits home. You will not ever again trade with the local citizens for anything, that is a direct order. I will be ordering every NCO in the outfit to keep a very close eye on you and the minute you step out of line, I'll be all over you like stink on shit, you hear me?"

"Yes, sir."

"Before you are dismissed, I'd like to give you two pieces of verse that I think apply to you. 'Don't bite the hand that feeds you; and he who laughs last, laughs loudest.' Now get out of my sight."

"Sergeant Major, what's on your mind today?"

"Well, sir, it's been three weeks since we last talked and still nothing has been changed. My men still escort ammo convoys and bring wounded back.

When the 1,800-man force was divided, 900 were designated for combat and the other 900 for non-combatant backup. Why can't the combat-trained men do just that and the other 900 do the convoy work? My guys are ready to fight, but they need to be given the opportunity."

"Sergeant Major, just what do you want me to do? I told you I have a regiment that opposes what you want and I'm having problems changing their minds."

"Colonel, all you have to do is order them into combat; you are the CO."

"Goddamn it, who do you think you're talking to? I am a colonel and you're a sergeant major and an enlisted man. You take the orders I give, like it or not."

McCaffery was clearly pissed. He reached for and lit a cigarette hoping to calm himself. He felt he had every right to be mad, nobody under his command had the right to question his authority, but he knew he had to be careful here. Even though Kennedy was an enlisted man, he was the highest ranking enlisted man in the Corps, plus being respected and well liked.

"Sergeant Major, I'm trying to fight a war on a regimental level. I also take orders. Why are you so dead set on seeing these men go into combat? Most would hope to avoid it."

"Colonel, these boys got off on the wrong foot. They were young and dumb and made a bad decision. We have all made bad decisions in our lives. Do these boys have to go to their graves without having the opportunity to redeem themselves? I have been with this group from day one at Parris Island, and I'm here to tell you that they are no different than any other Marine I have ever served with. I would lead them into combat myself if I hadn't been ordered to stay behind the lines. Please, sir, give them the chance to prove to the Marine Corps and themselves that they are no different."

"I read in your service record about this order that you stay out of combat. What's the story with that? I really didn't think much of it at the time, but you just mentioned it and now I'm curious."

"Well, sir, in conversation with the commandant and the president, they both made me promise not to go into the fight and I will keep that promise."

Colonel McCaffrey was a little overwhelmed with what he heard, but kept his composure. He finally got hold of his thoughts and asked, "Just what is your connection to these two very influential men, may I ask?"

"Both have had very close contact with this group from the very beginning. Both visited Parris Island and Camp Lejeune on several occasions to follow the group's progress."

"What you're saying is that you have the ear of the commandant of the Marine Corps and the president of the United States, are you not?"

"Yes, sir, that's true."

McCaffrey reached for the pack and lit another cigarette. He stared at Kennedy for several seconds trying to figure out if Kennedy was bullshitting him or not. *I wonder if this man is trying to bluff me. Let's just find out.*

"Sergeant Major, I get the distinct feeling that if I don't order your men into combat that you would use your influence in Washington to overrule me, is that a correct assumption?"

"Sir, I wouldn't use the word 'overrule,' I would ask the commandant and/ or the president to express to you their wishes to see these men fight. All I am doing here right now is telling you what I have been told by both of these men."

"And how do I know if this is all factual?"

"Colonel, all you have to do is pick up that phone, ask to be connected to the commandant and if he's not available, the White House and I'll show you."

Jesus H. Christ, he isn't bluffing one bit. After a few puffs on his cigarette he said, "Sergeant Major, give me a day or two to work on this, okay?"

"A day or two is just fine, sir."

Kennedy walked out of the office trying to keep a straight face. He knew he had won.

Charlie Company was tasked once again to escort an ammo convoy towards the village of Lo Bein, nearer the border. Radison was briefing his squad when Sergeant Ogden approached.

"Remind them of the info that was passed on reference to the civilians."

"No sweat, Sarge, just about to do it."

"Okay, First Squad, listen up. We've done this before; you all know the routine. The new wrinkle is that a couple of attacks have taken place south of here by civilians; men, women and children. Word is they walk the sides of the road and as the trucks pass they throw a grenade into one. What we plan is that when civilians are observed, unlock your weapons and be really alert to them possibly throwing a grenade. If they get it done we'll probably all be dead. Blow up a truck loaded with ammo and the explosion will kill them and us.

"If you don't feel you have the balls to kill a kid, then now is the time to speak up. If just one guy freezes we all could get it. If we run into civilians, this will be the drill. The truck driver, jeep driver, machine gunner and assistant will stay at their positions and we all dismount. Six of you walk one side and six the other side. We walk until the trucks pass the civilians. Any questions? Oh yeah, I forgot one thing. Sergeant Ogden and an ordinance guy will be in a lead jeep in front of the convoy. They will give us a heads up the minute they spot any civilians on the road. If he calls, we dismount and do our thing."

Riding in the back of a six-by loaded with a lot of ammo is not much fun or comfortable. It is better than walking in the rain, mud and humidity of the jungle. Because of the mud and fear of attacks, the trucks can only roll about fifteen miles per hour. In the first hour the squad dismounted four times because of civilians present on or near the road and each time the convoy proceeded without a hitch.

As the truck plodded along Radison sat staring at the canvas cover of the truck. It was stretched over metal rods that held it in place and the whole thing was half-round. He kept thinking a grenade couldn't stay on the top without rolling off. It would still cause a lot of damage when it exploded. The best place to ensure complete destruction of the truck, the cargo and the men was to heave it into the open rear of the truck. He reached for his radio and depressed the key.

"Blue leader, this is Blue three, do you read?"

"Blue leader, go"

"Blue leader, request a stop, need to talk."

"Blue leader, wilco."

The convoy came to a stop and Radison jumped out and walked to meet Ogden. When he reached Ogden he explained how he felt and said, "I'd like to leave one man in the truck to act as a catcher. When we're out walking because of civilians, the catcher is super alert. If a grenade were thrown into the truck, there's a good chance he could throw it out."

Ogden thought and said, "Okay, do it. Just remember it reduces our manpower outside the trucks by one, you realize that?"

"Yes, but with eleven men with automatics I think that's enough firepower don't you?"

"Yeah, I do, let's do it."

The convoy was getting close to the front lines. Artillery could be heard booming in the distance and every so often small arms fire. Sergeant Ogden called and reported three civilians ahead; an older man and two children, both girls, maybe ten and fifteen years old. "I don't like the looks of this one so be alert. It's too close to the front for these people to be near the road and so calm." First Squad leaped out and took their walking positions as planned. The walkers quickly saw the civilians. The man seemed to be maybe sixty, but with Asians it was hard to tell age. The two girls did look ten and fifteen and each carried a palm basket on their back.

The tension was overbearing and Radison could feel sweat trickling down his back. He wiped his brow several times to keep sweat out of his eyes. The first and second trucks crept past the civilians without any problem. As the first squad's truck passed the civilians, the girls dropped their baskets and in the blink of an eye, cocked their arms. Radison was on them in heartbeat and without thinking one bit, cut them down with a long burst of his automatic weapon. A second or so later two explosions rocked the area, but mainly where the three civilians had been standing. Apparently when the girls were hit by the gunfire, they dropped the grenades and it literally blew them apart.

It took Radison some thirty seconds to bring himself back to the situation at hand. For that thirty seconds he was just numb and his mind a complete blank. Once he cleared his mind, he leapt into action. Several squad members were already checking the bodies, what was left of them, and the rest were in positions to fend off further attack. When Sergeant Ogden got to the scene, he told them it was all over and felt sure nothing more would occur. "Great job, you guys, it went according to plan."

The squad mounted up and traveled on, with at least two men quietly asking if he did his job and just killed for the first time. Radison had no doubt what he had done. He knew he had fired first and that his aim was true. He knew that he was at least partly responsible for killing three people and two were young girls. He was starting to agonize when he suddenly realized those young girls were trying to kill him and his squad. That thought eased his pain.

After the ammo was off-loaded they all took a break. The wounded were not quite ready for the trip back, so the squad just sat on the ground near the trucks. Radison observed that nobody ate anything, nobody drank anything and nobody was talking. He gazed towards Romero and Martinez, both usually talkative and both as quiet as the rest. He felt he had to say something, but didn't know what. Remembering his role as squad leader he finally asked, "Is everyone okay?"

Everyone said yes or nodded so. Radison felt it best to let it go for now. That night he would seek out who fired and how they handled it.

Before the return trip started up Radison asked each man if he had expended any ammo and found that only he and Romero had fired. Gallo said he had fired one round, but it was totally out of fear.

"Hell, Gallo, we all shot out of fear. I had to check my underwear to make sure I didn't shit myself." Gallo knew Radison was only easing his embarrassment and thanked for him for it.

On the drive back Jim had a lot of time to reflect on the shooting incident. Romero had said he was standing at the rear of truck number two and had a perfect view of the three civilians. He, like Radison, had fired full auto at the three people and felt that he had cut them down himself. Radison felt the same way yet the bodies were too mangled to tell how many times they had been shot.

After the wounded were off-loaded the first squad returned to its hooch. Sergeant Ogden arrived and called the squad to him. "Is everyone okay? Any problems?"

No response.

"Remember if you need any help just ask, you're not the first in this kind of situation." Ogden nodded to Radison to follow him and they walked away. "Fill me in on the whole incident."

Radison did so, saying he felt and only he and Romero were shooters.

"Are you both okay with it?" he asked.

"Yeah, sure. We both needed some time to get over the initial shock of it, but we both agree that they wanted to kill us. I really don't see any problems from either of us."

"Okay. I've got to get going, but remember and the same goes for both of you; if you need help, all you have to do is ask, it's not all that unusual. I have to see the lieutenant, sergeant major and God knows who else and fill out an after action report."

With a lot of free time on its hands, the squad had constructed a camping area so to speak. It consisted of a decent bunker for each man, a fire pit and hammocks for each man to relax in. When Jim returned to the camp area he found the whole squad crapped out in their hammocks. A very small fire burned in the pit, no flame but enough heat to create smoke to keep the bugs away.

As it neared dark, one by one the squad hit the sack, leaving only Radison and Romero. "Juan, you really okay?"

"Yeah, man, I'm cool. Did I tell you I shot a guy when I was in the gang? It was only a .22, but I hit him in the leg. I was a big man in the gang after that.

What happened today was a lot different. I hit them with a lot of lead. I never seen bodies like that before, they were really fucked up."

"You feel bad about it?"

"No, I don't think so. Those motherfuckers were trying to kill us if we didn't get them first. I guess that's the law of the jungle, you kill first or get killed. How about you, Rad, this your first time?"

"Yeah. After we stopped firing, I must have stood there for a full minute frozen in fear. I was numb. When I finally got my ass in gear, I was back to being okay. I really felt bad at first knowing I killed two girls. But the more I thought about it, the better I felt. If one of those girls had tossed a grenade into the truck, we'd all be dead now."

From behind them came a voice saying, "You're damned right you'd be dead." Both men jumped to their feet as they recognized the sergeant major. "Relax, guys; you don't need to get up."

Romero said, "I need to hit the sack, unless you need me?"

"No, kid, go sleep well."

Kennedy looked at Radison and asked, "How you doing, son?"

"Pretty good, I guess. Once I got over the shock of it all I realized I did what I had to do to survive. I do feel something about those kids, but I can't place what it is."

"Son, it's the culture. The Asian doesn't look at life like we do; they don't value life as we do. In Korea they sent wave after wave to be slaughtered. If we killed off 100,000, they had plenty of replacements and it's 100,000 they don't have to feed anymore. You're going to see a lot worse before this is all over. What about Romero, is he all right with it?"

"Yes, sir, he's fine. We were just talking about it when you came, but I believe he and I both are fine."

"Well, listen to some advice from one who's been there before. You're going to dream about those two girls for the rest of your life. It's part of the process, nobody escapes it. Another thing, keep it here. Don't write to anyone in your family about killing, they just wouldn't understand it."

Kennedy stood and said, "I don't say this with any humor in mind, but go hit the sack and have your nightmares, you'll have more. I have a feeling that in the next couple of days you're going to the front lines to be real Marines. Good night."

"Sergeant Major Kennedy reporting as ordered, sir."

"Good morning, Sergeant Major, nice to see you. Coffee?"

"Yes, thank you, sir."

After fixing the coffee, Colonel McCaffrey sat down. "I've just finished reading the after action reports on your people's convoy duty yesterday. When I match up the reports from your people and ordinance man and the truck driver they all add up to a good job. The ordnance man and transportation driver said your people fought as well as any other Marines and were grateful as hell."

"Thank you, Colonel, that's what I've been trying to tell you."

"Yes, that's true, you have. Well, you have your wish. My staff is cutting the orders right now. Your four companies will be moving forward into the thick of it. They will replace or integrate with the line forces there now. I imagine it shouldn't take but another day or two to work it all out."

"Thank you, sir. Am I free to inform them?"

"Yes, you can."

"Anything else, sir?"

"No, Sergeant Major, that's all. I hope you'll remember that we all have major decisions to make and most are made with the majority in mind. Sometimes we don't get what we want and have to live with it."

"Yes, sir, I will remember that." As he left the regimental office Kennedy couldn't contain his smirk. He was happy for his troops. *I do wonder though, was it the action of yesterday or the threat of having to speak with the commandant or president that changed his mind? I'll probably never know.*

"Okay, listen up." Sergeant Ogden sat down next to a hooch counting heads. First Squad Charlie Company were all present. "We are leaving this resort tomorrow at approximately 1000 hrs. Able will leave at 0600, Baker at 0800 and if all goes as planned, we depart at 1000 on foot." Several "shits" were heard and Ogden just stared in their direction.

"You're Marines and an eleven-mile hike is nothing out of the ordinary. The bad part is that you will have a full field pack and all the ammo you can carry." Many "shits" were now heard and Ogden was about to lose his temper. "Will you kindly shut up, this ain't no picnic we're going to. Every goddamn round we can carry may save your ass or mine, so keep quiet and listen. Your field-pack better have everything it's supposed to and will weigh in around sixty pounds. Because of that, a six-by will accompany us and carry the extra ammo. There's only one road to where we're going, the same one we did the convoy duty on. We need to be super alert to civilians, as we already know.

"The base camp we're going to is just that, a base-type encampment where our four companies will bivouac. We will be going out in company-strength on patrols to interdict supply lines that the VC uses. They are sending in supplies from Laos via the Ho Chi Minh Trail.

"We will be updating our weapons because we know how well they work in the jungle. Aside from the BAR, one man will carry a SAW, squad automatic weapon. This is a new 50-cal-type auto that will enhance our firepower. Two shotguns will also be added to our inventory. What I need is for someone to take over the BAR as he is going to take the SAW. I also need two men who have had experience with shotguns to take them. Those men see me after we break, we fall out of 0930, full pack, weapons locked and loaded. Questions? Good, you know too much already. Oh I nearly forgot. Delta Company will be behind us by two hours, keep that in mind."

The march to the base camp started out just a few minutes late. Able and Baker reported that all was going well, except for the rain and mud. Charlie was to find the conditions no different, actually worse because the trucks mucked up the road. Sergeant Ogden kept roaming from squad to squad reminding them to keep their rifle barrels pointed down to keep the water out of the barrel. He also told them to keep them under their ponchos as much as possible. The first hour of the march proved to be more of an emotional strain than physical. The constant vigilance wore at them and the fear, mud and sweat only added to the discomfort. Radison's squad was no different, they were all jumpy and he did his best to keep them calmed.

At the first break, Romero made it clear he wanted to chat with Radison. They moved away from the squad, but still within visual range.

"What's up, Juan?"

"Listen, bro, I figured you needed to hear the scuttlebutt I'm hearing. Palmer been talking to another guy that he's thinking of giving up."

"You mean this march?"

"No man, to the VC."

"You're shitting me."

"No man, I'm not. The guy he told says he's been going along with all this so he could surrender to the VC. He figures they will make him a hero and do some radio and TV so he can tell the world what a bunch of baby killers we are."

"Okay, I'm glad you told me. I need some time to work this out."

The company marched on with nothing out of the ordinary happening. No doubt the rain and mud was as much of a pain in the ass to the civilians as it was to the Marines. When the first squad got to the spot where they had killed the three civilians, both Radison and Romero slowed up noticeably. It seemed like both were reliving it all over again. Sergeant Ogden was also aware of the location and was within sight of the first squad just in case. In no time the squad passed the spot and life went on.

After five hours of marching, Charlie Company came to the base camp. A few minutes after arriving, Lieutenant Brown and Sergeant Ogden showed up and gathered the squads together. They were told that the four companies they were relieving were going to stick around for another three days to get everyone acclimated to the area. Each squad would be assigned to a resident squad who would be their teachers. Those three days proved to be a best learning experience of all the training at P.I. and Lejeune put together. The mission was simple, but deadly. The task was to find the incoming trail that was going to be hopefully used, set up an ambush and execute it. The hazards were many, including the terrain, rain, heat, snakes and the fact that the VC was fighting in their own backyard.

They had years of experience and years to build an underground network of tunnels unequaled to anything in the world. Whole villages existed underground and each village housed hundreds of VC waiting to kill you. The newcomers were shown every type of device the VC used to cause death. The types of trip wires and punji sticks were countless in design and effectiveness. Every man had it pounded into his head that he needed to be one hundred percent aware of the booby traps because every day someone was tripping one.

Everyone was shown the base camp's defenses. Claymore mines were scattered completely around the base camp. There were paths to get around them and the newbies were shown where they were. Along with the claymores were large fields of land mines. After three full days the resident Marines were ready to depart. They had schooled the replacements as best they could. They only other thing they could have shown them was an actual ambush. The forward spotters, well behind the VC lines had reported no movement, so no actual ambush training could be affected.

As the departing troops were mounting up to leave, Radison approached his counterpart, a Corporal Bob Welker. "Bob, we can't say enough about your education ability. We sure owe you. Can I ask you a personal question?"

"Why not."

"You know who we are and our background?"

"Yes, I know."

"In the three days we've been together neither you nor your guys have ever mentioned it, why? We were expecting to take a whole lot of shit, but it just never happened and I'm wondering why."

"Since you asked, why not. Me and my squad could give a shit less about your past. That's all politics to us. We did talk about it and we all felt the same way. You're Marines and we're Marines. We all went through the same shit to get here, to fight. I don't care what you once did; you're in for the fight of your life. One out of three of you aren't going to make it out of here alive. We been here for thirty-eight days and we're happy as all hell to be leaving and getting some R&R. Trust me, man, we wish you nothing but the best. Semper Fi," he said, turned and walked away.

Radison began getting the squad assigned to positions as Sergeant Ogden had ordered. Four foxholes would contain three men each and Radison would grab whatever hole he was closest to at the time of need. As he went from hole to hole checking, Romero asked him, "Hey, bro, tell me again about this shit." He was holding up a machete and pointed to the grenade sump.

"Come on, Juan, you heard what they said as well as I did."

"Yeah, I did but I'm still wondering if they were bullshitting us, you know as a joke."

"Juan, I don't think this is the time or place to be joking with anybody, do you? That machete is for snakes. They said if it was a quiet day the snakes like to roam around and one could try and get into the foxhole. It's a lot easier to cut him in half than try and shoot him."

"Okay, we'll see if it's true. Now tell me again why you want us to line that sump with wood."

"I saw another hole that had it and asked about it. They told me that it makes it easier for a grenade to go deeper into the sump and will absorb the blast better."

"That sounds good to me then."

"Listen, Juan. If a grenade lands in your hole, kick it into the sump and press yourself against the wall of the hole. If it works the way it's supposed to the blast will mostly hit the sides of the sump wall and the rest go straight up like a chimney."

"Yeah, and if it don't?"

"If you live through it, build a deeper sump. Anything else, I gotta check another hole? The password procedure for now is, you challenge with Touchdown and the reply back is End Zone. Got it?"

242

"Yup."

"Be cool, guys, no first-night jitters."

Charlie Company got through the first night without a shot fired. It got through the next six nights exactly the same way. Nobody could figure it out. On the eighth day word was passed down that a regiment-sized force was roaming around the border. It was part of the 14th Division. It was assumed that they were going to protect the next convoy coming in with supplies for the South. Anticipation was growing.

As Radison was making his rounds he came upon Romero, who was reading a book. His mates were on guard watching the jungle. Radison asked him, "What in hell are you doing?"

"It's my sleep time and I can't sleep so I figured I'd read."

"What are you reading?"

"*The Sand Pebbles.* Vinny told me about it back at Lejeune."

"How in hell did you get it?"

"From the library at Lejeune."

"Don't you think its going to be a little overdue?"

"No, I didn't check it out, I just took it."

"Are you enjoying it?"

"Yeah, I really like the guy Red Dog bite-'em-on-the-ass-Shanahan."

"Good, Juan, you need some culture." Juan just smiled and went back to his reading.

At the third hole Radison saw Palmer. He jumped into the hole and asked the other two to take a break and leave them alone. Palmer asked, "What's up, Rad?"

"John, I heard some scuttlebutt that you're thinking of surrendering."

Palmer looked surprised and said, "Yes, I am. You don't have any need to know, but yes, it's true I'm going to surrender."

"Why, John? What's the point you're trying to make?"

"Rad, I am a true activist in the peace movement. I believe everything the movement stands for."

"Okay, but why didn't you tell someone before all the training and coming here. At least you would have had a chance of getting out of this."

"You don't understand, Radison, I wanted to come here. It was all part of my plan. This is our best chance for world press from the front lines of this mess. I surrender to the VC, and they use me to tell the world about how we are war mongers and have no right to interfere with another country's way of life. I'll probably be on radio and TV and who knows, if it all works out I could be up for the Nobel Peace Prize."

Radison leaned back against the foxhole wall and stared at Palmer. He needed time to formulate the words he wanted, but couldn't. All he could say was, "You're fucking crazy. It won't work because the VC will cut you down before you can speak to them."

"That's a chance I have to take, but to me it's worth the risk."

Radison stared at this man unable to fathom what he was hearing. He knelt down in front of Palmer and calmly said, "I am not going to let this happen, you hear me?"

"How can you stop me?"

"With a bullet if I have to."

"You'd shoot me?"

"You're going to bet your life on it."

"I don't think you could, Radison."

"Well listen real close, asshole. I am an expert with this weapon and I promise you I will put one round right in the back of your neck that will separate your head from your body. And that, my peace-loving friend, is a promise."

He crawled out of the hole and motioned the two men waiting to get back in. As the first man got in he changed his mind and asked Martinez to move away. He told Martinez what Palmer was planning and what he had said. "Listen, if I'm not able or not around I expect you to shoot him, you understand?"

Martinez didn't answer. "Hey, Martinez, you want that fuck to be telling the world that we're baby killers and all sorts of lies?"

"Okay, Rad, I hear you, I'll do it."

The first squad moved forward as planned. They were out on patrol looking for VC activity or evidence of recent traffic. Sergeant Ogden was along to assist and help school the squad at the same time. He was kneeling behind the squad when he saw Radison signal for everyone to stop. He slowly moved up and asked what was up.

Radison said, "Look there by that tree," pointing.

"Yeah, I see it."

"Now look there by that dead tree."

"Yup, I see it."

"I don't understand it, Sarge, it's too obvious."

"You're very bright, Radison, it's a VC trap. They want you to see them, they're probably fake and contain no explosive. If someone attempts to cut them, there's some type of signal sent out probably to a tunnel that there's action above them. They then pop up and rip you a new ass. Let me sneak forward and look around. If you see me signal to come forward, do it slowly and very quietly."

Ogden moved forward at a snails pace. Everyone was very tense and ready as they watched Ogden's every move. He suddenly stopped and knelt down. He backed up a foot or two and watched again. It was like watching a fox stalk a lemming. He finally signaled and the squad moved forward to his location. He signaled them not to speak and pointed to a spot not ten feet from him. He motioned to them by putting his hands together, palm to palm, making an open and closing motion. He was telling them he was seeing a hatch in the ground. They all looked very closely and all saw it.

Ogden pulled the pin of a grenade and crawled toward the hatch. He stood but still bending over as close to the ground as he could. He got a hand on the hatch and opened it slowly. When he had enough room he dropped the grenade into the hole and dove towards the squad. Just as he hit the ground the hole exploded and blew debris skyward. The squad all had their rifles pointed at the hole but nothing emerged other than smoke.

Ogden pointed at Romero and said, "Strip off everything from the waist up. Crawl into that hole with this," and handed him a 45-cal pistol.

Romero did as he was told and returned to the surface some five minutes later. "Three bodies pretty messed up from the grenade. The tunnel goes back that way about ten yards or so into an area maybe ten by fifteen feet. It looks like a sleeping and eating area and some small-arms ammo."

"Okay, get the ammo out and get dressed." While Romero was busy throwing up the ammo, Ogden was busy rigging up something. He finally showed the squad what he had done. "We rig this up into the hatch with four grenades and make a new hatch. We wire the grenades to the hatch and that's that. We can even pack their ammo around the grenades to make a bigger blast."

When the squad returned to the base camp, Ogden informed Lieutenant Brown what had taken place. The tunnel was marked on a map for future reference. Ogden said it was just an ordinary VC tunnel hoping to wipe out some Marines. Nothing of military value was found. Ogden told Brown he would pass on this incident to the other squads in the company. Brown would pass it on to the three other companies via their officers.

Later that day Radison bumped in Sergeant Ogden and got into talk about the patrol and the lessons learned. "One thing bothers me, Sarge, why did they have that hatch open?"

"Beats me, it was unusual. Maybe they got a bad batch of rice and got to farting so bad they had to air the place out." Both laughed. "Look, it was unusual, it's the first time I have seen it. They are very hard to see so we lucked out this time. A lot of Marines have been killed by those tunnel boys, keep that in mind."

Radison slid into the foxhole occupied by Romero and Joe Gallo. He was filling in for Cox, who was going to sick call for a slight infection. "Welcome to our house, bro," as Romero smiled at him.

"Anything going on? How you coming with your reading, Juan?"

"Not much time to read here. I'm to busy watching that no VC sneak up on us."

"That's a good man, it will keep us alive." Gallo dozed while Radison and Romero watched.

After a few minutes Romero asked, "You scared, Rad?"

"Damn straight I am. I wonder if it weren't for me being a squad leader and running around, would I crack up just sitting in a hole and thinking."

"No, you wouldn't. I spend a lot of time looking at the scenery and all the things that are alive out there. Yesterday I was watching a line of ants that were going in and out of a hole in the ground. They came into the hole carrying bits of green stuff and then come out and start over again. I watched them do that for most all day."

"Juan, you surprise me. For a city boy you're starting to notice a lot of things going on around you. Reading a book and studying ants, you're going to get all cultured up."

"Don't tell anyone, okay?"

Rad smiled and Gallo opened his eyes and said, "Nice story."

Romero looked hurt and said, "You heard all that?"

"Yeah, I did."

"Well, you better not give me any shit about it."

"Relax, Romero, I got more on my mind than busting your balls about ants and books."

"Yeah, I guess you're right, we all do."

Some thirty to forty minutes passed in silence. Radison finally broke it by asking Gallo where he was from. "Islamorada, Florida, in the Keys."

"In what, what are keys?"

Gallo knew Romero was not very educated in anything outside a city so he didn't make anything of his ignorance of the question. "It's a chain of small islands that run from the Florida mainland all the way to Key West about one hundred miles south of Miami. Each island is connected by a bridge."

"No shit, what do you do there?"

"We live like anyone else except we're surrounded by water. The water is our life. We fish, shrimp, dive and have a good tourist industry."

Romero thought a minute and said, "You know if we all get out of here I'd like to go and see these Keys. Could I come and visit you?"

"Sure man, I'll take you shrimping."

"How do you shrimp?"

"Well, big boats go out and trawl with long nets for commercial purposes, but we do it in small boats and you can even shrimp standing on land. We have a twenty-four-foot skiff with an inboard engine. You go out into the mangrove islands according to the tides, just before it changes and slightly after it turns. Sometimes it's two or three in the morning, sometimes late at night, but never in the daytime.

"We put a large square net off the stern and tie it off. Then we lower the outriggers and hang lights on them. They run off the battery and hang very low near the waterline. Then we stand on both sides of the boat with scoop nets and scoop them in."

"You mean they just come to your boat and let you them scoop them up?"

"No, not really. Shrimp hold onto the grass at the bottom while the tide runs. When they want to move they let go and then float with the slow tides. They can cover a few miles every time the tide turns.

"In late February and early March they are headed to the Dry Tortugas to spawn. If you shine a light upstream all you can see is orange eyes by the thousands on the surface of the water, all shrimp. Every so often you hear a very loud splash like a man falling into the water from a dock. It's tarpon chasing the shrimp. They can go up to 125 pounds or more and make one hell of a noise when they jump."

Radison piped up and said, "I'd like to see that myself."

"Well, you're both welcome to come, I got plenty of space."

Cox returned and told Radison that Sergeant Ogden wanted to see him

ASAP. Radison ran to the area he knew Ogden would be and reported in. "Intel says a large group should be heading our way tonight, probably using the trail they have been before we got here. They are moving from the border carrying supplies and heading south. Charlie Company has the ambush. Pass the word, we move out at 1500 to set up for the ambush. Make sure everyone carries at least three extra bandoliers of ammo each. The BAR and SAW guys go too, each with extra ammo. Got all that?"

"Sure do, I'll take care of it."

Sergeant Ogden led the first squad out early to pick out a good ambush site, then talked the company into the position. His experience made him the perfect choice to lead the squad for this assignment. By 1800 hours Charlie Company was in position for their first major ambush. Ogden went from squad to squad to make sure they were in the proper position and they all knew where everyone else was positioned. The worst-case scenario would be that they fired into their own troops because of poor positioning. Friendly fire accidents were all too common in combat and Ogden wanted none of it on his watch. If everyone did as they were trained and briefed; it would be a piece of cake.

The supply convoy was coming at Charlie Company from east to west. The first squad to come into contact was to let the convoy pass them until the last squad in line got sight and began to fire. If nobody got an itchy finger, the major portion of the convoy would be in gun sight all at the same time.

Five agonizing hours passed and finally at 2304 hours the first enemy came into sight. Each man was completely surprised by what he saw. The majority of the carriers were not soldiers, but civilians. They were carrying bundles on their backs, heads or two men were carrying a large load slung between them hanging from a bamboo rod, one end on each man's shoulder. Soldiers were at intervals of thirty-five yards or so, each carrying some sort of weapon, mostly AK47's.

It took nearly twenty minutes before the first shot was fired and then all hell broke loose. All the time the men had spent on the various rifle ranges paled to this experience. The noise level was deafening, yet not one man realized it. All they did was empty clip after clip and magazine after magazine into the line of cargo carriers. It was a slaughter. In less than two minutes the body count was eighty-seven enemy dead.

After the last shot was fired its seemed like an eternity before someone spoke. Radison hollered for the first squad to move forward and check for signs of life. All along the line individual shots could be heard, one at a time.

Some thought it was "take no prisoners," yet others felt they were just putting wounded out of their misery.

Sergeant Ogden appeared to check on the squad. Everyone was okay. The supplies that the enemy was carrying were broken open to see what they contained. It was mostly food with some medicines and small amounts of small caliber ammo. Ogden ordered the food scattered to the jungle and the rest burned. The ammo was not useable to the Marines so it was opened and scattered about. One day in the rain and humidly and it would rust, and make it unusable.

The march back to the base camp was one of euphoria. The Marines felt they had proven themselves in combat. They did not realize that the ambush was all one-sided; the worst was yet to come.

Over the next fourteen days, Able, Baker and Delta Companies conducted similar ambushes. The biggest surprise to everyone was that in conducting the four ambushes they only lost three men. One was KIA in actual fighting and the other two were lost to trip wire explosions.

Every squad leader in Charlie Company was called to a briefing one day after the fourth ambush. Lieutenant Brown and the senior NCOs let the squad leaders know what they should expect. Lieutenant Brown told them all, "The VC had lost four convoys of supplies in this area and we have to expect they are pissed. Their typical reaction is to send out a large group to kill off the raiders, us. Our forward intelligence should give us a heads-up on when their troops move out, but in the meantime we need to get ready.

"We start by adding more claymores to our perimeter and more land mines. I need a couple of tree climbers. We want to put colored panels as high up as we can to orient the killing field from us so when we call in air support we have a better chance. We have already called back to regiment for more ammo and it should be here tomorrow. The last thing is that one man from each hole is to be put into machine gun sites we designate. We have several 50-calibers on hand and I want them set up and used. I would hope we get at least twenty-four-hour notice on the troop movement, but you never know, they could be coming from any uncovered area and we could miss them entirely. Go back to your squads and get to work."

It took three days until the VC showed. Intel reported they thought the regiment-sized force was part of the 14th Division, all experienced fighters. During the first twenty-four hours of engagement, the fighting was squad-sized fire fights. It appeared they were probing the area of the Marines to find weak points, this also worked to find what defenses they faced. Small firefights could be heard from one end of the line to the other. Sergeant Ogden constantly visited the squads to tell them this was just a feeling-out process and they would be well aware when the real fighting starts.

And it did begin, with mortar barrages that seemed to last an eternity. With the jungle being so dense, it took time for the mortars to do the work the VC wanted and that was to clear out trees and at the same time kill as many Marines as possible. The barrage did slow when Marine air cover raids hit them, but only by a small measure.

The Marine Corps was the inventor of close air support and had just the right aircraft for it. AD-5's were propeller-driven World War Two vintage. With no fear of interference from the air, these low and slow aircraft arrogantly dropped their cargo of death so close to the Marines line that it was scary. After several air attacks, it did seem like the mortar attacks lessened, but they never stopped and they took a terrible toll.

Each morning the VC launched their first attack in force. The attack came at about the line where Baker and Charlie Company's line met. Both companies were heavily engaged in the fight that lasted for three hours before the VC backed off. Later in the day another attack against Charlie and Delta lasted ninety minutes before they backed off. The next day the attackers hit Able Company full force and both sides took heavy causalities. Word filtered back that Able took 19 KIA.

In the afternoon of the third day Radison was in a hole with Gallo and Romero. Cox had been assigned to the machine gun crew and Radison filled his position. They were all taking a breather from the action when Romero saw Sergeant Major Kennedy crawling up to their hole. Romero hollered, "Hey, Sergeant Major, you got any cold beer for us?"

"Wish I did. How's it going, guys?"

"Fine," Radison answered, "what are you doing here?"

"Just helping out, brought some ammo up and taking stretcher cases back. The brass don't know I'm here so keep your mouths shut."

"Will do, sir."

"You really all right? It's okay to be scared, in fact it's good. I'm scared just being here."

Radisson smiled. "We're really doing fine, Sergeant Major, and thanks for your concern. If there's a next trip, how about those cold beers?"

"No guarantee, but I'll try."

They all knew there was not a cold beer to be had for miles, but the thought of it was nice. After the sergeant major left, Radison commented to the others, "You know he's like a father out checking on his children."

Gallo said, "Well, I wish he'd stay here in this hole, I'd feel a whole lot better."

"Ain't that the truth," added Romero.

Late in the afternoon Able and Delta reported hearing many claymore explosions. The VC were sending out patrols trying to outflank the Marine line. Ogden came by and told the squads what it meant, the VC were getting pissed and would probably mount a massive attack sooner rather than later.

The third night proved to be an absolute bitch; everyone was strung out from fighting all day and lack of sleep, yet too tense to sleep. Around 0100 hrs Radison was startled by shouting down the line, not far from him.

He stood and heard someone shout, "Palmer, Goddamn it, stop."

He ran to the scene just as a flare lit up the sky. He saw PFC John Palmer walking towards the VC lines with his hands high up in the air. A shot rang out and Palmer grabbed his right arm and nearly fell. He turned and faced the Marine line, but keep backing closer to the VC line.

Radison raised his rifle up and at the same time shouted, "Palmer, stop or so help me, I'll kill you."

Palmer stopped for an instant and then turned and walked again towards the VC. Radison thought to himself, *God forgive me,* and fired two rapid shots into Palmer's neck. Palmer's body fell forward and did not move again. The flare slowly burned out and Radison walked back to his hole. Not one person said a single word.

Just after dawn on the fourth day, mortar fire started landing among the Marines. In between blasts Romero could be heard saying, "I got the feeling the shit's really going to hit the fan today."

After a twenty-minute barrage, the shit did hit the fan, in a big way. Like ants boiling out of a hole in the ground, the VC bailed out of the jungle in massive quantities. In less than a minute all hell broke loose. Rifle fire, automatic weapons, machine guns and hand grenades all seemed to be firing and it was deafening, yet nobody heard it. Each man was working on automatic mode without thinking about it. Like the explosions and fire noise, nobody could hear the screams of the wounded and dying. Every single man was in a zone of killing and survival.

The line of advancing VC came within thirty yards of the Marines until the last one dropped and the firing stopped, and the living returned to the present. The moans of the wounded then took over and most went to the aid of their comrades. As the wounded were tended to, Radison hollered to the squads to get one man from each hole to get replacement ammo.

Ogden appeared and asked Radison what his status was. "I got one KIA and six WIA, but mostly minor. Ammo was being dispatched and the squad was ready."

Ogden said regiment was sending up more manpower by truck with additional ammo. No air support was possible as the VC were too close to the lines. He wished them luck and ran to the next squad.

In the distance helicopters could be heard, but none landed anywhere nearby. Lieutenant Brown had called in medivac choppers for the wounded and they were now in the area.

"Mercy One to Ambush One, you read?"

"Ambush One, loud and clear. Can you help us out, we got a lot of wounded."

"Our motto is, you call, we haul, you all. Just tell us what and where."

"We have an LZ one click west of us. Right this minute we have a lull, but I have nobody to check the LZ out. It looks like we're completely surrounded, so we really can't get to the LZ anyway."

"Ambush One, let me call for some shooters and they can take a test run and rake the area if needed. Will call you shortly."

Ninety minutes later the VC started the second wave of their attack. The number of attackers registered in Radison's mind as compared to the banzai attacks by the Japs in WW2 and the human wave assaults of Korea. Nothing else registered in his head except to kill. Ten minutes into the battle Gallo took a bullet to the face and was dead in place.

Radison turned to get more ammo and what he saw nearly gave him heart failure. Not twenty yards away, Sergeant Major Kennedy was moving Cox's body from behind the machine gun and pushing it out of the pit. He then settled in behind the gun and commenced firing. With no time to think any more about it Radison turned back to the job at hand, kill and survive. Not long after, the battle appeared to die off. The mound of dead VC was now becoming an obstruction to the Marines, but also to the VC.

Again everyone turned to tending the wounded and re-supplying ammo. Radison told Romero that he was going for more ammo and to be alert. Radison ran toward the machine gun and the sergeant major. He stopped and said, "You're going to get your ass busted for this."

Kennedy was all smiles. "Son, this is what I'm trained for and I can't think of a better bunch to do it with. I'd like you to tell all the men that I now call them all Semper Fi. They won't know why I'm saying it, but I do. You do that for me?"

"Yes, sir, I will."

"Radison, do me another favor. If I don't survive, will you tell my wife and daughters that I love them very much and say I'm sorry that I couldn't keep my promise."

"Sergeant Major, you …"

"I know, but promise me you'll do it if needed."

"I promise. Will you do the same for me if it's necessary?"

"I'd be proud to, my boy, very proud."

"How in hell did you get here anyway? We're supposed to be surrounded."

"The flyboys were blowing the shit out of the VC, we just sneaked in between bombing runs."

The next attack came within minutes. Radison could not fathom where they got the manpower from. Wave after wave of humanity, but they did. This attack was the same as the first two and ended the same way. The dead VC was piled so high that they now seemed to work as a natural barrier in the favor of the Marines.

The VC knew it also and attacked the flank of Delta and wiped out some of their defensive line. They now turned toward Charlie's line. During the fight Radison somehow realized the machine gun seemed silent. He turned and saw the sergeant major slumped over the gun. He yelled to Romero to get to another hole and he ran towards the machine gun. The sergeant major was dead; a couple of very large holes in his chest and head attested to that. The machine gun feeder was trying to get the body out of the way to resume firing and Radison helped do that.

Radison yelled, "I'll fire, you feed, okay?"

The assistant gunner nodded his approval and they began killing again. After a few minutes the barrel of the gun seemed to be overheating. The assistant hollered he needed to replace the gun. Radison half-stood to help remove the gun out of the way when a bullet ripped into his neck, he was dead before he hit the ground.

The olive-drab C-130 rolled to a stop, but left its engines running. About seventy-five Marines marched out of its belly and formed up. They all saw the body bags lined up nearby with one lone Marine standing alongside them. Private First Class Juan Romero was the sole survivor of First Squad, Charlie Company. He had been given permission to see his comrades off. Sergeant Major Kennedy, Radison, Cox, Reinhart, Martinez and even Palmer and Perkins were all going home together. Romero brought himself to rigid attention and rendered the best salute he knew how. He muttered towards the body bags, "Semper Fi, guys," as the tears streamed down his face.

Chapter 18

"Good evening, ladies and gentleman of America. For the very last time I have this opportunity to spend some time with you. When I took office as your president nearly four years ago, I had a head full of ideas that I hoped to implement. None of those ideas were as large in importance as the thought I had mulled over for years.

"As an American first and later a politician, I had misgivings about the way our government was being run. For as long as I could remember the system was the same. The candidate lied to the public by saying he would do thus and such, but once elected, he did just the opposite. He always blamed partisan politics as the reason he couldn't keep his promises. In reality he joined the club that gave the appearance of doing the right thing for the public, but actually it was the right thing for himself. He did in fact get things for his constituency but at what price?

"That system has not changed right up to today. Each and every generation of politicians seem to all be for you, but he then joins the club and nothing gets accomplished. As I said, some things do get done, but only on the surface. That allows them to say, look what I got for our state or country. We still need more change.

"Many close friends knew my feeling before the election. When I decided to have the draft dodgers arrested, a second group joined us. We asked for the mandate to suspend the Constitution and began making the changes we all thought were needed to change the direction we were headed.

"The members of the second group are Senators Carl Concannon and

Craig Trowbridge, Assistant Secretary of the Treasury Catherine Carter, Congressman Sid Braverman, Supreme Court Justice Barbara Twell and Steven Ames, CEO of Parker, Ames, Love Brokerage. The seventh member of the group was recruited just before we asked for the changes. He is Charles Rose, a detective who retired from the Washington Metro Police Department. I owe these seven people a tremendous debt of gratitude and so do you. They worked very hard to assist me in making the changes.

"I am leaving this office feeling very proud of myself. Not because of myself, but for what these changes have accomplished for our country. From where I sit, from what I see, from what I hear, the changes have been very successful to a whole range of our people. I am very aware that there are always two sides to a fence. I know some didn't like the changes, but what was their motivation? If you're very high up on the food chain, you don't like changes. If you're at the lower end, anything that makes your life better you're in favor of. Unfortunately we have more have-nots than haves.

"We did something unheard of, unprecedented and as far out in left field as you could go. We suspended our icon of freedom and it worked. We have made changes in our society that should last for generations, depending on what you allow your next head of state to do. I agree with many of you that it's nearing the time to return to our Constitutional-guaranteed freedom, as long as we don't return to our former ways of running the country. The changes we implemented are working for the betterment of the majority and should remain in force.

"Nearly a year ago, I gave you a long list of numbers ands statistics on what the changes mean in quantitative terms, I'd like to read them to you again and update them as I do. The items I will cover are not in any order of importance.

"Our intelligence system is now one to be proud of. All intelligence is now housed under one roof, with one person in charge. Any agency that has need, can access it. Several people were removed from these offices last year, that's what it took to correct the problems.

"All foreign bases are closed and all U.S. troops are now based in the U.S. All of the countries involved are not happy but it was what we needed to do. If this policy is left this way, we said every five years we could repair aging infrastructure and in twenty years replace one hundred percent of it. We still feel that in the twenty-first year, income taxes could be reduced by ten to fifteen percent. We have no reason to change those figures.

"Death by auto was down 42 percent. It's now down 56 percent. Jail time due to motor vehicle violations was up 125 percent. It's now 74 percent.

"Adoptions were up 155 percent. That figure is now 210 percent. Mixed-race adoptions were up 168 percent, its now 203 percent.

"All crime was down 300 percent. It is now 433 percent. Killing by police was up 3000 percent that is now 900 percent.

"Unemployment was down 48 percent. That figure is now 61 percent. The minimum wage scale was a problem with all the new jobs created. We did get two increases of thirty-five cents each.

"Drug-related crime was down by 279 percent. That figure is now 327 percent. Armed robbery of doctor's offices, hospitals and pharmacies was up 406 percent. That figure is now 96 percent.

"Chain gangs are cleaning up our communities. We had increased minor crime arrests by 125 percent. It is now down to 48 percent. These chain gangs are still keeping our roadways clean and they are now building some things like playgrounds and low rent housing.

"There are many more facts and figures I could add, but not now. A fact sheet will be available to anyone who wishes it. One thing needs to be said here on this matter. There is an old saying that goes, 'figures lie and liars figure.' I have no reason to lie to you. I have been honest and upfront from day one and that still holds true.

"Several other areas need to be mentioned. We have opened numerous drug treatment centers throughout the country. There is one unique thing about these centers. They are methadone free. The drug abuser is getting off drugs completely. We no longer substitute one drug for another. This system is working very well.

"Our court system has no case overloads. We have no calendar backlogs. All cases are being heard within forty-five days of arrest. Our jail system is overloaded, quite obviously, but we have worked out some of those problems. . Every person sentenced to jail has the option to work within or even outside the jail depending on the severity of his crime. Most all non-violent criminals work outside the prison system and this seems to be working well.

"I would like to read to you three letters from among the thousands I've received. The letters are from three different cross-sections of our society, yet they bear relevance to what the changes have meant to them.

"'Mr. President. I would like to express my admiration for you and what you have done and are doing for our country. I not only admire, but applaud you. My colleagues feel exactly as I. Unfortunately we are cowards. You see, sir; we are elected officials from various states that have been put out of work by your mandate. I personally don't mind it that much; I can see why it's necessary. Because of party politics I must remain anonymous, for obvious reasons. Sir, you are doing the right thing, but the pressure exerted on us by upper level political leaders is tremendous and I'm not one of the rich politicians. I must feed my family, so I must abide by the partisan system. If you get feeling lonely, regale in the fact that you're doing a wonderful job. My hope is that one day I may stand up in public and praise your name and legacy.'"

The president put the letter down and gazed around the room. He seemed to have everyone's rapt attention. *Good,* he thought, *maybe some of these words are sinking in.*

He picked up the second letter and began. "'Dear Mr. President, I am a thirty-eight-year-old mother of two. These children are new to our household, thanks to you. My husband and I had been turned down for adoption several times due to my husband's health problems. His problems are not fatal only debilitating, but the adoption agencies said he could not be a good father. Thanks to you and your mandated rule changes, we are now the parents of a girl and a boy who just happen to be blood brother and sister. You have made four people very happy and we are proud to say you are our president. I wish I could give you the biggest hug. It is our opinion that you have done more for this country in the past two years than any president has done in the last fifty. If you should decide to run again, I am sure you will win in a landslide victory. God bless you." As he lowered the letter, he again glanced out to the audience. Those present seemed to be in a mesmerized state.

He reached for the third letter and said, "And finally the last letter.

"'It was my intention to write you a nasty letter about you thinking yourself a God. My nineteen-year-old son has been a car nut since I can remember. Being a car nut includes being a speed freak also. If you haven't guessed it by now, he got three speeding tickets and finally lost this car. He had a fortune tied up in that car. Because of your new laws, I had to drive him to work, back and forth every day. It's been a real hardship on me and I guess that's why I was going to rip you. Something happened between my son losing his car and this letter and that something is this. A truly good friend lost her son in a car accident. Her son was also a speed nut, but now he's dead. My boy may not be the best in the world, but he's all I have and I love him very much. I still have my son and it's thanks to you that I do. You have done good service to this mother and for that I need to thank you.'

"These letters represent three families. I don't like to play number games, but I hope there are many more such families that these changes have affected in a positive way. This is exactly what we hoped for when we conceived this idea. We do have our detractors, but the number people tell me the letters favor the changes at nearly twenty to one. There is one common theme to all the changes and effects on our people and that is common sense. I am seriously thinking that when I pass on I will have inscribed on my tombstone, 'He always believed in common sense.' You history buffs should remember that during our war for independence, Thomas Paine wrote his famous *Common Sense*. I like to think that maybe he and I have a common bond.

"I would like to now expound on a subject near and dear to my heart, the draft resistors. Nearly two years ago the draft resistor problem reached a pinnacle. Several of our most trusted allies told me that we had become the laughing stock of the world because of our draft problems. We looked like fools to the rest of the world and I guess we were.

"My group of close friends talked about this problem and from that talk eventually came the program we called 'Operation Roundup.' You should all know what happened next, so I won't bore you with the details. What you need to know is that this very large group of men was dumped into the lap of the Marine Corps and I mean dumped. The very short story here is that the Marine Corps did a magnificent job of making men out of this group. For twelve long weeks the Corps whipped these men into the beginnings of a fighting group that eventually did themselves proud.

"I personally kept tabs on them, so much so that I made several trips to Parris Island to see how they were progressing and ask the instructors how they were doing. I spoke with one platoon on a one-to-one basis, without any one present but them and me. I also became personally involved with several Instructors, of whom I will speak of shortly.

"After twelve weeks at Parris Island these men were transported to Camp Lejeune, North Carolina, for another five weeks of advanced training, learning the ways of war. I think I should digress here for a minute.

"When the arrests were completed, 12,362 were in custody. After all was said and done, only 1,800 of these men were designated for combat. Eight thousand or so were put into other branches of the service for their two-year tour of duty, to do whatever they could for the war effort. Some 2,562 men were not taken into the services for a variety of reasons such as religious beliefs, health, criminal records, sexual problems, etc. Of that 2,562, one hundred ninety-five were imprisoned for various reasons and sixteen died of injury or trying to escape.

"The 1,800 men chosen were integrated into the regular Marine Corps and most welcomed these men into their ranks. There were some who felt otherwise but by and large they were accepted.

"As it turned out, of the 1,800 men who went to Viet Nam, only half saw direct action. The second half was used to support front-line operations. Of the 900 who saw combat action, we have the following statistics:

> 287 were killed in action
> 485 were wounded in action
> 28 are missing in action

"These men did their thirteen-month tour of duty and returned with the following decorations:

> 1 Congressional Medal of Honor
> 2 Navy Crosses
> 9 Silver Stars
> 14 Bronze Stars
> 772 Purple Hearts."

Right up to this moment, the president wanted to tell his audience that at least three men had been shot in the back by their own. All three had openly stated that they intended to surrender. Of the other twenty-five MIA nobody could know if any surrendered. Military brass on his staff and the medical staff advised him that this fact should not be made public. Their thought behind it was that the families of the twenty-eight men missing will always wonder if it was their son who had been shot in the back.

What is, was the question put to the president, *so important, that you would put such terrible information out? What good would it do versus all the damage it could cause. Wouldn't it be better for the twenty-eight families to not have that question hanging over their heads? Let them go on believing their sons had died in action, defending their country rather then the stigma of being a coward.* President Barringer had lost sleep over this question. In fact right up to the present, he did not know which words he would speak. The time came and he continued his speech.

"Regarding the twenty-eight men missing in action, I would like to add this note. We pray they are safe. If they should be prisoners of war, we pray that our enemy treats them in the manner they are required to be treated by the Geneva Convention. Our government will go to any ends to trace these men and it hopes they can be safely returned home." He paused and looked up. He saw many members of his staff with smiles on their faces. They had won the argument. He agreed now, why pour salt onto the open wounds.

"Now let me now tell you about a true American hero. Sergeant Major James Kennedy was a Marine Corps icon. This forty-three-year-old husband and father of two will be the recipient of the Congressional Medal of Honor for his deeds and his ultimate sacrifice in Viet Nam.

"I met Jim Kennedy at Parris Island when our draft resistors were in recruit training. Sergeant major is the highest enlisted rank in the Marine Corps. Only a fraction of the very best can attain this rank. The sergeant major assured me in our talk that these men were not much different than any other American youth; they just got off on the wrong foot. He said that at that point in their training, the Marine Corps was happy and so was he.

"One thing you should know about Jim Kennedy was that he was a very intelligent man. He was the proud possessor of a master's degree in Latin. That degree is no small task for any man, let alone a serviceman. The last words we exchanged were when I asked him if he could call these men Marines. Without one bit of hesitation his answer was, 'Mr. President, I refer to them as Nondum Fidelis, which in Latin means Not Yet Faithful.'

"Sergeant Major Kennedy went with these men from Parris Island to Camp Lejeune for their further training. He personally asked me for permission to go with the men to Viet Nam. Being so valuable to the Marine Corps, I agreed with the provision that he not be allowed to go into actual combat. He was in a rear support area and moved from one location to another as needed.

"One unit of his men got into a very long and hard fight. This unit fought so long that it needed constant re-supply, mainly of ammunition. Many men were wounded in the re-supply and bringing wounded back from the front lines that eventually Sergeant Major Kennedy took it upon himself to lead this action. He made six trips in with ammunition and six back with the wounded. He received three wounds, but refused aid as his men needed more ammo and the wounded needed urgent medical help. On his seventh trip that unit was very low on manpower so the sergeant major took over operating a machine gun position. He preformed like the Marine he was. It is estimated that his fire was responsibly for 187 enemy dead before he was mortally wounded.

"About ten days after I was informed of his death, I received a note he had written before he went into his final battle. He said, quote, 'Sir, I can now report from firsthand knowledge they can now be called Semper Fi. I'm proud as hell of them.'

"There needs to be an asterisk to Sergeant Major Kennedy's story. A recruit squad leader in Parris Island was observed by the sergeant major. He excelled and was promoted to private first class upon completion of recruit training. At Camp Lejeune he again excelled and became a protégé of the sergeant major. Upon completion of training at Lejeune, he again was promoted to lance corporal and recommended to attend Officers Candidate School. The Marine Corps felt that only after Viet Nam would he travel the road to becoming an officer. Lance Corporal James Radison was married and the father of a two-and-a-half-year-old son. He was fighting very close to the sergeant major when he was killed.

"Lance Corporal Radison was the first man to reach the sergeant major. He then took over the operation of the machine gun. His squad mates reported Radison fought like a man possessed until his gun became too hot to fire. While changing weapons Lance Corporal Radison also was mortally wounded.

"He managed some dying words and they were as follows, 'Please tell my wife and son that I love them very much. Please try and get me buried next to the sergeant major.' It is my great privilege to tell you that Sergeant Major James Kennedy and Lance Corporal James Radison are buried next to each other in Arlington National Cemetery. The superintendent of the cemetery tells me their graves are the only two in that cemetery that contain a Congressional Medal of Honor winner and a Navy Cross winner side by side.

"The Congressional Medal of Honor is the highest military award our nation can give and the Navy Cross is the second highest award.

"I said previously that Lance Corporal Radison, even before View Nam was picked out as an outstanding Marine and a born leader. He was, as I said, one of only thirty-five men picked out of 3,000 to attend Officers Candidate School. By presidential order, Lance Corporal James Radison is hereby promoted to the rank of second lieutenant in the United States Marine Corps.

"As my last weeks wind down, your new president is working hard to assume the leadership of our country. He has said it is time for us to return to the Constitutional guarantees and I agree with him one hundred percent. I have told him I hope he keeps the changes in place and why they need to be kept. If you believe as I do, only you can make it happen. It's your government and your voice is what will make it run as you want it to.

"As you should remember, one of the changes we made was to get out of the United Nations and throw them out of New York. Let me give you something to think about. This very morning I received word that a report out of their headquarters in Brussels says they want us to rejoin the UN. Now let me tell you why they want us back; the UN is broke. While we were a member, we were paying half of their expenses and when we quit they went down the tube. That is exactly why we wanted more say in the UN, because we were paying too much in dues and we had less and less to say on how the UN operated. The waste and corruption is still eating up their funds. The handwriting is on the wall for all to read. We made a very good move in getting out of the UN and I pray we stay out.

"This is my last public speech as your president. Right now I can see no need for another. I am extremely proud of what we have accomplished. This administration, including every man and woman, has done a great service to our country. The numbers speak for themselves. Our nation has done a complete turnabout. I could not be happier to leave this office in the shape it's in. I thank each and every citizen in this country. Without you, these changes could not have occurred. I am proud of you. Good night and may peace be with us."

The president dabbed his eyes again. He stared out at his garden and could not stop the flow of tears. *I knew full well that when I took this job it could result in getting people killed, but why does it always have to be the good guys? Sergeant Major James Kennedy was one hell of a good man and I'm responsible for his death. He was all the good things I admire and more. Under different circumstances we could have been good friends. I must make sure I don't forget his family. I need to tell Marge to remind me to keep in touch with them, it's the least I can do.*

A soft knock at the door broke the sad moment the president was suffering. Charlie Rose peeked in. "You wanted to see me, sir?"

"Yes, Charlie, come on in."

As Charlie sat down he couldn't help but see that the president was returning his handkerchief to his pocket and the puffy red eyes. *I wonder what's got him so upset. Best to keep your mouth shut, Charles, and see what he says.*

"Do you have any idea what I was doing this morning?"

"No, sir."

"I awarded the Congressional Medal of Honor to Sergeant Major Kennedy's wife and daughters. Real nice family. I think awarding that medal is the greatest thing a president can do in his term of office, yet today I felt like a shit-heel doing it. Because of me, that lady and her two girls no longer have a husband and father. You never met him did you, Charlie?"

"No, sir."

"He was one hell of a man. He cared about his country and the men under him. We need more in this world like him, but they're hard to find that good."

Charlie could see and feel the emotion that the president seemed to be holding in. *That's why he was crying. Do I say something or just keep quiet?*

"In the same ceremony today I awarded the Navy Cross to two men who died with the sergeant major. One was Jim Radison, who Kennedy thought the world of. He was going to go the OCS when it was over and become a Marine Corps officer. He was married and had a young son. He took Kennedy's place on the machine gun when the sergeant major was killed and did a hell of a job also.

"The other Navy Cross went to a boy from Michigan named Dick Peacock. He was nineteen years old. He used his body to smother a grenade that landed in the midst of his squad. He gave his life for his buddies. Christ, Charlie, where do men like this come from? Truly magnificent men."

Before Charlie could think anymore, the president changed the subject and said, "Well, in three weeks I won't have go through this anymore. What have you been up to, Charlie, thinking about your future?"

"Yes and no. The team doesn't have anything to do and we're just waiting for you to disband us. I've been thinking about what I want to do, but haven't come up with any ideas except maybe to go on a vacation, somewhere it's warm."

"I guess you're right, I should tell everyone to go back to their normal lives. Our trip is over." The president stood and walked to the bar. "Care for a scotch?"

"No thank you, sir."

"I sure as hell need one." He poured two fingers worth and downed it in one long gulp. "That was for you, Jim Kennedy.

"Charlie, could I be so bold as to ask you a few personal questions?"

"Yes, sir, I don't have anything to hide, especially from you."

"Do you have a job lined up?"

"No, sir."

"A serious relationship?"

"No, sir."

"Well then, I have something in mind and now is as a good a time as any to lay it out. I would like you to be my aide. No qualifications needed aside from what you already possess. We are both bachelors so that makes it a unique situation. I would like you to move into my home. Your rooms will be anything you want. You will be my right hand, my bodyguard, my golfing partner and hopefully my friend."

Charlie was stunned. He sat staring at the president, speechless. All he could think was that the president of the United States, soon to be a civilian, wanted to be his friend. He idolized this man and had a growing fondness for him. He heard the president speaking, but didn't hear the words. He asked him to repeat it.

"You will receive a nice salary, special authorization to carry a weapon, all expenses paid and all the time off you want whenever you want it. The Secret Service detail will always be there, that goes with the presidency. Do you have any questions or doubts?"

"No, sir, not a one. I'm just stunned at your offer."

"Charlie, I have had the privilege to meet two very special men in the past two years, Sergeant Major Kennedy and you." The president extended his hand and said, "Charlie, please say yes." The two men shook hands.

"It will be my honor to say yes, Jim."

Epilogue

The subject matter for this book came to me more than thirty-five years ago when I was in my early thirties. At that time the Viet Nam war was going full bore and the draft resistors were in the headlines daily, so were the draft card burners, flag burners and bra burners.

Having had the great pleasure to spend the summer of 1958 at that world-famous resort, Parris Island, it came to me one cold and dark night while out on patrol in the community where I worked. The work portion of my life was that of a police officer. At that time and as of this day, if I had my way, I would have rounded up every resistor I could find and ship them off to Parris Island and let the Marine Corps retrain them spiritually and physically.

That idea fermented in my brain and I put some thoughts to paper and went about my life. On several occasions in the ensuing years the notes came to mind and I once took them out and added a few more lines. In general it was more important at the time to make a living and support my wife and children then it was to be fooling with a book.

I retired in 1990 and thought that now would be the time to get to the book. Wrong. Travel was important and golf became an obsession to me. After fourteen years of retirement, we still travel and I golf three times a week, but the book thought was haunting me. It was something I had started and never finished and I didn't like that. So in 2004 I began reading what I had once written and started to put ideas together and put some time into it. By 2005 I actually wrote the first chapter. Much of 2005 was spent in our normal activities, but I did put a lot of extra time into the book. I had it in my head that I would finish it regardless of how it turned out. If it was a hit, great my kids and grandchildren would benefit. All I wanted was to satisfy myself that it was completed. I naturally did complete it and I'm satisfied overall, be it winner or loser.

I don't think anyone can doubt where my mind-set is on the subject, but I need to add two postscripts here. The first is for all those who burned our flags during all those troubled years. I had another story about them in mind, but for now let me tell you this. If I had my way, I would have arrested every one who burned our flag and deported their young ass to some peace-loving country like Somalia or North Korea whey they allow that form of freedom of expression.

The second postscript follows this page. When I had just about finished writing Chapter 13 or 14, I received the first of two emails from friends. After reading the first I realized that it could have been written by me for this book. Two months later the second arrived and the very same thought passed through my head. Who or what was behind these emails? Was it God or some other power telling me something? Was someone or thing egging me on? Judge for yourself.

Received July 4, 2005

Wouldn't it be great to turn on the TV and hear any president, Democrat or Republican give the following speech?

My fellow Americans: As you all know, the defeat of Iraq has been completed. Since Congress does not want to spend any more money on this war, our mission in Iraq is complete. This morning I have the order for a complete removal of all American forces from Iraq. This action will be complete within 30 days. It is now time to begin the reckoning.

Before me, I have two lists. One list contains the names of countries which have stood by our side during the Iraq conflict. This list is short. The United Kingdom, Spain, Bulgaria, Australia and Poland are some of the countries listed there.

The other list contains everyone not on the first list. Most of the world's nations are on that list. My press secretary will be distributing copies of both lists later this evening.

Let me start by saying that effective immediately, foreign aid to those nations on list 2 ceases immediately and indefinitely. The money saved during the first year along will pretty much pay for the costs for the Iraqi war.

The American people are no longer going to pour money into third-world hell- holes and watch those government leaders grow fat on corruption.

Need help with a famine? Wrestling with an epidemic? Call France.

In the future, together with Congress, I will work to redirect this money towards solving the vexing social problems we still have at home. On that note, a word to terrorists organizations. Screw with us and we will hunt you down and eliminate you and all your friends from the face of the earth.

Thirsting for a gutsy country to terrorize? Try France or maybe China. I am ordering the immediate severing of diplomatic relations with France, Germany and Russia. Thanks for all your help comrades. We are retiring from NATO as well. *Bon chance, mes amis.*

I have instructed the Mayor of New York city to begin towing the many UN diplomatic vehicles located in Manhattan with more than two unpaid parking tickets to sites where those vehicles will be stripped, shredded and crushed. I don't care about whatever treaty pertains to this. You creeps have tens of thousands of unpaid parking tickets. Pay those tickets tomorrow or watch your precious Benzes, Beamers and limos be turned over to some of the finest chop shops in the world. I love New York.

Mexico is also on list 2. President Fox and his entire corrupt government really need an attitude adjustment. I will have a couple of extra tank and infantry divisions sitting around. Guess where I am going to put them? Yep, border security. So start doing something with your oil.

Oh, by the way, the United States is abrogating he NAFTA treaty – starting now.

We are tired of the one way highway. Immediately, we'll be drilling for oil in Alaska, which will take care of this country's oil needs for decades to come. If you're an environmentalist who opposes this decision, I refer you to list 2: pick a country and move there. They care.

Nearly a century of trying to help folks live a decent life around the world has only earned us the undying enmity of just about everyone on the planet. It is time to eliminate hunger in America. It is time homelessness in America. It is time to eliminate World Cup Soccer from America. To the nations on list 1, a final thought. Thanks guys. We owe you and we won't forget it.

To the nations on list, a final thought. You might want to learn to speak Arabic.

God Bless America. Thank you and good night.

Received Sept. 14, 2005

HOW TRUE!

I for one am praying that God will resurrect the deal Mr. Common Sense for our country's survival.

Today we mourn the passing of a beloved old friend, Mr. Common Sense.

Mr. Sense had been with us for many years. No one knows for sure how old he was since his birth records were long ago lost in bureaucratic red tape. He will be remembered as having cultivated such value lesions as knowing when to come in our of the rain, why the early bird gets the worm and that life isn't always fair.

Common Sense lived by simple, sound financial policies (don't spend more than you earn) and reliable parenting strategies (adults, not kids are in change.)

His health began to rapidly deteriorate when well intentioned but overbearing regulations were set in place – reports of a six year old boy changed with sexual harassment for kissing a classmate; teens suspended from school for using mouthwash after lunch; a teacher fired for reprimanding an unruly student, only worsened his condition.

Mr. Sense declined even further when schools were required to get parental consent to administrate aspirin to a student; but could not inform the parents when a student became pregnant and wanted to have an abortion.

Finally, Common Sense lost the will to live as the Ten Commandments became contraband; churches became businesses; and criminals received better treatment than their victims.

Common Sense finally gave up the ghost after a woman failed to realize that a steaming cup of coffee was hot, she spilled a bit in her lap, sued, and was awarded huge settlement.

Common Sense was preceded in death by his parents, Trust and Trust; his wife, Discretion; his daughter, Responsibility; his some, Reason. He is survived by two stepbrothers; My Rights and Ima Whiner.

Not many attended his funeral because so few realized he was gone. If you still remember him, pass this on; if not, join the majority and do nothing.

Glossary

A Possible: All the rounds fired hit the bull's eye, a perfect score.

Guide-On: Platoon standard bearer.

Grinder: Parade field, usually a very large paved area.

ITR: Infantry Training Regiment.

Lister bag: A canvas bag, some five feet in height. Holds fresh water for drinking. Usually hung from a large tree limb.

LZ: Landing zone.

Pogey bait: Anything sweet such as soda, candy or cake.

Rifle dope: Elevation and windage used to set the rifle sights to a particular distance or for a wind condition…

Salty: Brazen, acting superior.

Scuttlebutt: Gossip, the present gossip circulating at the time.

Slop chute: Enlisted man's club or NCO club, usually serving alcohol and snacks.

Top: Top sergeant, usually the senior sergeant of a unit.

782 Gear: A web belt with attachments; they are bayonet and scabbard, canteen and cartridge case.

Printed in the United States
66505LVS00003B/61-63